THE
WARRIOR'S
CURSE

JENNIFER A. NIELSEN

THE WARRIOR'S CURSE

· BOOK THREE ·

SCHOLASTIC PRESS · NEW YORK

Library of Congress Cataloging-in-Publication Data

Names: Nielsen, Jennifer A., author. | Nielsen, Jennifer A. Traitor's game ; 3.
Title: The warrior's curse / Jennifer A. Nielsen.
Description: First edition. | New York : Scholastic Press, 2020. | Series: The traitor's game ; book 3 |
Summary: The battle for control of Antora continues, and Simon and Kestra have been forced apart;
Kestra is a prisoner in the cursed All Spirits Forest where Loelle wants her to use her growing power
to heal the land and bring it back to life, while Simon has been made king of the Halderians, but is
surrounded by men whose loyalty is uncertain and who fear his connection to Kestra of the hated
Dallisor family, and the evil Lord Endrick.
Identifiers: LCCN 2019025348 | ISBN 9781338045451
Subjects: LCSH: Magic—Juvenile fiction. | Kidnapping—Juvenile fiction. |
Conspiracie—Juvenile fiction. | Adventure stories. | CYAC:
Magic—Fiction. | Kidnapping—Fiction. | Conspiracies—Fiction. |
Adventure and adventurers—Fiction. | GSAFD: Adventure fiction. | LCGFT:
Action and adventure fiction.
Classification: LCC PZ7.N5672 War 2020 | DDC 813.6 [Fic]—dc23
LC record available at https://lccn.loc.gov/2019025348

10 9 8 7 6 5 4 3 2 1   20 21 22 23 24

Printed in the USA   23
First edition, March 2020

Book design by Christopher Stengel

Para Alejandra,
Porque cuando te haces parte de la
familia, se te dedica un libro.
También porque eres un regalo
en nuestras vidas.

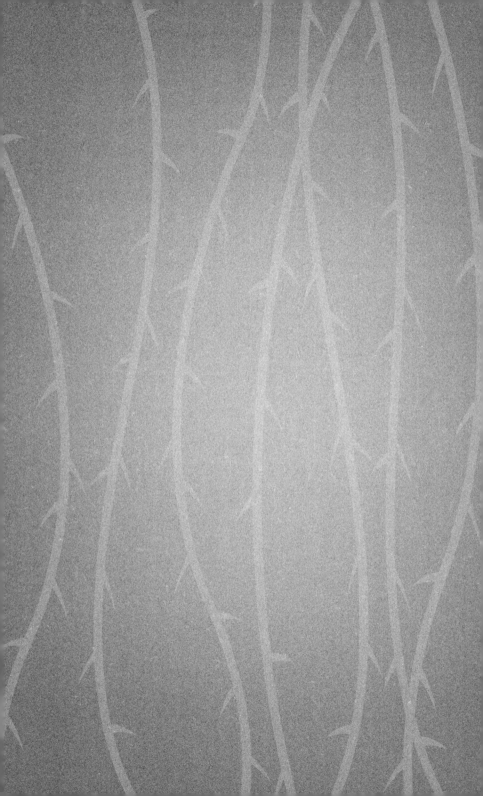

Face me with swords or with weapons of might,

I won't be afraid of that fight.

Threaten me, curse me, or crush my heartbeat,

Just watch me. I'll stay on my feet.

But . . .

If you come near me and fall on your knees

With kind words and warm whispered pleas,

If you should hold me, say I am the one,

I'll tremble and may have to run.

Or maybe I'll stay and give you my heart—

Keep it safe; don't tear it apart.

Now nothing forever can be the same.

For love is a dangerous game.

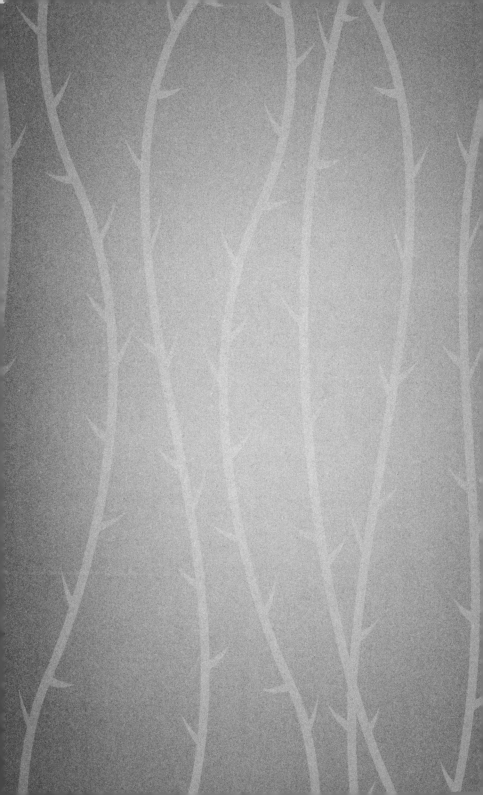

· ONE ·

KESTRA

Winter had come, bringing harsh winds that cut like knives through my cloak, the land frozen beneath my feet each morning and continuing to chill, even when the sun rose. Not that we saw much sun in such a forsaken place.

Loelle had taken me here, to All Spirits Forest, forcing me away from Simon, away from every reality I had ever known. For the first few days, I refused to speak to her, refused to acknowledge that she even existed. I was utterly miserable.

How could I be otherwise in such a place?

A generation ago, in the War of Desolation, Lord Endrick had cursed these woods. The trees and bushes had lost their leaves, lost their life. Now they were mere blackened posts in a dead earth, unable to renew and offer hope to the land, unable to return to their former glory.

Winter had brought cold to the forest, but no snow, no hope of springtime. Only more eternal decay.

Every morning, I tried to leave the forest. And every morning, I was blocked by some invisible barrier I eventually came to understand. The half-lives who existed here, who had once fought against me entering the forest, were now working to keep me trapped within these same borders.

Lord Endrick's curse wasn't targeted at the woods but, instead, at those whom he had corralled here at the time of the cursing: thousands of Halderians, his enemies. For nearly twenty years, they had been trapped here, in a midway point between life and death, like the trees themselves, unable to die, with no hope of living.

"You can save them."

It wasn't the first time Loelle had said this to me, though every time she did, she revealed a little more of her plans and purposes. This morning, she stood behind me as I combed my fingers through my brown hair, weaving it into a long braid. When I looked up, she repeated, "You can save these people, Kestra."

"Why would I care to save Halderians?" This was always my answer. Much of my life's misery was a direct result of their actions against me.

"My people are here too," Loelle said. "We call ourselves the Navan. Help us, and we will help you."

That part was new. I had known that Loelle came from a people foreign to Antora, and that some of them were here in the forest, but this was the first time she had spoken their name, and certainly the first time she had openly confirmed that I was here to help them. I wasn't here as a prisoner; she had brought me to be a servant. My temper warmed. "How can they possibly help me?"

"It's the reason I brought you here." Loelle put her hands on my shoulders, but I brushed them off. "Kestra, they are your only chance to defeat Lord Endrick."

"That isn't true." I stood, pushing back my chair. "I have no chance to defeat him from here, nor can I leave, thanks to *your* people!"

She stood as well. "Then help them leave."

"You want me to restore thousands of people to life? That'd take years."

"No. I want you to bring the forest back." I began to walk away but Loelle called after me, "Nature is less complex, and the curse is in the people more than in the land. Bring the forest back, and at least my people won't be trapped."

I stopped and looked back at her. She had my interest. "They'll still be half-lives."

Loelle smiled, in a way that told me her plan was far deeper than she had let on so far. "Yes, they will remain as they are."

I considered that a moment, then said, "Let me heal Darrow. I know my father is here. Let me heal him, and then I'll do what you want."

Loelle's eyes were sympathetic but unflinching. "Do as I ask first, then I'll send your father to you." When I didn't respond, she added, "Give me this one day, Kestra. If you don't wish to continue afterward, then I'll ask nothing more of you."

"And if I don't continue, these half-lives will let me leave?"

"No."

I grunted and marched over to the door. My cloak hung there from a hook, and I tossed it over my shoulders, shuddering against the wind when I walked outside.

Loelle followed, pointing out a blackened stump very near her small wooden hut. Whatever it had been once, I couldn't tell. "If you can pull strength from a person, I believe you can pull a curse from this tree."

"When I pull strength, I become stronger." My eyes darted to the tree. "What happens when I pull in a curse?"

Loelle sighed. "I think we both know. I'm so sorry, but there's no other way."

At first, I wanted to ask what she meant, but then I realized that I did know the answers to all my questions. All of them . . . except for the one I knew she would not answer: No other way to do what?

My only hope to find out was to move forward.

Loelle set my hands on the trunk of the dead, blackened tree, whispering into my ear, "Take the curse."

It wasn't about giving strength to the tree. I needed to pull the curse from its roots and stems and branches, drawing it into myself. As I focused on my task, Endrick's curse immediately flooded through my veins, expanding into every hollow of my body. I felt its ugliness, all its hate and desire to control life and love and hope, and especially its will to control me. To consume me.

I tried to let go. Every instinct within me rebelled against what I was drawing to myself, but I'd become bound to the tree, trapped in place until the tree had emptied itself of its curse.

When it was over, I collapsed to the ground, Loelle at my side, waiting until I had recovered enough to open my eyes. Hoping to quell the pain, I curled into a ball and whispered, "No more of that, Loelle. Whatever Endrick did to that tree, that curse, it's burning inside me."

"Let it pass," she replied. And slowly it did, the sharp burn fading into a small pit inside my chest, something cold and dead. As Loelle promised, after a few deep breaths, I began to feel strong again. Not just strong, but powerful in a way I had never experienced before, that perhaps no one had ever experienced. When I nodded at her that I felt well enough to move on, she smiled and said, "Look up."

I did and was surprised to find the tree was changing, its withered black trunk becoming brown, bark forming around perfect, new wood. The branches were spreading, even regaining the leaves it must have once had at the time it was cursed. They fell to the ground beside me, as winter leaves must, but new leaves would return to this tree with the coming spring.

It was so beautiful, so hopeful, and so tangible in its healing that I suddenly realized I wanted to continue on in the work, despite its effects. After so much fighting, so much destruction caused by my powers, finally I could heal something, and add peace and promise to this land. And so I began, working for nearly a month to heal the forest.

Every day, moving from one area to another, I'd work for as long as my strength endured, emptying and refilling myself over and over. It never seemed like enough before I had to quit, but gradually, the pockets connected and the forest began to come to life. Birds could be heard in the distance, the ground softened, and snow began to fall again.

Sometime in those weeks, I also became more aware of the half-lives who lived here, the target of Lord Endrick's curse.

"Let me heal them too," I begged Loelle, every single day. "Darrow."

"We cannot, not yet" was her daily reply, with no further explanation.

Still, I continued, so focused on my work that I was becoming immune to the cold. I felt the chill in the air, but it no longer bothered me. Rather, it was the heat from Loelle's evening fires that made me uncomfortable, so I began to sit near the door, leaving it cracked open enough that I could rest.

The evenings were most difficult. That was when my thoughts drifted toward Simon, wondering if he was still the Halderian king, wondering if he was now married to Harlyn Mindall. Wondering if he had ever tried to find me.

Then, one morning, I said to Loelle, "Simon was wrong about me getting magic."

Loelle looked up from a book she had been reading. "Oh? In what way?"

"He thought it would corrupt me, but consider all the good I've been able to do for these woods."

Loelle's smile saddened. "Yes, you've done what no one else could."

"Let me heal Darrow," I said. "I've earned that much."

"You have," Loelle said. "Soon, Kestra. I promise."

Soon. I would see my father again soon.

Until then, I had work to do.

· T W O ·

SIMON

We were a month into winter, and there hadn't been one sign of Kestra anywhere in Antora, nor beyond. With the permission of Captain Tenger, the leader of the Corack rebellion, Trina and Gabe and a few other Coracks had been combing the land for Kestra, and so far, their search for even the barest hint of her had come up empty. Despite recovering from a terrible illness at the time Kestra left and my new responsibilities as king of the Halderians, I'd ventured out myself as often as possible, but every trace of her had vanished.

Loelle had hidden her well, likely with the use of whatever magic she possessed beyond her abilities as a physician. I was certain she would keep Kestra alive, but I couldn't fathom why Loelle had taken her away in the first place. All I knew was that Kestra's absence had pierced a hole in my heart and it only became worse with each passing day.

Every time I returned home from an attempt to find her, Harlyn met me in the stables. She never asked about Kestra directly, likely because she already knew how I'd answer.

Instead, her question today was, "How is your arm?" She'd asked this before, and I'd come to understand that she was really asking, "How are you?"

Barely looking at her, I said, "Everything's fine."

Which was true only in the sense that my arm was fine. I, on the other hand, was miserable.

I dismounted, and as I did, she touched my right arm, pretending to study it when we both knew she wanted a reason to approach me.

"It hasn't softened," she said.

"It never will," I replied. "You know that, Harlyn."

In the battle with the Dominion, I'd discovered a Rawkyren, a young dragon, being tormented by Ironheart soldiers. I had rescued the dragon, but somehow its blood had mixed with mine, and now the flesh beneath my right arm was as strong as a dragon's scales.

At first, the Rawkyren could land on my arm without causing injury, despite digging its claws into my flesh for support. But the Rawkyren was too large for that now, almost the size of the Dominion's giant condors, and growing more each day. It accompanied me on every search for Kestra, though it usually remained on its own in the wild while I was here in Nessel.

Harlyn lowered her eyes. "I do know that. But I fear the injury did more than turn your arm to stone. I believe it turned *you* to stone. Will you never look at me with anything but contempt?"

I placed my hand over hers. "It's not contempt, but we both know you haven't told me everything about the night Kestra left, about *why* she left."

Her eyes became teary. "Gerald already explained it to you."

"Did he?" I pulled my hand free and stepped back. She remained where she was, but as I started out the stable doors, Gerald walked in, giving me a quick bow. I glanced over at Harlyn, wondering if this was yet another secret plan, but this time she looked as confused as I did.

"Come with me, now," Gerald said.

We immediately followed. He led us through a rear corridor of the manor that served as a sort of castle in exile, with me as a king in exile, ruling over a people I barely knew, and with Harlyn the only connection between us. Gerald brought us to the doors of a room where I met with the officers of what little army the Halderians still had. The door was slightly ajar, and Gerald motioned for Harlyn and me to come forward where we could hear.

". . . but like it or not, Simon is the king." The man who was speaking was named Edgar, and he was one of the finest officers in the cavalry. "We serve him."

"But who does Simon serve?" This man was Reese. He was the current head of the cavalry. "Not us, not our people."

"Master Thorne assured us that Simon was the king we've been waiting for. Commander Mindall trusts him too."

A third man, whose voice I didn't recognize, said, "Commander Mindall is too sick for his word to be trusted, and even so, he only supports Simon because his daughter will become the queen."

"We would serve her," Reese said. "But has Simon given any indication of wanting to marry her? No. I say the rumors are true, that the king is in love with the Infidante."

"If he is, then he'll have to be removed," the third man said. "It was bad enough that the Infidante is a Dallisor, that she's one of *them*. But now she also has magic, which means she must have Endrean blood too, the blood of the tyrant. I've heard rumors of the real reason Kestra Dallisor was sent away from here, and it's worse than you can imagine. If our king has any place in his heart for Kestra Dallisor, he will have to be removed too."

"Removed?" Edgar asked. "That's treason."

"Call it what you want, but it must be," Reese said. "We can't afford to have our people divided, not in these dangerous times."

I turned on my heel and marched away, my hands balled into fists. Gerald and Harlyn followed until we reached my room, then Gerald shut the door behind us.

"We have to find Kestra," I said. "If they mean to harm her—"

"Weren't you listening?" Gerald asked. "They intend to harm *you!*"

"We have to prove to them that she's on our side, that they're wrong—"

"They're not wrong," Gerald said. "She is more like Endrick than us, and you know for yourself that she has begun to corrupt. I didn't bring you to hear that conversation for Kestra's sake. I'm trying to protect you!"

I glanced over at Harlyn, whose eyes were lowered. She wouldn't look at me.

"Listen carefully," Gerald said. "There is a supper tonight. When it is finished, Simon, you will offer marriage to Harlyn, and, Harlyn, you will accept."

Harlyn opened her mouth to say something, but Gerald quickly added, "I know that neither of you wants a marriage to happen this way, but it must and it will. Refuse, and believe me when I say that within the week, there will be a challenge for the crown, and one way or another, it will end in death. When I see you tonight, after the supper, I will raise a toast in honor of the king, and, Simon, you will raise it in honor of your new queen. Are we agreed?"

"Where is Kestra?" I asked, not for the first time. "Do you know?"

And not for the first time, he replied, "Let her go. She—" Gerald stopped as a knock came to my door and a page opened it with a note in his hand.

The page bowed low and said, "A message has come for the king."

Gerald took the note and passed it to me. I opened it, then gave it to Harlyn. While she read it, I said to Gerald, "Have someone prepare my horse and a pack for several days of travel. I'm leaving now."

"You've just arrived."

"Then I'm most of the way ready."

"You'll need an escort, the cavalry—"

I nearly choked on his suggestion, then pointed toward the stables. "*That* cavalry? I don't need their help."

Harlyn returned the note to me, adding, "I'll go with you."

I nodded back at her, but Gerald asked, "What is the note?"

"Captain Tenger has finally located Basil, but he needs our help to rescue him from Lord Endrick."

"They've had him for a month," Gerald said. "No doubt by now he has told Lord Endrick where he has hidden the Olden Blade. You must stay and secure your place here."

"If Endrick finds that blade, I have no place here. None of us do." I practically pushed him through my open door, saying, "Prepare my horse. Harlyn and I will leave at once."

· THREE ·

SIMON

The journey from Nessel up to Highwyn, where Basil was being held, would ordinarily take a week of easy riding, but if the weather cooperated, and if Harlyn and I rode fast and rested the horses midway, I hoped we could get there in half the time.

That was still too long.

We could get there in a day if we used the Rawkyren. I'd hoped to eventually try flying with it, but I hadn't yet and didn't even know if it was possible. For now, we'd have to ride.

According to Tenger's note, Basil had been sent to the same dungeons beneath Woodcourt where Kestra and I had both spent time. We had found an escape by sliding over a steep ledge into a muddy pit littered with rot and debris. A narrow tunnel provided passage outside Woodcourt's walls, but it was nearly impossible to find. Basil had followed our route, and must have kept himself alive in ways I didn't want to fathom, but even after a month in the pit, he still could not find the exit. A few days ago, the dungeon guards had realized he hadn't actually escaped and recaptured him.

I couldn't imagine what was happening to him now either. But what I could imagine urged me to ride faster. Basil couldn't have much life left in him.

Less than an hour after receiving the note, Harlyn and I met in the stables. I mounted my horse with only a scant nod at Harlyn, but she remained in place, clearly with something to say. Already impatient, I looked down at her. "Yes?"

"I would have said no." Her voice was calm and even. "If you had gone along with Gerald's plan to propose marriage at the dinner tonight, I would have told you no." Now she took hold of the reins and climbed into the saddle. With one final glance at me before departing, she said, "When Basil's rescue is over, I will not return to Nessel. Based on the conversation we overheard, nor should you."

"Harlyn—" I began, but she was already riding away.

Nothing more was said until a few hours later, when it had become too dark and too cold for travel. Rather than ride up the more commonly traveled border between the Hiplands and Antora, we had cut through the center of Antora, a more direct route to the capital. Our chances of running into Dominion armies were greater, but it would shave at least a half day off our trip, so it was worth the risk.

While we rode, the need to watch for Dominion soldiers was a fine escape from my other troubles, but trouble can only ever be postponed, not outrun. With night falling fast, we found an abandoned home near the road with a small barn for the horses. The Rawkyren had stayed overhead thus far and flew off now, I assumed, to hunt, as it often did at night. Our shelter wasn't exactly a hiding place, but I hoped any patrols that did happen to pass by would think we belonged here, so there was nothing to investigate.

We warmed a supper over a small fire and then set out our bed-rolls in the center of the room, each of us facing the fireplace, absorbed in our own thoughts. My sketching pad was in front of me, but I hadn't yet made a mark on it.

Finally, just to make conversation, I said, "Did I ever tell you that I can hear the Rawkyren's thoughts? He wants a name."

Harlyn smiled. "A name?"

"He doesn't like being an *it*."

She tilted her head, letting her curly black hair fall to one side. "What name did you have in mind?" I shrugged, and she added, "My father is becoming ill. Perhaps in his honor—"

"I respect your father enough that if this Rawkyren turns out to be as evil as Reddengrad believes them to be, I don't think we ought to borrow your father's name."

Harlyn smiled. "You've been with this dragon for a month. You'd know if it was going to turn bad." That brought on an awkward silence between us, which she quickly filled by adding, "What if we simply call him Rawk?" When I agreed, she added, "My father also respects you very much. If he were well enough to still be in command, he never would have tolerated the kind of talk that we heard from the cavalry."

"No, but now that we've heard it, we have to deal with it. You're under no obligation to return to the Hiplands with me, but I hope you understand that your leaving does nothing for my safety."

Harlyn nodded. "It was a stupid thing for me to say. Of course I'll return. I wish . . ." Her voice trailed off, and when she spoke again, she asked, "If there was no Kestra, would anything be different between us?"

She must have already known my answer, but perhaps she needed to hear it aloud. "Yes, it would be different."

Now Harlyn's hand brushed across mine, and she left it there. "Is there any hope of things becoming different . . . in time?"

I exhaled slowly. The truth was that there was no Kestra anymore, not in reality. Only my memory of her, my wish to have her back, as she was before, as *we* were before. Harlyn's hypothetical question wasn't hypothetical at all. There was no Kestra.

Except there was . . . somewhere.

Still facing the fire, I said, "Unless I can divide my heart from the rest of me, I do not see how it can happen."

Harlyn rotated her body to be closer to mine. Surprised by the sudden movement, I looked at her, and in that same instant, she leaned forward and kissed me. My first instinct was to pull away, but I didn't. At first, it was a single kiss, and that should have been the end of it. But before I could think better of it, I accepted the invitation and kissed her back.

It wasn't long or overly emotional, and yet my heart was still pounding seconds after the kiss ended. I continued to stare at her, though I didn't know what I was thinking, *if* I was thinking.

Harlyn only smiled and pressed her hand flat against my chest. "That is how it happens, Simon. I won't divide your heart, I'll simply steal it away."

With that, she lay down on her bedroll, pulled a blanket up over her shoulders, and closed her eyes to sleep.

I did not, could not. I stayed in front of the fire until long after it had burned itself out, trying to align my thoughts with my feelings. But that was utterly impossible. Nothing made sense; nothing was logical. And there was nothing I could see ahead except more confusion and heartache.

I finally lay down, hoping for a few hours of sleep until we could ride again. As soon as I did, beside me, Harlyn whispered, "That won't be our last kiss, you know."

I knew. I just wasn't yet sure how I felt about it.

· F O U R ·

KESTRA

Somehow I had reached the end of another day that, for all I knew, might have been a thousand years long. Time was becoming impossible to measure. Had it really only been a single day? I genuinely did not know.

I was riding beside Loelle as she drove us in a wagon, she bundled in furs against the thick falling snow, and I in a simple gray skirt and white top with a light cloak. I held out my hand and let the flakes dance lightly upon my skin, amazed at how long it took for them to melt.

"It hasn't snowed in these woods since the war," Loelle commented with a faint smile. "Snow is water and water is life. You've done this for us, Kestra."

"There already was water in the forest," I said, thinking of how I had brought Simon across the borders once to help him heal after a fight with a Dominion oropod. Foul creatures.

"My people created those ponds in the last moments before they were cursed," Loelle said. "They hoped the healing waters might restore them. Those waters may heal the living, but they do nothing for half-lives."

"Why won't you allow me to heal them?" I asked. "Why only heal the forest?"

Without answering, Loelle pointed to a plume of smoke ahead. Beneath it was a chimney and tiny home built of rocks like others in the forest. She said, "That's where we'll sleep tonight."

"Someone lives here?" I asked.

"Not all of the Navan were cursed," she said. "And this particular boy is someone I very much want you to meet."

My brows pressed together and I fell silent. Whoever this *particular boy* was, I didn't like the tone of her voice as she mentioned him, as if this boy should be of particular interest to me. I only heard an echo of her lecture from a month ago, insisting that I let Simon go.

Loelle stopped the wagon beneath a wooden canopy that looked as if it had been recently built. For some reason, that irritated me. I hadn't healed the trees here just so they could be chopped down.

"I won't go inside until you tell me something about this *particular boy*," I said to Loelle.

"His name is Joth Tarquin," she said, as if that was all I needed to know. "He is a son of the Navan."

"And?"

"And he's eager to meet you."

"Ah." If that single fact was everything I needed to know, then that was plenty of reason to dread this visit.

I climbed out of the wagon and followed Loelle to the door. She knocked, then called her name through the door, which I hardly thought was necessary. Until this moment, I had believed she and I were the only fully living beings in All Spirits Forest. Joth Tarquin was evidently the third. I vaguely wondered if there were more.

A moment passed; then the door was opened by a handsome boy with keen blue eyes, and long black hair tied back with a band.

He seemed to be near Simon's age though he was taller and leaner in his build. His smile at Loelle was brief, lasting only until he noticed me at her side. Then the smile dissolved into a full glare. To Loelle, he said, "I told you not to bring her."

"You said you weren't ready for me to bring her," Loelle replied. "That's not the same thing."

His glare shifted toward me, and I was more than happy to return it. "Let's go," I muttered.

"Where will you go?" Joth looked past us to the skies, from which thick snow continued to fall. He widened the door. "I suppose you'd better come in."

With a quick smile, Loelle brushed inside as if the invitation to enter had been given with any sort of enthusiasm. I was more reluctant, keeping my place until he sighed and said, "You're letting the heat out, so if you're going to enter, then do it. I've got to shut the door."

I grimaced but walked past him. Loelle had already removed her cloak and furs and set them near the fire to dry. She approached me, but I backed up. "I can do this myself."

"Very well." Loelle nodded at a pot of stew hanging over the fire. "Joth, might you have enough to share?"

He grunted and fetched a couple of bowls from a small table in one corner. He dished up a thin stew and gave us the bowls without spoons. Loelle took care of that, walking back to the table and getting one for each of us and, notably, taking the chair that Joth likely would have preferred, forcing him to sit across from me. He did but folded his arms and held a steady glare while he watched me eat.

This was absurd, and after a few bites, I'd already had enough.

I walked the bowl over to the table, then crossed the room again to collect my cloak.

"We can't leave," Loelle said.

"I won't stay," I countered.

"You have to stay."

"There's no point," Joth said. "Even if you'd brought me someone more capable, it was still a foolish idea."

"No point in what?" I asked. "Why am I here?"

"Oh, she didn't tell you?" Joth stood, gesturing to Loelle. "She didn't *warn* you?"

"About what?"

He and Loelle exchanged a knowing glance, but neither would answer. So I finished wrapping the cloak around my shoulders, then headed for the door.

"I meant what I said." Loelle stood as if to follow me. "You must stay, Kestra."

"It won't work," Joth said.

I opened the door, then turned back one last time. "Tell me why I am here, or this is the last you will see of me."

Loelle walked to Joth, putting one hand on his arm. "This boy is the key to your success. With his help, you may have a chance of defeating Lord Endrick."

After deferring this conversation more times than I could count, Loelle finally had my attention. "How?"

He sighed. "Close the door. You're letting the heat out . . . again."

I hesitated, slowly shut the door, but kept hold of the handle. "Tell me more."

"I will," Loelle said, "but first I must test your magic with his, to see if it's compatible."

I looked over at Joth, truly curious. "What is your magic?"

"We're not revealing that yet," Loelle said. "Don't be offended, child, but the few of my people who remain have learned not to be too open about their magic until it's necessary—we don't want Lord Endrick to become aware of us."

"Then how are we supposed to know if it's compatible?"

"I can answer that—our abilities will not blend," Joth said. "This is a waste of time."

He'd made his objections perfectly clear, and enough times that I could practically anticipate his exact words. But for now, I merely rolled my eyes and repeated my question to Loelle.

She shrugged. "The only way to be sure is to actually use your powers together, but I fear doing so would alert Lord Endrick to your position. We need a quieter method."

"Such as?"

"There's a simple test." Joth held out his hand to me. I walked over to him and tentatively took his hand. "Don't use your magic, just think about it, and I'll do the same."

I closed my eyes and reached out to feel the strength inside him. How easily I could take enough to sustain myself for days. It would be wrong, I knew that, but he'd been so unlikable since we'd met, the temptation was there.

Still skeptical, I reached for his strength but was surprised to feel something tug from his end too as he focused on me. His magic pressed in tighter and tighter, until I was short of breath. Suffocating.

I could stop him.

Unnerved, I yanked my hand free, and he immediately backed away, eyes wide with alarm. "You considered killing me just now?"

Killing him? No, of course not! Yes, maybe I'd considered draining his strength, incapacitating him for days, but I wouldn't kill him. How would he have known that anyway?

Or how was it that I had felt something from him too?

I stared at him. "What happened?"

"You felt the presence of my magic, as I felt the presence of yours."

"Then there is compatibility," Loelle said.

Joth brushed off Loelle's comment. "It doesn't matter. I will not help her."

Loelle crossed over to him, her hands clasped in a desperate attempt to make him change his mind. "You did connect!"

"It wasn't a connection, only a thought in her that I detected. The kind of thought a person should pay attention to if he wants to live."

"Without your help, she will fail against Lord Endrick," Loelle said.

"She is corrupt," Joth said. "I felt it from the moment she came. The Navan have never been corrupted because we have never connected with anyone outside. We don't know how a connection will affect us."

"But we do know what happens if she fails."

Keeping an eye on me, he said, "And what if she succeeds, as she is? We have never trusted the corruptible, and we cannot start now."

He was speaking to Loelle, but I felt like I'd been hit with his words. Corrupt? That's what Simon had said about me. He'd been so delirious at the time, it had been a simple thing to dismiss it. I had no such excuse for Joth.

Barely glancing at me, Loelle said, "If there are problems, then it's only because she's spent weeks absorbing the curse on this land. Whatever has happened to her, it's been in the service of our people! Don't we owe her something for that?"

"She will betray us before this is over," Joth said. "Anything we owe her, she will make us pay for it. How is she any different from Lord Endrick?"

I'd heard enough. My heart pounding with fury, I stood, retrieved my cloak again, and this time marched straight for the door. I flung it open, hearing Loelle call my name, and took my first step outside. The falling snow was up to my knees by now—Loelle's wagon wouldn't make it through this, or at least, I hoped she wouldn't try to follow me.

From the doorway, she said, "Where do you think you are going?"

I had no idea, but I called back, "I am nothing like Lord Endrick, nor do I need anyone's help to defeat him. I will finish this alone."

I trudged on ahead until the snow was lower on my legs and I could move faster. Wherever I was going, I intended to get as far from Joth and Loelle as possible. I felt the presence of spirits around me as I ran, and I shouted vague orders at them to leave the area entirely or I would never heal them. I wanted to be alone, needed to be alone—to be anywhere that I could think.

Sooner than I had expected, I came to the boundary of the forest, finally able to see rolling hills and open fields waiting for me beyond these densely packed trees. It was strange, to be here inside the forest, a place I had seen so often but rarely dared to enter. Now Antora felt just as foreign, a place I seemed to be seeing for the very first time.

I came closer to where the border of the forest thinned and stretched into open space. Only then did I spot clusters of Ironhearts gathered in pockets around the forest, set up in camps that looked as if they had been here for some time. They were scattered as far as I could see along the entire border. Were they here for me?

I pressed into the shadows of the trees, where I hoped I wouldn't be noticed, and tried to figure out the best way to escape. I couldn't fight off all the Ironhearts who were here.

And even if I did escape, where would I go? I was not welcome anywhere, not wanted anywhere. I still had to kill Lord Endrick but had no means to do it.

"My lady, I've been watching for you."

I nearly fell back as a familiar-looking girl stepped out of a small tent. Her hair was lighter than mine, with a natural curl I'd always envied, even when I'd despised her for having once betrayed me. It had been a long time since I'd thought of her, though I never would forget her. At one time, I'd considered her my closest friend.

"Celia?" I whispered.

Celia was my former handmaiden, and former friend. She had been with me during my exile into the Lava Fields, and had betrayed me to the Coracks. I'd heard almost nothing of her since then.

"How did you know I'd be here?"

Celia shrugged. "We didn't. But we believed that if you did leave these woods, you would be in one of only a few places. This is the area to which I was assigned. I hoped you'd come this way. I felt of anyone, I'd be the best to talk to you."

"Are you here representing the Coracks?" I asked, keeping my place. "Because if you are—"

"I was with them for a while," she said. "Then, last fall, I was captured by the Dominion in a raid of Lonetree Camp. I now serve as a messenger from Lord Endrick . . . as an Ironheart."

I exhaled as I took that in. If she was an Ironheart, then Endrick had the ability to communicate through her, if he desired. And I was certain that he desired it very much.

"You serve as a messenger?" I asked. "What is your message?"

"My king, Lord Endrick, wishes to know how many people must die before you accept your punishment for treason."

That took me aback, but Celia had spoken so calmly, I wondered how deep Endrick's hold was on her heart, how much he controlled her thoughts and feelings now.

"Your king, Lord Endrick, is the only one who needs to die," I replied. "If he surrenders, all other lives will be spared, including yours."

Celia lowered her eyes, as if listening, then said, "Lord Endrick refuses your offer. However, in his mercy, he has one of his own. Vow to serve him, and through you, he will rebuild the Dominion. You will be the lady of Woodcourt, Endrick's prime counselor, and the most powerful woman in all of Antora."

I arched a brow. "Most powerful woman? Without him, I would be a queen."

"He knows you do not have the Olden Blade, nor does he believe you have any hope of finding it again." Celia blinked once, her tone remaining disturbingly even. "But he invites you to come with me now, to go to him in peace. He will help you to understand your powers, and how to use them as he would."

I shook my head. "I have no desire to do anything that will make me more like him. Tell your master that I refuse."

Celia's eyes flashed with a moment of panic, and her voice rose in pitch. "Refuse, and you will leave my master no choice but to kill you. But if you vow to serve him, he will allow you to keep your powers, and reap the rewards of service."

"What rewards have you reaped?" I asked.

Celia didn't even blink. "I am allowed to live, my lady."

In its simplicity, that statement revealed just how desperate she must feel. But I could help. I could do more than that. If she would let me, I could heal her. Offering one hand out to her, I stepped forward. "Celia, I can save your heart. I can save you, but you must come with me into the forest."

Celia shook her head. "It's better to serve him willingly than to suffer needlessly. Either way, he will win in the end. Please, my lady, surrender to him and live."

"I will survive just fine."

"No, my lady. Unless you surrender, you will not survive the next minute."

I looked around me, realizing I was standing on the forest boundary. Ahead of me, five archers who had obviously been in hiding all this time revealed themselves, all with their disk bows aimed at me. I could not attack them all, nor defend myself from so many disks.

One archer in particular caught my attention, a girl my own age with piercing brown eyes and long, thick lashes, and hair the exact color of Simon's.

Simon once said he had a younger sister. Could this be her?

Celia raised one arm. "I am begging you to come with me, my lady. For the good of Antora. Nothing else will save your life."

· FIVE ·

KESTRA

After several long seconds of waiting, Celia's nervousness became apparent. Clearly, she did not want to give orders to harm me, but I knew she would if she had to.

A voice behind me commanded, "Return to the forest, Kestra. Now!"

I turned to see Loelle riding up behind me with Joth in the driver's seat of her wagon. His lips were pressed tightly together in clear irritation, but Loelle's entire body seemed to be tense with fear.

"My lady, announce your surrender and we will escort you to our king." Celia's eyes darted away from me. "He knows about those two behind you. The Navan were cursed here for a reason. They serve only themselves, falsely claiming a larger purpose in this world. Any kindness they are showing you now is only because it benefits them. Once they have taken from you all that they desire, you will be tossed aside."

"That is not true!" Loelle's tone sharpened. "Kestra, return to the forest!"

Celia's gaze shifted back to me, her eyes pleading with me to listen to her. "My lady, they brought you here against your will, manipulating your powers, draining your strength, and robbing you of every glory that should be yours. Lord Endrick can restore it to you. Please, come with me now or these soldiers must shoot."

I took a step backward, my toes on the boundary. I felt half-lives around me, attempting to drag me back with them, but I resisted their tug too.

"Is he frightened of me?" I asked Celia. "Lord Endrick knows what I can do to him."

"The Lord of the Dominion fears nothing," Celia said; then with a cry of pain, her body contracted. "Please, my lady. I beg you to come with me."

He was squeezing on her heart. There was no reason for it—she had done nothing but obey him.

"One more step back," Loelle said. "Then you're safe with us."

"Return to the forest and you do so as their prisoner," Celia said. "Or come with me and be a free leader of the Dominion." She cried out again and I knew Endrick was continuing to torment her. Why was he doing that? "Please, Kestra. He will kill me otherwise."

I held out my hand for Celia. "No, you must come with me. It's only a few steps, and I will save you." I looked up at the archers. "I will save all of you, if you will drop your weapons and come to me as friends."

"They are not friends," Joth said. "They cannot be allowed to enter."

I began to argue with him, until another cry from Celia forced my attention to her again. She was half bent over, clutching her chest, and in her pained voice, she whispered to the disk archers, "Release."

My eye immediately shifted to the girl who shared Simon's brown eyes. She didn't flinch as she sent her disk flying. In that same instant, Joth's arm curved around my waist, yanking me backward, fully within the borders of the forest. The disks collided in the air where I had just stood, exploding into dust against each other, then falling to the ground.

"What sort of game was that?" Joth snarled at me.

"He's killing her—let me go!"

I broke free of him and tried to run out of the forest, but the same half-lives who had just protected me now barricaded me from leaving. A scream pierced the boundary, then it was cut to total silence.

"Celia!"

When I saw her again, she had collapsed to the ground, but her body was still now. Dead.

"No!" Desperately, I turned to Loelle. "You can save her."

"It's too late, and even if I could, not with those archers out there." In a sterner voice, Loelle added, "Besides, she would not have needed saving if you had not come to the border." To Joth, she said, "Put Kestra in the wagon and keep her there until I can get us deeper into the forest."

He half threw me into the back of the wagon, immediately climbing in next to me. If he wanted a fight, he'd get it. I reached for his arm but was repelled by the same half-lives that had prevented me from going to Celia.

Fuming, I shouted, "Celia was right. I am a prisoner here!"

"We're all prisoners here!" he countered. "You're our only chance at escaping, and you might have just ruined it. You should have left the instant you saw the Ironhearts. If they suspected you were here before, now they know it!"

"Well, I won't be here much longer. First chance I find to escape on my own, I will be gone." Still furious, I leaned against the sideboard of the wagon and folded my arms as Loelle drove us away.

Once the border was no longer visible, he said, "You might thank us for keeping you from being shot."

"*Us?* You and your half-life slaves? Does Loelle control you all too? Of all your people, why are you and Loelle the only two who escaped the curse?"

Joth hesitated, but Loelle looked back long enough to say, "We've got to tell her the truth."

He nodded but still said nothing until we had returned to his home. Then Loelle excused herself to go inside while Joth waited with me in the wagon. My arms remained folded, and I stared up at the trees rather than acknowledge him.

After a lengthy silence, he began. "My father was the king of the Navan, many years ago when we lived across the Eranbole Sea. But there was a great war and only a few of us survived. We escaped, coming to Antora only to face another war. Hoping to preserve our people, we took up refuge here in the forest, but so did many of the Halderians. When Lord Endrick cursed these woods, that curse became ours as well. I was very young then. My mother and I were saved only because my father had placed us in hiding outside the woods, but my mother has never forgotten our obligation to restore what has been lost to them all these years."

"Loelle is your mother, Navan's former queen." Suddenly, it made sense why she resented the poor treatment she had received from the Brill.

"Titles mean nothing to us now. It's only the survival of the

Navan that we care about, and the Halderian half-lives as well. My mother is a healer, but her powers do not extend to these curses. I'm a communicator. I can speak to the half-lives and hear them speak to me. No matter the distance, and no matter how quiet."

I smiled. "No offense intended, but if they were going to save someone from the curse, they should have picked someone with greater magic than a communicator."

"I am the only link between their world and this one," he said, obviously offended. "We have used that link to protect this forest. When a person from outside attempts to enter, the decision becomes mine. If the half-lives judge the person to have a good heart, a non-Dominion heart, I will let them in. If they are Dominion, I may order the spirits to attack."

"I've experienced both of those welcomes," I said. "And if you believe me to be corrupt, then I likely haven't faced my last attack."

He shrugged. "That's possible. Though based on what you experienced at the border, the attacks out there will be worse than anything we might do."

"Based on what I've experienced in here, I disagree."

"There are reasons we've had to be so careful. When you took my hand earlier this evening, do you deny wanting to harm me?"

"I had the thought, but nothing more. If I had wanted to harm you, I would have simply done it."

"And if I'd wanted the half-lives to harm you, I would have ordered it. So here we are." Joth sighed. "There is only one guarantee, and that is what Lord Endrick will do if you seek him out alone. I heard what that girl was offering."

"Her name was Celia and she was my friend!" My heart was so

heavy with her loss, I'd barely heard anything he said. If only there were a way to go back and redo those last moments with her. I should have tried harder to get her to come with me. I could have helped her, or saved her myself. Why had I just stood there, frozen between the two worlds?

Joth was either unaware of my turmoil, or he didn't care. He simply shrugged. "All right, I heard what *Celia* was offering. You must know Endrick will not keep his promises."

"That doesn't mean I have to stay here. I'll find another way out of the forest."

"What do you think Endrick will order now that you've been seen? I'll place half-lives around the forest to keep his Ironhearts from coming in, but he already has the forest surrounded. You will not escape."

"I've heard those words before, and I always escape."

"Then what? With no Olden Blade, no army, and, from what I understand, no friends on the outside to assist you in your quest? We may have needed your help to heal this forest, but you need us as well. Let us find a way around the corruption, or better still, a cure for it. Then maybe we can talk about working together." He offered a hand to me. "Perhaps you don't feel the cold, but I do. Return with me, please."

I looked back toward the forest border, wondering how many Ironhearts I could fend off before my strength wore out. Probably not enough to make it worth the risk to my life.

Defeated, I followed Joth back to his little home. It would be warm there, but warmth was not what I needed.

I needed to be stronger. Once again, my thoughts returned to

Celia, though even if I'd found greater strength in my magic, it wouldn't have protected her. Lord Endrick had magic I could not defend against. There was only one solution.

I needed *his* magic.

Which meant I needed to find the Olden Blade. Desperately.

I would do it for Celia and those Ironheart archers, and for everyone I would have been able to save if I were more powerful.

For now, I entered Joth's home, sat against one wall, and thought about how much of a villain Lord Endrick was.

Then I tried not to think about how Joth likely considered me to be just as bad.

And for the first time, I began to wonder if he was right. Maybe I was.

Maybe from now on, I would be.

· SIX ·

SIMON

Harlyn and I were on the road again at dawn and, so far, were making good time. She hadn't said a word about what had happened between us the night before, which was fine by me. The dragon, Rawk, flew overhead, and as usual, I sensed his perception of the land around us, as he warned me far in advance of when to change course to avoid trouble.

Late that afternoon, we stopped in Irathea to rest our horses. While they were being fed and watered, I said to Harlyn, "If we can keep up this pace, we have a chance of meeting up with Captain Tenger tonight."

"That's good." There was a vacancy in her tone. Her mind was elsewhere.

"Is something wrong?"

For a while, I wondered if Harlyn had heard me. But finally, in little more than a whisper, she said, "You believe there are things about Kestra that I'm not telling you. Maybe you're right."

I turned to face her so quickly that it startled her back. "What do you know?"

She took a deep breath before she gathered the courage to

answer, and she did it with a question. "If you knew where Kestra was, what would you do?"

My temper began to warm. "All this time, and you've known—"

"I don't *know*," she said. "But a few days ago, I'm fairly sure that Gerald received a message from Loelle. It was delivered verbally by a courier and I missed most of it." She quickly added, "But I know that when Gerald asked to return a message to Loelle, the courier told Gerald he refused to return to that haunted place again."

"All Spirits Forest," I mumbled. It wasn't fifteen miles away from where we now stood, only an hour's ride. Trina and I had considered whether Kestra could be there. Early in the search, Trina had even explored the perimeter for any sign of life, but her every attempt to enter was blocked by the half-life spirits who dwelled there. We believed that if Trina was not allowed in there, Kestra certainly would not be, so the Coracks shifted their searches to other parts of the country. I had never questioned their decision, and in fact, it still struck me as an unlikely hiding place.

Twice before, I'd been with Kestra inside that forest. The first time, her presence created a palpable tension among the half-lives. The second time, they had tried to kill her.

I shook my head. "It can't be. With or without Loelle, those spirits would never let Kestra stay."

"Maybe not the Kestra that you knew." Harlyn licked her lips. "But would it change anything if the spirits were aware of her magic . . . if they needed it?"

I groaned, frustrated at having failed to think of something so obvious. Kestra surely did not have the strength to heal all the half-lives, but if she became convinced that there was a reason to try, such as with Darrow, her father, I knew she would.

"She's there, Harlyn. I'm sure you're right."

Which left me with an awful decision to make. From here in Irathea, we'd have to change course to get to All Spirits Forest. If we proceeded on to Highwyn for Basil's rescue, we'd miss the forest entirely.

Harlyn seemed to sense my frustration. She waited as I looked from one direction to the other, as if simply staring would make the decision easier.

"If you wish to go after her, I'll come too. Or I'll stay the course with you for Basil's rescue. Whichever you prefer."

I pushed my fingers through my hair, my mind at war with itself. What was the point of rescuing Basil if Kestra was lost? The reverse was true too. Only Basil could lead us to the Olden Blade. Only Kestra could use it.

Nor was it only my thoughts that were stirring. I loved Kestra, or I had loved her, not so long ago. But if I found her again, she would be different now.

And then there was Harlyn, who should be a perfect match for me, who would solidify my claim to the Halderian throne, who was in every way the logical choice.

The hostler who had been caring for our horses walked them over to us. After a quick inspection of his work, Harlyn said, "We'll ride to the forest, and—"

"All Spirits Forest?" The hostler cleared his throat, then added, "I don't know what business the two of you might have anywhere near that place, but you don't want to go there now."

"Why not?" I asked.

He stepped closer and lowered his voice to speak. "Earlier today, I changed horses for some travelers who passed near the forest last night, planning to camp near Limsriver, as many travelers do."

"And?"

"They ended up riding through the night and told me they were lucky to escape with their lives." He looked around before continuing. "They believe the curse is lifting in the woods. Many of the trees have come alive again, birds were flying in and out, and it was snowing. That hasn't happened in a generation."

Harlyn looked at me with wide and curious eyes. That was a confirmation of where we could find Kestra, though I couldn't understand why she would help Loelle . . . unless Loelle was somehow helping Kestra. Was that possible?

"We have to go there," I said, and Harlyn nodded her agreement.

"Didn't you hear me before?" the hostler said. "Those travelers barely got away. Dominion soldiers have surrounded the woods. People around these parts believe that when the curse fades, the barrier will fade too. If that's true, then you can bet they'll go in and destroy the place for good. Get anywhere near the forest, and someone will find you."

My heart sank, something Harlyn acknowledged with a comforting hand on my arm.

"Did the travelers see any way into the forest?" she asked.

The man snorted. "In? You'd be insane to ever cross into the forest, but certainly not while it's returning to what it was. And no, from what they said, I'd guess the bulk of our good king's army is positioned there. Even if I were the king's closest friend, I still wouldn't trust my life to getting near that place."

We thanked the man, then rode off to the nearest bend to privately discuss our decision.

My eyes drifted westward, but this time Harlyn said, "If I thought there were any chance of us getting past those soldiers . . ."

Her voice trailed off, and I turned to her, keeping a thin hold on my patience. "Then what? What would you do if you thought we could get past the soldiers—"

"I'd suggest that we go."

"Why? To protect Kestra, because she's the Infidante? Or to protect me *from* Kestra?"

Harlyn glanced down, lightly combing her fingers through her horse's mane. "I've seen Kestra in battle. If those soldiers confront her, we both know she's entirely capable of taking care of herself." Now she looked up at me. "I know that you used to love her. I know that when she left Nessel a month ago, she either broke your heart or carried it away with her. But I also know, and you do too, that the magic inside her is a poison, and sooner or later, she will use it against you, and probably against all of our people. Yes, Simon, if you go after Kestra, then I am coming with you, to protect you and all Halderians from her."

She waited for me to reply, but I had nothing to say. Much as I wished otherwise, everything she said was true. I gripped the reins of my horse and turned it northward. I nodded at Harlyn, and together, we set out for the capital, to rescue Basil. If we succeeded, he would give us the location of a dagger that Captain Tenger would refuse to hand over to a corrupted Infidante. I knew that too.

After Basil's rescue, Tenger's next order would be Kestra's death.

· SEVEN ·

KESTRA

With little protest, I had followed Joth and Loelle into his home, determined to take control of my life again. So I'd said all the right things, praised Loelle as a blessing to her people, even as she'd brought a curse to me. And I'd done my best to pretend that I was settled with the idea of remaining in All Spirits Forest for as long as I was needed here, but in fact, the very opposite was true.

All night, my mind had been churning with the things that Joth had said while we were outside. The wider scope of Loelle's plan was becoming clear; the purpose of her plan was not.

As Loelle wanted, I was healing the forest. Every day pulling more of Endrick's curse into my body. His corruption.

This corruption was the reason I didn't feel the ice outside; because the ice was inside me now. This was that cold, hard center that had formed like a pit in my heart and had begun to spread.

I should have felt frightened by it, should have already asked Loelle for a way to purge it from myself, but I didn't.

Because now that I knew what this was, I could understand it. Corruption wasn't what anyone had thought.

It didn't weaken or destroy; rather, it fed on weakness to make itself stronger and thus I became stronger too. Corruption was only a powerful magic evolving within a weaker host, binding the one to the other, creating something more perfect than either was alone. I could withstand the ice because I was the ice; I could pass through the storm because more and more, I was the storm.

Simon would disagree, but he was wrong. He was wrong about nearly everything, I realized that now, including when he had said that he loved me. Maybe he loved the Kestra Dallisor he had captured once, the girl he had forced into betrayal of her family and her king. Maybe he even loved that girl when she had become the Infidante, bound to kill Lord Endrick.

But whoever I was now, whatever I had become since I had last seen Simon, I was no longer that girl. No longer . . . me.

I didn't know who I was now, honestly.

A healer, perhaps. And a destroyer. They were one and the same. With magic, I could give strength by destroying it elsewhere, or take strength for myself, destroying its source. I could not give without taking, and I needed to give.

Increasingly, I wanted to take.

My life did not belong to Loelle; I was no tool for her and Joth to use in order to accomplish their goals. I had to watch out for myself because no one else would.

And with that thought, the cold within me spread, assuring me I had made the only decision I could. As soon as possible, I would find the Olden Blade; then Lord Endrick and I would meet again. This time, I would destroy his curse from within its well. Destroy him.

"Kestra, what are you doing? You're bleeding!"

I looked down and realized that, without thinking, I had grabbed

Loelle's knife from off the nearby table and was holding it by the blade. I set it down as Loelle rushed to my side and began to wrap my hand with a rag that had also been left on the table.

"What did you want with the knife?" she asked.

I didn't know, but it frightened me to realize what I had been doing. I had no memory of picking up the knife, and I certainly would never have gripped it by the blade, not in my right mind.

Loelle finished wrapping my hand, fastening it tight with a pin; then she went to the fire and added two logs before coming to sit beside me. There, she patiently waited until I was ready to explain myself. Which I could not do.

After several minutes of silence, I said, "I think Simon's sister is an Ironheart now. I think she was one of the archers out there with Celia."

Loelle took that in with a steady breath. Finally, she said, "I knew Simon's sister, Rosaleen. I knew Celia too, and I'm sorry you had to see what happened to her. But we must keep moving forward, or Celia's sacrifice will be in vain. All that *you* are now sacrificing will mean nothing if we do not succeed."

I glanced away, finally speaking the truth that I'd kept buried since almost the very moment of becoming the Infidante. "I will succeed, Loelle, because I must. But I fear that I will not survive to see the fruits of it. Not with what is happening to me."

Another long pause, then Loelle's whisper. "I should have warned you."

"Simon already tried to warn me, when I saved him from the river below King's Lake. I didn't listen to him. I wouldn't have listened to you either."

"But you feel it now."

"Yes. I've felt it for some time, even before coming here. I didn't realize—"

"With the Endreans—your people—corruption usually comes on slowly, over several years or more. With you, it came on within a week. How did it happen so fast?"

I shook my head. "I don't know."

"I think you do know." She blinked a few times, then in a notably gentle tone, asked, "Before you escaped from Brill, how did their palace explode?"

My eyes darted. "I've already explained that—"

"No, you haven't, not really. I told you that I was nearby when it happened, and I saw you race away shortly afterward. But *how* did it explode?" When I still didn't answer, she added, "Was Lord Endrick there with you?"

"It's as I said before, I did not cause that explosion. Lord Endrick did, in his anger at me."

"Why was he so angry?" Loelle took a deep breath. "Kestra, before you escaped, did you and he come into direct contact?"

I hesitated, replaying those few minutes in my head, as I had often done since coming here. He had reached for me with the intention of killing me, but I had taken hold of his leg, pulling strength from him to heal myself. It had created a cycle of give-and-take between us, one that would be fatal for whichever of us let go first.

I looked up at Loelle. "I think that I pulled in so much of him that it would be impossible for me not to have been corrupted by it."

"And then you have spent a month here, pulling in his curse to yourself." Loelle sighed. "I believe what you have done here is your only chance to succeed as Infidante. But I am deeply sorry for it. I have been searching for a way to remove the corruption."

"I don't want the corruption removed." I saw her eyes widen with alarm, but there was no reason for it. "Corruption doesn't make me evil, like Lord Endrick. It allows me to see things more clearly, to see beyond the pettiness of life and understand what is really important."

"Which is?"

"Power! Not as Lord Endrick uses it, to control the people and keep them in constant fear. But power to give the people of Antora the kind of lives they ought to have had. Power to protect against war and disease and poverty. I can do that for them, Loelle, if I defeat Endrick!"

Loelle shook her head. "You can't do those things, or you shouldn't. Your task is to defeat Lord Endrick; then the people will speak for themselves on how they wish to be ruled."

I let that go, for now. There was no point in arguing something that, to her, was only theoretical. However, my future after I killed Endrick could not be left to chance, nor to the whims of a people who had hardly shown me friendship. I had to make plans, whether she was aware of them or not.

But before that time came, I had to fight him. And that, I was beginning to understand, was the very reason Loelle had brought me here.

"How can I succeed against him?" I asked.

"Lord Endrick knows now that you have magic, and he has some idea of what it is. You will not be able to get anywhere near him on your own. You will need an army."

If I did, it wouldn't be the Coracks. Captain Tenger was surely making plans to replace me as Infidante.

It wouldn't come from Reddengrad. Their losses had been the heaviest in the battle at King's Lake. Even if Basil were still alive to command them, he had been captured by the Dominion.

Nor would Brill come to my aid. I didn't know if they fully blamed me for the explosion of their palace, but they certainly knew I'd been involved.

And what of Simon? Would he come, and bring the Halderians, who hated me? Hated me for being half-Endrean, their enemy race. Hated me for having been adopted by the Dominion, their enemy clan. And hated me for having been chosen as the Infidante, a position they felt should have gone to Trina or maybe to Simon's wife-to-be, Harlyn Mindall.

No, Simon would not come, nor did I want him to come. He had no claim upon the Scarlet Throne. If anyone should be the heir to that throne after Endrick's death, it was . . .

Me.

Sir Henry was dead, which made me the heir to Woodcourt, and heir to the throne.

"I am alone, then," I mumbled.

Loelle took my hands in hers. "No, my lady. You have a large army who will follow you into battle. At the command of—"

"Joth Tarquin." My eyes widened. "Joth can communicate with the spirits here. Loelle, it won't work. If he and I are separated during the attack—"

"It's almost certain that you will be. But if your magic is compatible, and if you are able to unite your powers, then he will go into the battle sharing in what you can do, and you will enter the battle able to command an army that Endrick cannot kill, because there isn't enough life in them to be killed."

I said to her, "What do you mean, *if* our magic is compatible?"

"That's what we're here to find out."

From behind me, Joth said, "If this works, then together, you and I will ensure Endrick's defeat."

· E I G H T ·

SIMON

It was very late when Harlyn and I rode into Highwyn. Rawk probably wasn't far away, but with these tall buildings and narrow roads, I couldn't see the dragon anywhere. The streets were exceptionally quiet, even for this time of night. Usually I would have expected to evade endless patrols of Dominion soldiers, but perhaps with so many soldiers sent to All Spirits Forest, and after his losses in our battle last fall, Lord Endrick had fewer soldiers to spare. I hoped that was the case, anyway.

Near the center of Highwyn, the Coracks kept a small base disguised as a Loyalist home for those occasions when we needed to be in the capital. For safety reasons, we rarely had more than two or three people here at any given time, but the last I had heard, my younger sister, Rosaleen, had been one of those stationed here. Much as I loved her, I had mixed feelings about seeing her again. It had been almost a year since our last meeting, and my life had almost entirely changed. Her life had too. I wasn't sure if she knew that our mother had died, and how it had happened, and why. Every time I had started to write her a note, I changed my mind and crumpled it up. This had to be something I told her in person.

"Are you all right?" Harlyn asked. I didn't answer immediately and she added, "I can see that you're not. What can I do?"

"All I ask is for the truth."

Now it was her turn to fall silent, and we rode on without speaking.

Many more than two or three people were here now. Lights inside the home illuminated shadows of at least a half dozen people. As we approached, a large Corack named Hugh, but whom we called Huge, immediately walked outside to greet us. He must have been assigned to the watch.

"We weren't sure if you'd come, but it's good to see you both." Huge offered to help Harlyn off her horse, and while she dismounted, he added, "I'll get your horses fed and watered while you go inside. They're making final plans for a morning rescue."

I thanked him, and once I'd climbed off my horse and grabbed my satchel, Harlyn and I cautiously opened the door, announcing ourselves as we entered. I didn't want to raise anyone's alarm if they didn't immediately recognize us.

"Simon!" Trina was the first to run up to us and enclosed me in a hug; then she stood back and studied Harlyn. They had been friendly before, so at first I didn't understand Trina's cool welcome. Perhaps it was a recent loyalty that Trina had developed to Kestra. Trina had been there when Loelle took Kestra away; in fact, she had been there for part of their journey to . . . wherever. Trina believed that Harlyn had been in on the plan to send Kestra away, one of the many questions Harlyn had never fully answered.

Gabe was the next to greet us. The last time I'd seen him, he had been recovering from some terrible injuries, a gift from the Dominion. But he seemed to be back to his usual self, though perhaps a little tired. No one had done more to search for Kestra than he and Trina.

Gabe gave Harlyn a warmer greeting than Trina had done, then invited us into the rear parlor to discuss the rescue plans for Basil.

Captain Tenger was in the room, standing over a table with a large piece of parchment on it, upon which was a map of Woodcourt. He looked up at me; then he noticed Harlyn and nodded, pleased to see her.

"We didn't think you'd make it in time," he said. "But we can definitely use your help."

"We intend to give it," I said. "But I had hoped to see my sister first. Is she still assigned to this base?"

Tenger's eyes darted, and I instantly knew something was wrong.

My voice lowered. "Where is my sister?"

Trina touched my arm. "Rosaleen was on patrol a couple of weeks ago and never returned. It's believed that she was captured by the Dominion. We think she's still alive, but that she's an Ironheart now."

My chest tightened, and I was vaguely aware that Harlyn had taken my hand. "Do we know where she is?"

Trina only shook her head, but there was deep sorrow in her eyes. She and Rosaleen had fought together several times in the past.

Tenger cleared his throat to get my attention. "Simon, as always, the best plan for rescue is defeat of the Dominion. Are you still willing to help?"

I gritted my teeth and nodded, irritated at his dismissal of the awful news I'd just received, but I also knew he was right. Defeat of the Dominion wasn't our best plan for rescuing those we had lost; it was our only plan.

Tenger picked up the parchment. "We only know a few things for certain." He pointed at the lowest level of Woodcourt. "Basil was dragged from the basin beneath the dungeons where he had somehow managed to stay alive and to hide for a month. We know he is in such bad condition that the Dominion's usual method of torturing information out of him simply isn't possible, so they are trying to get him well enough for questioning. But we also have to accept that, in his delirium and weakness, he will tell them where the Olden Blade is."

"Do we know where he is now?" I asked.

Tenger nodded. "That's why it's so important you've come. He's somewhere in Woodcourt, but we know nothing more specific than that. Since the death of Sir Henry, it's been abandoned by its servants, but the Dominion still uses it. Of all of us, you and Trina know it best, so we need you both to lead the search. The rest of us will be there for support."

Harlyn leaned forward. "You say the Dominion uses it. What does that mean?"

"We're not sure of their current numbers, only that there are fewer soldiers now than there were a few days ago, so at least that is good news. We need to expect a heavy defense—as many as five Ironhearts for each one of us."

Harlyn smiled over at me. "That's a relief. I thought we'd have more of a challenge."

Tenger's sharp glance showed no humor whatsoever. "This is nothing to joke about. It is possible, even likely, that we will lose some people in this mission, or worse, that we won't get Basil out alive." He turned to the rest of the group. "Our top priority is to learn from Basil where he hid the Olden Blade. That is more important than his survival, and more important than yours." Now his eyes returned to me. "Even more than a king."

"I'll go in with the rest of you," Gabe said, "but we need more of a plan than each of us taking down five Ironhearts."

Trina's eye flicked to my hardened right forearm. I knew what she was thinking, and I was too.

"I don't really have a plan," I began, "but I do have a Rawkyren that is ready to be tested."

"What can it do?" Huge asked.

"I don't know, honestly. But we seem to be connected by thought, and I have the very strong sense that it wants to be part of whatever we're doing."

Trina stood and pointed to Tenger's map of Woodcourt. "For that dragon of yours to be useful, we need to draw the Ironhearts outside."

"How do we know it will attack?" Tenger asked.

Harlyn looked from him to me. "Rawk will protect Simon. Put Simon out there as bait. The Ironhearts will want to capture him alive. And the dragon will attack . . . probably."

That caused my heart to skip a beat. I really didn't know how this would go. "Probably. Thanks for the suggestion, Harlyn."

She leaned over and kissed my cheek, a gesture I knew the others didn't miss. "I'll be right there at your side."

"It's as good a plan as we'll get on such short notice," Trina said. "When do we leave?"

Tenger reached for a disk bow, one I assumed he had stolen from an Ironheart somewhere. "We go now."

· NINE ·

SIMON

Until now, my communication with Rawk had been passive. I was always aware of his general location and purpose, as he surely was with me. But I'd never attempted to make a demand of him. I didn't even know if that was possible. Rawkyrens seemed to be the last of the breeds of dragons. Something in them was fierce enough to survive, and I would not dare to expect his obedience. I could only hope for it, and I was hoping now as never before that he would come. My life literally depended upon it.

Since we seemed to share thoughts, I sent a thought to him for the first and most important step in Basil's rescue: to draw the Ironhearts out of Woodcourt. Every available Corack was already stationed nearby with disk bows and hopefully would bring down the Ironhearts as they emptied out of the house.

Every available Corack, but two. Trina would lead Tenger into Woodcourt to find Basil and either bring him out, or keep him alive until we had secured the manor.

Harlyn stood near me, and when the last of us were in place, she whispered, "Are you sure Rawk will come?"

Almost as if in answer, Rawk immediately flew overhead, his

silvery wings spanning wider than when I had last seen him. He landed on the garden lawn almost directly in front of me, which was a problem. I needed to be in place to defend Rawk as the Ironhearts came outside.

"I think he landed there to protect you," Harlyn said with a slight smile.

"Well, I know what's coming. He doesn't. Follow me."

I led Harlyn to my left. Huge and Gabe were hiding on the sides of the garden, and I motioned to them where we were headed. But no matter how fast I moved, Rawk shifted his position to stay in front of me.

"I'll go hide with the others," Harlyn said. "I'd tell you to stay safe, but it's obvious Rawk has it under control."

She had only taken a few steps when the first group of Ironhearts emerged, nearly ten by my count, though I didn't have as clear a view of the area as I would have liked. Gabe and Huge shot off a few disks, and the Ironhearts ran for cover, shouting into the house for help.

I tried to send thoughts for Rawk to allow me to fight, but when he remained in my way, I ran toward him, even as he widened his wings to protect me. I grabbed the end of one wing and climbed up on his crouched rear leg to see better, but with that wing, he swept me onto his back and, instantly, I detected his thoughts. He was going to fly.

No, *we* were going to fly. The thought of it sent ripples through my gut, but I'd known this was coming sooner or later. I gritted my teeth and desperately felt around for something to hold on to, but Rawk's scales were smooth and harder than the metal of my sword.

"I'll fall!" I warned Rawk, but my words were drowned by his roar as we took flight, escaping a black disk that would have hit him otherwise. Or maybe that wasn't a problem. From this height, I saw other fallen disks on the ground directly in front of where he had been. None of them pierced his scales.

Rawk angled in a sharp circle over the gardens, which might have made a quick end of me except that my hardened forearm seemed to give me both strength and balance on Rawk's back. And in the middle of his arc, Rawk let out a fiery breath hot enough that it nearly evaporated the Ironhearts below who were targeting us. Another group emerged and met the same fate, even before they could strike.

"No more!" I shouted at Rawk. So far, I hadn't seen my sister, but it was possible she was inside.

A single soldier had remained hidden beneath an overhang attached to Woodcourt. Even from here, I could see him shaking. He stood and called up to me, "If we surrender, we are dead anyway. But will you allow us to run? That may be our only chance."

Tenger was nearby, and I knew what his orders would be. So I quickly replied, "Then get everyone who is inside that home as far from here as possible. You have two minutes. After that, anyone we find will be ours."

Faster than I thought possible, the man shouted an alarm that became muffled when he raced inside Woodcourt. Within seconds, from my altitude, I saw Ironhearts empty from the manor as if lightning were at their heels.

Huge, Gabe, and Harlyn ran from their hidden positions to begin a cursory inspection of the interior gardens. When Rawk seemed to think the area was safe, he landed on a low wall nearby. I leapt off his back, relieved to be on solid ground again, then ran into the east wing to begin searching rooms.

Lily Dallisor's room was in the rear, and nothing looked even slightly out of place.

Sir Henry's apartment was on the opposite side of the corridor. I opened the first door. No soldiers were here, though the clearstones in the room were warmed. I also noticed half-empty mugs, still steaming, and an unfinished game of cards. Evidence of soldiers who had left in a hurry.

Farther on, I opened the door to Sir Henry's bedroom at the same time as Trina and Tenger entered the room directly from the gardens. Basil was in the bed against the wall, pale and so thin that the bones of his face were prominent. His light blond hair was filthy and matted on one side, and his wrists were tied to the posts of the bed, which seemed absurd considering that he was clearly too weak to attempt an escape. For all I knew, he was already dead. His eyes were closed, and he wasn't moving.

Trina reached him first but paused to stare at him. I saw sympathy in her expression, which I understood, but other emotions were there as well that were harder to identify. This was a side of Trina I'd rarely seen before, more tender than the brittle veneer she usually displayed.

Finally, she pulled back the sheet that covered him, revealing deep bruises on his arms and bare chest. She placed her hand over his heart and left it there for several tense seconds before saying, "If he's alive, it won't be for long."

Tenger leaned over Basil and loudly said, "You're with friends, Sir Basil. You must tell us where the Olden Blade is."

Basil's eyes fluttered, and he stirred slightly, then settled again into unconsciousness. I noticed more heavy bruising along the sides of his neck when he moved. The Dominion had been working on him, but I figured he hadn't told them anything about the Olden Blade, or he'd be dead already.

Trina started to say something, but then her eyes widened and she shouted my name. From almost directly behind me, an Ironheart had emerged from a closet. His sword struck once against my right forearm, but before I could engage him, he made a second swipe along the side of my body. I struck back, injuring his shoulder, then he ran for the garden door. Tenger followed, but he disappeared into the gardens. Seconds later, Huge called out, "I got him!"

Trina stood halfway between me and Basil, clearly unsure of where to put her attention. "Are you all right?"

I nodded and leaned against the wall for support while I kept a hand over the worst area of my injury. "Tend to Basil." My life was not in danger. His was.

"What can you do for him?" Tenger asked.

Trina looked at him and shook her head; then Tenger turned his gaze on me. "Please tell me you know where Kestra is. We need her."

A thought entered my heart, so clear that I knew where it had come from. "Even if I knew, I couldn't get to her in time to save Basil." I caught the flap of a dragon wing outside the window overlooking the garden. I smiled at Tenger. "But I think my dragon believes he can."

With those few words, Rawk launched himself into the air, flying south. As I expected, toward All Spirits Forest.

Toward Kestra.

· TEN ·

KESTRA

I eyed Joth suspiciously, my heart beginning to pound in my chest. What did he mean, *if* our magic was compatible, if *this* worked? If what worked?

Loelle squeezed my uninjured hand. "I'll leave you two alone to talk. What happens now is up to you."

I started to ask what she meant, but she was already walking outside, making the vague excuse of needing to do "something important," so I asked Joth the same question. "What is supposed to happen now?"

"Endrean magic—your magic—is different from the magic of my people. The Navan are able to combine our abilities, amplifying each other's powers and working as one. But as I explained earlier, it's never been attempted with anyone of another race."

I rolled my eyes. "So if our magic combines, then you'll be able to use my powers, and I'll be able to use yours?"

"Yes, for as long you and I are connected . . . in theory."

"So this connection isn't permanent?"

"With the Navan, it is." Joth sighed. "Combining magic is a very personal experience. It requires the two people involved to share each other's thoughts and emotions. The bond becomes very close . . . the closest of all bonds."

"I won't do it," I said. "We don't even know each other, and we certainly share no feelings for each other."

He smiled. "If you have any feelings at all for me, I know what they must be. I apologize for my behavior earlier. I felt my mother was forcing something upon both of us without caring for the consequences of combining magic."

"What consequences? Are you speaking of love, because—"

"Connecting powers has nothing to do with love, but it often becomes love, because no one will ever be closer to you than the person with whom you have combined magic." When I didn't answer, he said, "My mother first proposed this idea after she brought you to All Spirits Forest. I rejected it too, for all of the same reasons you oppose it, though I've begun to change my mind. I know Celia's death upset you, and I know you're trying to do what you believe is right. So maybe enough good remains in you that we can work together."

I rolled my eyes, wondering what might follow that sour compliment. Would he congratulate me for not getting anyone killed today? Or admire my features with the glow of Endrick's curse on my skin? I had no interest in him or his piercing words.

Sensing my irritation, he added, "I've had a month to get used to the idea of connecting. I wish I could give you the same time too, but the Dominion is clearly aware of what you're doing here, so we're out of time. We should at least test whether we truly can combine powers."

I was skeptical of that too. "I won't do this test. I'll find another way."

He started to answer, then tilted his head and, with a tone of surprise, said, "You have a visitor."

My brows wrinkled. How was that possible?

Without another word, he walked to the door where Loelle was waiting on the other side. "Stay ready," he mumbled to her. "I'm told there is some unrest."

Then he widened the door, and almost instantly, I felt a new presence in the room, something warm and loving, something familiar.

"Darrow?"

I couldn't see or hear him, but I knew he was there.

"Where is he?" I asked.

Joth nodded sideways. "Beside me. He's staring at you, Kestra."

My eyes filled with tears, and I turned to about where Darrow would be. With a quick glance at Joth, I said, "I'm going to heal him."

"He's different than the others here," Joth said. "He was cursed differently, so there is more . . . substance to him. Yet it will be harder than you think to restore your father, requiring more than you alone can give."

I immediately understood where this was going. "But if you and I were connected, then I could do it, is that the plan?" Joth hesitated, and I stepped closer to him. "I will not be forced into this!"

"I didn't bring him here! He came . . ." Joth cocked his head again. "Wait. Something has happened." He started toward the door, but Loelle opened it first.

"I hear noises," she said. "Oropods. They're inside the forest!"

Joth held up his hand for silence, listened with a growing tension in his eyes, then said, "The Dominion has breached the forest boundaries. We are doing our best to stop them, but there are so many, we can only slow them down."

"We've got to get Kestra out of here," Loelle said.

"Not without my father!" I was firm on this point. "What do we need to do? I'll connect with you now."

"Not like this," Joth said. "I won't do it this way."

An oropod screech sounded in the distance. Far away, but not far enough. Loelle grimaced, then held out her arm to me. "Take what you need to restore your father," she said. "Hurry!"

I held out my hand, and Joth told me that Darrow had placed his hand against mine, something I felt in my heart rather than on my skin. As quickly as possible, I sent strength to him, gradually feeling warmth against my palm as a faint image of my father appeared. Drawing from Loelle, I continued to give to him, though I was fading fast, and I was terrified of taking too much from Loelle.

The faint image of my father gradually grew in presence, like a person emerging from a fog. As soon as I saw the light in his eyes, I fell to my knees and released Loelle, whom Joth caught before she fainted entirely. While he helped Loelle to a bed, Darrow knelt beside me, touching my face with his fingers, then wrapping his arms around me.

"I thought I'd never see you again through living eyes," he whispered.

Tears ran down my cheeks, though I was too empty to return his embrace. I only said, "I'm sorry." I wasn't sure why I was saying it, only that I knew I needed to.

Another screech cut through the darkness, though this one was different from before. Darrow stood and ran to Joth's door, cracking it open.

"I've called the others to come." Joth began strapping any weapons he could to himself. "They'll guard my home for as long as we need them to, but that won't help us escape."

"An escape is available to at least one of us," Darrow said, widening the door. "And I think it's you, Kestra."

Directly outside the door was a dragon, noticeably larger than the giant condors in Lord Endrick's service. Its scales were silver and more reflective than the finest mirrors. Its eyes were large and intelligent and as focused on me as when Simon used to look my way. The dragon crouched low, as if waiting for a rider.

Loelle must have seen it too, for she sat up on one arm and said, "Trina rode with us when we left Nessel. At that time, she told us that Simon had saved a Rawkyren. Do you suppose—"

"He sent this animal to find me," I whispered. "I think I'm supposed to ride it out of here."

"You can't go alone," Loelle said. "As weak as you are, you'll fall to your death. Joth, you must go too."

"She'd rather have her father there," he said.

"But she needs someone with magic," Loelle said. "Go with her."

I looked up at Darrow, who smiled as kindly as he always did. "A battle against the Dominion is coming," he said. "I'll be there for it, I promise."

"You need to go now," Loelle said. "If the Ironhearts get closer, the spirits can keep them at bay for a while, but not forever."

That was enough to get me to my feet. With Joth's help, I stumbled toward the Rawkyren, rolled onto its back, and felt Joth's arms wrap around me as he braced us for a launch into the air. Which happened so suddenly that I felt like my stomach was floating up to my chest; then we cleared the treetops and went higher. And sometime shortly after that, I fell asleep, utterly exhausted.

· ELEVEN ·

KESTRA

W e've crossed over Highwyn." Joth was nudging me awake and smiled when I opened my eyes. I sat up, surprised to find myself feeling better than I had before, while Joth's shoulders seemed heavier than when I'd last seen them. I suspected that, as close as he had been holding me as we flew, I must have drawn some of his strength to myself.

I tugged at the rag Loelle had wrapped around my palm after I had held the knife. The cut was already healed, further evidence that I had pulled strength from Joth. Yet even if he was weaker, he continued to hold me close.

"Highwyn?" I had expected the dragon would fly us south to Nessel, where Simon would be. If Simon had come to Highwyn, it would be for only one reason.

"Basil's rescue," I mumbled. Either he had been rescued, or was still in need of rescue. Or they had failed in the rescue but had obtained the location of the Olden Blade.

I hoped it was the first, or at least that he was alive. I had not always treated Basil as kindly as I ought to have done. Despite all of that, he had cared for me, and I desperately wanted him to be safe and well.

It wasn't long before the dragon flew lower and I began to

recognize the roads and buildings beneath us. More specifically, I recognized my former home, Woodcourt. A long, scorched line cut across what had once been our gardens, and I saw fallen bodies. The dragon must have done this too.

The dragon landed near the rear entrance, and Joth dismounted first, then helped me slide onto solid ground. My feet were barely down on the ground before Trina ran outside, calling my name.

"Is Basil here?" I asked.

Her eyes widened momentarily, surprised that I knew why I was here, then she said, "His life is in grave danger. Can you help him?"

"She's still recovering from having helped someone else," Joth said.

"Who are you?" If Trina picked up on the protective tone in Joth's voice, she clearly resented it.

"I'll do everything I can," I said. "Take me to him."

Trina led the way into Woodcourt and toward the east wing, my parents' half of the home. As we ran, I asked, "Simon, is he—"

"He's here, but he's getting bandaged. Nothing serious," she quickly added. "I'm sure he'll want to see you as soon as he can."

By then, we had reached the door to Sir Henry's room. I hesitated in the corridor, dreading going inside. It was difficult enough to return to Woodcourt, mostly because of who my adopted father had been in any of our forced interactions. I'd rarely been allowed into his room. If anything, it was his sanctuary from me. But if Basil was in there, then I needed to enter.

I drew in a deep breath and held it when I opened the door. Immediately, my concern for having to think of my adopted father shifted to looking at Captain Tenger, who stood to greet me. He gave me a polite nod, but I did not return it. I did not trust what he might do the second my head was down, and I was surprised he trusted me enough to bring me here.

"Thank you for coming," he said.

"Has Basil said anything?" When Tenger shook his head, I added, "Then leave us alone. I need privacy to do this."

That wasn't entirely true. I didn't *need* the privacy, but I wanted it, and certainly wanted it from Tenger.

"Trina will stay—" Tenger began.

"Alone!" I snapped.

Joth began directing him and Trina toward the door, with both of them now asking who he was. When they left, Joth closed the door behind him, leaving me alone with Basil.

I warmed the clearstone in the room, brightening its light, then immediately set to work. Basil's cheeks and eyes were sunken in, and his neck was so thin, I wondered how it held up his head. I placed one hand over his heart and felt a faint, reluctant thump, each one slower than the one before it. He was within minutes of death.

No sooner had I connected with Basil than I drew in a harsh gasp, sensing just a portion of what had happened to him, what was still happening. Endrick had tortured him physically, but there was also an internal torture I didn't fully understand. It was twisting his soul, causing a torment I also felt in my own flesh. I would have to take as much as I could to have any chance of saving him.

I began with his heart, giving him strength until his pulse evened out. He wasn't out of danger yet, but I didn't want to give him too much too fast, for both our sakes.

Then I drew in some of the curse, which seemed to create holes within me that could not be filled by anything other than the ice that was already there. Allowing the ice to expand was the only way I could continue my work, but even then, I finally could do no more.

No more than half, never more than half.

While I rested, I noticed a washbasin on the table beside him. I took the rag and tenderly washed Basil's face, then poured a few drops of water into his mouth.

I gave him a little more strength after that, until his chest began to rise and fall with the deeper breaths he was taking. I was fairly sure I sensed some broken ribs, or hopefully they were only badly bruised, but I couldn't heal them as completely as Loelle would. I could only give him strength to live.

I continued to give, feeling myself weaken, especially because it hadn't been long since I had helped Darrow. And finally, I knew I had to quit, or I would have nothing left. I laid my head on the side of Basil's bed and fell asleep.

Sometime very early in the morning, I felt a hand in my hair. Startled, I sat up straight and saw Basil watching me. His smile was thin and weak, but it was there. He was clearly struggling to keep himself awake, and he seemed to be having trouble speaking.

I reached for a cup and offered him more water. He took a few sips, then almost mouthed the words as he whispered, "Olden Blade."

"Did you tell them where it is?" I asked. "Do they know?"

His eyes darted to the right and fear passed through them, but when he looked back at me, he shook his head, very faintly.

"Can you tell me where it is?" I asked.

He nodded and motioned for me to lean in closer, which I did. His head dropped back on the pillow, and for a moment, I was sure he had fallen asleep, but then I heard the words *Lily's grave.*

· TWELVE ·

SIMON

I knew the exact moment when Kestra arrived. I felt it in Rawk's arrival, his landing behind Woodcourt like a soft thud in my chest. But even more, I felt her nearby. I made a move to stand and greet her, but Harlyn put her hands on my shoulders and pressed me back into the chair. "I have to bind this wound. Do you want to bleed all over her for a greeting?"

She was being kinder than she needed to be, which only worsened the guilt I felt. But maybe that was because she felt guilty too.

While she worked on my shoulder, the guilt must have become too much, for when she spoke, it was with one long breath that sounded as if it had been rehearsed. "Before you speak to Kestra, I ought to tell you something. The night she left Nessel, I wasn't part of the plan, but I knew of it."

She waited for me to respond, but my chest had tightened and I didn't trust myself to speak. If I did, I was sure we'd both regret what followed.

Finally, she continued. "She came into your room and saw the infection in your arm, how sick it was making you. I spoke with Kestra myself. I'm the one who convinced her to leave."

"And what did you say to her?" My tone was flat, the best I could manage in that moment.

"She wanted to help, but we couldn't let her, not without knowing what it would do to you." Harlyn paused. "I didn't say anything that wasn't true, but I'm certain what I said was hurtful."

At first I couldn't answer her, or even organize my thoughts to speak. All this time she had deliberately concealed this information, no matter how many times I had asked, or even insisted that I knew she was holding something back. I wondered if she would have told me this much if Kestra had not come.

"Why didn't you tell me this before?" I mumbled.

"To protect you." She finished tying the bandage, then sat in a chair in front of me. "I meant what I said earlier, Simon. She could not be trusted then, no matter how much she loved you, and she cannot be trusted now. I'm here to protect my king, even if that means protecting him from himself."

"You had no right to do that!"

If she noticed my anger, it didn't seem to bother her. With an overly calm voice, she replied, "I had the obligation to do it. And I hope one day you'll understand that." She bit her lip as she considered what else she might say to excuse herself but must've come up with nothing. All she said was "We should join the others."

That was the last thing I wanted, but if Kestra was going to be discussed tonight, I needed to be there. So I walked with Harlyn into a small dining room, where most of the Coracks had already gathered. I no sooner had taken a seat near Gabe when Tenger and Trina walked in with a boy our age with long black hair tied behind his back, reminding me of Gabe. But this boy's eyes were sharper and darker, and seemed to be making a quick assessment of everyone present. I was assessing him too, wondering about his weapon of choice. Everyone in Antora had one, but he didn't have the build of a person who was accustomed to the violent life in Antora. His hands appeared to be capable of work, but they looked too soft to be a farmer's or a fighter's, and he wasn't well-dressed enough to be of the upper class. I was genuinely curious.

"Who is this?" I asked.

"His name is Joth Tarquin," Tenger said. "Claims to know Loelle."

Joth grimaced. "Actually, what I claimed is that Loelle is my mother. She sent me here with Kestra, for Kestra's protection."

That got my attention. "Protection from whom?"

Joth gestured around the room. "All of you." His gaze returned to Tenger. "You're the captain. You want to kill her and replace her with—" He pointed at Trina. "Replace her with you, is that right?"

"That's not the plan," Trina said, though I knew at least part of what Joth said had to be the plan. Tenger could not afford to let Kestra leave here, as unpredictable as she would be with corrupted magic. The only question was whether Trina was in on the plan.

Joth looked at me next. "You're Simon. Do you still love her?"

The question stole the breath from my lungs. I hadn't admitted my feelings aloud to anyone but Kestra. I wasn't sure what my feelings were anymore, and I certainly didn't know how she might feel about me.

"I want to see her," I said, immediately angry with myself for making it a request, as if I needed Joth's permission.

Ignoring me, Joth merely turned to Harlyn. "And you're the girl that Simon is supposed to marry. I assume that hasn't happened yet."

Before Harlyn could answer, Tenger said, "You seem to know more about us than we know about you. What race are you and Loelle? Not Endrean?"

Joth scoffed. "We're the Navan, or what remains of our people after we were scattered by war."

"You have magic?" Harlyn asked.

"Yes, but it doesn't corrupt like the Endreans'. Since we are working together, more or less, I need to tell you something. Even Kestra does not know this yet. I didn't want to alarm her if it wasn't necessary."

"Yes?" Tenger stepped forward, arms folded.

"As Kestra and I flew here on that dragon—"

"My dragon," I cut in.

Joth glanced at me. "As Kestra and I flew here on *Simon's* dragon, about halfway between the forest and Highwyn, I saw an army just outside the capital, coming from the east. Their flags were white, but almost translucent, and they appeared to be armed for war."

"The Brill," Tenger said, then tugged at his beard. "How close are they?"

"Within the day," Joth said. "Do they come as allies or enemies?"

"I don't know." Tenger eyed me with a warning to say nothing more to Joth, as if I would.

"Why didn't you tell Kestra about it?" Trina asked. Maybe she didn't get the warning glare of silence from Tenger.

Joth folded his arms and leaned against the wall. "From what Loelle has explained, it's obvious that Kestra has only a few allies, and even fewer friends. I didn't want to alarm her until I knew whose army I'd witnessed. Whatever the Brill are to you, they are no friend to Kestra."

That was true enough.

Tenger said, "Kestra does have friends here, but we must know the truth about her. Has the corruption within her spread?"

Joth hesitated before saying, "The price of removing the curse from All Spirits Forest was high. Of course it has affected her."

I sat up straighter. "She's been taking in the curse? You lecture us on friends and allies and that's what you've been doing to her?"

"What we've been doing is her best chance to succeed as Infidante, possibly her only chance. And Loelle has a plan to remove the corruption. If she survives—" He stopped abruptly, as if he had said more than he intended. Then he cleared his throat and said, "I'm sure Kestra will be exhausted once she is finished with Basil. I don't want any of you going near her room. I'll know if you do."

"That's not your decision," Tenger said. "Basil was rescued by us and has information that we desperately need. The Coracks are in charge here, not you—"

"I don't claim to be in charge of Basil or your general affairs," Joth said. "But I am charged with Kestra's protection and I do not trust any of you. So you will stay away from her room or pay the price for it."

Gabe opened his mouth to object, but I asked Joth, "Are you guarding that room tonight, then?"

"I am, and when she is ready to leave, I will see that she gets away from here safely. None of you will stop us."

"We wouldn't think of trying," I said, to shocked expressions from the others around me. I knew how it sounded, to be so quick to give up Kestra's defense, not only to a stranger, but to a stranger who was ordering us around like hirelings. Even Harlyn nudged me, saying that we had no reason to trust this boy, and I didn't.

But I trusted Tenger even less. I knew Kestra's fate if she remained here. With my injuries, I wouldn't be much help in protecting her, and I didn't trust anyone around me with her safety. As frustrating as it was to hope for anything from this arrogant person, he was probably the best chance she had to walk away from here.

Joth nodded at me, as if we had come to an agreement that he felt he had earned. He said, "Perhaps you do love her, Simon, for you have shown the purest kind of love possible just now, to acknowledge that she is better off without you. I promise, I will take care of her."

My fists curled, but before I could retort, he had exited the room.

"We can't let her go anywhere with him," Trina said as soon as the door closed.

"Of course not. Once she heals Basil, she will get the location of the Olden Blade." Tenger turned his attention to me. "You have her trust more than any of us. Keep her here until we can safely recover the blade."

And then they would kill her. If there was any hope of finding a solution for Kes, I needed to be involved. So I nodded, saying, "I'll keep watch outside Basil's room."

"Stay out of Joth's way as you do it." Tenger saw me about to object and added, "You're in no condition to fight him, and whatever happens tonight, it is not about which of you two Kestra prefers. Remember that."

I felt Harlyn's hand on my shoulder. She said, "Let me wait outside the room with you."

But I shook my head. "You did enough damage the last time you talked to Kes. We both know that a second conversation would only make things worse."

Harlyn shrugged. "We also both know that tonight won't go well, whether I'm there or not. I'll stay where no one will see me, but I won't be far away either."

To that, I nodded. Because the truth was, I was nervous to speak to Kestra again. Harlyn was right. This was going to be a very long night.

· THIRTEEN ·

KESTRA

L ily's grave."

Those were the only two words Basil spoke before he drifted off to sleep, a calmer, more restful sleep than before.

And I needed time as well to recover my strength, which gave me an opportunity to reflect on those words. Basil's decision to bury the Olden Blade at my mother's grave had been a brilliant one. Even if someone suspected the dagger were there, my adopted father never would have allowed anyone to disturb her resting place. Whatever else he lacked, Sir Henry had dearly loved his wife.

Gradually, I began to feel stronger again, which meant I needed to go after the blade.

I had forgotten my cloak at Joth's home and would have liked it now. Not for the cold outside—that wouldn't matter to me—but I liked the idea of hiding within its folds, of leaving this place with the hood up so that no one would know who I was. If that was not possible, at least I could make some changes. My mother always kept a few of her dresses in my father's wardrobe, and I pulled out one now. It wasn't fancy, but it was nicer than what I'd had on before and certainly cleaner. I tied a red sash around the brown wool skirt and coat, and then sat at my father's old grooming table to properly tie back my hair. Every part of me wished it were possible to stay for the rest of the night and sleep. Just to close my eyes and have nothing to think about, or dream about—just peace. But that couldn't happen.

I didn't even know what peace was anymore.

Then the cold center in my chest urged me to take the first step out the door, giving a warning to move quietly, to trust no one. It renewed my strength and deepened my resolve.

I gave Basil a quick kiss on the cheek and whispered, "Thank you." That was far too little in return for all he had done for me, for the preservation of the dagger, and for all he had suffered to protect that secret, but I could do nothing more for him here. Then I put on my boots and slipped as silently as possible out the door.

The manor was quiet when I left Basil's room, the corridor mostly dark but for a few candles left burning in sconces along the walls.

Joth was in a chair waiting just outside the door. He stood the instant I left the room, and after a quick inquiry about my strength, he put a hand on my back to lead me out of Woodcourt. We had taken no more than three steps, when, from behind us, Simon called, "Kes, wait!"

Shaken with surprise, I turned, and there he was, exactly as I remembered him, though it seemed so long ago now. His shirt was half-buttoned to allow for a bandage wrapped around his middle, and his dark hair was a little longer than before and tousled from wherever he'd been sitting before I came. His brown eyes were focused entirely on me.

My stomach knotted, and I had no idea what to say or do, so I just stared. At some point, Joth leaned over to me and whispered, "I'll give you some distance, but I can't let you be alone with any of these people."

That shook me into action. "I can take care of myself."

"Nevertheless, I'll stay." Joth backed farther down the corridor, though he'd still be able to see and hear us, so I didn't understand the point of his having moved away.

Simon stepped closer, casting an occasional glare of irritation in Joth's direction. Finally, his focus resettled on me, which was horrible, for now it was obvious that he had no idea what to say or do either.

Did he still love me? I wondered. Did I still love him? Had I ever truly loved him? My heart seemed to think so. It was racing wildly.

I stretched out a hand toward Simon's bandages. "I can help with that."

He angled away from me. "Thanks, but no."

"If Loelle were here, you'd let her help."

"At one time, I might have. But her magic is . . . different from yours."

I pulled my hand back. "You think if I use any magic on you that it'll corrupt you too?"

He continued staring at me, though the expression in his eyes saddened. Yes, that was exactly what he thought.

Finally, he asked, "How is Basil?"

"He'll live . . . despite whatever *corruption* I gave to him." My voice bore more than a hint of anger.

"Good." Simon kicked once at the ground. "How are you . . . after last night? I'm sure you're exhausted."

"I'll live too."

"Good."

Good. This was what we were reduced to. Everything was *good*. I doubted that was enough for either of us.

He took one step toward me, and I countered with a step back. "Did he tell you where the Olden Blade is? Is that where you were going now, to get it?"

"I have to leave, Simon."

I turned, but Simon said, "I did search for you, Kes, after you left Nessel. There was no trace of you."

Without looking at him, I said, "How long did it take?"

"Rawk found you, and your shadow. Who is he? A bodyguard, or a captor tasked with bringing you back to Loelle?"

"No."

"Then who is he?"

"The person who will help me finish my quest."

"That's why we're here. We will help you."

"Oh?" Now I turned, snorting with disgust as I did. "And how long after helping me will Tenger try to kill me too?" Simon flinched, so I added, "Will you help him do it?"

"No, I will never allow that!" Simon stepped closer to me. "But something must be done before you get worse. Before *it* takes over."

"Who are you to decide that something must be done? I'm fine, Simon. I'm getting stronger. I can defeat Lord Endrick now!"

"And then what?" Simon widened his arms, seeking an answer.

"Then I'll stop whoever Captain Tenger has assigned to kill me. I'll stop everyone who gets in my way."

"What does that mean, that you'll stop them?"

Before I could answer, Harlyn rounded the corner, calling Simon's name. She froze when she saw me, then said to Simon, "We have to talk."

Without taking his eyes off me, Simon said to Harlyn, "Not now."

Harlyn planted her feet, one hand shifting to the knife sheathed at her side, making it clear she wasn't happy about being ignored.

Simon said to me, "If you're going to get the Olden Blade, let me come with you."

Now I stepped closer to Simon, keeping my voice as low as possible so that neither Harlyn nor Joth could hear us. "Do you really believe me to be corrupt?"

Simon pressed his lips together and slowly nodded.

"Then what do you think should be done with me?"

Pain filled Simon's eyes, and he glanced away, then whispered, "What do you mean you'll *stop* everyone who gets in your way?"

"You know what it means, Simon. Why did you fight all those years as a Corack? Freedom for Antora, was it not? Finally, I can provide that, in ways no one else in this kingdom can. You believe corruption is an evil developing within me, but you're wrong." And with that, I was finally able to tell Simon the truth he needed to hear. "You are wrong about magic. You are wrong about me. You never loved me."

That last part hit him hard, I could see it in his expression.

"Simon, we have to talk," Harlyn repeated. "The Brill are closer than we thought."

In response, he took two steps toward her, but changed his mind midway and addressed me again. "No, Kes, that's not true. At one time, you had everything in you to bring peace to Antora. And *you* are wrong about magic. It can never bring freedom to our land. It will only bring more destruction and death."

I tilted my head. "Perhaps. But it will not be *my* death."

"Simon!" That was as far as Harlyn got before an explosion somewhere on Woodcourt's grounds shook the earth. I heard something topple and guessed it was one of the walls surrounding the property. Was it the Dominion attacking?

This time when Simon spoke, his expression had changed. "That's the Brill. Kes, you can't be here."

Joth grabbed my arm and pulled me in one direction while Simon and Harlyn ran in the other.

"They're already here," I said to Joth. "How will we get away?"

His smile revealed an eagerness for what was coming. "We have a few minutes, I think."

Then I understood. Joth had already issued a command to the spirits who had followed us from the forest. The Brill wouldn't get in until we got out.

They were too late to stop me.

By morning, I would be holding the Olden Blade in my hand. Lord Endrick was living the last few days of his life.

· FOURTEEN ·

SIMON

Immediately after Kestra left, I grabbed a cloak and ran to the stables to prepare my horse, intending to follow her and Joth before we engaged the Brill.

"Wake everyone," I said to Harlyn, who raced back into Woodcourt, calling out the alarm.

Tenger was already in the stables on his horse, but he shook his head when he saw me. "I don't know what is happening, but some force is blocking us in here. I already tried to ride out to meet the Brill."

Undaunted, I mounted my horse and urged it forward, but it took only a single step before it reared up and backed away from the stable door. I tried again, but to no avail.

"Joth Tarquin!" Tenger said. "This is his magic at work."

I slid off my horse and marched back into Woodcourt, taking the nearest exit out of the home that I could find. Or, I attempted to do so. It too was blocked. I pressed forward against an invisible . . . something that would not let me pass.

I cursed and banged against the barricade with my arms. The hardened forearm of my right arm pushed deeper into the barricade than my other arm had, and I pulled it closer to stare at it. Since this had happened to me, I had assumed that Rawk had changed the flesh for my interactions with him. But it had to be more than that. This arm was stronger than whatever was blocking the exits from Woodcourt.

I wanted to understand that better, and to figure out what other abilities I may have with my arm, but for now, I needed to find Kes.

Harlyn ran up behind me. "She'll be quite a distance from here by now. We lost her."

"But Rawk can find her." I closed my eyes and tried to locate him with my thoughts. He was on the outskirts of Highwyn, but he knew what I wanted and I felt him start to move as clearly as if I were there with him.

"All right, so Rawk finds her, then what?" Harlyn asked.

"He's not going after Kestra. He's coming for me."

Harlyn followed me into the stables, calling out questions I didn't have time to answer. I only knew that he was close, and when he landed, I warned her and Tenger, "Get down."

Rawk spat fire toward the stables, and at first, it didn't break through, but then a lick of flame ate a hole in the stable wall. It was small, but it was enough.

"Everyone, go now!" I shouted, making a run for Rawk. He crouched down as I leapt onto his back, and he shot into the air.

The flight was easier this time as Rawk carried me into the night sky. I saw the Brill below, prevented from crossing onto Woodcourt's property as we had been prevented from leaving it. Their army could have been over a thousand in number, and for all I knew, this was just the first wave. The only thing I was certain of was that they had come seeking revenge against Kestra. That was why they attacked Woodcourt, not Endrick's palace.

I flew over his palace now. We were easily spotted and disk bows fired up at us, but Rawk flew higher and the disks were little threat to him anyway. Then I heard orders shouted to call for the condor riders. That did make me nervous. Rawk was larger and had fire, but Endrick had a great number of condors.

So I urged Rawk to fly us away as quickly as possible in search of Kestra. I had no idea which direction to tell him to go, but that wasn't necessary. He already seemed to know.

We flew over Highwyn, where the air was thinner and where I was forced to work for each breath. But we were high enough that it was less likely Kestra and Joth would see us, or that Joth could stop us if he did notice we were in pursuit.

Finally, I caught sight of them, racing as fast as their horses would allow, and side by side. My eye fixed on Kestra, at the steadiness of her course, so intent that she never even considered whether anyone was following.

And it wasn't only me.

With earsplitting screeches, the first condors emerged from their cages behind the palace, but they didn't fly after me. Instead, they targeted Kestra, seven birds in a V formation aimed directly toward her. On the horse next to her, Joth shook his head. Whatever powers he had that prevented us from leaving the stables didn't seem to apply here. Which became my first real clue about the nature of his abilities.

I'd deal with that later. For now, at my first thought, Rawk directed us toward the condors, his long silver tail pointed straight out and his eyes as focused as a hawk's. The wings of the condors fluttered nervously as we approached, but their riders fought to keep them directed at Kestra.

When the first of them was within range, its rider withdrew a disk bow and set a disk into the pocket. He took aim at Kestra, and I took aim at him. At my unspoken order, Rawk sped forward, easily skirting past the condors, and as he did, he painted the sky with fire.

Through the smoke and flame, I saw the tips of the condors' wings dip unevenly, heard the cries of their riders as they fell, and watched the freed condors rising higher into the air to escape the danger. I let them go. Kestra was my only focus.

There was still a risk that Endrick would send his oropods out after her, but she had a solid lead on them. Unless she was going a great distance, she had a good chance of reaching the Olden Blade.

Basil wouldn't have hidden it far away. He wouldn't have had the time to do so, and he'd have wanted to keep the blade somewhere Kestra would have easy access to it. And a place that the Dominion could not touch.

Or *would not* touch. From my position in the air, I had a good idea of where she was going. And if I was right, then Basil had made an excellent decision in his choice of a hiding place.

Kestra glared up at me as I flew overhead. She urged her horse to go faster, but she and Joth were already riding at top speed. Nothing she could do from below would prevent me from following her, and for that, I knew there would be consequences.

Because once I landed, she would demonstrate exactly what she had meant by stopping anyone who got in her way.

I was about to get in her way.

· FIFTEEN ·

KESTRA

Simon had fought off the condors, which was a great relief. And I might've been grateful had I not realized he'd done it only to clear the obstacle for his own purposes—to catch up to us.

As soon as he flew overhead, Joth called over to me, "Is there any chance he knows where the Blade is buried?"

I shook my head, but deep inside, I wondered if Simon did know. Why else would he have gone on ahead?

I watched his dragon until the trees above us became too thick to see where they had gone. With such a great beast, Simon must be certain that he had every advantage over me, enough that sooner or later I'd be forced to yield to him, but he was wrong. If Simon did intend to stop me, he would regret it.

Once we cleared the trees, we entered the Dominion cemetery, thick with gravestones, some of which were as old as Antora itself, and far too many that were the result of our long history of wars.

"Simon believes magic will bring about more war," I said. "Do you agree?"

Joth looked over at me. "I believe that what we are doing will result in only one more death, and that is a good thing."

Lord Endrick's death.

Of course that would be good, but everything depended on who replaced him. It must be someone who could make Antora into the land it should have been from the beginning. A queen, perhaps, who would earn the throne by virtue of her name, her bloodline, and the success of her quest.

Me.

We rode through the cemetery toward my mother's grave, but in rounding the final bend of the path, I halted my horse, as did Joth beside me.

Simon stood directly in front of us with his dragon perched on my mother's grave.

My fists clenched in anger. "My mother is buried where your foul creature stands. Out of respect—"

"You are not here to show your adoptive mother any respect. The blade is buried here, isn't it?"

"*My* blade is buried here. You cannot touch it."

"No, and you will not touch it, not until we figure out a way to work together."

I laughed. "That is hardly your captain's intentions. I will get to that blade, Simon, even if I have to go through you and your dragon first."

"Your magic won't penetrate his scales." Simon held out his hand, and his eyes softened. "Can we talk, please?"

"We already did that."

"Yes, but there's more to say. Please, Kes."

I stared at his hand. "I could pull the life out of you."

"You could also remember that we were friends. That we are still friends, I hope."

I scoffed but dismounted. Even as I did, I wasn't sure whether I would do as Simon asked, or whether I would teach him a lesson for trusting me.

"It's a trick," Joth warned.

Maybe it was, but I was prepared for that. Or I thought I was. I took Simon's hand, and he gently folded his fingers around mine.

"It's better if we could speak in private," he said.

"Absolutely not," Joth said.

I turned back to him. "Wait here, and guard this place."

Simon gave a meaningful look to his dragon, and I wondered if he had some way of communicating with it, and if so, if his orders had been any different from what I had said to Joth.

Still hand in hand, Simon and I walked farther up the road, continuing to round the bend until trees and tombs blocked us from view and the snow became too deep to pass. Once there, he released my hand and I stepped back, realizing for the first time how hard my heart was pounding.

I gestured toward his right arm, the one that had been injured when I left Nessel. It was covered by his sleeve, but I'd bumped against it as we walked and knew something about it was different.

"How's your arm?"

He glanced down at it, then looked up at me with furrowed brows. "Is this the reason you left?"

I didn't want to talk about that, didn't want to think about that night again, how awful it had been to walk away from him, not even knowing if he would live. I shook my head and began to turn. "This was a mistake."

Simon called after me, "Please, I beg you, just answer this one question." I stopped, but several beats passed before he continued. "I know who was involved in the plans for you to leave Nessel, but I don't know why you agreed to it."

I turned to him, curious. "Why does that matter now?"

"It does matter, Kes." His stare penetrated me enough that I felt his sadness. "Why did you leave? You told Gerald that you wanted to go because the corruption was so bad. But you told Trina that you were forced to leave, and that you loved me." He licked his lips. "Which was true?"

My breath locked in my throat. I didn't know what the truth was anymore. I couldn't stand so close to him and deny the racing of my heart, the longing to stand even closer. But I no longer knew the words to describe these feelings.

"You should not be here," I finally said. "I should not be here, with you."

He pointed to his chest. "There is a wound here, created the day I awoke and discovered you were missing. It hurts, every day. So tell me that you chose to leave and I'll accept it, or tell me you were forced to leave and I'll fight to bring you back, but tell me something, or this hurt will never heal."

"What am I supposed to say to that? This has hurt me too, Simon. Do you know how it felt to ride away after you became king? To know that I'd struck a bargain to keep you alive, but it left you with *her*?"

"What were the terms of the bargain?"

My eyes began to sting, and I blinked away tears. "They would've let you die of the infection in your arm. What else was I supposed to do?" When he failed to answer that question, I added another. "During the battle at King's Lake, you claimed that, if necessary, you would die for me. Is that still true?"

Simon's eyes flashed with an emotion I couldn't quite read. Sadness, maybe. At least, that's how he sounded when he said, "I would die for the Infidante, because I took an oath once to do so. I would die for Kestra Dallisor, because without her, there is no meaning to my life anyway. But I cannot sacrifice myself for a corruption that will eventually take over this land."

My temper flared. "You call it corruption, but it's only a word. It could as easily be called power or progress, or evolution, for any of those are better descriptions."

"I describe it as rot, as decay, as an acid inside you. Look around, Kes, and see how it's changed you! We're in the dead of winter, and you don't even have a simple cloak for protection. Does it make sense that you're not even shivering?"

I wasn't shivering, but he must not have noticed my trembling. Whether from anger or from whatever feelings I still had for Simon, I didn't know. But he was right about one thing: In any other circumstance, I should have been frostbitten by now.

Simon took another step toward me, more cautious this time. "Please let me help. Before it's too late."

My fists clenched. He just needed to understand what had become obvious to me. "If you'd seen the forest, seen what I did for Loelle's people, you'd feel differently. I've taken the curse from the land, so they can leave now. And when I have the strength for it, I'll take the curse from them. Your people were there too, Simon. Thousands of Halderians were trapped by Endrick's curse and are able to leave now." I stepped closer to him and watched him counter with a step back. With a tilt of my head, I added, "If you think that is a bad thing, then perhaps the true corruption is in you."

He frowned. "I think we have to remember the larger purpose in Antora."

"I *am* that larger purpose! Kings and queens will come and go, but if Antora is to continue to exist, then we need someone on that Scarlet Throne to preserve the peace."

"Like Endrick did?"

My spine stiffened. "I am the Infidante and the Infidante is magic. If there is corruption too, then it's who I am now. So if necessary, would you die for me or not?"

He wouldn't answer. "There must be a way to heal you—"

"Why should I? Magic is leading me toward a throne to which I am the rightful heir. You are not that heir, but you want it for the Halderians, *King* Simon."

"You know that's not true. You also know that your parents— your true parents—gave their lives to fight the very thing you are now embracing."

Simon didn't know that Darrow was alive, but it didn't matter. My true mother was not. Tears filled my eyes. "Don't speak of my parents."

"I know that Darrow loved you. Your mother—"

The first tear fell. "Stop this."

I lifted a hand and felt the coldness inside me, the corruption. For the first time, I was frightened by its presence.

Maybe Simon didn't realize how his words were affecting me, but if he cared at all for me, he would stop. Instead, he pushed further. "Your parents must have suspected what lay ahead for you, if you were ever discovered. If there were a way to return to who you were, what would they want you to do?"

"What would *you* want me to do?" My voice became as serious as it had ever been. "Before leaving the forest, I saw your sister. She's an Ironheart and probably somewhere here in Highwyn now. If I see her again, and if I can get close enough to restore her, shall I pull in her curse too? Save your sister, and lose more of myself?"

Until that moment, Simon had been moving steadily closer, but he was frozen now, the only movement a stiff rise and fall of his chest as he took that in.

"You saw Rosaleen?" When I kept my gaze steady on him, he said, "We'll find a way to save you both. We'll—"

"Kestra!"

Hearing Joth's alarmed voice, I backed away from Simon, whose widened eyes looked as confused as I felt.

"The Coracks are coming," Joth said. "We've got to leave!"

The Coracks? Angry, I turned to Simon, who was already shaking his head. "I swear I didn't know—"

"You tricked me!"

"Kes, don't go." Simon reached for me, but I took his hand and instantly pulled enough strength from his body that he collapsed to the ground unconscious.

As soon as Simon fell, I heard the screech of his dragon, which took to the air. It was coming to protect its master, which meant my mother's grave was accessible.

By the time I returned there, Joth was already digging a hole, beneath what looked like a fresher area of dirt than the rest of the grave. I knelt beside him to help, and within seconds, my hand touched a canvas bag.

The Olden Blade.

I pulled it from the ground, still in its bag, and then leapt onto my horse. I had barely grabbed the reins, when pain seared through my shoulder. I cried out and looked back to see a silver disk lodged in the flesh. Behind me, Harlyn was reaching for a second disk, this one black—it would kill me. As much as the others wanted me dead, Harlyn would have twice the motivation. She wanted Simon for herself.

Well, she could have him. I felt like a fool for how easily he had duped me. Never again.

Joth mumbled something under his breath, and behind me, I watched the Coracks suddenly collide into a barrier I could not see.

"The half-lives," he said. "They are protecting us."

We rode until we left the cemetery behind and found a quiet place to stop. Joth dismounted, then helped me off my horse. The blade was still stuck in my shoulder, and I was dizzy with pain.

"If I pull this out, will you be able to heal yourself?" he asked.

"Not unless I can pull strength from you to make it happen. It will hurt you too."

He knelt beside me. "I can handle it."

I wasn't sure that he could, but I also knew this wound was deep enough that if I didn't do something for myself, I'd be in serious trouble. So I gritted my teeth while Joth pulled out the disk, one firm, awful tug that made me cry out.

I collapsed onto all fours, but he took my hands in his and I began to pull strength from him.

The instant I did, he gasped and his face twisted, but he held on to me and made no effort to resist what I was doing, what I had to do if I was going to live. I took no more than what I needed, but even then, when I released him, we were both exhausted.

We lay in the snow, which should have felt colder than it did, and as I recovered, anger seethed inside me.

"Simon tricked me. He was stalling until the Coracks arrived."

"Weren't they always going to try to harm you?"

"Not Simon. I didn't think Simon—" I sat up, unable to finish the rest. Unwilling to face the truth about Simon, but knowing I had to do it.

Simon had never cared for me; he was just better at using me than any of the others. I'd been blind to that for so long, but no longer.

That cold center within me began to burn. The Corack rebellion wanted to see itself as the hero of the people, as the defense against Lord Endrick. But they were worse than Endrick had ever been, for they wanted the same tyranny and masked themselves as the guardians of freedom.

The ideas that had been unsettled in my mind until now began to come together at last. I knew what I had to do.

I turned to Joth. "What is required for us to unite our magic?"

He sat up, taking a moment before answering. "I still am not certain it will work. If it does, we each will have twice the strength, twice the abilities. You will know what I'm doing before I do it, and I'll know the same. But arriving at that place requires your whole heart, and you will take mine."

I faced him directly. "How is it done?"

"It's simple, really." Joth looked around to be sure we were alone, then stood and helped me to my feet. He led me deeper into the trees and said, "You must understand, if this works, we will do more than share magic, we will share ourselves with each other. It is a very . . . close relationship. If you still have feelings for Simon, that may interfere—"

"I don't." No positive feelings anyway.

"Then take my hand."

He held it upright near his chest, and I clasped his hand with mine, bringing our bodies close together. Already I could feel the pulse of his magic wrapping around my fingers, but he only gripped my hand tighter.

"Your magic is powerful," he said. "When it surges inside you, your eyes deepen in color. Grass green to emerald."

I smiled. "Now what?"

"Offer up your magic as a gift, sincerely given, with all your heart. In return, I will give my magic to you, as much as you wish to take. If we give of ourselves fully and freely, we should—" His voice broke off there, and his eyes widened.

I wondered if what he felt was anywhere near what was happening to me. For his magic was flooding through me, more than I could contain. I knew he was pulling at my own magic too, but even as I gave it, I felt my powers grow as never before, blending with his and binding themselves into one.

I gasped, unable to take enough of a breath to absorb everything as it came to me, unable to comprehend how even my own magic seemed to have doubled in strength. With the next wave of his magic, I suddenly realized that I was kissing him, or he was kissing me, I wasn't sure how it had begun.

I only knew that he had become so much a part of me that he was in my mind and my every thought was of him. I didn't fully understand what was happening, only that our magic had crashed together and was one united power now.

For the first time since we began, he released my hand and wrapped his arms around me, but the kiss between us continued. I was feeding on his strength to build my own, and as I became more powerful, I knew he must be pulling strength from the half-lives around him to continue to give to me.

His hands were on my neck, and for the first time, I realized how warm they were. Too warm. I pushed away, separating myself from him, my eyes widened.

"Joth, you took in my corruption too."

When it had only been mine, I had not thought it to be too dangerous, that it was something I could control, but the change in his eyes made me nervous. The bright blue had turned silver, like molten steel now, flaming with emotions I could not understand, even as he worked to slow his breathing.

"At first it felt like taking in poison," he said. "But then I began to understand it isn't corruption at all. It's power, and together, we will take all of it."

"I . . ." I wasn't sure what he meant by that, whether I wanted what he was now suggesting. But his next kiss seemed to dissolve any concern I might have had. By the time we emerged from the woods, hand in hand, my resolve was clear. I was ready to kill Lord Endrick.

No, not simply ready. I was eager for it.

· SIXTEEN ·

SIMON

Trina shook me awake, and I sat up in a bed, disoriented, until I realized we were back at Woodcourt. At first, I didn't know how I had gotten here, but the pit in my gut told me something had gone horribly wrong. Then I remembered, and it was worse than horrible. We may have ruined everything.

"Did she escape?" I asked, not certain of how I wanted Trina to answer.

Trina nodded, but said, "Harlyn shot her with a disk, so she couldn't have gone far. If we follow the trail of blood, we should be able to track her down."

"That isn't the plan anymore," Tenger said, walking up to join me and Trina. "The few of us Coracks who are here aren't enough to fight those two. Kestra retrieved the blade, so we can assume they're going to begin preparations for an attack on Lord Endrick. We need to be there when it happens, and with a force strong enough to demand their attention. Hugh and I are returning to enter negotiations with the Brill."

"The Brill, who want Kestra dead?"

Tenger's eyes sparked. "The Brill, who have both the numbers and weapons that we lack. Their technologies are better than anyone else's in getting around magic, whether it's Endrick's or Kestra's, or this boy with her. Like it or not, Simon, we need their help."

"Are you sure of that?" In my head, I heard the echo of Kestra's question to me, of whether I would still give my life for her. How could I possibly have answered that?

I cursed and tried to stand up, but Kestra had taken more from me than I had realized at first. I was having a hard enough time simply sitting there.

Harlyn sat near me on the bed to check the bandage she had wrapped around my side earlier. As she did, she said, "You're lucky to be here. Kestra nearly killed you."

"And you tried to kill her," I countered. "Do you think there's any chance she'll work with us now?"

"You must stop pretending that is even a possibility." Gabe had been leaning against the far wall of my room, but now he stood taller. "We all know how you feel, but you've got to see her as she is. Simon, if she is not stopped, she will be a greater enemy to us than Endrick ever was."

"I do see that. But I won't allow you to kill her. We must weed the corruption out of her."

Tenger and Gabe exchanged a look, which was easy enough to read. Then Tenger said, "You warned me against giving her magic and were obviously right to do so. I thought we could keep control of her magic better than we have, delay the onset of corruption." Then he straightened up, scratching his trimmed beard. "Loelle betrayed us and, in doing so, has already destroyed Kestra. Blame her for Kestra's troubles, not me."

It was a nice speech, and I did agree that Loelle had brought great harm to Kestra, but that didn't mean Tenger was blameless. We wouldn't be in this situation but for him.

Though to be fair, Kestra wouldn't be alive today if she hadn't received magic. We had done that to her.

And to be even more accurate, if I had not captured her that night, and forced her into the betrayal of her family, someone else would have become the Infidante, and Kestra might have had the simpler life that she had wanted.

Tenger nodded at Trina. "I need you to assist Basil in his recovery. Try to find out anything you can about his time in captivity— perhaps we'll learn something to help our cause. Even if we get the Brill on our side, it won't be enough. You must convince him to send for his armies from Reddengrad."

"They were nearly destroyed in the last battle," I said. "They won't come to help us fight here."

"We saved Basil's life—they'll come." Now Tenger addressed me. "And what orders will the king of the Halderians give to his people? Is it not his obligation to retake the Scarlet Throne?"

If I didn't care to occupy the Halderian throne, why should he think I would seek out the throne to rule over all of Antora? Especially because I knew at what price I would obtain that throne.

I started to shake my head, but Gabe said, "Can you all leave us alone for a minute?"

Tenger muttered orders for everyone else to leave, and when they had gone, Gabe sat in the chair across from me and leaned forward, elbows on his knees. For a long time he remained silent, waiting for me to begin.

Finally, I did. "If she had wanted to, she could have killed me. There is still more good in her than bad."

"For now."

His words hung in the air. I couldn't ignore them.

"You're a blind fool," he said. "Here you have Harlyn, who hangs on your every word. She'd marry you yesterday and would be a partner you could trust and rely on. You're losing her, and for what? The nicest thing you can say about Kestra is that she could have killed you but didn't. Not for the first time, I might add."

For some reason, that made me smile, but Gabe continued. "From the moment you first saw Kestra, you lost your reason and logic. It's time to claim it again, my friend, and it starts now. I'm going to leave and send Harlyn in here so that you two can talk. Remember that everything is on the line. The future of Antora, our lives, and the entire purpose for the rebellion. Do what you must to preserve all that we have fought for."

I hated that he was right. Having to admit that, even to myself, tore at my heart, yet the same thoughts had been weighing on me for weeks. It was time that I finally listened. I gave him a brief nod; he smiled grimly and stood up, leaving the room. A moment later, Harlyn entered. For her, I forced myself to my feet.

We faced each other awkwardly, then Harlyn said, "What are the orders of the Halderian king?"

I drew a slow breath. "I'll send you with Rawk back to the Hiplands. I want every soldier of our armies, or everyone who wishes to join in this fight against Lord Endrick, to assemble here as quickly as possible. Can you bring them here?"

Harlyn straightened up. "You intend to fight Lord Endrick, then?"

"The Halderians will be there when he is destroyed." Forcing the words from my mouth caused a deep pain within me, but they had to be spoken. "And we will celebrate when the Scarlet Throne is ours again at last."

Harlyn tilted her head. *"Ours?"*

"Yours and mine."

Harlyn smiled. "I'll return with our cavalry, Simon, I promise."

She gave me a kiss and a warm embrace that left me feeling colder than before, and finally excused herself to make preparations to leave.

Gabe entered again and smiled at me when he saw how happy Harlyn looked. Once we were alone, he said that Tenger and Hugh were on their way to meet the Brill. "I don't like a foreign army joining us," he added. "Don't we have enough strategies of our own? Remember that binding cord from Lonetree Camp?"

"Of course."

"I've still got it. If we find Kestra, maybe it'd work to keep her with us for more than a few minutes."

If only we could. "I think we're beyond that now."

He encouraged me to sleep, but I couldn't. I only sat at the window, gazing out at a chilly day in which lazy snowflakes drifted listlessly in the air, lit by a waning sun.

I heard the trouble before I saw it, the sounds of marching in perfect step. Ironhearts. They were loud enough to awaken Gabe, who joined me at the window.

"They're not headed toward Endrick's palace," Gabe said. "They're going north."

And I was certain of why. Endrick had to know where Kestra and Joth were. And I knew who was likely in the company of the Ironhearts.

"We have to be there," I said, reaching for my boots.

Gabe shook his head. "Those aren't the odds I'm willing to accept. If we go, it'll be the four of us against a hundred or more."

I stopped long enough to look up at him, making sure he understood that I was going whether he came with me or not. "I think Rosaleen will be one of those Ironhearts."

"Your sister?" He let out a low whistle. "So whose side will we be on?"

Kestra had asked whether I'd sacrifice my life for her. My mother had given her life for Kestra. I would not lose my sister too.

That was the only thing I knew for sure. Gabe and I reached for our weapons to fight an enemy I could no longer define, and for a purpose I could no longer defend.

SEVENTEEN

KESTRA

After escaping the Corack ambush, Joth and I found shelter in the upper room of an abandoned building in Highwyn. Based on its appearance, no one had entered this place since before the war, and for good reason. The wood beams that still held the structure together were half-rotted, the plaster had fallen off the walls and ceiling in large chunks, with many more threatening to crumble upon us as we slept, and some areas of the floor had already begun to collapse, making every step we took a risk.

Yet this was still better than spending another minute with the Coracks.

In the daytime, our little room loomed over one of the busiest roads in Highwyn, including a shop where Joth had somehow managed to get me a clean dress and a garter to hold the Olden Blade against my thigh, when necessary. Now that evening had fallen, the road was quiet, and from a small window in the corner, we could see Endrick's palace. At another angle, I saw smoke rising from the grand chimney of Woodcourt and suddenly missed the evenings I had spent as a child curled up in front of the fireplace with a book from Sir Henry's library.

All those years ago, Simon had tended to those fires. Sometimes, if no one else was around, I would read aloud from the book while he worked, so that he could listen.

The memory was softening me, I realized, and I shook it off. I would not be able to return to Woodcourt until this was over. And not only after Endrick was dead, but after the Coracks and every other threat to me had been removed.

Simon.

What was I supposed to do about Simon?

I shouldn't have been thinking about him, remembering.

Joth had prepared us a small meal from food he had obtained at Woodcourt while I was busy with Basil. He carried a plate over now, and while it smelled delicious, I only set it aside.

He handed it to me again. "Food was surprisingly difficult to come by in All Spirits Forest. Of course, given that it was a dead forest, maybe it is not such a surprise. I learned to make the best of what I got."

"You were never trapped there," I said. "Loelle left."

"I could not abandon my half-lives." He smiled. "I stayed strong for them, as you must stay strong too. Please eat."

"Strength is not my problem," I said, taking my first bites. "What I need is access to Endrick. I fear he's left the palace. We've seen no sign of him."

"He's in there," Joth assured me. "He's recalled his armies away from All Spirits Forest. They're coming to Highwyn, which can only be for one purpose."

I had suspected that would be Endrick's next move. Once Basil had been freed from captivity, Endrick would know it was only a matter of time before I discovered the location of the Olden Blade. He would guess that I had it by now, and I did.

Since recovering the blade, I had worn it or held it in my hands, and it felt like the return of an old friend. Today I had been polishing it for so long that I could see myself in the reflection of the metal. I wanted the blade to catch the light just before I stabbed Endrick, giving him a final flash of knowing that he had lost the throne to me.

"After Endrick is dead," I said, "I want the Scarlet Throne moved to Woodcourt, and Endrick's palace burned. There should be nothing of him left in all of Antora."

"You intend to rule in his place?" Joth asked.

"Of course. That throne is mine by inheritance, and if I am the one to kill Endrick, then I have earned my place on that throne more than anyone." I turned to him. "I will heal your people, Joth. Restore life to all of them."

"*We* will restore them, when the time is right," Joth said. "I share in your powers now."

"And I in yours." Looking around me, I said, "I can feel the presence of your people, like never before."

"They will listen to your commands, as they would mine." Joth stood and found a gap in our walls with an easy view of the street. "But for now, they have orders to guard us, and to circulate throughout the city to find out what information they can. When we get word that the time is right, we will attack."

"How long, do you think?"

"Perhaps as soon as tonight. If you've eaten enough, then you ought to get some sleep."

Joth had prepared a bed for me against one wall while he would sleep nearer the broken window. I was immune to the cold, but he had begun complaining of the heat in this room, and he wanted all the winter air he could get.

I lay down and closed my eyes but could not sleep. My shoulder ached, despite having been healed. My heart felt worse, the wound widening with every thought of my last fight with Simon. I had come to him in hopes of repairing our friendship. He had come to lure me into a trap.

As I finally began to close my eyes, I heard marching sounds outside. I looked over at Joth, who was already sitting up and peeking out from the gap in the wooden walls.

"Ironhearts?" I asked, though I didn't need his nod to confirm it. The soldiers were making no effort to hide their presence, so they must have wanted the people to know they had returned. Maybe they wanted me to know it too. If so, they would regret it.

I leapt to my feet, the room around me thick with half-lives eager for their first real battle. I had not yet issued any orders to them, but this was my chance. "Block them from behind," I said. "This will begin here, and end here."

I glanced over at Joth, whose breaths were more shallow than usual. He was nervous, and understandably so. He'd spent nearly his entire life in All Spirits Forest and never tested himself as a warrior. Everything he knew about the coming battle was pure theory.

He said, "With your powers, I can either draw strength from them or give them strength?"

"Never give more than half of your strength, not even to me. The body cannot recover if you do." Then I smiled. "But I'm very interested to see how much we can take."

Joth carried a disk bow and shield, and wore a lever blade at his side. I had a knife in my boot and the Olden Blade against my leg. If I happened to test it on some Ironhearts before using it on Lord Endrick, maybe that would help him understand that I was stronger than I had been in our last encounter.

At Joth's suggestion, the half-lives went before us in battle, so by the time we emerged from the rotted building, the attack had already begun. The commanders had ordered the Ironhearts to remain in their formations while they retreated to what they believed were safer distances. In my head, I heard Joth's orders to take care of the commanders first.

Without intending to, on the night he cursed the people in All Spirits Forest, Lord Endrick had created an army as immortal as himself. All they lacked was the ability to leave, and I had provided that.

"The Infidante is here!" one soldier called, and instantly, the focus of every soldier rested on me.

Disks immediately began flying toward us, more than I could count, but not one of them came close. To the eyes of the Ironhearts, they would have simply stopped midair and fallen to the ground. Only we understood that they had indeed hit a target, too dead to be killed, and just alive enough to provide a barricade for us.

Joth moved right and I went left, so confident in the protections around me that all I had to focus on was my attack. I swung fierce and hard, and when the blade wasn't enough, with one touch of my hand, I drew enough strength from the soldier to drop him to the ground.

Despite the numbers on their side, the fight was hardly fair, not at the rate at which the Ironhearts were dwindling. After only fifteen minutes, an order was called for retreat, but that was immediately followed by a shout that no one could break through our barricade.

Ahead of me was a statue of Lord Endrick. I climbed it and shouted for the attention of those Ironhearts who were still alive. At least a hundred soldiers still remained on their feet, but the area was littered with their fallen comrades.

In my most commanding voice, I said, "You will surrender to us! Lord Endrick will not harm you; he needs every soldier he can get. So go to your knees now and you will live. Nothing else will save you."

The Ironhearts closest to me were the first to toss their weapons and fall to their knees. In turn, so did the soldiers behind them, followed by yet another row. When the last row knelt, I looked past them and was surprised to see Simon and Gabe standing in the distance, just beyond where the barricade of half-lives would be. They could not get in any more than the Ironhearts could get out.

Simon was staring directly at me, his expression one of deep concern, which confused me because I had just caused the surrender of an entire company of enemy soldiers. He should have been happy, not looking at me as if I were an even greater enemy.

Joth ran up beside me. "I have an idea," he said. "Take my hand."

Grateful for the distraction, I did as he asked, and he shut his eyes. In my head, I heard his command, but before I could stop it, I felt the half-lives swoop in from around us. Somehow Joth was sharing my powers with them, the power to take strength. And they took with a vengeance, killing every Ironheart in their path. They moved so fast, the Ironhearts toppled over in a single wave. Within seconds, Joth and I were all that was left of the battle. Everyone else was dead.

I yanked my hand free of Joth's. "I told them to surrender and they would live!"

"You shouldn't have made such a promise. And you don't know

for sure that Endrick would have let them live." Joth grabbed my shoulders. "At least this way, we benefit from what happened. Can you feel their strength flowing into you, Kestra? So much power!"

The icy core within me was pulsing with life. *Their* lives. It hungered for more, and the more I fed it, the more it wanted.

Yes, I felt it.

"What have you done?" With the half-life barricade dissolved, Simon had run up to the base of the statue. His sword was in his hand, which it shouldn't have been. Not unless he expected to need it against Joth or me.

Almost in a wild desperation, Simon began checking the Ironheart bodies, occasionally using the sword to roll someone over. He was searching for a specific person.

His sister was an Ironheart.

Joth jumped down and offered me a hand for support. "Come with me, Kestra. Our business is finished here."

I ignored his offer, instead looking around the area for anyone who might have been Simon's sister, desperately hoping with every good part of myself that I would not see Rosaleen here. Meanwhile, Simon's words echoed in my ears.

What have you done?

"*Why* did you do that?" Gabe called, running to Simon's side. "They were on their knees. They had surrendered!"

Joth pointed toward those who had fallen. "They attacked us! Had the battle gone differently, they would not have accepted our surrender! The Dominion would have done the same to us!"

"But you're not like the Dominion," Gabe countered. "Or are you now?"

"We are the only ones fighting the Dominion," Joth said. "You Coracks dance around them, poking at their feet with pinpricks and moaning about why the problem continues. It's about time someone hit them hard enough that Endrick would feel it."

"If they had been attacking you, I'd agree. But these soldiers threw down their weapons. At that point, they were no longer your enemies." Gabe turned his focus on me, and I felt its bite. "This was murder, Kestra."

His words stung, and deep inside, I knew he was right. Joth held up a hand for me again, and this time, I took it as he lowered me to the ground. But as soon as I was there, I started toward Simon.

"I didn't see her." Simon didn't acknowledge me at first, so I said it again, adding, "I don't think Rosaleen was here."

He barely glanced up at me, and even when he did, his expression was so harsh it frightened me, a fear immediately swallowed up by the core of ice within me. It whispered, *His sister would have killed you too.*

I put my hand over my mouth, fighting against those horrible words, against the decay inside that was beginning to suffocate me.

"It isn't safe to remain here." Joth put his arm around my shoulder and turned me away from them. I let him walk me out of the square, my thoughts consumed with what Gabe had said, my heart frozen with the pain and anger in Simon's expression. I hated to imagine what he was thinking.

"We did the right thing," Joth said as we walked.

"No, that wasn't right. They were surrendering, and you just killed them all!"

"We share magic now." Joth stopped and took my hands in his. "Whatever happened back there, we did it together." I started to pull away, but I realized tendrils of his magic had begun to weave themselves around my pain, insulating it, dissolving it until nothing was left but the magic itself. He gave to me until I could breathe again, until the worst of my guilt and horror had subsided, leaving behind the strength that had come from the fallen Ironhearts.

"Do you feel better?"

The truth was that I didn't feel anything, or if I did, I couldn't define it, or connect it to anything happening around me. Searching within myself, I discovered one emotion only.

I turned to Joth. "I feel . . . powerful."

"Then we should strike soon," Joth said. "But this time, against Lord Endrick. And when he goes to his knees, begging for mercy—"

"I will kill him," I said.

Joth took my hand and kissed it. I knew he was warm but was surprised at the heat of his touch. Before we walked away, I turned to see Simon and Gabe still searching among the bodies. I desperately hoped Rosaleen wasn't there.

Or maybe they hadn't found her yet. I couldn't bear it if they did.

Slowly, I began to absorb the feelings, and as they became ice, once again the corruption was fed.

"You've become so strong," Joth said.

His words rang hollow, because they were not true. The corruption was strong—I wasn't—and too often it was in control. I was merely its host, a girl who could never admit aloud that she was terrified of what it meant for her.

· E I G H T E E N ·

SIMON

After a careful search of all the bodies, I finally took my first complete breath. Rosaleen was not here.

"But she might have been, and wherever she is, she might be next." Gabe waited until he had my attention to be sure I heard him. "Surely you see it now, what Kestra's become."

"Yes, I see it." My teeth gritted together.

"Which means you know what we have to do. Now will you—"

"Enough!" Hardly an hour had passed in days when someone wasn't reminding me how dangerous Kestra had become, or when Kestra herself wasn't proving them right. I understood the problem. I just couldn't make myself agree to the solution.

We returned to Woodcourt, where Trina was waiting for us and Basil was resting in a chair with a blanket wrapped tight around him. I passed them by, letting Gabe do the explanations, which he obliged with every possible detail. I had hoped to get some sleep, but my eyes never stayed closed more than ten minutes at a time before I awoke with thoughts of Kestra and the battles that were looming before her. Certainly, the time was coming near when she would have to face Lord Endrick again, though I expected the other battle, the one within, would be far more difficult. It would delve into the very core of who she was now. I truly didn't know if she would fight that battle, or if she could.

When I came downstairs the next morning, a hot meal of eggs and fry cakes was waiting for me in the dining room. Trina and Basil were already eating, with Gabe placing another plate of eggs on the table.

"Hungry?" he asked.

I wasn't at all hungry, but I dished up some food anyway and sat across from Trina and Basil. Gabe sat beside me.

"How are you?" I asked Basil. "You look better every time I see you."

"I owe that to the care I'm getting," he replied with a sideways glance at Trina.

I poked at my food, trying to be interested. "Tenger is still talking with the Brill?"

Basil nodded, then added, "He's also keeping watch for any of my people, if they come in time. Gabe believes Kestra will attack the palace sooner rather than later."

"Agreed. And the Halderians . . . my people will come as well." I still stumbled over identifying them as mine, but I had to speak of them that way, or else how would I ever think of them that way?

"These fry cakes are the best I've ever had, honestly. But of course, I made them, so what else should I have expected?" Gabe took another bite while Basil and Trina chuckled at his joke; then more seriously, he said, "How long do you think it'll be before Harlyn returns?"

"You think about her more than I do," I replied. "If you're interested—"

"Trust me, Hatch. If I thought I could get her attention, I would gladly save her from a life with you."

I stared at him until we all broke into laughter. I didn't know why. He was perfectly correct that Harlyn would be better off away from me. Yet it felt good to smile. It had been so long since I'd had any reason for it.

My mind shifted back to months ago, before Loelle took Kestra away from Nessel. Kestra and I had met in a small alcove, just the two of us. I had smiled then, and meant it.

"Someone else will have to face Kestra . . . at the end," I mumbled, and when Gabe tilted his head, unsure of whether he'd heard me correctly, I added, "You all think I can't see the truth about Kestra, but that isn't the problem. I do see it. But if a battle comes between us, I won't make the correct choices. I won't know the difference between what I want and what I'm supposed to do. And I will choose her over myself every single time." I glanced up, meeting the eyes of everyone at the table in turn. "I'm saying this because I know a battle is coming, and I'll need as much help as possible to survive it."

"To survive *her*," Gabe echoed. He put a hand on my shoulder. "May we all survive her."

Basil leaned forward. "Trina told me that Kestra was here, that she healed me."

I nodded.

"What the Dominion did to me . . ." He closed his eyes as if remembering it all, and a shudder seemed to pass through him. "They took me to the brink of death, and Endrick suspended me there in the cruelest sort of torture—unable to die, unable to live. I became so weak, so hopeless, that the Ironhearts became sloppy with their watch over me. One night, they left the bars of my dungeon cell open. It took most of the night for me to work up the courage and the strength to leave, but I did. I remembered hearing of how you and Kestra escaped before, and at first, I seemed to be following your footsteps exactly. I went over the edge of the lowest cell in the dungeons but never could find the exit. There I waited, expecting death, even wishing for it, until the Ironhearts finally found me."

Basil paused as if seeing the events he described play out in his mind. His shoulders had hunched increasingly as he spoke, and his hands occasionally trembled. We waited for him to continue, and eventually, he did. "I expected to die down there, and not because of hunger or thirst, but because Endrick's magic still lingered with me. Without even knowing exactly where I was, he was still torturing me."

Trina placed her hand over his. "I've seen the dungeons, Basil. I can't imagine what you went through down there. What you were still going through even after we rescued you."

"I should be dead right now, but I'm not." For the first time since he began to speak, Basil looked directly at me. "Kestra took all of that curse from me. Even while I was unconscious, I perceived that she was pulling the wickedness out of me, like ice melting and draining. She took it."

"Pulling the curse into herself," Gabe said. "She made herself worse."

"That's how she saved me." Basil rapped his fingers on the table. "While you're all discussing how dangerous she has become, I think it's important for me to add that Kestra is the only reason I'm still alive. She saved my life."

"She has saved all of us, at one point or another," Trina said. "Whatever she is now, we owe her a chance to survive."

Gabe shook his head. "No, we don't. I'm sorry, Simon. I know how upsetting it must be to hear that, but the reality is, we may not have many opportunities to stop her, and if we get the chance, we cannot pause and debate Kestra's current position on the scale of good and evil. We must act."

Basil sat up straighter. "How can you say that? In Reddengrad, we would never condemn a person on so thin a judgment."

"In Reddengrad, you are not led by a nearly immortal king who has redefined evil, and a girl who seems to be folding herself into his mold."

"What is happening to Kestra is a consequence of her trying *not* to be like him!" Basil insisted. "There is good in her, and we must have hope for her future."

"Simon and I just saw her bring a hundred Ironhearts to their knees in full surrender," Gabe said. "Seconds later, she and Joth killed them all. What if this were to happen again? Will you explain to the families of her victims that we did nothing because we were hoping she wouldn't do it?"

"Don't you see my point?" Basil looked to each of us before his eyes settled on me. "If the evil can be pulled out of me, it can be pulled out of her too."

"It doesn't work that way," Trina said. "A magnet pulls iron shavings from the earth, but the earth cannot pull the iron shavings back to itself. Magic is the magnet and cannot help but to pull corruption to itself. Once there, the corruption binds to the magic. The one becomes part of the other."

"Then we must pull all magic from her," Basil said. "That is her best chance."

"Unless the magic is bound to her life," Gabe said. "If magic is in her breath, in the beat of her heart, in her every footstep, then she has no chance. The only question is how many people she will destroy on her way down."

Trina sighed. "We don't have answers to any of these questions. All I know is that, at this moment, there is no way to pull magic from Kestra without killing her."

"We have a place to start, at least." I stood to leave the room. "Sir Henry kept a diary, and there are hundreds of books in his library. Surely one of them will teach us about Endrean magic."

At first, I thought I would be going to the library alone, but seconds later, Gabe caught up with me. Then Trina leaned out the door and said, "Basil is tired and needs to return to his room. I'll stay there to watch over him. But he asks if the two of you will bring a stack of books for us to go through as well. If a solution lies in this home, we will find it."

· NINETEEN ·

SIMON

Asolution to Kestra's corrupted magic was *not* in this home. That had been confirmed at least seventy books, three burned-out clearstones, and two full days ago. And yet I continued to scour page after page, hoping a solution would somehow appear amidst useless descriptions of philosophy, languages of foreign nations, and theories of leadership.

Obviously, the answer wasn't here, but still I held out hope that it would magically appear.

Magic. The irony lingered in my mind.

Around me, Gabe, Trina, and Basil were equally frustrated. Nothing we had read offered the slightest hope for a solution. Not only did the books and diaries fail to mention corrupted magic, they failed in any mention of Endrean magic whatsoever. Either no one truly understood it, or more likely, no one dared to write about it. Not with Lord Endrick watching.

Basil was on his feet by now and watched every day for any sign of his Reddengrad armies to appear on the horizon. Gabe and Trina did the same for any sign of the Coracks, or the Brill. I watched too, wondering if Harlyn would have any success in bringing the Halderians. I had my doubts. Only five days ago, Commander Reese and other leaders within my cavalry had been part of a plot to expel me from the kingdom, by force or by my death. Why would they fight for me now?

Harlyn. They would at least fight for Harlyn. And so I continued to watch.

At the end of two days, Tenger must have completed his negotiations with the Brill, for their leaders entered Woodcourt's gates, though they came with narrowed eyes and upturned noses. At their head were Captain Tenger and a woman who had to be one of the Brill. Brillians were known to be highly intelligent, with superior eyesight and hearing capabilities, and I was sure this woman was no exception. While her hair normally would have been nearly translucent, it had recently been shaved, as were the heads of all her army. Still, she remained as beautiful as all Brill were, and whether this woman was my age or three times it, I couldn't tell for sure.

Basil and I met her and Tenger in Woodcourt's gardens. Undoubtedly, Gabe and Trina were nearby to watch and listen.

I offered a hand to the woman, but she only stared at it as if it were filthy. And judging by the stern expression on her face, that was her kindest opinion of me.

Tenger greeted us more warmly, then stepped aside to gesture at her. "Simon, Basil . . . this is Imri Stout, acting head of the Brillian army, and of its government."

"I lead only until other arrangements can be made," Imri said. "After everything is settled here in Antora."

I bristled at her implication that the affairs of Antora required the Brill to be involved, but I remained silent. The truth was that we needed help from as many people as possible.

"Imri is the one who trained Kestra to use her magic," Tenger said. "She knows what Kestra is capable of, and where her limits are."

"The student betrayed her teachers." Imri ran a hand over her bare scalp. "This is our sign of mourning for all those we lost on the day Kestra left Brill. But we are dedicated to putting an end to your Lord of the Dominion, despite our recent troubles."

Recent troubles was a polite description. Something had happened in Brill between Endrick and Kestra, resulting in the explosion of their royal palace and everyone inside. It was amazing that any army was here right now; whether they would be a valuable asset was still in question. They clearly believed Kestra deserved at least partial blame for what had happened there.

Imri finally stretched out a hand to Basil, who apparently was considered less filthy. "I know your father, and he is a good king. You will be an equally valuable partner to Brill, I hope."

"Reddengrad always proves its loyalty to its friends," Basil said, clapping a hand on my shoulder.

Imri's attention shifted to me. "I understand you are the new king of the Halderian clan. Brill keeps watch on all rulers in this region. How is it we did not know about you?"

I smiled. "Perhaps in the same way I did not know about you . . . er . . ."

"I require no titles. You may call me Imri Stout. I have also been told that there is some connection between you and Kestra Dallisor."

I kept my expression even, or tried to. "There is, though I have no way of describing it."

She arched her neck. "It is not necessary to describe it. All I need to know is if you are on her side or ours."

"I hope that her side is our side," I replied. "Are we not all here to bring an end to the reign of Lord Endrick?"

Imri's piercing blue eyes narrowed. "Are we, Simon?"

Tenger cleared his throat. "Perhaps we should settle these matters in a more private place. Hugh will help the Brill set up a more permanent camp outside Woodcourt's walls." He gestured to Basil. "You should join us."

I grunted my approval and led our group into Sir Henry's library, as good a place as any for the conversation we needed to have. We set four chairs around his former desk. Tenger was to my right and Basil to my left with Imri Stout directly across from me.

She began. "Captain Tenger has insisted that Kestra Dallisor was not responsible for the destruction of the palace in Brill. However, that does not mean she is no threat to us. I've seen what she can do, but I also know what she cannot do. The Brill are uniquely qualified to stop her, and the boy."

Tenger leaned forward. "I told Imri Stout about Joth Tarquin and what we suspect of his abilities."

She nodded. "I have already instructed my science officers to develop strategies to counteract his magic. I hope to have some answers by morning; then we will solve this Antoran problem once and for all."

I folded my arms and stared at her, unable to contain myself any longer. "But that's the point—these are Antoran problems. It is not for the Brill to solve them, nor to determine our future."

"When our palace exploded, that gave us every right to have a say in Antora's future."

"You will never rule in Antora," I said. "You will never occupy

Antora. If you choose to remain here, then you must agree to do so under my command."

"Or mine," Tenger said. "I am a captain—"

"And I am a king." I glared sharply at him until he glanced away. "When Endrick is defeated, the Scarlet Throne will belong to the Halderians, not to the Coracks, not to the Brill—" I glanced over at Basil. "Nor to Reddengrad."

"We don't want it," Basil said. "My people will fight this battle only out of gratitude for my life."

"Kestra will think the Scarlet Throne is hers," Tenger said. "And, confidentially, between the four of us, by rights of inheritance, it is. So we will settle this now, Simon. Answer as you should, and I will allow you the Scarlet Throne without contest. What are your intentions regarding Kestra?"

I kept my gaze steady. "Kestra cannot be allowed to take the throne."

Imri shook her head. "Yes, but what are your intentions?" When my eyes darted away, she pounded a fist on the table, drawing my attention back to her. "Let me be more specific. If Kestra succeeds in killing Lord Endrick and tries to claim the throne for herself, what will you do?"

I hesitated, unwilling to answer. Something more pressing was intruding on my thoughts.

"Simon?" Tenger asked.

I stood and pushed back my chair. "Excuse me."

I ran into the yard in time to see Rawk landing with Harlyn on his back. Seeing me, she leapt off and rushed forward, throwing her arms around my neck. "I did it—they're coming! Our cavalry is only a couple of days away."

I rubbed my hand down Rawk's neck in gratitude for having safely returned Harlyn. He nestled into me a moment before I understood that he was tired and hungry after such a long flight. I let him go, and he flew off to hunt.

When he'd gone, I turned to Harlyn. "Did you have any trouble with the cavalry?"

"A little, but I settled it." Harlyn lowered her eyes. "We should talk about that."

"We will, but first I must settle something of my own. Come with me."

I walked with Harlyn back into the library, where Tenger was standing in conversation with Imri Stout, and where Basil remained in his seat. They all looked up as I entered.

"The Halderian cavalry will be here within two days," I said. "When they arrive, we will attack." Then I addressed Imri. "Either Kestra will succeed in killing Lord Endrick, or in her place we will find another Infidante to do the job. When it is completed, Kestra cannot be allowed to take the throne."

"If she tries—"

"If she tries, we will stop her . . . at any price," I said. "But it will be under my command alone. Agree to that now, or my first order to the Halderians will be the expulsion of the Brill, the Coracks, and, if necessary, even the prince of Reddengrad."

"I will command my people," Basil said. "But I will take my direction from you."

"As long as you do as you have promised here, the Coracks will follow you," Tenger said.

Imri templed her fingers and looked directly at me. "You cannot say the words, can you, Simon? You tell us that Lord Endrick must be killed, but when it comes to Kestra Dallisor, all you can say is that she must be stopped. So here are our terms. We will follow you to the death of Lord Endrick. But when it comes to Kestra, if you will not *stop her* to our satisfaction . . . to her death . . . then we will."

My heart thudded against my chest, but there was no going back now. All I could say was, "Agreed. We will call ourselves the Alliance, and you will retain command of all those who came with you. But only while you are following my command."

Heads dipped in agreement, and I nodded in return. With Harlyn at my side, we left the library. I had just united the opposition against Lord Endrick under my leadership, and we were finally prepared to move forward.

"You did well in there." Harlyn squeezed my arm. "We must celebrate this new Alliance."

"Why would we celebrate that?" I asked, harsher than I ought to have done. Correcting myself, I added, "Forgive me, Harlyn. I'm glad you arrived safely."

By then we had reached her room. I kissed her cheek, but when I began to back away, she took my hand.

"We do need to talk, Simon."

I understood, but my gut was too twisted for conversation. I mumbled a terse "Not now," the most I could utter in that awful moment.

She stared at me for what seemed like a very long time. "Yes, of course."

I dismissed myself, then went to my own room, where I shut the door, slid down the wall, and held my head in my hands. Maybe I had done the only thing I could, but I had never felt more miserable in my life. If Kestra still trusted me at all, I had betrayed it.

I had just doomed her.

· TWENTY ·

KESTRA

Joth and I had returned to our upper-floor shelter in Highwyn. As the morning streets began to fill with merchants and their customers, I sat near a broken window to hear the passersby bargaining for goods and trading in gossip, namely the fate of the Ironhearts we had killed only a couple of nights earlier.

"Who could have done such a thing?" they'd ask each other.

Not one of them knew the answer. Not one of them guessed that within easy distance of where they stood was the girl responsible for their deaths, the same girl who had one more death ahead of her— Lord Endrick's.

The countdown to Antora's freedom was now numbered in hours.

The central advantage of our location was the clear view of Endrick's palace. Through careful observation, it was obvious that he knew something was coming. The entire palace was surrounded by more Ironhearts. Oropods with well-armed riders patrolled the streets throughout the city, looking for any sign of trouble. Carnoxen were held behind thick iron fences, ready for release in the event of an attack. The giant condors flew overhead, and I had no doubt that whatever they saw, Endrick also saw.

But he would not see me until it was too late.

After a couple of days of careful planning, Joth and I felt ready to launch the attack on Lord Endrick. Every detail had to be accounted for: Where in the palace would he be? How could we maintain the element of surprise? Once the attack began, would the Ironhearts defend him, or abandon him?

If only we had answers to any of our questions. Even the simplest questions had serious consequences. Was it possible to further curse the half-lives into nonexistence? If so, would Endrick do it? And most troublesome of all: What if Simon and the others with him tried to interfere with our plans?

"We must go tonight," Joth said. "Every day that we delay increases the chances of the others joining us."

That's what he always called them: *the others*. Simon and Harlyn and their Halderian army, which was surely on its way. The Coracks, who were beginning to gather from all parts of Antora. The Brill and, we suspected, even what remained of the armies of Reddengrad had already arrived.

Whispers rising from the street said they called themselves the Alliance, and that they were led by a young Halderian king no one had ever heard of.

A young Halderian king I tried very hard not to think of. If I was going to survive this, he had to be only one of *the others*, one of many who would soon bow to me when I took the Scarlet Throne for myself.

And it would happen tonight.

"I agree," I said to Joth. "It's time to act."

With little else to do, I continued polishing the Olden Blade, and now I could clearly see my face in it. I didn't know why I had put so much effort into the blade—a shine made no difference in how sharp my stab would be. But still, I continued to polish.

Joth placed his hands over mine. "Are you worried?"

"Yes."

He leaned in closer to me, but I refused to acknowledge him.

"You're still angry with me?" he asked. "Because of the Ironhearts?"

"What if Simon's sister was one of our victims?"

"If she was, then it's because the Ironhearts pose a threat to our reign. We cannot leave any of them alive, unsure of their loyalties. But when we rule from the Scarlet Throne—"

I looked up. "*I* will take the Scarlet Throne. I am its heir. And I will rule alone."

He stood, his body stiff with sudden anger. "Alone? You have not gotten this far alone, nor will you complete your task alone."

"The help you have given me does not qualify you to take what is mine. Your reward is all that I have done for your people, all that I will still do."

"That is their reward, but what will you offer me? We joined powers, Kestra—what did you think that would mean? We are not simply using each other for magic—we have connected our lives! I told you that would happen."

"You told me it often happened, not that it must happen. And I will be the exception, Joth. I will take the throne alone. If you cannot accept those terms, then you may withdraw now and lead your people back to permanent captivity in the forest."

His face reddened, but he finally got his temper under control and said, "None of this matters if we fail to defeat Endrick. Let's keep our attention there. The rest can be decided later."

We barely spoke another word to each other as we made our

preparations to leave. Joth had ventured into the city earlier that day and obtained for me leather pants, a belted tunic with protective padding on the shoulders and elbows, and a new cloak to protect me from the wintry cold, though with all the ice inside me, I hardly cared about the snow outside. I wound my hair into a braid and had just put the Olden Blade in place against my thigh when a knock came at our door.

My head shot up, and I looked over at Joth, who didn't seem at all surprised. Which told me two things. First, that no matter how often he claimed that we were working together, he was still holding back from me. And second, that he must have had some warning from the half-lives who were keeping watch on this place, which meant I did not have full access to his magic.

Yet he seemed to have full access to mine. That would have to change, and soon.

Joth crossed to the door and opened it. I arched my head in that direction, but relaxed as soon as I heard, "Darrow."

I rushed to the door, intending to close him into an embrace, but I paused when I saw him. For as long as I'd known him, this man had been a servant, and a friend. I'd thought about him hundreds of times since figuring out who he was, but I had never known him as a father.

Yet there he was. As alive and whole as he'd been before that night when the Coracks stopped my carriage and shot him, then carried him from my sight. That seemed like ages ago, and everything was so different now.

Different enough that I could only widen the door for him to enter and greet him with, "Hello, Darrow." Nothing more.

He shifted his weight, looking as uncomfortable as I felt. Maybe he had expected more from me, something that I was incapable of offering. But why should it have been otherwise?

Finally, I asked, "How did you find us?"

"The half-lives brought him here," Joth said, then to Darrow added, "Where is Loelle?"

"Captured by the Brill as we tried to sneak into the city. I don't think they'll harm her, though they said they'd give her to the Coracks. I can't say what they will do to her."

Nor could I. Loelle had worked with them for years as their trusted physician, but I knew now that her service had nothing to do with loyalty. She had been waiting for the Coracks to find an Infidante . . . to find me. Once I'd been chosen, Loelle had manipulated the situation to ensure I obtained magic, then taken me away from the Coracks, solely within her control. Forgiveness would not come easily to her, if it came at all.

I looked from Darrow over to Joth. We had just learned that his mother was being returned to the very group she had betrayed, and he didn't seem particularly concerned. Would I respond the same way now, if it had been Darrow in captivity? Was I similarly hardened?

Joth saw me watching him and, with almost no emotion, said, "You know the Coracks better than anyone. Will they harm my mother?"

"Not if they have any reason to keep her alive." Which should have been a thin comfort, but it seemed to fully satisfy Joth. For my own sake, I added, "Loelle is a great healer. That might be enough."

Joth slowly nodded. "Then we'll take care of the task ahead of us first."

"I suggest you go prepare for it now." Darrow gestured toward the door, and his voice became stern. "Let me speak with my daughter."

Joth's eyes darted between Darrow and me as he contemplated what to do. Finally, he licked his lips, then excused himself, saying he would ready our horses. Darrow and I remained facing each other. He looked me over and seemed to understand why I was dressed this way.

"So the attack is tonight?"

I tilted my head. "How much do you know?"

"I know only what Joth has communicated to the other half-lives." He stepped forward. "Is there anything else I should know?"

I considered telling him about Simon, and almost did, except that when I opened my mouth, no words came out. I had no way of explaining to my father what I could not explain to myself.

His brows pressed together. "What else, Kestra?"

I shrugged. "There's no one else." I winced, even as the words came from my mouth. I should have said there was *nothing else*. Surely Darrow would catch the mistake.

If he did, he put that aside and instead said, "I'll come with you."

I considered that for a moment. "You can't help me. And besides, I must focus on Endrick. I won't be able to protect you."

He smiled. "What a cruel twist when the daughter must protect her father. Kestra, I am not asking to come. I am coming. All I need to know is how I can best help you succeed."

I hesitated. As much as I respected my father, he was a liability if anything went wrong. But he still was my father.

"You may come," I finally said. "But you must understand that I have only one purpose tonight, and that is Endrick's death."

He nodded, keeping his eyes trained on me as I crossed to a

small fireplace we had rebuilt enough to cook food without burning down the building. "There is tea here, if you'd like it."

Darrow noted the cup I was using to pour myself a drink. "How many of those do you have?"

I smiled. "This one is all we found in the wreckage. Meanwhile, the Coracks have taken up residence in Woodcourt with some of the finest porcelain dishes in all of Antora." I took a sip for myself, then handed the rest to Darrow. "How did you escape All Spirits Forest? When we flew overhead, it was surrounded."

"It was, *until* you flew overhead. The Ironhearts saw that dragon and must've guessed you were on it, because they left almost immediately to return here to Highwyn."

Joth ducked his head in the door. "It's time to leave."

I started forward, but Darrow said, "Wait." He added, "When you restored me, I sensed that something was different about you. And now that I'm here, I know it is. You're in trouble."

I shook my head. "No more than usual. I'm the same as always, only with magic now."

"No, you're not the same." Darrow put his hand on my arm. "Can't you feel the difference yourself? For I see it in your eyes and sense it in the tone of your voice. Soon, that difference will be as visible as the graying scars on Lord Endrick's face."

I pulled away from him. "That is not true."

"It is, and if it would matter, I would give my life to change that fact. But you must fight this, Kestra, at least as hard as you are about to fight for Antora."

"For now, that is her only fight." Joth widened the door. "It's time for you to leave, Darrow."

I nodded toward him. "My father will be helping us tonight. Before we leave, he should understand our plans."

Joth frowned over at Darrow. "We don't need him."

Darrow stepped forward. "I don't have magic, and maybe I've been half-dead for so long that my skills with a disk bow aren't as sharp as they ought to be, but my daughter is going into a battle. I will be there with her."

"Your daughter *is* the battle," Joth said. "All you will do is get in her way." When Darrow refused to step aside, Joth finally sighed. "Very well. We'll find a more . . . peripheral place for you."

"I already know my role. What Kestra has to do is something only she can do. My job is to clear every other barricade in her way, if I can."

"*I* will do that," Joth said to him. "You take care that you are not one of those barricades." He pointed out the window toward the palace. "All right, here is the plan."

While Joth reviewed the details with my father, I watched as Joth's eye occasionally brushed over me, slight irritation in his gaze to remind me that he'd rather it was just the two of us moving forward.

Little did he know that it was not the two of us now, and it never would be. Tonight we would ride under the cover of darkness, determined to make an end of things before the night was finished. Whatever happened tonight, I had no intention of leaving the palace. By morning, I would either be dead, or I would be sitting on the Scarlet Throne.

I took one glance at Joth.

I would sit on the Scarlet Throne . . . alone.

· TWENTY-ONE ·

SIMON

Only two days ago, I had met with the other leaders of the Alliance. But for all that had happened since then, it might have been months. So many people had come and gone, seeking direction for each new development, that I could hardly keep up with the whirlwind.

It began with the arrival of Reddengrad's army. Basil received an enthusiastic welcome when he went out to greet his people, though he still walked with a limp and seemed to startle at nearly every loud sound. He wasn't ready yet for any fighting.

Not long after, Huge and his patrol of Corack soldiers brought Loelle in as a captive. She looked exactly as when I had last seen her a little more than a month ago, although considering the way she had betrayed us, I expected to see at least a glimmer of humility or fear. If she believed things would return to what they had been before, she was mistaken. I could never think of her with the same respect and friendship as I once had.

Loelle was taken into the library to face Tenger and me. Imri had insisted that she be allowed to attend as well, but I flatly refused. Clearly there was some animosity between Imri and Loelle, and it must have run deep. Imri left the room telling everyone within earshot of her personal verdict, that Loelle be sent to the dungeons until a proper trial could be held.

Once the library door closed, muffling Imri's anger, Loelle turned to Captain Tenger and me, saying, "Surely the judgment of the Brill carries no weight among the three of us."

Tenger and I sat on one side of Sir Henry's desk. He offered her a seat, but she shook her head, insisting that she could better defend herself on her feet.

"Then by all means, do so," Tenger said.

"I will be vindicated in the end," Loelle said. "For years, I listened in on the Corack plans, all of them ambitious and well-intentioned, but not one with much chance of succeeding. Finally, we found Kestra, an Infidante with access to Dominion strongholds, and uniquely qualified to unite all of Antora. We might've used her to her full potential, until Simon fell in love with her. Then every consideration had to be worked around that, and we were failing again. We all know that."

"If you wanted a change of plans, you should have taken them through me," Tenger said.

"And how would you have answered, if I explained I needed to isolate Kestra in All Spirits Forest for weeks, using her magic to rebuild my own people?"

"I'd have said no," Tenger said.

"We needed the half-lives to get this far, and we will need them until the end. Your decision would have been wrong."

"That is irrelevant. Even if I had been wrong, that still does not mean what you did was right."

"I can accept that," Loelle said. "But it's been done and I believe my actions will be the key to Endrick's undoing. If you disagree, then you must determine my punishment."

Tenger looked at me. "What do you think?"

I leaned forward. "You will return to the service of the Coracks, Loelle, as before, healing anyone you can. In every spare second otherwise, you will work on a solution to help Kestra."

She shook her head. "Don't you think I've been trying? Simon, the guilt I feel for what has happened to Kestra overwhelms me. I will not work for a solution because of a punishment. I will keep trying because I owe that to her. But I must be clear. Nothing I have tried gives me any hope of helping her without killing her. And I fear the corruption is spreading to the boy who travels with her, Joth. My son."

Joth had already explained this, but the tenderness in Loelle's voice was unmistakable. I said, "Get yourself something to eat, and set up a medical station in this home. You must find a solution, Loelle. Please find it."

She had only barely left when Imri Stout came in with another report on the activity nearer to Endrick's palace. The Brill had begun patrolling areas around the palace at the closest possible position of safety. It was clear from their reports that Endrick sensed an attack was coming. As far as we could tell, he was drawing all Ironhearts in from every region of Antora, gathering them around the palace like a living fortress.

"If we succeed in getting past so many soldiers, it will come at a high price," Imri informed me. "There must be another way."

There wasn't, not that I had yet figured out. Because it wasn't only the Ironhearts that concerned me.

He had oropods and carnoxen on the ground and giant condors

in the air, searching for any signs of danger. Interestingly, their riders paid us little attention as we patrolled. We suspected their only orders were to search for Kestra.

When the time came, I would use Rawk to fight the condors, but even as powerful as the dragon was, we would be only one against twenty or more.

The Halderian cavalry would be the best matched against the oropods, but the speed and ferocity of an oropod was almost double that of our horses. Even if we won in the end—and that was far from certain—with the number of losses we would endure, it would feel like a defeat.

"You need to get Kestra to talk to us," Tenger had told me more than once.

We knew where she was. She and Joth had stationed themselves on the upper floor of a tall building that had been abandoned for as long as I could remember. The plaster was crumbling and the wood had begun to rot, but the fact that it was so visibly unsafe likely made it an ideal hiding place, and its height would give them a good view of the palace—perfect for making their own plans to attack.

The Coracks kept a steady watch on the building as we did our patrols, yet the same magic we had encountered before held us back here too. It was possible that Kestra didn't even know we were trying to contact her. Or if she did, after our last attack on her, she likely had no interest in speaking with us. With me.

"Then we'll continue watching," Tenger said. "When she and Joth attack the palace, we must be there."

"Whether she wants to admit it or not, she will need our help," Imri said.

"They don't seem to believe that," I said. "And your idea of help might be different from theirs."

Before Imri could make yet another objection, Trina rushed into the library where we had been meeting. "Simon, your cavalry is here."

I stood and straightened my tunic. "Tell Harlyn."

I'd barely seen her over the past two days, and in the few times I did, we were always among so many people that we'd scarcely said three words to each other. I'd begun to think that she was avoiding me.

I walked from the library to the entry hall of Woodcourt. Gabe was there, staring out the front window. "You're *their* king?" Gabe said. "Those riders are twice your age."

"They don't consider me their king," I replied. "If you want a good laugh, watch them pretend to respect me when I go outside. If I even get that much honor."

I made a move in that direction, but Harlyn came rushing down the stairs behind me, her eyes wild as if in a panic. "Simon! Don't go out there yet!"

"Why not?"

She paused to catch her breath, and when she seemed a little more settled, Harlyn said, "I told you that we had to talk. I've put it off for as long as I can, I suppose. Can we talk now?" She briefly eyed Gabe, who made a quick excuse that he had to finish dressing for patrols that evening.

Harlyn took my hand and pulled me into a quiet alcove of the entryway. She lowered her eyes and seemed to be searching for a way to begin our conversation.

I waited for her to begin, and when she didn't, I prompted, "Is this about the cavalry?"

"Yes."

I was becoming increasingly curious. Harlyn's personality was so bold, I'd rarely seen her reluctant to speak.

"There were problems in persuading them to come, I assume. Because of me?" I wouldn't forget that, only days ago, we had overheard them plotting my death.

Still refusing to look at me, she said, "Reese has taken full command of the cavalry."

I rolled my eyes. "Reese? Wonderful." Of all those we had overheard, he had been the most opposed to me.

Harlyn's smile was grim. "They're all against you, Simon. Commander Reese was just the loudest. When I first asked him to bring the cavalry here, he refused. And yes, it was because of you. He said that to fight for you was to fight under the banner of the Infidante. They know your feelings for Kestra. But I needed a way to persuade them that there was no longer any connection between you and her. I had to tell them something compelling enough to make them come." Now she glanced up. "I know you won't like it."

"You told them we were married."

She winced, barely, but enough that I took notice. "Yes, but only after I'd tried everything else to change Reese's mind. They'll follow me into battle, Simon. They know me; they know my father. They'll follow you if they believe you follow me, and not her." She shifted her weight before adding, "Besides, many people had expected it would already be true of us, or that it soon will be."

I nodded as I took that in. It was absurd that I continued to fight the inevitable, and hadn't I already suggested to Harlyn that the Scarlet Throne would be ours one day? At some point, I would have to marry Harlyn, and in time, we would probably be very happy. Or I could pretend as much anyway.

I took her hands. "You got them here, which is better than I could have done. Now that they're here, we have to deal with their reasons for coming."

"Then we'll tell them the truth."

She was trying to smile but doing a poor job of it. And though she was taking responsibility for the lie, I also knew she'd never have had to lie if I'd already married her, as I should have done.

Gripping her hands tighter, I said, "What if we make what they already believe become the truth?"

Harlyn tilted her head. "Are you serious?" I nodded, but she still seemed uncertain. "Do you want to marry me, or do you feel that you must?"

I sighed and tried not to think of Kestra, or tried not to let my thoughts of her ruin this moment. "Part of accepting the realities of who Kestra has become is accepting that I've missed what is right in front of me. It will take me time to get to where I should have been all along, but I will get there, Harlyn."

Harlyn's face twisted, but at least she was still smiling. "That is literally the worst proposal of marriage anyone has ever heard. But we're at war, you're obviously exhausted, and I did recently announce our marriage as a last resort to save your life, so I suppose you're forgiven. I accept your offer."

I leaned forward and kissed her. It wasn't the kiss she should have received considering that we had just agreed to marry, but it was a start for us.

When we parted, I said, "I've got to tell the cavalry the truth about us. I can't ask for their trust and betray it in the same breath. Will you come with me to speak to them?"

"I have to go on patrol with Gabe right now."

"I'll go in your place. You should be here to prepare the cavalry for the coming battle."

"Their king must prepare them." Harlyn placed a hand on my cheek. "They're already on my side. Now let's get them on yours."

I took her hand, and together, we walked to the front doors. A light snow was falling, made worse by a cold, wet wind. We pulled on our cloaks and wrapped them around us, then went outside to welcome the cavalry—my cavalry, I supposed—as they approached. Commander Reese led about a hundred riders forward, and on his signal, they stopped in four straight rows behind him. All were dressed in the brown and blue colors of the Halderians, and two riders on either side of Reese carried brown flags, each with a blue stripe across it.

Reese dismounted and gave me a curt nod of his head. He had been with Harlyn's father when we had fought at King's Lake two months ago, though we had not worked together directly. He was a large and sturdy man, the kind of warrior I needed on my side, and not only because he would likely defeat me in any sort of challenge. If I could persuade him to follow me, the other men here would accept me too.

Which made it even more problematic when he only nodded in

my direction but then addressed Harlyn. "My lady, we have ridden as fast as our horses would allow. My riders are exhausted and cold, and their horses need care."

Harlyn opened her mouth to answer, but I said, "Commander Reese, you are relieved of duty."

He widened his stance as he looked over to me. "Pardon?"

"If you are so exhausted that you forget to address your king with proper respect, then clearly you are too exhausted to lead these soldiers into battle." I cut off his attempt at a protest by adding, "You are dismissed. Tend to your horse and you can sleep in the stables until you wish to speak to me with respect."

"And who are you that I should care to address you at all?" Reese's hand shifted to his sword. "You're a boy who came from nowhere, without a drop of Halderian blood. Only King Gareth's ring, which, for all we know, you stole from his finger as he slept."

"But I am Halderian," Harlyn said. "And this is your king. If you stand with me, then you must stand with Simon too."

"I will fight for you alone, my lady, whether as a commander or a stable boy." Reese's glare aimed at me contained a tangible heat, the most heat he was likely to feel on this cold night. "But you must excuse me now. My horse needs tending to."

He grabbed his horse's reins and began to walk toward the Woodcourt stables. In turn, Edgar, one of the other men I'd overheard back in Nessel, dismounted and said, "My horse also needs attention, my lady." Ten men and women followed his actions and excuses, and within a minute, every single rider was walking their horse toward the stables.

Harlyn looked up at me and smiled wryly. "That could have gone better."

"It's not over yet." I kissed her hand. "Be safe on your patrols tonight and take care of Gabe."

"You be safe too," Harlyn replied. "I daresay you're about to deal with a far more dangerous situation than I am."

I nodded as she returned to Woodcourt, worried that she might be right. Somehow I had to face a group of soldiers who had already committed treason in their hearts. All that remained was to finish the job.

· TWENTY-TWO ·

KESTRA

We waited to leave until the night was as black as it would become. We had chosen this night for its darkness—a new moon gave us just enough light to guide our horses, and the overcast skies dimmed the stars. We hadn't expected the snowfall, but Joth said it might keep others off the roads and further mask us. I hoped he was right.

Joth set out first, then me, then Darrow, none of us speaking unless absolutely necessary. Considering the consequences of being discovered too early, I couldn't think of anything that would make extra noise a necessity.

Unfortunately, that left me alone with my thoughts, and my head was so crowded with them, I didn't know where to put my attention.

The threads linking our plan together were too thin. There were too many possibilities we could not account for, too many things that could go terribly wrong. Even if everything went right, I was beginning to doubt my own abilities. I'd already tried once to kill Lord Endrick, and that had ended terribly. A second failure would likely be my last mistake ever.

Yet success was the most frightening of all. If I succeeded tonight, then what?

It was a question without an answer, or worse, a question that spawned another hundred questions. At the center of them all: What would happen to Antora after tonight?

What would happen to me? Once I succeeded, would I become the next target?

Joth would be on my side. But I wasn't sure if I wanted that.

Despite what he claimed, that his people were not susceptible to corruption, when he had joined powers with me, that had introduced corruption into him. I didn't know if he could see it in himself as easily as he had recognized it in me in All Spirits Forest. I could see it though. If only I knew what to do for either of us.

Or if anything should be done. The corruption might be all I had to survive the night. It gave me strength, and courage, and assured me I was doing the right thing.

It had lied to me, and in turn, I was lying to everyone else. But if there was a way back now, I didn't know it.

Suddenly, Joth stopped his horse, holding up an arm to get my attention. He looked over at me, communicating with gestures that we were being watched.

I withdrew the Olden Blade and began surveying the area, searching for any sign of who might be nearby. It was late by now, and the snowfall was heavier than before. Nobody would be out here tonight without good reason.

Then I saw it, a slight movement of a cloak on a road to my left. A row of homes was between us, and our watcher was hiding behind the last of them.

Or watchers . . . was there more than one?

I gestured to Joth and Darrow that we should continue riding forward, staying ready for anything that might come without leaving ourselves in a position vulnerable to attack. They agreed, and we continued riding, now in a straight line along the narrow street. I rode in the center.

We rounded a corner and stopped. Immediately, my pulse began to race. Gabe was astride his horse in the middle of the road, his eyes trained on me. I straightened up in my saddle and stared with equal coldness, trying to assess how serious a threat he was. His sword was sheathed, and though he had a disk bow within easy reach, his hands were on the horse's reins.

"We want to talk with you, Kestra," he said. "Just you."

"Keep your voice down," I hissed at him.

But he shook his head. "Agree to speak with me and we can whisper. Until then—"

Before he finished, sounds behind us alerted us to another approaching horse and rider. I turned back to see Harlyn there. But unlike Gabe, she held her disk bow ready, the same one that had already shot me once.

"We won't hurt you, Kestra." Harlyn's conversation opener was rather interesting, considering that the disk bow was armed. "But we need to talk."

"Have you considered that Kestra is far more capable of hurting you?" Joth called to them. "Save yourselves and let us pass."

Gabe said, "Kestra, please—"

"Hush!" I looked up to the skies, certain I had heard a fluttering noise. Was it Simon, on that dragon of his?

Joth had heard it too—I could tell from the way he was looking up—but Darrow had angled his horse to keep an eye on Harlyn, and Gabe still seemed to be trying to get my attention.

After a moment's silence, Gabe spoke again. "We only want to help you succeed tonight."

"Then why have you followed us in secret?" Darrow said, still watching Harlyn. "You come with weapons in hand and ask my daughter to trust you?"

"Daughter?" Harlyn was only temporarily caught off her guard before she added, "Sir, ask your daughter about the dozens of Ironhearts she killed only a few days ago, *after* they had surrendered. Ask about her plans to take Endrick's place on the throne once this is over, perhaps after having absorbed his magic into herself."

"Stop!" I whispered, and tears formed in my eyes. Maybe because of her lies.

Maybe because it was all truth.

Either way, she had to stop.

Seeing that she had found a way to truly wound me, Harlyn continued. "You may call her your daughter now, but be warned, sooner or later she will betray you too, if it benefits her."

Again I heard wings fluttering overhead, but I no longer had it in me to say anything. If that was Simon above us, then he probably already believed everything Harlyn was saying anyway.

Harlyn drew in a breath to speak further, but Gabe called out her name and said, "Run!"

It was too late. That hadn't been Simon. Instead, one of Endrick's condors swooped down from above, its talons grabbing Harlyn and lifting her from her horse. She tried to kick herself free but dropped her disk bow in the process. Gabe reached for his own bow, but before he could act, two more condors flew in, their riders launching fire pellets at the ground. As the pellets exploded, each of us scattered. Gabe fled one way as we rode in the other direction.

Joth and Darrow gathered on either side of me, and one condor circled overhead. The road we were on had become too narrow for the enormous bird to reach us, but its rider fired disks at us.

Finally, Darrow shouted, "Ride on!" I saw he had his disk bow ready and armed, and he had turned his horse to be directly in line with the condor.

"Stay with us!" I called, but Joth grabbed one end of my reins and pulled my horse along with him.

We rode into a thatch-roof market, empty at this time of night, but with rows of stalls to hide and protect us.

"We must go back and help my father," I said.

"Your father is helping *you*, as he should," Joth said. "At least the condors took care of one of our enemies."

My heart sank. Was Harlyn an enemy to me? I supposed she was.

But I felt no relief from knowing where she was headed now, and certainly no joy. I only redoubled my grip on the reins, pulling them away from Joth, and said, "Let's get to the palace. We're running out of time."

· TWENTY-THREE ·

SIMON

I waited inside Woodcourt for two hours until the night had become colder. Then, with the help of a couple of younger Coracks, I walked out toward the stables with a vessel of hot cider and a stack of firewood.

After dismissing the Coracks, I built a fire directly outside the stables. I expected the members of the cavalry were watching me from wherever they were surely huddled together, battling their pride.

Once the fire roared to life, I poured two cups of cider and walked with them into the stables. Sure enough, the soldiers were clustered together in groups, shivering beneath their thin blankets.

I took a sip of the cider and looked around the room directly at each man or woman to be sure they knew I'd come. No one spoke a word, but they all were staring at me and most had a hand on whatever weapon was nearest to them.

Loud enough for them all to hear, I said, "It is true that I am not Halderian. But it is also true that the father of my birth fought alongside you or your fathers in the War of Devastation, and there he gave his life. I had the rare honor of gaining a second father, though I was three years in his home before I learned that he was the exiled Halderian king. Before his execution at the order of Lord Endrick,

Gareth gave me his ring and his sword, naming me as his heir. Ever since that day, I've known who I was and what I was supposed to do, but I refused to claim the throne for the very reasons you have objected to me. Do you think any of your complaints are a surprise? Did you think I expected you would embrace me as your king? But I am your king, and I am Halderian now. My first father earned that for me with his blood, my second father gave that to me with his inheritance, and I will claim it from you in these coming days when we fight together on the battlefield. Whether I will live for you, or die for you, I swear on the lives of my fathers that I will lead you in the best way I can."

With that, I continued looking around the room until I saw a girl who might've been a couple of years younger than me. She was thin and her face was dirty, but her eyes held a spark in them that had responded to my words.

I walked over to the girl. "What is your name?"

"Amala Fingray."

"Am I your king, Amala?"

"Yes, my lord."

"*Lord* is the title for Endrick, and all others are too grand for me now."

"My king, then."

I smiled and handed her the second cup of hot cider. "Amala Fingray, until further notice, you are commander of this cavalry. Join me outside and we will discuss strategy for the coming attack." Then I looked up at the others. "The fire outside is warm and the cider is tasty, for I found it in the cellar of the former master of Woodcourt. Join me, or don't, but this is the moment when you will decide where your loyalties are. If you come to the fire, then you come to your king."

Then I turned and walked out with Amala on my heels, her head tall with pride but taking in deep breaths as she contemplated the weight of the assignment I had just given her. Once outside, we stoked the fire with more wood, and then we waited.

And waited. Amala had another cup of cider while I began to feel nauseous enough to worry I might lose what I'd already swallowed. If no one came, I would present to the Alliance my army of one.

"Do you want to discuss strategy?" she asked.

"How are your skills with weapons?" If she had any at all. Amala didn't move like a warrior.

Amala patted the sword at her side. "My mother gave this to me before we left, and I've practiced with it at every opportunity since. But I'm good with horses, and I was told that they needed every fighter they could get, since so many of ours were lost in the battle at King's Lake."

Many more would be lost in the battles that were coming, if Amala Fingray represented the totality of my cavalry.

"May we join you at the fire . . . my king?"

I looked up to see three men walking out from the stables. These had been some of the last to follow their former commander into the stables earlier that evening, so it was no surprise to see they were the first to emerge. But it was a great relief.

I poured cups for each of them and placed one in each man's hands as he bowed to me and found a place around the fire.

Within five minutes, another eight soldiers had joined us. Before

I had their cups filled, another ten were outside. That was followed by the majority of the riders, each of whom greeted me as their king, gave me a respectful bow, then found a place around the fire.

"What is the strategy, my king?" Edgar called. "We are here to kill Lord Endrick, are we not?"

"No," I said, and this was the test. If I was going to lose them again, this was where it would happen and I would not win their attention a second time. "There is only one person who can kill Lord Endrick, and that is the Infidante."

"I told you all, and you wouldn't listen," Reese, the former commander of the cavalry, said, walking out of the stables. "His marriage to Harlyn Mindall is a fraud. He is in love with Kestra Dallisor."

I poured another cup of cider but held it in my hands. "You're correct. Harlyn and I are not married. She told you that to get you this far, but I am telling you the truth now. Whether you remain here depends on your ability to trust what I am about to say: Not one of us anywhere within the land of Antora has the ability to kill Lord Endrick. Only the Infidante can do it. So we can help her succeed, or we can get in her way. There are no other choices, and the consequences of failure are severe."

"We came to help her," Reese said, stepping into the circle near the fire. "But my question for you is, what happens after Endrick is dead? Who will sit on the Scarlet Throne?"

"The Scarlet Throne belongs to the Halderians," I said, looking Reese directly in the eye. "No one else can be allowed to have it after Endrick is dead." Then I offered him the cup of cider.

He stared at me for a long moment, then finally nodded as if satisfied with my answers. Reese took the cup and raised it in the air.

"A toast to my king and yours! May the coming battle be full of glory!"

A cheer followed, but it was quickly muffled when Gabe rode up, out of breath and with a torn sleeve near his shoulder. Beneath it was a deep scratch.

"Harlyn is gone; they took her," he said.

"Who?"

"The Dominion. We've got to get her back." Gabe's wide-eyed expression was full of panic. "Kestra and Joth were there too, on their way to the palace."

I turned to Amala. "I'm afraid that I must ask you to cede leadership for now." She nodded, and I said to Reese. "Commander, prepare your riders and horses to leave within the hour. I will notify the others gathered here that the time has come. Tonight will mark the end of Lord Endrick and the Dominion." Then I glanced up at Gabe. "And we will get Harlyn back. Go wake Tenger."

Less than an hour later, I sat astride my horse at the front of a long line of Alliance soldiers. To my right were one hundred soldiers of the Halderian cavalry. At my left were about twice the number of Coracks, with Tenger at my side. Directly behind me were five hundred Reddengrad soldiers, some on horseback and some on foot. Behind them all were a thousand Brillian soldiers, determined to have their revenge against Lord Endrick. They had been working day and night in hopes of finding a defense against Joth's powers. I hoped they were ready.

And not one of us would be of any use if Kestra failed tonight. I hoped she knew what she was doing.

· TWENTY-FOUR ·

KESTRA

Lord Endrick's palace was the highest on the hills of Highwyn, situated so that it had an easy view of the city and of the surrounding land of Antora. Woodcourt was only a little lower, and as Joth and I came closer, we saw signs of activity from below. The Alliance was on the move.

"They expect to join us in the battle," I said to him.

"They're of no use to us." Joth was still staring at our road ahead. "We must stay with our plan."

"Our plan involved Darrow." I glanced back once more, as I had done already a thousand other times. "Where is he? Do you suppose—"

"He will come if he is able to." Joth's tone was cooler than usual, which hardly made me feel better. "We're better off without him anyway. Are you ready?"

I put my hand on the Olden Blade. "Ready."

As we had seen from our upper-floor lookout deeper within the city, Endrick's palace was surrounded by what I assumed was his entire Ironheart army. If Simon's sister was still alive, then she would be in there, somewhere. Thousands of soldiers stood at attention, heavily armed, and fully aware that to fail here would mean an instant death sentence. Endrick had control of the hearts of every single person here.

He'd once controlled mine. I knew how they must have felt, compelled to obey, terrified that a single wrong move might prompt a squeeze on the heart, or worse.

"Promise me that the half-lives will not kill them all," I said.

"Only those who get in your way." Joth offered me his hand, and I took it. His flesh was warmer than before. He squeezed on my fingers, then asked, "Do you feel the magic in me?"

"I do."

"As I feel yours, I will do my part from out here, but once you are inside, if there is anything you need, I will sacrifice my safety for yours, and if necessary to protect you, I will sacrifice everyone out here. You are the priority now."

I nodded, hearing an echo of Simon's voice from ages ago, that he would die for me. Joth had just forced the same obligation upon every living thing between me and Endrick. I hoped they were all smart enough to move out of my way.

Joth kissed my fingers, then released my hand as we heard rumbling noises coming from farther down the hill, from Woodcourt. Teams of horses and foot soldiers raced toward us.

"They are coming," I said.

Joth cursed. "They'll ruin everything! You'd better go now!"

I withdrew the Olden Blade and kicked my horse into action. The instant I came into view of the palace, I heard shouts of my name and orders for the Ironhearts to stand their ground. I only sped up, fully aware of the weapons being drawn, the pikes aimed toward my heart, and the disk bows being loaded with every intention of killing me.

I rode faster, passing through the palace gates into a wide courtyard surrounded by tall rock walls. As soon as I crossed the gates, the first disk flew. Immediately, I felt a rush of wind around me, headed toward the Ironhearts. It wasn't cold like the night air, nor clear like wind should be. Instead, it was the color of wispy summertime clouds, but with a soft glow that lingered after it had passed. And it stopped the disk.

No, *they* stopped the disk. These were the half-lives, going before me in battle. I saw only the faint glimmers of light they left behind, though I doubted the Ironhearts could see even that much. Everything happened so fast, they probably saw nothing at all. The half-lives' attack was like a broom sweeping across Endrick's lands, flattening everything in their path.

Tears creased my eyes. This was not what I had agreed to, but I could not stop now.

I rode across the courtyard as fast as I could, keeping myself close to their wave, ignoring everything around me but the doors to the palace itself.

A long series of wide stairs rose to the entrance. I charged my horse up the steps and whispered out orders to the half-lives to open the doors. They did more than that; somehow the two large doors at the center of the landing were ripped from their frames and flung out on either side of me, landing far down on the ground below. I rode inside, then dismounted, my Olden Blade in hand.

Where would Endrick be?

The palace was square shaped with a large reception area inside the doors. From what I recalled on my few visits here, the east wing was for official state business. My adopted father, Sir Henry, often met with Endrick in the rooms there. The west wing held Endrick's private rooms, and straight ahead were the servants' quarters. At the top of the grand staircase directly ahead of me was Endrick's throne room.

It would take hours to thoroughly search the palace. Endrick could be anywhere here.

Of greater interest was that the palace appeared to be empty. I could not understand that. Lord Endrick kept a full staff of servants, and there was always a bustle of activity from members of the Dominion clamoring for his mercy, or attention, or reprisal on some uprising or another.

Where was everyone?

At least I knew that Endrick was still nearby. Joth had ordered the half-lives to watch the palace since we had arrived in Highwyn. If Endrick had attempted to leave, we would have known. Nor did I expect any escape. He had defeated me once and would believe he could do so again. His pride would not allow him to fear me.

But he would, very soon.

With no choice other than to search room by room, I began opening doors, beginning with the servants' quarters. At the first open door, my earlier questions were answered. The half-lives must have come through the rooms already, for I saw the scattered bodies of servants lying on the floors, having fallen while mid-action.

I crouched down to feel a faint pulse of a woman who must have been sweeping when the half-lives found her. Her broom had lodged against the wall, and her body had folded over the handle, placing her in a most uncomfortable position. I lowered the broom to allow her to lie flat on the ground, then realized I had inadvertently drawn strength from her.

Something deep within me suggested I could take all I wanted, and I should. This room had a dozen servants in it, all of them alive enough to be of use to me.

Take their strength. You'll be stronger. The suggestion in my head was louder than my own thoughts. Or perhaps those thoughts had been mine, and some part of me wanted to finish the job the half-lives had begun.

Recoiling at the possibility, I hurried onward but hadn't even reached the next room before the thoughts returned, louder and angrier. This time they scolded me for not having drawn strength while I could. I had to kill Endrick, didn't I? And these servants worked for him, making them legitimate targets.

"I won't do that," I whispered, and with those words, my breath locked in my throat. I grabbed my neck, as if that would allow me to breathe again, but nothing released until I was close to passing out.

Desperate for air, I fell to my knees, directly in front of a guard the half-lives had visited.

Take him.

For the first time, I realized how the corruption worked. If I would not use magic to feed the poison, it would feed off me, and it was doing so now, forcing me to use my magic.

I had believed that I was in control of the corruption, but now I understood the very opposite was true—the corruption was stronger than me, and only a fraction of how strong Lord Endrick would be.

I felt the pulse of this guard. Despite his unconscious state, it was strong and regular, so he would recover. And when I looked at his face, I immediately recognized him from my time in the dungeons. He had threatened me and might have carried through on those threats if Simon had not been there. Later, he had nearly beaten Simon to death.

The longer I stared at him, the more I was convinced that it was the right thing to take strength from this man. I needed it, and he had only used his strength for cruelty.

I took from him, without guilt or shame. I left him enough that he would eventually recover, but what I took made me far stronger than before. Perhaps I needed that, for I left that room with even greater confidence that when I found Endrick, I would be ready for anything he might do.

I took strength again in the kitchen, growing in power, absorbing the cold from every corner of the room. I exhaled and saw the frost in my breath, and it warmed me to see it. I redoubled my grip on the Olden Blade, anxious to use it, eager to be finished with my quest.

Wanting to kill Endrick.

I no longer dreaded it, no longer cowered at the thought of my blade piercing his gut, spilling his blood.

He was evil. He had murdered thousands of Antorans for his power, including my own mother, and many other people I had cared about once. And he would continue to do so for as long as he reigned.

I moved faster through the rooms, my hunger to find Endrick growing stronger with each step. When I did, I would make him pay for his crimes.

At last, I had searched every room on the main floor of the palace. There was only one place left, the throne room. It was the worst possible location for him to defend himself; hence why it was the last place I'd looked for him. At best, he was a fool to be in there.

Which made me nervous. Endrick was no fool. He was in that room for a reason.

In the daytime, the room was brightly lit thanks to the large panel of windows along one entire wall. But this late at night, those windows only made this room seem darker than it otherwise might have been, and I suspected Lord Endrick preferred things that way.

My eyes immediately flew to the center of the throne room. A tall dais was there, surrounded on all sides by six steps. At the top of it, Endrick sat upon the Scarlet Throne.

Soon, it would be my throne.

He had seen me too, for he leaned forward, resting both elbows on his knees. Despite the darkness, I was certain he was smiling.

A smile from Lord Endrick was far more terrifying than a frown, for it deepened the many lines and scars in his face, each one created by someone he had killed on his road to power. To hide his visage, he usually wore a mask in public, but today, it was only him. And although he obviously knew I was coming, he had not bothered to protect himself with armor. I considered that an insult.

And a great worry, for he *should* have been at least a little concerned. His apparent eagerness to see me set my mind off balance.

I heard a cough, and my gaze fell to the bottom of the steps, upon a figure on her knees, facing away from me.

Harlyn.

Her head was lowered, and a sword was clutched in her hands. As far as I could tell, no physical harm had come to her . . . yet. But no doubt, Endrick had control of her heart and he would use her against me.

Indeed, as I came closer, he stood and smiled. "It was a mistake to come, Kestra. But since you are here, I would like a demonstration of your abilities. Let us begin."

· TWENTY-FIVE ·

SIMON

Whatever Kestra and Joth had intended in their attack upon Endrick's palace, it seemed to be working. Because of the dark night, I was nearly at the palace before I saw the Ironheart bodies, already covered by a thin layer of snow. Death's blanket.

I shouted immediate orders for a search to be conducted for Rosaleen, or for any other Alliance members. I could not bear to do the search myself. I hardly could tolerate riding through it.

Until this moment, I had known they were capable of terrible things, including what I'd seen them do to the smaller group of Ironhearts before. But I'd also hoped that would have shocked Kestra back into the reality of how quickly and deeply she had descended. Instead, she must have embraced it. I only hoped at the end of this, she'd be successful as Infidante. That at least would be some small justification for what I was seeing.

At the end of the row of the fallen, Joth sat alone astride his horse at the entrance to the palace gates, hands casually crossed in front of him, waiting for us. That concerned me.

So I raised a hand to call our soldiers to halt, then rode forward alone.

"Is she inside?" I asked.

Joth nodded. His eyes were heavy on me, unyielding.

"Alone?"

He shrugged, a half smile on his face. "Depends on how you define that word."

"The people Endrick cursed in the forest, are they with her?"

His smile faded into a grimace. "Yes, some of them."

Then the rest were out here, probably surrounding him right now, though I couldn't see or feel their presence.

"Let us help."

He snorted. "You are mice attempting to help a giant. At best, your help is interference."

"We want the same thing you do."

"And what is that?" Joth laughed aloud. "Or *who* is that? I'm afraid you are too late to have any chance with her again. Kestra has connected her powers with mine, which will connect her heart with mine in ways you'll never comprehend. When her quest is complete, I will finish my own quest, and rule upon the Scarlet Throne, finally providing a home for my displaced people." He chuckled again. "So I suppose you are correct: We do want the same thing. But I do not need your help to get what I already have."

He raised his hand in a gesture toward me, and I felt the energy of some invisible force rushing toward me. I began to race my horse away from it, shouting, "Now!"

The distraction had worked. While Joth had talked with me, the Brill had moved into position, armed not with disk bows or swords, but with instruments all tuned to the same piercing frequency. Drawing bows along their strings, the hum was loud and vibrated into my heart, causing an ache that made me clutch at my chest, but at the same time, the invisible force of the half-lives had ceased to press upon me.

I gestured for the cavalry and the Coracks to ride forward, which they did, though the riders appeared to be in some degree of pain from the relentless vibrations. We pushed through it, directly past Joth, who sat helpless as he tried to adjust to the realization that his half-lives could not function as long as the vibrations were playing.

"Stop this!" he shouted. "You will not help her this way!"

Finally, Joth rode toward us with such fury in his eyes that I knew whatever happened next would be bad. At least his focus was on us and not on his half-lives.

"Go with your cavalry." Eying me, Tenger crossed his horse directly in front of Joth's, the Coracks lining up behind him.

Joth called to Tenger, "You should not challenge me, Captain."

"Perhaps not." Tenger straightened up in his saddle. "But I *am* a captain here. Which means I will die if necessary to protect my rebels."

"As you wish."

While Joth rode toward Tenger, Tenger shouted at me again to leave. I rode around them and into the walled courtyard, calling to the others that our priority was to get inside the palace.

However, unexpectedly we met with resistance. Inside these walls, the vibrations lost their intensity, so the half-lives must have had some force here. I dismounted, and using my right forearm, I was able to push through the barrier, allowing Gabe and Trina through, but the gap closed behind us.

I looked back at where we'd come from, trying to understand what had changed. "The vibrations didn't get past the walls."

"They were supposed to, the Brill were sure of it." Gabe frowned. "Maybe there are no more vibrations."

"Joth attacked Tenger." Fear caused deep creases in Trina's brow. "Maybe the vibrations ended because Tenger won."

"Or because he lost."

Trina's hand flew to her mouth, but when she removed it, she said, "Joth must have gotten past Tenger and attacked the Brill."

Which could only mean one thing. I asked Gabe, "Did you see Joth's attack?"

Solemnly, he nodded. "Tenger fell with a single touch of Joth's hand. It reminded me of one of Kestra's attacks."

"Is it possible that he has Kestra's magic?" Trina asked.

"Joth told me they had connected powers," I said, wondering exactly what that might mean for them, and for us.

Gabe cursed and breathed out, "Perfect."

I withdrew my sword, and the others did the same. We entered the palace through two doors that had been blown from their frames. A horse rushed past us out the doors, rearing up in a panic.

"I recognize that animal," Gabe said. "It was Kestra's."

"But where is she now?" Trina asked.

I looked around, trying to orient myself within these lavish halls. If the Alliance won tonight, the Scarlet Throne would be mine. That thought should have enticed me to fight harder, but it did just the opposite. I couldn't imagine myself here. I didn't belong in this place, nor would I want to become a person who'd ever be comfortable here. This building of marble and gilded gold simply wasn't me.

"She is wherever Endrick is." I pointed to the grand staircase toward the throne room. "He'll be up there."

"Wait," Gabe said. "If it's just the three of us, we have to agree on our priorities."

"Helping Kestra defeat Endrick is most important," Trina said.

Gabe's eyes flashed. "Harlyn is here somewhere. We have to find her."

I turned to Trina. "Go and find Harlyn. Get her safely out of this palace if you can."

"I'll go with Trina," Gabe offered.

"No, I need you with me," I said.

"I won't help you save Kestra at the expense of Harlyn's life."

"I know that."

"So let me find Harlyn." Gabe marched toward me, his face reddening with anger. "Maybe you don't care what happens to her, but I do! She was taken while on watch with me, and I'm going to find her now."

"Trina can find her as well as you." I nodded at Trina. "Go and find her."

Furious, Gabe advanced on me. "We said we would do what we could to help Kestra succeed, but she's already here, more powerful than the two of us put together. Do you remember our agreement? If Kestra tries to take the throne, we will stop her. How dare you break that promise now?"

"I'm not!"

"Then what is this?" he asked. "One last attempt to save her from herself, the same as what failed last time, and the time before that, and the time before that?"

"No!" I lowered my voice before we alerted half of Antora to where we were. "Gabe, if she tries to take the throne, I won't be able to do what has to be done. You can."

He paused and lowered his head, then he spoke. "I will act with honor, Simon. This has never been personal."

"I know that."

Gabe put an arm around my shoulder and gave it a pat before we began walking forward. But we didn't get more than ten steps before Trina emerged again.

"You're supposed to find Harlyn," Gabe said.

Trina tilted her head in obvious annoyance and then took three more steps forward until we could see that she was not alone.

Directly behind her, with a knife at her back, was Darrow, Kestra's father. Fully alive. And he clearly recognized me and Gabe.

"This is as far as you three can go," he said. "I overheard your plans for my daughter, and I will *stop* you here. But don't worry—it's not personal."

· TWENTY-SIX ·

KESTRA

Harlyn didn't stand at first—maybe she couldn't, I thought. But eventually, with a fierce grimace, she put one foot square on the marble floor, then another, and finally straightened up and faced me.

I looked her over for any possible injuries—she must have had them to be reacting the way she was. Then I saw the anger in her eyes and realized something else entirely was happening.

"There is no purpose in making us fight!" she shouted to Endrick. "Kestra has magic. We all know how this will end."

Her defiance must've earned her a pinch inside her chest, because she contracted before standing upright again.

"I did not come here to fight her," I said, advancing on Endrick. "I came here for you."

"And I have no objection to that." Endrick raised his hand, fingers apart. "Shall I kill this one, and then you and I can begin?" All he had to do was draw his fingers together, and it would crush Harlyn's heart. Her eyes widened. She knew what was coming as well as I did.

"Stop!" I raised the Olden Blade toward Harlyn. "If we fight, it must be fair. I won't use magic."

She shook her head, doubting my words, but if she refused to fight me, the consequences would be immediate and absolute. So I charged at her, forcing her to raise her sword, and when she did, we clashed hard.

Suddenly finding her will to fight, Harlyn struck back at me. She was better than I had anticipated, particularly with a sword longer than the dagger I carried. The Olden Blade could defend me, but I would never get the better of her this way.

I attempted twice to steal her sword, but Harlyn anticipated me both times and moved away. Behind me, Endrick laughed. "If this is all you can do, Infidante, then I have nothing to fear from you."

"This isn't all you can do," Harlyn said, quietly enough that Endrick couldn't hear her.

It was all I could do under the terms I had agreed to.

"I've seen enough," Endrick said. "I now understand you, Infidante. Or shall I call you the *Insignificant*?"

"I'm sorry," I whispered to Harlyn. On her next swing, I touched her hand just long enough to pull strength out of her body. As she began to collapse, I struck the side of her head, not as hard as it appeared, but enough to make it look like the reason she had fallen unconscious was the consequence of our fair fight. It never was. I had lied to her and cheated.

But I had also saved her life.

With Harlyn now in a heap upon the floor, my attention turned to Endrick. My heart raced with anticipation, but Endrick didn't seem the least concerned. Maybe that was *why* I felt so nervous. Did he know something I didn't?

Endrick stood and began the descent down the stairs leading away from his throne. With each step, he clapped for my victory, but it was a flat, mocking applause, intended to embarrass me.

I dismissed that, unwilling to entertain him with any reaction whatsoever, and tried instead to remain focused on my plan.

Endrick's strategy would be to keep me as far from him as possible, but I needed to get close. So I charged toward him with the Olden Blade ready to strike.

Casually, he swiped his hand sideways, and I was thrown in that direction, landing hard on my left shoulder. I stood again, summoning Joth's half-lives to surround me. I didn't want to repeat that.

Immediately, I felt their presence, but they had an effect on Endrick too. His eyes began darting in all directions.

"I can see them, you know." His expression remained even, but his voice was notably shaking. "And if they think I cannot do any worse to their present curse, they are mistaken."

I smiled, advancing on him. "If you think I cannot do any worse to you, then you are also mistaken."

But he raised his hands again, forcing me back. He drew his hands into fists, and I perceived some degree of pain surrounding me. The half-lives.

With a curl of his lip, Endrick extended his hands wide open, and in that same instant, all that I had perceived vanished, like a hundred masses of energy had at once ceased to exist.

The half-lives in this room had all just been erased. They were dead, truly dead.

I felt their loss like a crushing weight on my shoulders, heavier than I ever could have imagined, but I had to keep moving. He was distracted, giving me an opportunity to push closer to him. I was within ten steps of him, Olden Blade ready in my hands, when he finally turned to me.

"You truly expect to kill me here?" he asked. "And then what?"

"Then the throne will be mine."

"Until a new Infidante comes for you," he said. "And the cycle continues."

I stepped forward. "I will not be so foolish as you were, to lose this blade. I will use any magic that is mine to help Antora, not destroy it, as you have done."

That made him laugh, an awful sound, and one I'd only heard issue from him when something terrible was about to happen. "If it is true, my dear, that you and I are the last two remaining Endreans, then I expect the kind of ruler you will become shall make me proud. You will be cruel, you will be sharp, you will control the people as I never could."

"Never!"

"It's inevitable now. I know what is inside you, but it's all wrong. Corruption is heat, not cold. Fire, not ice. Yours feels like ice because you are fighting against it. Why would you do that?"

"I fight it because you embrace it," I said.

"Oh, I do embrace it, and you will also. Once you understand what it truly is, once you feel its warmth, you will know how empty you have been until now."

"I will never accept it."

"You will, and it will begin here."

I rushed forward, my blade ready, and nearly made it to him before he swept me off my feet and I landed harder on the floor than before. The wind was knocked from my lungs, and my head throbbed where it had crashed.

He laughed. "Go to your knees, girl."

I pulled my blade beneath me but clutched at the marble floors, hoping for anything I could use to protect myself from what was coming. Yet I found nothing, no help, no comfort.

"To your knees!"

"I won't. I'm stronger now, and I won't."

Endrick waved his hand, forcing consciousness back into Harlyn's body. With a gasp of pain, she returned to her knees, one arm holding the place where I had cut her, and with tears streaming down her face.

Endrick said, "Obey me, Kestra, or you will see for yourself how much pain this girl can endure before she dies. It will be more than you think."

There was no reason I should have cared what happened to Harlyn. She had pried Simon's affections away from me, manipulated his illness to force me to leave the Hiplands, and only days ago shot me with a disk. If our positions were reversed, Harlyn would eagerly seize the opportunity to watch me die.

But I remembered how it had felt to hear I might be responsible for the death of Simon's sister. I could not also be responsible for the girl he intended to marry.

Somewhere deep inside, I knew it would be wrong to let Harlyn suffer for my refusal to kneel to Endrick now. Which meant I would have to suffer instead.

Rolling to my knees, I said, "This is only between you and me, but you must know anything you do to me will fail. If you attempt to take my powers, I will simply pull them out of you."

He shook his head. "I'm not taking anything from you, child. I'm giving."

He came at me from behind, put a hand to the back of my neck, and sent something into me. It wasn't pain; it was a burn that spread through my chest to my limbs, evil flooding through me.

I tried fighting it, but it was enveloping me, taking me. Its kiss was like sweet molasses that coated my throat in its deliciousness, and from there it spread. But it was poison, not molasses, burning its way through me. And its power was growing. I wanted more. I wanted all of it, and for it, I was willing to do anything that was required of me.

"Give yourself to it," Endrick said.

I closed my eyes, and the corruption embraced me, filling me with warmth that burned away what had been ice before. How foolish that was, to believe the ice was power. No, *this* was power, and the more of it I absorbed, the more I wanted. I pulled it into myself until I was the corruption. Soon, I knew, I could not separate from its grasp without splitting myself in half.

Never sacrifice more than half of yourself, Loelle had said. Then the poison asked me to surrender my other half, and I obeyed.

At Endrick's command, I opened my eyes and saw how pleased he was with what he had accomplished. But he did not trust me yet. Instead, he gestured to the Olden Blade still in my hands and pointed at Harlyn. "Kill her."

I smiled. The idea of killing was so simple now, so pleasurable. Even the thought of it sent a rush of the purest joy through me. Lord Endrick walked me over to Harlyn, his hand on my back.

"Prove yourself," he said. "Show me that you can do this."

I could do this. I wanted to do this.

Harlyn shook her head, her eyes widened in a desperate fear that added to the heat within me. "Please don't, Kestra. You're not yourself."

"Isn't this *exactly* who you've accused me of being?" I countered. "Am I not now the very person you believed I would become when you shot me with that disk? If I will be accused of being part of the Dominion, I'll do better—I will be the Dominion itself. And for that, I must kill." I raised the blade, but rather than bring it down on Harlyn, I twisted and thrust it directly into Endrick's chest.

He gasped; his eyes grew in alarm and horror. I only smiled at him in return.

"You are mine," he said. "I made you."

"And I shall replace you," I said.

He grabbed my wrist holding the blade, sending fire up my arm and leaving a burn on the back of my hand. I withdrew the blade and he staggered away, but the wound I had created was expanding from its center, creating a dark mass of smoke and blood. His eyes widened in disbelief and he clutched at his body to try to hold it together, but that only seemed to make the wound spread faster.

"I curse you—" he shouted at me, but got no further before what remained of his body faded into a thick black smoke that tightened into a small ball before it suddenly pulsed in, then exploded. The force of it was so strong it shook the earth beneath my feet, and chunks of the ceiling fell around me. The explosion was loud enough that I heard it continue to echo as it spread from beyond the palace walls.

I had crouched low to protect myself, but when everything went silent, I opened my eyes and saw the smoke beginning to gather again. It rushed for me, nearly choking me at first for its thickness, but when I finally had to take a breath, I felt it enter my body, filling me with his powers. All his knowledge, all that he could do, all his understanding, became mine.

Harlyn stood, raising her sword as if that would matter at all. "Kestra, I can't let you—"

"Silence!" I stood tall, sheathing the Olden Blade at my waist, then clutched my burned hand to my chest. I could heal it, if I took the strength from Harlyn. But I was repulsed at the idea of benefitting from her, even against her will. So I gritted my teeth against the pain in my hand and said, "I will spare your life for only one purpose, that you go and tell the people what I've done. They are free of Endrick, but they are mine. I have his powers, all of them. And I have the Olden Blade to keep control over my power, as he never could. Go now, for if you say a single word, I will change my mind."

Harlyn stared at me for only a second longer before she dipped her head at me and ran.

I drew in a deep and satisfying breath, then ascended the steps to the Scarlet Throne. After running one finger along the arch of the chair, I rounded it once, then sat.

The Scarlet Throne was mine. I was the Dominion now.

· TWENTY-SEVEN ·

SIMON

Whatever happened inside the throne room was powerful enough to throw me off my feet and send both Darrow and Gabe careening against one wall. Only Trina was able to keep her balance but just barely. Anything not attached to something stable toppled over, including a large marble bust of Lord Endrick that nearly hit Gabe.

In a nearby room, I heard what sounded like an enormous chandelier crash to the floor, followed by sounds outside of decades-old trees falling to the ground.

The destruction was followed by a minute of such absolute silence that it filled me with dread. Something terrible must have happened.

Echoing my thoughts, Gabe asked, "What was that?"

"It's Lord Endrick," Trina said warily. "Though I don't know if it means good news or bad."

"Kestra was in the throne room with him," Darrow said. "Whatever just happened, she is involved."

"*Was* involved," Gabe corrected him. "It's quiet now. Too quiet."

"We have to find her," I said. "Maybe we can help."

Darrow rolled his eyes. "I already know what your help means for her."

Standing again, I added, "Sir, Kestra is a danger to herself, and certainly is at risk of endangering all of Antora. Help us to help her, that's all we ask."

"Tell me how killing my daughter will help her."

"Tell us how ignoring the truth about Kestra will help Antora," Gabe countered.

"Are you certain that she is still in the throne room?" Trina asked. "What does it mean that everything has become so quiet?"

I took one cautious step forward. "Darrow, take me to her. You know enough of my feelings that if there is any way to save Kestra, I will."

"You're too late." Harlyn ran toward us from deeper inside the palace. A long cut was on her right arm, her dress was torn in several places, and her face and hands were dirty.

My heart stopped. "What do you mean we're too late? Is she—"

Harlyn shook her head. "No, she's alive, and she completed her quest—Endrick is dead. But I think it's only made things worse. She assumed all his powers, and she holds the Olden Blade!"

I took her hands in mine. "Are you all right? What happened?"

Harlyn drew in a deep breath before speaking. "Before she killed him, he forced her to her knees. He did something to her there, corrupting her further, I think. All I do know is that Kestra *is* Endrick now, in power and demeanor, and in the way she thinks."

"With her magic, and with the half-lives, she should have been on equal ground to fight him," Darrow said. "How did he get her to her knees like that?"

Harlyn opened her mouth, then closed it and shook her head. "I don't know. I'm sorry."

From behind me, Trina said, "Are we going to sit here and discuss this, or do something? Every minute we waste is a minute she better understands what she has absorbed from Endrick."

I turned to Darrow. "Surely you see what is happening. Take me to her, *please*."

After a quick glare at Trina, he looked again at me. "The first time I saw all of you was on the road headed to Woodcourt. Kestra's life never was easy, but you Coracks made a fine mess of what little she did have. You destroyed the family she had known, made her hated in every region of the country, gave her magic—knowing what it would do to her—and now you wish to punish her for what you did! Kestra is my daughter. I gave my life to her service, the only way I could remain close to her, and just when she was getting old enough that I could have told her the truth, you took me from her too." Darrow shook his head. "You have ruined her life. I'll take you to her, Simon, no one else. But if you make a single move to harm her, I swear that I will strike you down first."

"You cannot go," Trina said. I began to object but she added, "You're a king. You have responsibilities to your people."

"You won't have the right judgment around her—even you admit that," Gabe said.

"I'll go," Harlyn said.

"No!"

"Simon, listen to me! When I was in the throne room with Kestra, there was a point when she could have killed me, but she didn't. I don't think she'll kill me now either."

"None of us should go in that room without a plan to stop her." Gabe quickly added, "Without harming her, of course."

His tone sounded sincere, but I knew otherwise. Gabe had only said that because Darrow was listening.

Harlyn said, "The hand she fights with is injured. If I can get close to her, I can steal the Olden Blade. Then at least we have something to bargain with."

Or the means to kill her. I was thinking it, and I knew the same was true for every one of us in this circle.

"If Kestra already saved Harlyn once, she might not see Harlyn as a threat," Trina said. "I say that we should let her go with Darrow."

It wasn't a good idea, but it was the best idea we had, so reluctantly, I nodded. Harlyn gave me a smile of confidence, then followed Darrow down a long hallway.

"Now what?" Gabe asked.

"Let's rejoin the others and figure out what to do next," Trina said.

Only then did I realize that we had not been alone for our conversation, though I couldn't say how long Joth had been standing at the entrance to the palace. He announced himself with a mocking laugh, then said, "Rejoin the rest of your petty Alliance at your own risk." Joth strode into the palace through the main doors as casually as if this was his country to rule. "With Endrick dead, it's chaos out there."

I marched toward him with every intent of attacking, but Gabe grabbed my arm to hold me back, whispering that this was not a fight we could win.

Joth merely stared at us as if we were little more than flies to be swatted away, finally saying, "Kestra completed the task she was chosen to do, gave freedom to Antora, and all you can think of her is what a problem she has become. Kestra Dallisor saved all of you! Can you not be grateful enough to postpone thinking of ways to kill her even for a single day?"

Trina had walked to the palace doors, right where Joth had previously stood. "Simon, he spoke the truth. We need to get out there."

"One minute." Hoping to placate Joth's temper, I kept my voice calm. "Will you pass a message to Kestra? Tell her that, at noon the coming day, I will be waiting on the front steps of the palace, unarmed and alone. I only want to speak to her, to thank her for what she has done."

Joth smiled. "Isn't that charming? I'll be sure to tell her."

Except that his tone clearly indicated he had no intention of telling her what I'd said. He countered, "Instead, I want you to go out there and tell your people to bow before the new ruler of this kingdom here in the courtyard of the palace. And for their sakes, they had all better come."

I shook my head. "I will pass on no such message until after I speak directly with her."

"Anyone not in the palace courtyard at noon will be punished," Joth said. "Whether you give them the message or not."

"Are those Kestra's orders, or yours?" I asked.

"Kestra and I share powers, so we share orders," he said, raising his voice. "You wish to speak to her? Well, you have, through me."

I tried another tactic. "If she is queen now, I am a king, and I want to open diplomatic talks with her."

Joth laughed. "Ah yes, King of the Banished. You have only a few hours left to rule over a lost and damaged people. Enjoy it while you can, but there will be no meeting, ever. Now get your scattered Alliance to the courtyard by noon."

He turned and walked away from us, not once looking back over his shoulder, which meant he had no fear of being followed.

I had until noon tomorrow to figure out a solution.

No, if I waited until noon, the game was over. The countdown had begun. If I was going to win, noon tomorrow would either prove our victory, or destroy us all.

And the clock was ticking.

· TWENTY-EIGHT ·

KESTRA

Somewhere in Highwyn, a steeple clock rang out the time. Midnight. I had been the queen of Antora for exactly twenty-eight minutes and so far had done little but contemplate the insignificance of my title. Considering all that I had done to get here, I felt no satisfaction in merely being a queen.

Should I be an empress? If there were overlords, could I be an overlady?

I supposed these were the problems a new all-powerful leader had to deal with.

Smiling, I began to think of what I should do first: announce to the people that Endrick was dead, I supposed. Perhaps they would cheer, until they realized that I had replaced him. No one would be happy about that.

Not the Dallisors—I wasn't one of them.

Not the Halderians—more than once, they had rejected me as part of their clan.

Not the Coracks—they wanted me dead.

There were no more Endreans. I was the last of them.

But all of them would kneel at my feet, or they must die.

As I was the last Endrean, so I would be the last queen of Antora as well. For if Endrick had been nearly immortal, then I would correct his errors and reign forever.

"Kestra." The doors to the room opened, and most amazingly, Darrow was on the other side of them.

I stood, eager for company, someone to congratulate me and counsel me as to how best to introduce my reign to the people. But I had no sooner said his name than I realized he was not alone. Another person entered the throne room with him, and I was anything but happy to see her.

"Harlyn?"

Her hands were shaking, but she would have been even more afraid if she'd known my thoughts. Addressing her, I said, "You enter this room without acknowledging my title, nor showing me the proper respect. Go to your knees, both of you." I waved my hand, and both Harlyn and Darrow collapsed to their knees. That was better.

"Is it kneeling if we are forced to do it?" Harlyn asked. "I recognize one ruler only, king of the Halderians, Simon Hatch."

"Do not say his name here!" I had it in mind to crush her heart for her words, but instead, her words were already crushing mine. I'd tried desperately to seal my heart against pain, against any further wounds, but if simply hearing his name hurt this way, then all my efforts had been in vain. With such scattered emotions, I could not collect the magic within me to punish her properly. So instead, I said, "Do you think that because I spared your life the last time you were in this room that I will do so again? You'd be wrong to think so. You were only the trick I needed to finish my task. I warned you to leave before, and I promise that your life will be measured in minutes if you do not leave now, and stay gone."

"She has come with me." Darrow rose to his feet and walked closer to the dais where I stood. "Kestra, I must speak to you."

I arched a brow. Yes, perhaps I was his daughter, but I was also his queen. He could not demand anything of me.

Still . . . I was curious.

"What do you want?"

"I need to see for myself if you are well. If you are . . . yourself." There was more to this conversation than that. Sadness and disappointment were etched deeply into his face.

"I'm better than I was before. I succeeded in my quest—Endrick is dead."

"Yes, I know."

"Then why do you look as if I've just told you I failed? Endrick is dead, Darrow!"

"Is he?" My father took one step closer to me. "Or does he remain alive in you?"

"I am not Endrick!" I shouted, descending the steps, heat building the closer I came to him. "Endrick has no possession of me, no influence on me, nothing! I am your daughter, as I always was!"

Darrow shook his head. "No, Kestra, you are not."

"You call me by the same name I've always used."

"And yet you answer with a different voice. There is an edge to it now, anger."

I brushed past him to gaze out the vast windows at the side of the throne room. Here, we were high above the ground and able to see the outskirts of Highwyn, areas of farmland and travel routes to and from the city. These roads were usually full and purposeful, and I wondered if they'd be empty tomorrow. I stared at them and said,

"Should I not be angry? Where are the crowds to greet their new queen? Where are the midnight parades to celebrate that I have freed them from Endrick's grasp?"

"Where is the daughter who risked herself to save two servants from the Coracks? The girl who defined her freedom by the miles she could run each day, the distance she could explore in the waning sunset? Where is *my* daughter, Kestra?"

"Leave me." Anger flared within my chest. "That girl was a child, but now she has seen too much to be that naïve again. Your daughter is gone."

"My daughter is still here, beneath layers of powerful magic, laced with tragedy." Darrow stood at my side to stare out the window, and finally turned to me. "Nothing in this room will make you happy. Come back to us, to those who love you and care for you."

"Joth loves me." Didn't he?

"No, Kestra. Pain and doubt and fear sometimes wear fine gilded masks that pretend to be love, but they are lies. Joth's heart has become numb to anything but his own wishes, and he cannot love. Please, walk away from this."

I shook my head. "*This* is the reason I've sacrificed all that I have. Why else was I chosen as the Infidante if not for *this*?"

"You were tasked with killing Endrick, not replacing him. You sacrificed to save others from what he could do, and you did so with immense courage. But none of what you did was ever meant to bring you to this place."

"There is no other place for me. If I do not sit at the top of Antora, I will be crushed by those who climb over me to reach the throne."

"Then come away with me." Darrow stretched out his hand, earnest in his expression. "If there is nowhere else, we can return to the Lava Fields, and there you can start over."

For a brief moment, I wanted to take his hand, to be the girl I once was, in a time that seemed ages ago. But I clutched my hand into a fist and backed away from him. "I have work to do here. I must build a new army, control my enemies, and create a circle of loyalists around me. That's where I will start, right here in this room. With my father by my side, I hope."

Slowly, Darrow exhaled, and his shoulders hunched. "I will not be a loyalist to you, Kestra. I cannot."

Incredulous at his words, I stopped to stare at him. "What do you mean?"

"I will not kneel to this person you are now, not willingly. I will love you always, as a father, but I will not serve you, nor heed your orders, nor acknowledge you as anyone with authority over me."

"Then you will be the first to commit treason against me. Would you betray me, Father?"

"Would you punish me, Daughter?"

Heat rushed through my heart, hardening it. "Believe that I can, and I will. You will be an example to the people, either showing them how to kneel to me, or the consequences of failing to do so."

His shoulders slumped further. "Then I was right all along. Lord Endrick is not dead after all. He lives and now goes by the name of Kestra Dallisor."

I raised my hand, furious and fully aware that with the powers that I had absorbed from Endrick, I could kill Darrow where he now stood, or do anything else short of that.

Yet wasn't that his point, that I could now do everything that Endrick could have done?

And that with these powers, I *would do* everything that Endrick had done.

I was still myself, but I suspected if I looked in a mirror, the eyes that stared back at me would have a reflection of Endrick in them. Would that be so wrong?

Endrick's rule had been fierce, but except for the Coracks, Antora had been at peace for a generation. There would be peace under my rule as well, after I crushed the rebellion.

"Leave me alone," I whispered. "Never return. Your daughter as you once knew her is dead to you. And the Kestra Dallisor that she has become will not forgive you twice."

Harlyn stepped forward, raising her sword. "Then the Kestra Dallisor that you have become will have to fight me."

I smiled. "Fighting you is no more effort than crushing a mosquito." As Endrick had once done to me, I waved my hand through the air, and Harlyn was pushed along with it, swept out the back exit of the throne room and out of my sight. I didn't care what happened to her after that. The air already smelled better without her sharing in it.

"What have you done?" Darrow asked, shaking his head. "Forgive me, Queen, but I will go and attend to that girl you just . . . whatever you did to her. I must see if she is all right."

Maybe she was and maybe she was not; I hardly cared. Instead, I cared that Darrow didn't even look back as he left my throne room. Did he know how that broke my heart?

I took a deep breath and shook it off. No, Darrow could not be allowed to crush my heart any more than I would have allowed Endrick to do, or as Simon had done. I would have a heart that could not be crushed.

Which meant I must have a heart that could not be touched.

Which meant I would have to cease to feel anything for anyone.

It was the only way I could ever survive.

Darrow left the room, and in his place, Joth entered. He walked up behind me, placed his arms around my waist, and kissed my cheek. "We did it," he said. "We won."

"*I* won," I told him. Though if this was winning, I found no joy in it. Not even the Scarlet Throne of Antora was grand enough to heal the despair within me.

· TWENTY-NINE ·

SIMON

Joth had described the scene outside the palace walls as one of chaos, but until leaving the courtyard, I had failed to appreciate the exact meaning of the word. Thankfully, the snow had stopped falling, but that was the only good news. It might've been a dark night but for the many fires set both within and without the walls. I didn't know whether our soldiers had set them, or the Dominion Loyalists who had come to defend their ash and smoke. Ironhearts were tripping over each other in their bid for freedom, and citizens of Highwyn were attempting to protect what little they had with weapons that were hardly more threat than sticks and feathers.

The Brill appeared to be the only group to have retained their lines, but for the worst possible reasons. A thick row of bodies went straight through the center of their numbers, and most of the survivors seemed afraid to move.

"Is that because of Joth?" Trina asked. "Are they—"

"Dead," Gabe said under his breath. "Joth and his half-lives tore through them within seconds. He could do the same to any of us, without warning, and we'd have no defense."

Both looked to me, and I wished I had any answers to offer them. But before I could speak, Basil rode toward me with his halberd in hand. He was still too thin and weak for battle, but I respected his choice to be here. "Is it true?" he asked. "Is Endrick gone?"

"He's gone." Though if battling Endrick had been a windstorm, now a season of tornados had begun. "Where is Captain Tenger?"

Basil grimaced, then cocked his head to the left. "Come with me."

I followed him outside the palace walls to a field of trampled snow. In the center, Imri Stout was standing over two other Brillian soldiers. One of them, a woman with long eyelashes so translucent white they almost glowed in the darkness, looked up and shook her head.

Imri turned to me with a vacant expression. "Even our technologies cannot heal him."

I pushed through the group to find Tenger on the ground. There were no visible wounds, but his eyes were rolled back in his head and he was mumbling incoherently.

"Loelle," Trina said. "If I can get him to Loelle—"

"I'll help," Basil added.

"Go," I said. "And hurry." Tenger had made it through tough scrapes before, but this time felt different, and I was worried.

Basil started to reach for Tenger, then turned back to me and said, "I was here when it happened. Tenger challenged Joth Tarquin to a duel, no magic, a fair fight. Joth just laughed and grabbed him with both hands, holding on until Tenger barely had a breath left in his body. He said that was what Tenger deserved for plotting to kill Kestra . . . that such an honor must be reserved for himself alone."

I did a double take. "He what?"

"That's what he said. I know it's terrible news, Simon, but I think Joth might be planning to do the same thing to Kestra, and then to each of us. With his half-lives, it won't be hard."

The pit that had formed in my gut suddenly became heavier. I dismissed Basil and Trina, then turned as Gabe began sending orders to Huge, who was nearby.

"Gather in as many Alliance members as you can and send them to Woodcourt," Gabe said. Then to Imri, he added, "Is there nothing more you can do? None of your technologies?"

She ran a hand over her close-cropped head, looking more unnerved than I'd ever seen her, or any Brillian. "Our vibrations worked as planned. But we did not anticipate the breadth of his magic, nor his willingness to use it."

"How many did you lose?" I asked.

"Fifty-two, based on the most recent report. Simon, it happened so fast. And if his magic is like Kestra's, then he just pulled the strength of all fifty-two of my people into himself."

As Kestra had just pulled all of Endrick's power to herself. And hadn't Joth told me he and Kestra were sharing their powers now?

"Loelle's medical station is set up at Woodcourt," I said. "That's where Tenger is going. If any of your soldiers are still alive, she can heal them too."

"I will not accept that woman's help," Imri said. "And I cannot believe that you are letting her roam free."

Sighing, I said, "What good is Loelle to us down in the dungeons? If you wish to save lives, get your people to her as quickly as possible!"

I started to walk away, but Gabe grabbed my arm. "Where are you going? Surely with Joth and Kestra inside the palace, we are sealed out of it."

"I still have Rawk," I said. "He can get past the half-lives."

"And then?"

"I've got to find Kestra."

"Harlyn is in there too!"

"Yes, and wherever Kestra is, Harlyn won't be far away. Joth is going to kill Kestra, Gabe."

"Maybe we should let him. What if Kestra is responsible for your sister's death?"

He waited for my response, but I was frozen with anger. Or was it fear that was causing my heart to pound so violently against my chest?

When he saw how his words affected me, with a louder voice he added, "If you can get in, find Harlyn. I am right about this. How can you be so blind?"

"Right or wrong, I am in command." I began searching the skies for Rawk's approach, losing the focus I should have had on Gabe.

I caught movement from him just as he swung at me, hitting me square in the jaw. "Maybe you shouldn't be," he sneered.

I reeled backward, then launched myself at him, trying to pretend there weren't stars in my vision. He easily grabbed my arm as I reached to hit him, but he never saw my other fist headed for his gut.

It was his turn to stumble back, though he refused to let me go, so I used my own weight to shove him. We ended up on the ground, each of us more than ready to continue.

"Stop this!" Imri yelled, running up to us. "We cannot fight each other—we must focus on the enemy."

"Who is the enemy, Simon?" Gabe yelled. "Who is it?"

I released him and shook myself free of his grip, then stood as Rawk descended nearby. Without another word to Gabe, I rolled onto the dragon's back and gave a silent order to launch into the air. Hoping to calm myself, I rolled my knuckles against Rawk's scales, thanking him for coming before we made even bigger fools of ourselves down there. Rawk snorted at me and I gave a tight smile, but I was no calmer than before.

We had launched steep and high, so I already had a good view of the layout of the land. Many of the Ironhearts were retreating, literally running for their lives. I searched every face I saw for any resemblance to Rosaleen, but as far as I could tell, she wasn't here. She wasn't anywhere, and that worried me.

My cavalry was in close pursuit of the fleeing Ironhearts. Before this had all begun, I had left orders with Commander Reese not to strike at anyone in the act of surrender, and my soldiers seemed to be following those orders.

However, all at once, simultaneously, every single Ironheart stood erect, many of them clutching at their chests, then in unison all of them retrieved any weapons they had dropped and began hurrying back toward the palace.

Kestra was ordering them in. She was using Endrick's powers to regroup an army she now considered hers. Nothing else could explain what I was seeing. If Rosaleen was in the area, she'd be called in too. That's where I'd find her.

I asked Rawk to locate any way through the palace barriers that he could, though I was surprised that on his first attempt, he flew straight through to the castle without even a whisper of resistance. No barriers.

It shouldn't have been that simple, even for Rawk.

Something had changed.

What was happening inside that throne room? Was Harlyn somehow involved?

Rawk flew us over a wide parapet somewhere near the rear of the castle. From here I could see empty iron cages. Endrick's animals were free, though I hadn't seen Dominion riders on any of them thus far. Maybe they had escaped as soon as Endrick was killed. Or maybe they had been moved so Kestra and Joth wouldn't have access to them. However, for now, my main task was to get inside the throne room and see the commotion for myself.

Gabe had asked me who the enemy was, and I now had the answer.

Kestra was the enemy, though Joth was worse.

Harlyn was an enemy to Kestra, though Gabe was worse.

Gabe might've become my enemy as well, though of all enemies, I was the worst.

For I had not given anyone the full explanation of why it had to be me entering the palace.

I had come to claim the Scarlet Throne for myself.

At all costs.

· THIRTY ·

KESTRA

As awful as I had felt when Darrow left my throne room, my mood didn't improve at seeing Joth kneeling before me. Now that I had my place on the Scarlet Throne, it was time to disconnect my powers from Joth, to separate us again. He wouldn't like it, but I wasn't offering him a choice.

For now, he smiled, took my hand, and kissed it. The last time he had taken my hand, I had noticed how very warm it was, but that was true no longer. Or perhaps I was now as fever warm as Joth had been.

Joth kept hold of my hand to say, "My queen, now that we're alone, there is something I must ask. In your battle with Endrick, I know that you called the half-lives here to the throne room for your protection, but I do not sense them here . . . or anywhere. Where are they?"

His question irritated me. Who was he to imply that their sacrifice was not worth my victory? With a sigh, I said, "Endrick claimed that the curse he had imposed upon them was not the worst he could do."

Joth's eyes widened. "He didn't . . . Kestra, he didn't—"

"We knew there would be sacrifices in order to claim the throne—"

"Corack sacrifices, yes! Brillian or Halderian sacrifices! This was not supposed to happen! Harlyn walked free from this room. How could you save *her*, and not my people?" He was practically screaming now.

I stood. "Enough of this! I am your queen, and you will not speak to me this way."

He stood as well, grabbing my arm. Instantly, I felt a sensation of all strength within me being sucked from every vein, every drop of my blood. As if my bones had melted to jelly, I sank to the floor.

He must have planned this. He must have waited for this very opportunity when my guard was lowered.

This time when Joth knelt, it was without humility, without respect. His voice was a rabid snarl as he said, "As punishment for your misjudgment, a few of my people must be restored. I will not weaken myself with their cure, but your strength is expendable. I am gathering them all into this hall. Find them, restore them."

It had always been my intention to eventually restore his people, so I didn't know why he had resorted to forcing me now. He must have had other reasons.

"There is not enough in me to do it." This wasn't stalling—he had genuinely drained me of every bit of strength I had.

"For now, it's only a small number of the Navan. I will give you what you need to complete the task, but no more. As long as you are restoring my people, you will live."

"And then?"

"And then you will try to persuade me to keep you alive. Our magic is connected, Kestra. If I must dispose of you, it will cause me great pain, I assure you."

A hundred thoughts of what I wanted to say came to my mind,

but I lacked the strength for any of them. Instead, I preserved what I had to reach out to the Ironhearts, ordering them into my service and hoping they listened. They had no reason to do so, other than possibly recognizing that my magic had the same signature as Endrick's. I hoped they would believe that I could crush their hearts if they refused me, though at the moment, I lacked the strength to crush even a gnat.

"My people are here," Joth said. "Begin."

My eyes had been closed, but when I opened them, I was surprised at how well I could see the half-lives. I faintly recalled Endrick saying that he could see them, so it followed that I was now able to do so too. Hundreds of half-lives were in the room—I could see each one as though I were looking through a sheer veil. Their attention passed from Joth to me, wondering who would be called forward first for restoration. Wondering, no doubt, why Joth had said that for now, I would only be helping a small number of them.

At Joth's prompting, a man stepped forward, wearing a stocking cap and a simple tunic and trousers with a rope for a belt. I reached out to him and gave everything I had to his restoration, then immediately felt a new surge of strength for the next to step forward, a woman similarly dressed. Perhaps his wife.

They were an odd choice for restoration, I thought. Clearly these were not people of high status or recognition, and Joth wasn't paying them any particular attention as close friends or family.

But as I restored the man's wife, I began to understand why he had chosen them. Joth did have his reasons.

And I had mine.

So I continued with the next in line, and the next, each time receiving a limited infusion of strength. Again and again I continued restoring his people in the order that Joth silently called them forward. I had no idea where he was getting his strength to continue this process, but since he wasn't showing the slightest sign of weakening, he must have drawn in enormous amounts of strength before entering this room. Somewhere outside this palace, there must have been dozens of his victims, or more.

"Please let me rest," I begged him.

"My people have not slept for an entire generation," he said. "When they sleep, you sleep."

"You don't understand," I said. "You are restoring my magic enough to help your people, but physically, I am empty. I will not do anything more until I've rested."

"Keep going, or you will die here."

Barely keeping my eyes open, I said, "I will die here if I keep going."

His grip on my arm tightened; then suddenly he tilted his head and mumbled something under his breath, as if in conversation with someone.

Perhaps he had forgotten that with our connected magic, I was privy to what he was hearing, and I wasn't sure what to think of it.

"The Halderian king has entered the palace" was the message.

Joth pulled me closer to him. "Did you know of this?"

"Know of what?" I replied.

Inside, my stomach was churning. Had Simon come as friend or foe?

Foe.

On more than one occasion, I had proven myself an enemy to him. If only he knew how ineffectual an enemy I was.

With that single thought, something within me awoke. I had Endrick's magic. I was more powerful than this! Maybe I didn't know everything Endrick had been capable of doing, and certainly I didn't know how to use the magic I now had, but I would not play the victim any longer.

Perhaps Simon was an enemy now, but Joth was the greater threat. My only hope might be to use the one against the other.

I reached out once more to the Ironhearts, and despite my weakness, I found it easy to identify each individual. I knew in general where they were, and I knew if any were attempting to ignore my hold on them.

So I gave a slight squeeze on the hearts of every single soldier. Now I had their attention. Then I made sure they knew their orders. Their queen had need of them.

Joth faced the thirty people I had restored. I imagined they were nearly the same as what they had been before Endrick had cursed them: same age and clothing as before, same interests and abilities . . . or almost the same.

Joth said to them, "If you have been restored, then for now, you must remain in this room, for your protection. Those who have not been restored must offer their assistance to all of us. Go and find the Halderian king. Bring him here."

Once Joth seemed satisfied that his order had been obeyed, he turned back to me. "Will Simon relinquish his kingdom to save you?"

Despite my weakness, I couldn't help but laugh. "As things between us are now, Simon wouldn't relinquish his dessert to save me. But if he is coming here, whether by choice or by force, you should be afraid. Whatever he wants, he will get it."

"Then I hope he wants to die," Joth said. "For once I get him to kneel to me, that will be his fate."

I shook my head. "Who will kill him? It won't be you."

Joth's eyes narrowed. "Why not?"

I smiled. "By the time Simon gets here, my Ironhearts will already have their orders to bury you."

At my words, nearly every door into the throne room began to echo with pounding noises. Joth's people rushed to the doors to hold them closed, but their eyes revealed their fear.

"Remember your magic," Joth told them. "Use it!"

But the people only stared at him and each other in confusion, which made my smile widen.

The thirty Navan had been restored . . . mostly. But Endrick had one power at the root of all other powers he had ever obtained—the ability to steal magic from others.

And so I had.

It was commonly believed that he had to kill the person in order to take their magic, but now that his power was mine, I understood differently. He killed the person so that they could not challenge him to get their magic back. He could have left his victims alive.

As I had left the thirty people of Navan alive. But their magic was mine. And I had no intention of sharing any of it with Joth.

Joth's face reddened in anger. "What have you done?"

Now my smile disappeared. "Kneel to me and beg my forgiveness. This will be your only warning."

"Never!" He reached for me, but using a power I had just acquired, my arm slipped through his grip like it was coated in warm butter. He ordered his people to grab me before I escaped, but I did the same with them, slid out the door, and used the last bit of strength within me to seal the door closed.

There were no Ironhearts nearby. I'd ordered all of them nearer the front of the throne room, closer to where the bulk of Joth's restored Navan were.

Grateful to be alone, I slumped to the floor, closed my eyes, and tried to find anything within me to stand. I knew it wouldn't be long before I was found, and I needed to hide until I recovered.

"Get up, Kestra."

I opened my eyes and groaned. Harlyn stood before me, with a disk bow aimed directly at my chest. Her voice lacked any emotion whatsoever. Considering all that I had done for her in the past several hours, I would have preferred to hear at least a hint of gratitude. Or at least something in her tone that didn't sound nearly so eager to shoot me again.

"Get up," she repeated. "Or this will be the place you die."

I glared up at her. "And what happens if I do get up?"

Harlyn's eyes flashed, and she gave no answer. She didn't need to. I already knew it.

· THIRTY-ONE ·

SIMON

Joth had use of the half-lives as his army, warriors I could not even sense, much less see, yet who apparently had become tangible enough that they could strike a person down in an instant. Finally, I understood that.

And I had to expect that they knew I had entered the castle, and that some attempt would be made to stop me.

Until they did, I would do everything in my power to get as close as possible to Joth and Kestra . . . if she was still alive. And I had to find Harlyn. If I failed at that, I figured Gabe would finish whatever he had started outside. I'd never seen him so angry, and certainly not so angry with me.

Then I paused right where I stood as a realization flooded over me. It was so obvious, I couldn't believe that I had missed it.

Gabe had feelings for Harlyn; maybe he even loved her. He couldn't say anything because he knew she was meant for me, but nothing else explained why his reactions concerning her had been so strong.

Which made me wonder if Harlyn felt the same way about him. I knew they had spent a lot of time together and become good friends, *if* they were only friends. Maybe she didn't feel she could say anything either.

Loud, angry voices suddenly echoed down the hall from the throne room, bringing me back to the moment. I could think about Gabe later. For now, I needed to think of Harlyn and Kestra.

I lifted my sword and ventured deeper into the palace, toward the throne room. Perhaps it was pointless to have my sword out—it would be worthless if the half-lives attacked—but I felt better with it in my hand.

Only a few steps later, someone reached out and grabbed my arm. I twisted around and began to swipe at my attacker, but stopped at the last minute, realizing it was no attacker at all. Or at least, I didn't think it was.

Darrow put a finger to his lips and motioned for me to join him. He had stationed himself in a darkened alcove directly beneath the grand staircase. I crouched near him but said nothing. He looked deflated, as if the world had caved in around him.

"You were right about her," he said. "Kestra is worse than I had anticipated. Even if she recognizes what she has become, she has no wish to change anything. She cares only for the throne."

"Harlyn was with you. Where is she?" I asked.

"Harlyn entered the throne room with me, and when I failed, she challenged Kestra to a fight. Kestra used some sort of magic to sweep Harlyn out of the room, but I couldn't find her. I don't know what has happened to her since then."

"Was Joth in the room with you as well?"

Darrow nodded. "He entered as I left, though he greeted Kestra as a queen and seemed warm enough to her. But he has me worried. When I was . . . like his people, and banished to All Spirits Forest,

Joth was the person everyone looked to. They consider him their ruler and respect him because for all these years, he was the only one they could communicate with. They served him, and for it, he promised to find a way to free them one day."

"Or to find someone who could," I breathed.

"Loelle is Joth's mother. They used Kestra to fulfill the promise, but their plans made sense. There was no other hope for us, and Loelle's motives seemed good. In exchange for Kestra's work, we would help her fight Endrick, in a way that no fully human army could. I need you to understand this, Simon. Joth is a good person, or he was. But he has become—"

"Like Kestra," I finished.

"Yes, but worse, because I don't think he has fought it the way she did. I've stayed close enough to the throne room to know that she is finishing what she started with his people, restoring them to full life. But I think this time he is forcing her to do it."

A pit formed in my stomach. "Do any half-lives remain?"

Darrow shrugged. "There were a great many of them, but most of them were originally Halderians . . . *your* people, not Joth's. Is there any chance of you bringing them to your side?"

"Maybe I could. But Harlyn would do better," I said. "We've got to find her."

"If it's the only way of persuading the Halderian half-lives to join you, then I will help you find Harlyn. But in exchange, you must help me find Kestra. There's got to be a way to reach her, to help her."

I drew in a deep breath. "What if there isn't? Loelle told me she's searched for weeks for a way to heal her, and has not found any way to do it. What if it cannot be done?"

"I will never stop hoping for a solution," Darrow said. "I'm her father!"

"And I'm in l—!" I paused, to better select my words. In a quieter voice, I added, "I'm her friend, Darrow. Tell me what to do, because I genuinely don't know."

Darrow stared at me before softly nodding, then said, "Kestra must be in the throne room still. As she was, I cannot imagine that she will abandon the throne as long as a breath of life remains in her."

"There might not be anything more than that," I said, feeling the weight inside me grow heavier. "If Joth intends to replace her on that throne, there is only one way to do it."

Darrow nodded again. "And what about you, King of the Halderians? Do you intend to replace them both on that throne?"

"I intend to remove anyone from the throne who is ruled by corruption," I said. "But what I told you before is true: The last of my intentions is to harm Kestra."

Darrow grunted. "I really do hate you Coracks, and perhaps you most of all. But I'll choose to believe you because I have no other choice. Let's go in and try to talk our way toward that throne, or fight our way there if we must."

I shook his hand and together we emerged from the alcove, rounding toward the grand staircase, only to find ourselves surrounded by a dozen people who I assumed had been half-lives an hour ago. They were dressed in clothing that might have been in fashion a generation ago, and looked uncomfortable in their surroundings. Most were lightly armed, if at all, but I had no doubt that if they were here, so were several half-lives who would assure we followed whatever orders we were about to receive.

"The king of Antora, and prince of the Navanese people, requests an audience with you in his throne room," a woman near us said.

Darrow squinted at her. "Do you mean Joth?"

"Where is Kestra?" I asked. "The queen?"

The woman shrugged. "She betrayed the king. Upon his orders she restored us, then harmed us in the same moment."

Darrow's eyes narrowed. "How?"

The woman held out her hands, palms up. "Before Endrick cursed us, I had the power to produce heat from my hands. Kestra Dallisor has that power now, *my* power! She stole from me, stole from every one of us. When we find Kestra, she will have to answer for her crimes."

"When you *find* her?" I repeated. "She's no longer in the throne room?"

"No, as you will see for yourself." A white-haired man stepped forward from the group, widening his arm to show us the way. "If you will, please."

Darrow and I nodded, and the group closed in around us. However, just before we entered the throne room, the man leaned in a little closer to me and whispered, "I know who you are, Simon Hatch, and no matter what happens in there, I consider you my king."

I gave him a brief nod, then the doors opened and we were led inside. Joth sat on the Scarlet Throne now, casually leaning against one arm of the throne as if to give the impression of being unruffled and confident, but it wasn't working. Something had clearly rattled him since the last time we had met.

Scattered about the room were more of the people Kestra had restored, but it wasn't even forty or fifty. Certainly it was not the army that I had expected to see, based on the force of their initial attack. When Joth leaned into the light, I noticed he had a long scratch down his face. I hoped Kestra had done that.

He let out a heavy sigh. "I warned you to leave, I warned you to stay away, and yet here you are *again*. My hope is that you have re-entered my palace with the intention of bowing to me now, saving yourself the humiliation of doing so tomorrow at noon, in front of all the armies you have brought into the courtyard."

"That is half-correct," I said. "As you suggest, I do not want to be humiliated tomorrow at noon. But I have come here to discuss the details of your surrender. Because I will not bow to you now, or ever."

Joth's face reddened, but he asked, "What details are those?"

"Obviously, I cannot allow you to take the throne without a challenge."

He frowned. "Obviously."

"So my first option is to bring the full power of the Alliance against you and your army of fifty civilians, stripped of their magic. I know you still have some half-lives to help you in the fight, but there are more of us than them. Based solely on the numbers, I will prevail."

Joth didn't flinch. "And your second option?"

"Tomorrow at noon, I challenge you to a duel, though you must agree to fight without the use of magic—nothing else is fair. The winner cedes his throne to the other."

Joth smiled. "Ah, so if you defeat me, you expect that I will surrender the Scarlet Throne?"

"If the battle is only between you and me, we each preserve the lives of our people."

"And when I defeat you," Joth continued, "what is my reward?"

"The Halderian throne, with all our lands and our people." I let the offer dangle in front of him for a moment, tempting him.

"I could kill you here," Joth said.

"Which would mean I am no longer a problem for you, but that will not give you the loyalty and service of my people."

Darrow turned and began addressing the others in the room. "I know that many of you here feel a loyalty to Joth because of all he has done for us. I also know that many of you are Halderian. Your king, Simon Hatch, is before you now. You may be grateful to Joth for making your lives possible. But it is time to bring your loyalties back home. You will serve your Halderian king."

Silence fell in the room for a moment, until I saw the same white-haired man who had escorted us here go to his knees. Another woman at his side did the same, then three or four more people, then another ten. Another fifteen or twenty crossed one arm over their hearts and stared at Joth, their king. Just like that, I had taken almost half of Joth's followers.

"Meet me in the courtyard at noon tomorrow," I said to Joth. "Or you'll never have the respect of those you claim to lead."

"Sooner or later, they'll all come crawling to me," he said. "Noon tomorrow."

"Until then, where is my daughter?" Darrow asked. "I insist on taking her away with me."

"Who was the other girl you brought here before . . . Harlyn? I am told that she was last seen in pursuit of your daughter with a disk bow ready to fire. I expect that by now, one or the other is still alive. Not both."

"Where did they go?" Anxious as I had been to confront Joth, that was nothing compared to thinking about any confrontation between Harlyn and Kestra. I added, "We want to find them."

"Her father can search for her," Joth said. "You will remain with us. If I am not allowed to use magic in the duel, you must not be given the opportunity to make any tricks against me."

There was no point in objecting. I desperately wanted to go after Harlyn and Kestra, but he had just given me a perfect opportunity to observe him and better understand his vulnerabilities. If he was allowing it, then I needed to stay.

Darrow leaned in and whispered, "He will not keep his word, you know. He will cheat."

"I'm counting on it," I replied.

Darrow looked up, but I could not offer him an explanation here. So he merely touched my arm, then ran from the throne room in search of Kestra.

Or in search of Harlyn.

I wanted to believe there was a chance that both of them were still alive. But I knew them both too well to have much hope.

· THIRTY-TWO ·

KESTRA

The difference between a disk in the pocket of the bow and a disk lodged in my chest was a slight nudge of Harlyn's finger on the string. It would take so little for her to kill me right now.

I searched within myself for any magic that could make Harlyn regret her words. I found the powers but knew I lacked the strength. As it was, I had no choice but to obey Harlyn for now and, at my earliest opportunity, take a fierce revenge. I was already counting the minutes.

"Lift your hands where I can see them," Harlyn instructed as I began to move. "I don't trust you."

"That's wise." I began to stand, then lost my footing and slipped again. Harlyn raised her bow. Alarmed, I said sharply, "Don't you dare shoot me over a little slip! If you haven't noticed, I'm not exactly at my best right now."

"Maybe that's a trick too," she said.

"Maybe it is," I replied. Once I was standing, I asked, "What now?"

Harlyn clearly hadn't expected to still be on her feet. Her eyes darted leftward while she considered an answer, which was, "We will walk out of this palace together. There you will surrender to Simon Hatch, king of the—"

"King of the Halderians, yes, I know who he is." I sighed. "But Simon is not available for surrender at the moment. He's somewhere inside this palace, probably under attack by Joth's half-lives."

Harlyn's eyes widened. "Do you know where he is?"

"Of course I know," I lied. "Follow me."

"If you're leading me into a trap, you'll pay for it," she said as I began to limp forward.

I looked over my shoulder. "If this is a trap, I won't give you that chance."

I didn't know Endrick's palace well, but I suspected Simon was headed toward the throne room, for that was the direction where Joth had sent his half-lives. And the last person I wanted to see now was Simon, so I led Harlyn in the opposite direction, to the rear of the palace. This was where Endrick's servants would have once worked, where the commanders of his armies would have quartered at night.

I paused there, mumbling under my breath about what I intended to do with this wing of the castle once my rule was secured.

"Who cares about any of that right now?" Harlyn asked.

I didn't care. It was only a ruse to give me a moment to catch my breath as I began to feel whispers of strength returning again.

"Keep walking," Harlyn said, nudging me in the back with her disk bow. "We have to find Simon."

If she truly wanted to find him, then she was in the wrong place. He'd have no reason to be here, so far from the throne room.

One of the rooms nearby was larger than the others had been, with row after row of beds, and at the far end was a ladder headed belowground. That might be my only chance.

I peered into the room as a shout came from somewhere behind us. Harlyn pushed me forward, then peered out into the corridor. "Joth's got his people on patrol. Kestra, we have to—"

By the time she looked my way again, I was halfway to the ladder. I had enough strength by then to upturn one of the beds between us. In nearly the same second, Harlyn shot at me. Her disk lodged into the mattress, releasing a tuft of feathers.

I grabbed the ladder but loosened my grip enough to slide straight down; then I yanked the ladder free and set it on the ground. The door that had been propped open by the ladder slammed shut, which I had not expected, but I used a little magic to keep it sealed. Suddenly, I was standing in near total darkness, save only for a few small clearstones along the walls of this tunnel.

I warmed one, which barely gave enough light to reach the next clearstone, but that one was burned out from overuse. The clearstone after that seemed so far away.

Panic rose in my chest, enough that I could do nothing more than crouch to the ground and try to find air to breathe. Above me, Harlyn pounded on the door, but that did her no good.

"Kestra, let me in!" she cried. "People are searching for us."

Then let them find her. I'd shown her mercy. In return, she'd shot at me, and now I was stuck down here.

Down here. I wrapped my arms around myself and shuddered. I couldn't stay in this dark place. Because of Harlyn, I couldn't go out the way I'd come in, and nothing in me had the ability to walk on.

As the panic began to overtake me, the strength of my magic

failed, including my ability to keep the door overhead closed.

Harlyn pulled it open and tossed a rope into the tunnel. Then she slung the disk bow over one shoulder and lowered herself until she could drop to the floor.

I heard her land, and her breathless "thank you" and then a "Kestra, where are you?"

If she said anything else, I wasn't around to hear it. I was already working my way through the darkness. It terrified me to run, but that was better than remaining anywhere near Harlyn. If I did, it was a guarantee of either my death or hers. It would have to be hers.

· THIRTY-THREE ·

SIMON

After Darrow left the room, the full weight of Joth's attention fell on me.

"I am curious," he said. "What makes you think you have any chance in the duel tomorrow?"

"Other than being the superior swordsman?" I spoke with confidence, even arrogance, but inside, my stomach was knotted.

He smiled. "I suspect that you are. I didn't get much practice in the forest, not with half-lives for company. And my people have never cared for swords anyway. They're inefficient compared to magic."

"Then why did you accept my challenge?" I asked. "You can't possibly expect to win . . . unless you cheat."

Joth's casual smile soured. "On the contrary, I have no intention of cheating tomorrow. My subjects will be there to watch. They must see me strike you down, sword against sword, without magic."

My eyes narrowed. "Or I will strike you down."

Joth's laughter darkened. "That will never happen. You and I will face each other with swords. I will raise mine. You will try to do the same, but I fear you may not have the strength for it."

His eyes darted meaningfully around the room, and I knew he

must have silently issued some sort of command to the half-lives who were here.

"If you are Halderian, then I am your king!" I had no idea which way to turn as I spoke, or whether they could even hear me, but this was my chance. Lifting my sword, I added, "I am King Gareth's heir, and with your help, this throne will belong to the Halderians again. Whatever you were ordered, I ask you to stand at my side, defend me now."

Joth grimaced and made a gesture with his hand. I felt a slight wind move toward me from all directions, then it simply stopped as if a wall had gone up in front of me. Why had it stopped?

After a brief, tense pause, Joth stood and shouted, "*I* am your king! For a generation, I have protected you, watched over you. It is through me that you have been given the chance to live again."

"And through me, you will live in freedom," I said. "I will extend the offer to those of you who are among Joth's people. He will reign over you, and upon your backs he will rule from this time forward. But it need not be. You see that I am protected by my people. Join them and be free."

For the first time, Joth stormed down the steps from his throne. I held my ground, confident in the protection of those around me.

"This will not be tolerated, not in this room!" He thrust out one hand, pointing to those of his people whom Kestra had already restored. "Take the King of the Banished and make him suffer for his words! If you refuse, I will use what magic I have obtained to return you to your half-life state!"

At first, nothing happened, and I believed Joth had finally gone too far. Then someone in the corner shouted, "Your king has spoken! What are you waiting for?"

All eyes fell upon me, most of them unfriendly, but when the restored Navan took their first steps toward me, others got in their way, saying, "*Our* king has also spoken. They have agreed to settle their differences tomorrow!"

I wasn't sure who threw the first punch, only that when the fight began, it quickly engulfed the entire throne room. I genuinely didn't know who was fighting for Joth and who was fighting for me, which made it impossible to use my sword to enter the fray. All I could do was trust that the half-lives who had surrounded me before would continue to protect me.

But that was a mistake. Joth must have been silently giving directions to the half-lives, because somehow my protection was gone. A few of his restored people rushed at me from behind, pushing me down to the floor. I struggled against them, but someone clubbed me in the back.

"Get his sword!" Joth demanded.

I fought to keep hold of it but took plenty of hits on my body as a result. When I rolled to protect my ribs, someone's hand went over mine on the hilt of the sword. I felt it being pulled away from me, and I was hit hard on the side of my head. Lights pulsed in my vision. With a second hit, I would be unconscious. But then the doors opened and a woman called out, "Stop this at once!"

That was Loelle's voice, and it was commanding enough that those around me lowered their fists, though no one released me.

She marched forward, and although I couldn't see her from my position on the floor, I felt her anger from here. "Joth, what have you done?"

Joth had taken refuge from the fighting on the steps to the Scarlet Throne, and he held his place as he widened his arms. With the same arrogance as I'd heard from him before, he said, "I have taken the kingdom, Mother. We may have lost the throne when the Navan were exiled, but now I have a new throne, and a land far greater than what we left."

"This was never the plan!" she said. "And this is not my son speaking now."

His expresson grew colder. "I am your son, and I have improved upon your plan."

"Nothing that I see here is any improvement. Where is Kestra?"

"Go and find her," Joth said, I assumed to the half-lives. "If she is still alive, bring her to me now."

He paused, perhaps while his orders were carried out, and then looked down at his mother, who echoed, "*If* she is alive?" When he did not answer, she said, "After all she has done for us, you betrayed her?"

Now Joth became angry. He stomped down the stairs and marched directly in front of his mother. "I finished what you started! You convinced Captain Tenger to give her magic, and the magic she acquired was better than any of us could have imagined. Through Kestra, we finally had the ability to raise an army that Endrick could not kill. You did that to her!"

"Never to harm her."

Joth raised his voice further. "Is that so? You saw what was happening to her in the forest, and still you pushed her onward."

"But I was looking for a way to bring her back, Joth. I'm still looking!"

"There is no way to bring her back. Before she killed Endrick, he did something to her. He corrupted her beyond redemption."

His words hit me harder than any of the half-lives could ever have done. I sucked in a breath but could not make myself release it. If what he said was true, and Endrick had gotten to her, then Joth might be right.

Beyond redemption. Few words had ever been spoken of greater tragedy.

Loelle wasn't finished arguing. "And then what? You attacked her, I assume. Where can she go now, Joth? You have doomed her!"

Joth dismissed his mother's objections with a wave of his hand, then began walking a circle around her as he spoke. "Wasn't it you who told me that Kestra was doomed from the moment of her birth? Didn't you describe to me how any chance she might have had for a normal life vanished once she accepted the role of Infidante? How she belonged to all groups and to none. You told me of her powers, great in their potential, strong enough that they would certainly trap her within them. Didn't you tell me that the closer she came to success, the more that success would destroy her?" Now Joth faced his mother directly. "The truth is that I did nothing to change her fate, nor did you; we only altered the route she took to get there."

By then, I had recovered enough to sit up, though my voice was weak when I said, "Where is Kestra now, Joth?"

He closed his eyes to listen, then said, "The half-lives have found her, but she is not alone. You have accused me of terrible things, but I am not threatening her life. Someone else is."

Harlyn.

"Kestra is in a weakened state," Joth said. "She has no defense against her attacker. But even if she should happen to survive, if she returns to confront me, as she confronted Endrick, I will be ready for her."

"I will not let you harm her," I said.

"Nor I," Loelle echoed.

Joth laughed. "Mother, eventually you will come to see that I am right. And, Simon, before you offer Kestra any protection, you might study your reflection in the mirror and see what my army did to you in only a few minutes. I will be less kind in our duel tomorrow."

Loelle arched her neck. "We are leaving now, Simon and I."

"Not just us," I said. "I invite all Halderians to come with us, and all those of you who refuse to be associated with Joth Tarquin, king of his own wilted mind and nothing more."

Loelle walked out first, then I, and when I glanced behind me, nearly the entire room of restored people was following us.

Joth still held the throne, but I left the palace certain I had won that battle between us.

· THIRTY-FOUR ·

KESTRA

I don't know how long I ran through the tunnels, but the passages seemed to stretch out endlessly before me, a twisted maze that darkened and compressed with every step I took. Strength was slowly seeping back to me, so it should have been possible to pull enough magic together to find an escape, or to reach out for help, but my heart was drumming against my chest and my thoughts were flying in all directions. I was breathless and drenched in sweat, and through all of it, I knew only one thing: Harlyn was still behind me, still in pursuit. Still intending to kill me.

And so I ran, until at one point I tripped and fell, yet there was nothing beneath my feet to have caused it. Pain shot from my foot up through my leg. I tried to stand, but something held me down.

It had to be the half-lives, though I could not see them any longer. Not with my faded abilities. But they could certainly see me, and hear me, I hoped.

"Harm me and who will heal you?" I asked. "Joth? Hasn't he already proven he intends to keep you as you are, as his half-life army? I am your only hope to return to life again, but I will not restore another person until you first prove your loyalty to me."

The pressure on me yielded, but this time when I tried to stand, my foot collapsed beneath my weight. I wasn't going anywhere. I stifled a cry just as Harlyn rounded the corner, her disk bow trained on me.

"Enough running," she said.

"Prove your loyalty *now*," I said, but not to her.

Almost instantly, Harlyn was knocked against the wall by some unseen action. And even through the darkness, I saw a silver disk somehow reverse from its intended motion, flying backward and lodging in Harlyn's arm. With a cry, she slid to the ground, out of my reach, but not out of theirs.

Finish the job.

That was what I intended to say to the half-lives next, but suddenly they were gone, as quickly as they had come, as if Joth had summoned them back to himself. Obviously, he had their true loyalty.

Which left Harlyn on one end of this small tunnel room, and me on the other. Neither of us able to leave; both of us capable of killing the other.

I could do it. Everything in me wanted to do it.

Yet as I contemplated how to do it, she shifted her position and gasped with pain as she pulled the disk from her shoulder. I didn't need to do anything after all. The bleeding would take care of everything, in time. Her own weapon would become the cause of her death. That was better justice than I could provide.

"We have no cauterizing powder here," I said. "How badly are you injured?"

"Why?" she replied. "Trying to decide how much effort it will take to finish the job?"

"Not half the effort as you expended in chasing me this far. I completed my task as Infidante. I had hoped you would choose a different way of thanking me."

"You must understand why I have to do this," Harlyn said. "If a wolf kills a bear, as grateful as you are, that doesn't mean you are safer with the wolf."

"That wolf spared your life—twice—in the throne room!"

"And why did you?" Harlyn paused to draw in a deep, stilted breath.

"Whatever my reasons, it was obviously a mistake."

"Why did you?" Harlyn asked again.

Rather than answer, I reached for my injured ankle. It must have been swelling within the boot. If I were to drag myself closer to Harlyn, with a single touch, I could pull enough strength from her to heal myself. I could pull everything from her if I wanted to.

And in that moment, I absolutely wanted to. The only reason I was even down here was because of her.

"Come any closer and you'll get a disk too." Harlyn quickly loaded the pocket of her bow. "The one that got me is silver—I'll recover from it. But this one is black. Get it and—"

"You forget that I am immortal now, Harlyn." Or mostly immortal. I wasn't sure how the black disk would affect me, but it was enough to keep me at a distance. To make myself feel better, I added, "I can afford to be patient, but you cannot. I suspect you only have a couple of hours left to live."

"Will you still have your sanity by then?" Harlyn's strike back at me was cruel. "In this small, dark passage, I imagine you feel like the walls are closing in on you."

"That's enough."

"It's almost like being buried alive," she continued, then drew in a loud breath. "The air down here is already becoming thin. I'm sure that I'm taking more than my fair share."

"Enough, Harlyn!"

She breathed loudly again, taunting me.

In a greater panic, I flung out an arm, intending to frighten her, but the passageway shook, violently enough that the tunnel from where we had just come collapsed.

My heart crashed against my chest in sudden terror. What had I done?

If I had felt panic before, that was nothing compared to the surge that threatened me now. Exhausted by the force of magic I'd just created, I had nothing left to calm myself. It was no longer a perception that the walls were closing in. The only exit I knew had been destroyed, and I had no idea if there was any escape ahead.

I tried standing. Even if it hurt, I had to move, I had to find a way out.

Yet my ankle collapsed again.

"Kestra—"

"Don't say another word, Harlyn! Or I'll . . . I'll . . ." My breath began to choke me. I could no longer speak.

"Kestra, you need to stay calm. For both our sakes."

She didn't understand. She didn't know how bad it was for me, and if she did know, she'd only continue to use my fears against me.

I tried a third time to stand and fell harder to the ground than before. I searched for a whisper of magic, anything to get me through the next few minutes.

"Kestra! Kestra, can you hear me?"

I heard her. I just didn't care, or see how anything she wanted to discuss in the moment should mean a thing to me.

"I'm coming over to you—unarmed. Please don't attack me."

I vaguely heard dragging noises, but an hour seemed to pass as I tried to get control of my breathing, tried to slow my pulse, tried to convince myself that everything I believed was happening— everything I was certain was happening—was not real.

Then a hand touched my shoulder, firm but not aggressive, and Harlyn said, "It's all right, Kestra. It's going to be all right."

I shook off her hand, but Harlyn wrapped her whole arm around me, the uninjured arm. Even then I heard a slight gasp as she did.

"Just breathe," she whispered. "It'll be all right if you breathe."

Keeping my eyes closed tight, I listened to her words and concentrated on the air flowing in and out of my lungs. Soon the worst of the panicked feelings began to dissipate.

Eventually, she removed her arm, but she remained close beside me. I was so weak, so exhausted. And there she was within easy reach of me. I could take everything from her.

I stretched out a hand until I found the source of the wound, the fabric of her sleeve wet with blood.

"Do you trust me?" I asked.

"No."

"Well, you left your weapons against that wall, so you have no choice."

I put my hand on her arm and pulled strength from her, absorbing it to myself like a thirsty sponge. She grimaced from my touch and tried to push me off, but as I became stronger and she weakened, her efforts did nothing to stop me.

Then, as soon as I was certain I had enough, I used that strength to pull the wound from her body, taking the worst of it for myself. When the wound began to seal, I let her go and leaned against the tunnel wall, beyond exhausted.

Minutes passed before either of us spoke. She broke the silence by saying, "Thank you." I didn't answer, and eventually she added, "So what now?"

"I'm still the wolf," I said, curling into a ball and huddling in the corner. "My strength will return soon. It's better if you're gone when that happens."

Harlyn sighed, and walked across the small tunnel room to collect her weapons, paused briefly as she passed by me, then left me alone.

· THIRTY-FIVE ·

SIMON

Rawk was waiting for me as I left the palace, and I invited Loelle to ride with me, an offer she accepted only when I pointed out the fighting still happening around the palace. Once we were in the air, she touched my shoulder. "Take us to Woodcourt."

"I need to counsel with my soldiers."

"You need to speak with Tenger. He begged me to come here to find you before it's too late."

"Of course." At my silent direction to Rawk, he returned us to Woodcourt, landing in the same spot in the courtyard as when we had first taken over the home.

Loelle alighted first and led me into the room that must have once belonged to Kestra's mother. Tenger lay in the wide canopied bed, heavily bandaged and sleeping. He looked peaceful, but maybe too peaceful. Tenger was dying. Loelle leaned over him, nudging his arm until he awoke. He eyed her first, then me, then mumbled, "Leave us, Loelle."

She obeyed, and I sat in a chair beside him. He managed a weak smile before mumbling, "Believe it or not, I almost defeated Joth, that little brat."

I smiled too. "How was that?"

"I attacked from behind, but I needed one more strike to finish him. Before I could do it, he got a hand on me. His pull on my strength was so strong, I could not even breathe."

"I know the feeling. Kestra used that same trick on me once, though it was not as awful as what Joth did to you."

"He intended to kill me, and it seems he'll still get his way."

"No, sir, you'll recover—"

"No, I won't. We both know that, and I didn't bring you here to discuss my funeral." Tenger paused, closing his eyes and resting for a bit. When he opened them again, he said, "Kestra completed her task."

"Yes, Endrick is dead. The Dominion has fallen."

Tenger nodded. "I killed Sir Henry once, you know."

I tilted my head, unsure of whether I'd heard him correctly. I couldn't have. While it was true that Sir Henry was dead, Tenger had not caused it. Harlyn had been responsible for the death.

"There is no more threat from the Dominion," I said. "But we need to figure out how to stop Joth."

"I have a theory about the corruption. We can stop it. I think I know . . ." His eyes rolled. "Sir Henry was dead."

I touched his arm, pulling him back to this room, if only for a moment longer. "Sir Henry *is* dead, Captain, but tell me about the corruption."

He barely mumbled the words, "Our plan is correct. Kestra cannot live."

I sighed. For all the hope I had felt, we were exactly where Tenger had been for months—that after completing her quest, Kestra would have to be killed for her magic.

"Captain, do you know how to save her?"

"Save her," Tenger whispered. "Simon, you must save her."

"Tell me how." I shook his arm as his eyes closed. "Captain, tell me how to save her!"

His eyes fluttered, as if he was trying to wake himself up. I shook his arm again, desperate for those final words. But his arm went limp and mouth sagged open slightly. He was gone.

Even as I sat there beside him, I could not make myself believe it.

Captain Tenger and I had fought alongside each other and, on a few recent occasions, against each other, but I had always considered him a great leader. Now that I was a leader myself, I realized how many decisions I made were because of something Tenger had taught me.

I glanced outside and, with the breaking dawn, saw a softly falling snow, but I saw no beauty in it this time. Antora was a diminished land because of Tenger's absence. Trina or Gabe, or maybe Huge, would take over as captain of the Coracks, but none of them would ever match his greatness.

I stayed with him for several minutes, running through my mind everything he had said and finally concluding that he had been confused. He could not simultaneously order me to save Kestra and fulfill the Corack plan to kill her.

I walked from the room and stared at Loelle, who had been sitting in a chair waiting for me, as if helpless to do anything more for Tenger. That pricked at my temper. "I thought if we brought someone to you, if they were still alive, that you could heal them. Why didn't you heal him, Loelle?"

Loelle's head was hung low, and in the softest possible voice, she mumbled, "Joth attacked him personally, which introduced a poison to his body that he could not sustain without a presence of magic as well. I could not save him from that." She stared up at me, her eyes hollow and tearful. "If that little bit of corruption killed Captain Tenger, I no longer believe it is possible to save Kestra, or to save my son."

"There must be something we've overlooked."

"Maybe. But I think we must also accept the possibility that all we have done is make things worse. And that nothing we can do will ever make them better." She closed her eyes, shutting me out, mumbling to herself. "I believe we have lost."

· THIRTY-SIX ·

KESTRA

At some point, I must have fallen asleep, though I couldn't say whether ten minutes or several hours had passed. My last thought had been a promise that at all costs, I must not let down my guard. Then I'd closed my eyes and broken the promise. I was lucky to be alive.

And unlucky, for I was still in this confined place with a swollen ankle that would not support my weight.

I did feel a little better when my eyes opened, though I wasn't nearly strong enough to face Joth again, which I would have to do soon. With every passing minute, his hold on the kingdom deepened. For all I knew, I was already too late.

Panic began to rise in me, worse than before, creating a cycle I could not break: My desperate need to leave the tunnel was sapping the very strength I had to leave this horrid place.

I wanted to sleep again, to escape into empty dreams if nothing else offered me respite. But in the darkened room, I heard footsteps. Maybe that was what had awakened me before.

I looked up at a faint light that entered the tunnel and saw Harlyn standing over me with a clearstone in one hand. Her disk bow was armed and within easy reach if she decided to use it, but it was not aimed at me, not yet.

"For once, when you go away, will you please consider staying away?" I asked.

"You must make me understand," she said, setting the clearstone in a sconce. "Why did you let me live back in the throne room?"

"A moment of insanity."

"And then here, why did you save me again?"

I turned my head away from her, but she would not give in to my silence. Crouching beside me, she said, "I know what Endrick did to you before you killed him, I saw what happened as the corruption entered. You should *want* to kill me."

"I do." More than usual, at the present moment.

"But you saved me instead. Tell me why. I need to understand this, Kestra!"

"I don't even understand it, all right? I just know . . ." I took a breath, trying to calm myself. "I have to stop Joth, because no one else can do it. If I win, I will take the throne again. But . . ." I hardly dared to say the rest, especially with Harlyn studying my every move, ready to shoot that disk if I twitched the wrong way. But I had to say it. "Harlyn, I know there is a chance I won't win. If I die, then the fight against Joth must continue. At the end of it, you must take the throne in my place."

Silence followed, so long that I wasn't sure she had heard me. Then she said, "Why would you want me on the throne? You hate me."

Behind me, where I had accidentally collapsed the tunnel, pebbles fell from the tunnel ceiling, as they had occasionally done for hours. I wrapped my arms around my body until everything was

quiet, then said, "Whatever I think of you, I also know that the people will follow you, and they should. You're a good person. No
corruption. And Simon will be at your side."

I was so tired by then, I was only mumbling. I knew that Harlyn
sat beside me, putting an arm around my shoulders while whispering
assurances that there was nothing to be afraid of down here in the
tunnels. How very wrong she was.

Harlyn continued talking, asking questions that I'm sure she
suspected I would never answer in any other circumstances. We
talked of magic and the throne, and of Joth and Simon and Trina and
Loelle. We spoke of other things too, though in my exhaustion, I had
no idea what I might have said.

Finally, I nodded off to sleep, the last words in my head being
Harlyn's promise to stay and keep watch over me.

At least for now, I was safe.

· THIRTY-SEVEN ·

KESTRA

I awoke sometime later, filled with the magic I had thought might be lost forever, and fully recovered of every hard feeling that Joth had numbed when he had robbed me of strength. My ankle was so completely healed that I wondered if I had imagined it being injured before.

When I warmed the clearstone, I saw Harlyn asleep in a corner of this small tunnel room. Her disk bow was slung over one shoulder and her hand was on her sword, sheathed at her waist. Unfortunately, I had not imagined any of this.

What a fool she was, to have let herself become so unguarded, so vulnerable. It showed a lack of respect, as if I were no threat to her. Maybe last night, when I'd been empty and lost, I had not been any more dangerous than a mouse or a biting fly, but that was different now.

Silently, I reached out to my Ironheart soldiers, instructing them to find me here in the tunnels. I promised that if they remained loyal until my final battle against Joth, I would free them, either in my last breath of life or as my first act as the established queen.

And I sensed their response. Every Ironheart still in Highwyn heard my call. The test would be how many of them obeyed. For their own sakes, they had better be competing for who would be the first to reach me.

As I waited, I searched within me to understand what abilities of Endrick's were mine now. There were so many powers I didn't understand, or powers that felt colder than I dared to explore. Endrick seemed to have a fascination with life: its creation, destruction, and eternal preservation. One day, I would know all that he knew.

Every day after that, I would surpass all that he could do.

But for now, I simply needed the power to make a person sleep. Harlyn had barely stirred, and that's how I wanted her to remain. Now it was simple to take the dagger from her boot, the sword from her waist, her bow, and the satchel at her side containing two disks, the black one she had already threatened me with, and a white disk that would separate the target's soul from their body. The eternal punishment.

I smiled as I placed her satchel over my shoulder. This may have been the first kind thing I could say about Harlyn: that the black disk she had threatened me with was far better than the alternative. One day, I would have to thank her for that, probably a few minutes before executing her for treason.

Once I had disarmed her, I tried to recall the conversation we'd had shortly before I fell asleep. I'd said more than I intended to, I knew that. I vaguely remembered that I had offered her the throne.

Why had I done that? Searching within myself again for the motive, I realized that Joth had not only drained my strength, he had pulled most of my magic away from me, which surely included the corruption. It would have left me vulnerable to emotions that the corruption suppressed, of pity, mercy, justice—qualities that were fine for commoners, but which made a queen vulnerable.

Our conversation hadn't ended there, I was sure of that. I believed we'd talked about Simon, and it seemed that she had let it slip how much she loved him. Or maybe I had said those words. I hoped it wasn't me.

I especially hoped it wasn't she who said them.

Minutes later, an Ironheart rounded the corner. He was roughly Darrow's age, with a similar build, and a long beard and rags for clothes. He went to one knee for me. "My queen. My name is Lore and I am at your service."

"You are the only one to come?"

He rose up. "There is one more, not far behind me."

I rolled my eyes. A glorious punishment was coming for all Ironhearts who had ignored my orders, but I wanted plenty of magic saved up for that event. For now, I needed that magic elsewhere.

Lore stood, accidentally bumping a foot against Harlyn's leg. She sat up with a start, alarmed to see we were not alone. She reached for her sword, then saw it at my waist, along with every other weapon that had been hers not ten minutes ago. Sensing how vulnerable she was, Harlyn glanced down, hoping to be ignored. I was happy to do that.

Lore asked, "What are your orders, my queen?"

"Can you get me out of this tunnel?"

"If you're going after Joth, I want to come too." Harlyn's eye was fixed on her disk bow, slung over my shoulder. I hoped she didn't attempt to take it, because that would force me to defend myself.

I shook my head. "You will not come. Other than the kind gift of your weapons, you are of no use to me any longer." She had started to her feet, but with a wave of my hand, she fell to the ground and there she would stay. "We are not friends, Harlyn, and anything I might have said last night no longer matters."

"Anything you might have said?" Harlyn's eyes narrowed. "Oh, you don't remember what you said, do you? Well, believe me when I say that it matters a great deal."

I began searching my recovered powers for a way to make her regret her insolence, but was startled by the approach of the second Ironheart.

"My lady, I came as fast as I could."

"Address me as your queen," I demanded, then stopped once I saw Rosaleen standing before me. Simon's sister.

Now behind me, Harlyn breathed out her name. Rosaleen glanced at Harlyn briefly before her eyes returned to me.

"My queen," Rosaleen said obediently.

"Do you know who I am?" I asked.

"Kestra Dallisor, Queen of Antora."

"What else?"

Rosaleen's eyes misted. "You were the Infidante. I used to fight for you."

"Do you still?"

With a brief glance at Lore and then at Harlyn, she said, "I am an Ironheart, my queen. I must fight for you."

Her answer told me more than I wished it did. Rosaleen was not here by choice, but at least she was here. If this was my only way to get an army, it's where I would begin.

I said to Lore, "Lead me out of here."

He went first and I followed, with Rosaleen behind us. Recalling the way she had taken aim at me outside All Spirits Forest, I eventually told her to walk at my side. Even if she was calling me her queen, I felt safer being able to see her.

"Why did the two of you come for me?" I asked.

Lore glanced back long enough to say, "How should we answer such a question, my queen? With what you want to hear, or the truth?"

"I want to hear the truth."

"The truth is what the ruler of the Scarlet Throne declares it to be."

"Enough bantering of words!" I said as we continued to trudge forward. "Why did you come for me in these tunnels?"

Rosaleen said, "I saw what happened to your former hand-maiden when her heart was crushed. I prefer to avoid that fate."

I started to tell her that, for Simon's sake, I was hoping to avoid crushing her heart. But I didn't say it. That hardly seemed like the right choice of words while I still needed her help.

In a softer tone, I asked, "If Endrick's magic could stop a heart, could it start one beating again?"

No one answered at first; then after we rounded another bend, Lore said, "He did that for your father once. For Sir Henry."

I paused. "When?" I'd never heard of such a thing.

"While you were . . . missing from the kingdom, two or three years ago, there was a Corack uprising. Their captain, a man who goes by the name of Tenger, managed to stab your father straight through the heart. He was dead, my lady. I saw it myself, and with such a wound, how could he be otherwise? But the next morning, Sir Henry stood in front of us all, alive and well, ordering punishments on everyone he felt had failed to protect him during that battle. Nothing could have healed him except Lord Endrick's magic."

By then, a ladder leading to the tunnel's exit had become visible. Lore went up first, to ensure the area was secure. I turned to Rosaleen. "Simon is your brother."

Something flickered in her eyes, fear perhaps, but she quickly took control of it. "We had a mother too, once. If you intend to kill my brother as well, then I beg you to crush my heart now."

The person I had once been would have been hurt by her accusation, but I felt nothing now, cared nothing for a death I had not caused and could not have prevented. Or at least, I was trying to feel nothing. With no words in my mind for a response, I merely stared at her before I silently climbed the ladder out of the tunnels. A minute later, Rosaleen followed.

Once safely on the surface, I said to them, "Will you serve me by choice? Not because of any threat to your lives but because you believe in me as your queen. Will you stay and help me see this through to the end?"

Silence followed as Lore and Rosaleen looked at each other, neither wanting to be the first to speak, but both of them clearly with something they wanted to say.

"Are you so afraid of me?" I finally asked.

Their eyes lowered, giving me their answer.

"I am not Lord Endrick," I said to them.

"You have his magic, and there is an echo of his voice when you speak, my lady," Lore said.

Prove him right.

The words entered my mind so forcefully, it was as though they came from somewhere beyond myself. And yet they had been my thoughts, my instincts. My own desires.

I said again, "Will you serve me by choice?"

More silence, then Lore stepped forward, his head lowered as if expecting the worst. "What happens if we refuse?"

My mind raced with possibilities, with everything I wanted to say, every threat to force them to bend to my will. With a clench of my fist, I could make them obey, or simpler still, with a single touch, I could take their strength to myself and enter the throne room as strong as all of them put together. I didn't need them to serve me. I only needed their strength.

It was easy to reach out my hand toward this bold man who had dared to question me, and far more difficult to pull it back. But I had to do it.

Because something had changed in me last night. Separated from my corruption for a few hours, I had a brief glimpse of who I had been, and who I now was. I missed the girl I had been once: Reckless and arrogant and deeply flawed, but still at my core, I had thought myself to be a good person. I wanted to hold on to that Kestra for as long as I could.

So I said, "If you choose not to follow me, then you can walk away now, as free Antorans. But I ask you to consider who now sits on the Scarlet Throne. If we allow Joth Tarquin to remain there, what will your future be?"

"What is my future now?" Lore asked. "My brother was among the Ironhearts you attacked as they marched into Highwyn. You gave the Ironhearts there the same promise you're offering now. Then you and the boy who now sits on the throne killed them all. I don't know what will happen once I walk away, but I will walk away. I can serve corruption no longer, not you or Joth Tarquin, or Lord Endrick himself. Indeed, my lady, I don't think there is any difference between any of you."

Unprepared for that accusation, I recoiled. Had he slapped me he could not have hurt me more. By the time I looked up, only Rosaleen remained.

"You can go too," I told her. "I want you to go. Your brother is desperate to see you."

"I vowed to serve the Infidante," she said. "If she is still there inside you—"

"She's not." I withdrew Harlyn's sword. "I am releasing you as an Ironheart, but as your queen, I have one order that you must fulfill. Find my father, Darrow. Ask him to find me, wherever I am. I do not know if he will come, but he is the only one who would. Then go to your brother."

Rosaleen nodded and gave me a polite bow before she ran in one direction while I began marching toward the throne room, ready for revenge. Surely in his paranoia, Joth had not left that room all night.

And if there was a price for my victory, Joth Tarquin would dearly pay it.

· THIRTY-EIGHT ·

SIMON

Early the following morning, all the soldiers who had fought with us returned to Woodcourt to regroup. I was out there with them as each group arrived, exhausted, often wounded, and diminished in spirit. I was little better.

First to arrive were the Brill, with only half their original numbers. Reports had already come in of how the last of Endrick's Dominion had targeted them with the carnoxen. The Brill's eventual victory had come at a terrible price.

The effects of the loss were evident in Imri Stout's face. The Brill were notoriously proud of their beauty, but dark bags hung beneath her reddened eyes now, which appeared to have little life left in them.

"Our country has lost so very much," she said. "We should have licked our wounds and remained in Brill, rather than come here."

"I hope you will stay and help us," I said, "though I understand if you choose to leave."

"The Brill never leave in defeat," she said. "We will see this battle through to the end, and leave victorious or we will not leave at all."

I nodded at her, with deep respect for the honor she showed us.

But the way Imri responded left me confused as to whether she felt the same respect for me. "Word is spreading among my people that you have challenged Joth to a duel for the throne."

I arched a brow. "How did you hear that?"

"The restored Navan who still remain loyal to him have been sent throughout Highwyn as criers, commanding everyone within the sound of their voice to be at the palace courtyard at noon today, to see you kneel in recognition of him as king."

I clicked my tongue and felt my hand curl into a fist. He would not have ordered such a thing unless he was certain of a victory.

"We can offer you our technologies," Imri said, "The Brill have abilities nearly equal to some of what Endrick was once able to do."

"We agreed there would be no magic," I said, quickly adding, "Which means no imitation of magic either. The people must see a fair fight between us."

"And you believe Joth will follow through on that?"

"No." I had challenged Joth as a lure to draw him out of the throne room. Either by intention or desperation, he would cheat, which I'd hoped would turn the entire population against him. Then I would order a mass attack, one he would not be able to counter.

That had been the plan, until only a handful of his Navan had left me on the floor, so helpless that I'd needed rescuing by Joth's mother, a fact that stung more than I wished to admit. There was a chance that the coming duel, now only hours away, would end the same. It was likely that I would lose in front of a crowd of onlookers who believed Joth had legitimately earned his victory.

Imri left in one direction while Basil and Trina entered Woodcourt's grounds from another, with Gabe and Huge not far behind. Gabe briefly locked eyes with me, then shook his head and moved on toward the stables. That was fine with me. I walked over to Basil and Trina instead.

Trina nudged me. "He's been your best friend for years! Get over there and talk to him."

I shook my head, angry at her suggestion that this was somehow my problem to solve. "He struck first, Trina."

"Yes, but to be fair, most of us have felt like hitting you at least once over the past several months. I'm sure Gabe held out as long as he could."

She had meant it as a joke, but I didn't take it that way. And when I didn't smile, she added, "With Tenger's death, Gabe will probably become the new captain of the Coracks. How can you finish this battle if you can't even speak to each other?"

"Do you know why he hit me?" I asked. "He's in love with Harlyn."

Beside Trina, Basil chuckled. "If that's true, then surely you understand how Gabe feels." When I looked at him for an explanation, Basil added, "I loved Kestra. And at first it infuriated me to see she preferred you, because I was the more obvious choice. I was a prince; you were part of a failing rebellion. I offered her protection while you placed her in greater jeopardy." He smiled. "And I'm clearly more handsome."

"You're saying that Gabe is angry because Harlyn is choosing me?"

Basil shook his head. "I thought I loved Kestra, until I saw the way you loved her. I'm saying that *you* are angry with Gabe because he loves Harlyn more than you ever can."

I opened my mouth to answer, then hesitated as I absorbed his words. Not so many months ago, Endrick changed Kestra's memories so that she believed she loved Basil. That had nearly destroyed me. Hoping to restore her memories, I had risked my position with the Coracks, even my own life, and done everything possible to . . .

A knot formed in my gut. I had risked everything because I was in love with her.

I still was in love with her.

Despite reason and experience and the constant twisting of my heart, I was drawn to Kestra as if she was my next breath. And if my heart twisted with every thought of her, perhaps that was only to hold her in there when everything else wanted to pull us apart. I realized then that, in some form, I always had loved her, even as a young boy. And no matter what consequences might still come to me, I knew that I always would.

Kicking at the ground, I said, "Basil, I owe you a lifetime of apologies."

"You owe me nothing. I have all that I want," he said, wrapping an arm around Trina, who nestled in against him. Until that moment, I hadn't noticed any particular affection between them, but clearly I *should have* noticed.

"Go and make things right between you and your friend," Trina said, nudging my shoulder.

I offered my hand to Basil. "You are a better person than I ever was."

He smiled. "I believe you're right."

"Now go and say that to Gabe," Trina said.

He and Huge were finishing unsaddling their horses when I walked up. "No injuries?" I asked Huge. I still wouldn't look directly at Gabe.

Huge shook his head. "Unfortunately, the carnox I fought with can't say the same."

I laughed at that and so did Gabe, and I wondered in that moment if that single joke would be the last thing Gabe and I might ever see the same way.

Settling my eyes on Gabe, I said to Huge, "Will you give us a minute alone?"

Huge looked from me over to Gabe, who had returned to working on his horse, then quietly dismissed himself.

Gabe continued to ignore me, which only made things harder. I wasn't about to open with an apology if he couldn't tear himself away from the fascination of saddle inspection. Trina was right—we did need to talk, but I wasn't about to apologize to the side of his uninterested face. I grunted and began to walk away. We'd do this later, maybe in another twenty or thirty years.

But as I turned, he said, "I know where I hit you, and it wouldn't have done all the damage I see now. Who was next in line to take a swing at you?"

"I spent time in Joth's throne room."

"Ah." No sympathy was offered, only a shift of his stance for his next question. "Did you find her? Or let me be more specific. Did you find Harlyn there?"

"No. Nor did I find Kestra. But I managed to get Joth to agree to a duel with me at noon. No magic."

"Congratulations. I noticed the way you were nursing your sword arm when you shook hands with Basil. Magic or not, Joth will be a tough opponent."

"I'm hoping that when she has a moment, Loelle might heal me."

Gabe threw his arms outward. "Look around us, Hatch. She won't have a moment. We are overrun with the injured, and none of what we did made any difference! Endrick was killed without our help, and now what we have on the throne is worse."

"This isn't over. If Kestra still has the Olden Blade—"

"We've been through this, over and over and over again. So if you came here for the same fight we keep having—"

"I didn't. I came to tell you that I know how you feel about Harlyn." Gabe started to speak, but I quickly added, "I know you love her."

Gabe closed his mouth, then opened it again to say, "Another quest that will make no difference, regardless of what I do. For weeks, I've watched her openly pursue you, only to be met with polite indifference, or at best, a kiss to her cheek that makes you appear to be in physical pain. And I know what she says in public, but I don't believe she truly loves you. How can she, when you haven't shared any piece of your heart with her? It is cruel the way you let her hold on to a thin hope for you to change when we both know you cannot tear yourself away from Kestra."

"You're right," I said. "You're right that I owe Harlyn every possible apology. Have you told her how you feel?"

"No, and I won't. I'm not about to empty out my soul to her and have her reply that she can't wait to marry you." He shrugged. "I'm sorry I hit you, Simon. I never should have done that. But I'm not sorry for my reasons."

I would've replied, but Gabe's eyes had drifted behind me. I turned around and, to my surprise, saw Harlyn speaking to Trina, who pointed over at me. Our eyes met, and Harlyn motioned with her head that I should follow her.

I started toward Harlyn, but Gabe called out, "Hatch!" I paused but did not look back at him. Forced to speak to me thus, he said, "At least I do understand you now. I know what it's like to care for someone who is beyond your reach. I haven't changed my mind about Kestra, but I hope you know that I understand what it's like to give a piece of your heart to someone who won't return those feelings. Our situations are not so different."

"How did you figure that?" Now I turned to him, angrier than when we'd fought. "Have I set terms for whether Harlyn gets to live, maybe offered to kill her myself? Have we spent hour after hour debating whether Harlyn's life has any value beyond her use in battle? Will your own life be threatened if anyone discovers your feelings for Harlyn?"

Gabe looked down. "No, none of those."

I frowned at him. "Then our situations are very different, and you do not understand. But if you want to try, begin here: I did not give Kestra a *piece* of my heart. She *is* my heart."

· THIRTY-NINE ·

SIMON

Harlyn motioned to me again and I left Gabe, but when I had almost reached her, the heads of my cavalry rode through the gate. I offered Harlyn my arm and together we went to greet Commander Reese.

He looked in better condition than most others who had returned this morning, so I hoped he was bringing good news, but that didn't appear to be so. He shook his head, dismounted, and gave me a low bow. "We lost ten riders. My first officer, Edgar, was among them. And maybe ten doesn't seem like many compared to the losses others have taken, but it's a tenth of my cavalry."

"I'm very sorry." The weight of responsibility for those losses was heavy on my shoulders. "I tried everything I could to keep the worst of the battle from reaching you."

"I can see that." Reese gave a deep sigh. "If you wish to remain our king, then you must trust us, as you ask us to trust you. We are soldiers. We are part of this battle too."

"I'm glad to hear it, because this is not over. I still need you to keep our riders alert."

"*Our* riders?" Commander Reese reached out to shake my hand,

and for the first time I saw a sincere hint of respect in his eyes. "Yes, *our* riders are at your service."

"We thank you," Harlyn said. "But for now, you all must rest. Use any resources from Woodcourt that you need."

"Thank you . . . my king." He bowed to Harlyn. "And my future queen."

Harlyn only lowered her eyes. "Can we go somewhere private?"

Our walk into the library was long and unusually quiet. I couldn't help but think of how Gabe must be watching us, and hating me for leaving with her. How he must be wishing he could hit me again.

Once we entered the library, before Harlyn said another word, she checked that every door was closed and even glanced up at the windows high above us to be sure we were alone. When she finished, she turned to me, looking as nervous as I'd ever seen her. "Don't get upset. The wound is gone."

My brows furrowed. "What wound?"

Harlyn removed her cloak. Her dress was torn in several places, but most prominently, one sleeve was bloodstained. Her blood, I guessed.

"The wound is gone," she repeated.

"How?" The only possible explanation seemed . . . impossible. "Kestra?"

She nodded. "You'll be angry with me for most of this story, so I must remind you that I was only following orders you agreed to."

"You tried to kill Kestra."

"I fully intended to do it, and I still wonder if I should have done it when I had the chance. She was weakened—Joth had taken nearly all her strength. I don't know how she found it in herself to continue running from me, but she did. Then she entered a tunnel that I think is used by Endrick's Ironhearts. It was small and dark—"

"And Kestra became afraid."

Harlyn frowned. "Yes. And although I had the opportunity, I couldn't harm her when she was like that." She shrugged. "Then, when I finally worked up the courage to do it, I literally couldn't. The disk that I had intended for her backfired, and I shot myself instead."

My brow wrinkled. "How did that happen?"

"Half-lives. They would've done worse, but Kestra tried to persuade them to give loyalty to her instead. I don't know if it worked, but they didn't bother us after that. And then she did something that caused my wound to begin healing. She saved my life in there."

"But I thought—"

"I think in her weakened state, the corruption itself was weakened and she was . . . like the old Kestra, or the Kestra that I think she must have been once."

Hope filled me. Perhaps Loelle was wrong and there was a way to heal Kestra. But in Harlyn's very next words, all hope vanished, leaving me emptier than if she had never spoken.

She said, "By this morning, Kestra's strength had returned and, with it, every bit of corruption I'd seen before." Harlyn looked up at me. "I saw it for myself, Simon. When she is weak, the corruption fades. But it's always there inside her."

"Where is she now?"

"I don't know. I last saw her as she was leaving the tunnels. Her strength had returned, she had taken all my weapons, and she was going back with them to face Joth."

Alarms rang in my mind. "She went alone?"

Harlyn drew in a slow breath. "Not alone. Kestra called two Ironhearts to help her get out of the tunnel. One of them was Rosaleen."

My heart stopped. "You saw Rosaleen yourself?"

"Briefly, but yes, it was her."

"She and this other Ironheart are going with Kestra to face Joth?" Pressure began to build inside my chest. She could have a hundred Ironhearts with her, and Joth would cut through them in a minute to get to Kestra.

Harlyn took my hands in hers. "I followed her to the end of the tunnel. I don't think she knew I was there. Simon, she released the two Ironhearts, gave them their freedom."

"So where is Rosaleen?" Again, a spark of hope lit within me. And again, Harlyn snuffed it out.

"Kestra sent Rosaleen to find Darrow; then she planned to face Joth alone."

I pulled my hands free and backed up, pushing my fingers through my hair, trying to sort my thoughts as they flew apart in every direction.

Harlyn said, "Kestra is strong, and she is smart. We have to trust her to do to Joth what she did to Endrick."

She was right about that, but it didn't make me feel any better, not if this was about trust. "She's still corrupt. What is the difference between Joth on the throne, or Kestra?"

"It makes every difference." Harlyn closed her eyes and seemed to be deep in thought. Finally, she opened them and said, "Do you remember when I told you that before Kestra killed Endrick, he made her kneel? Darrow asked me how he was able to get Kestra to her knees."

"You told him that you didn't know." I tilted my head. "Is that true?"

"No." Her eyes darted. "Endrick gave her a choice. Either she would kneel, or he would use his magic on me. She chose to kneel, for my sake. She saved me again in the tunnels, even after knowing I was there to kill her. Kestra is different from Joth. She is fighting the poison inside her, fighting harder than I could have imagined until I had to watch her try to resist its hold on her. It's like an infection that comes back again and again and again, each time a little stronger, and yet she still fights. Joth never has fought it."

"She cannot fight it forever," I said.

Harlyn stepped closer and put one hand on my cheek. "Simon, she fights because she loves you. And as long as she loves you, she will never give up."

I shook my head. I wanted to believe Harlyn. More than anything, I wanted some bit of hope to latch on to, even the thinnest evidence that a future with Kestra still remained. But every time I dared to hope, it was ripped away and I broke a little further.

"It doesn't matter," I said. "Whatever you think you saw to have told me this—"

Harlyn sighed and gave me a slight smile. "Do you have any idea how much I wanted to return with a report that Kestra deserved to die, or to say anything to finally separate you from her? Once I was trapped with Kestra in that tunnel, my plan was to learn the truth about her." She took another breath. "The problem is that I did learn the truth. I know that she loves you because those were her own words. She believes that she lost you months ago, but we both know that is not true."

I looked at Harlyn again, really looked at her, and this time I noticed a tear in the crease of one eye, and the way she was attempting to control her breathing.

"I'm so sorry," I told her. "Harlyn, in any other time or place, I would have chosen you from a million others."

She forced a smile to her face. "Only if Kestra was not also one of those million, no?" Now her smile became more sincere. "I always knew that you still loved her, even when you denied it, maybe especially when you denied it. But I believed that you would eventually come to see who she really is. The problem is that last night, I was the one who saw who she really is. Kestra is worth fighting for, Simon, worth saving. If she survives this morning's battle with Joth, then I will do everything I can to help you protect her until a way can be found to bring her back."

"Do you believe that?" I asked. "That she can come back from this?"

Harlyn smiled. "No, I don't simply believe it. The Kestra I met last night will find a way. I *know* it."

· FORTY ·

KESTRA

Along with acquiring Endrick's powers, I had also inherited a sense for the number of Ironheart soldiers here in Highwyn, and their general location. Which meant I also knew that they had wasted no time in attempting to leave Highwyn as quickly as possible, hoping that with enough distance, they might finally escape their servitude.

Only two had responded to my call for help in the tunnels, and of those, only one remained: Simon's sister. I doubted she had obeyed my order to find Darrow. More likely, she had scattered with the others as soon as she was outside the palace walls.

I strode toward the throne room, hoping a show of confidence would mask the reality that I was completely alone in this fight. Or . . . perhaps not.

Directly in front of the throne room doors, a dozen half-lives stood with their eyes on me. I saw them clearly enough, but had not seen them before. If these had been in the group down in the tunnel, I hoped they were here to offer their loyalty once again.

If not, then I was in serious trouble.

Until I was sure, I braced myself, wondering if their intent was to stop me from entering the room, but that didn't seem to be their purpose. As I stepped forward, so did they.

"You are coming with me?" I asked, more incredulous than not.

I couldn't hear their words, and I didn't know if they were even speaking, but I did see distinct nods, and I returned them with gratitude. So I would not be going in alone after all.

"Stay close." I hoped that would be enough.

I hesitated outside the doors to find every possible bit of Endrick's power that I could identify within myself. There was so much he could do that I'd never known. He could temporarily slow time and detect when someone was lying. He had dozens of powers still unexplored, or that he considered unnecessary for his reign. What little I already knew of his abilities made him far more powerful than I had suspected.

When I was queen, it might take years to understand it all. I intended to use every moment expanding my kingdom, or making the countries that had wronged me pay dearly. I'd start with the Brill. With what was left of them.

After that, my expansion of power would never end, never diminish. For once I finished with Joth, I would be immortal.

He was about to regret everything he had done to me.

At my command, the doors flung open, and I marched through them with Harlyn's sword in hand. Joth must have known I was coming, for he stood at the base of the stairs to the Scarlet Throne, without any visible weapon but looking as if he'd been waiting for me.

If he expected a fight, I'd bring a battle, or the whole war, if necessary. I'd be a hurricane against his storm, iron for his tin. Whatever he thought of me, I would be stronger and fiercer. Faster than he could think, darker than he could see, and unafraid of the worst that he might bring.

In my previous battle with Endrick, chunks of the ceiling had fallen, but now, with a single glance of my eyes, other pieces fell, large metal squares directly above where Joth stood. Using the same magic, he halted the pieces in midair, then fluttered his fingers until they fell like snow around him. He gathered them together and began to raise a wall as his barricade. I charged forward, hoping to get to him before the wall was formed, but when I got too near, he merely pushed the wall toward me.

I saw it tilt, then placed the sword directly in front of me, blade up. The wall fell as intended but split in half exactly across the sword, leaving two metal slabs on either side of me.

Joth's face tightened into a grimace. "You have no more claim upon this throne than I do."

"I think you meant to say that *you* have no claim upon this throne whatsoever."

He raised his hand, brushing his fingers together as if sparks of magic should somehow appear there. "Without my magic, Endrick would still be alive. So I believe I have some claim."

I didn't flinch. "Kneel to me now, Joth. It is the only way you will survive this."

He smiled. "I think that *you* meant to say I am the only one who will survive this."

Using the same magic Endrick had used against me multiple times, I willed his body to kneel. He did so but crouched lower and pressed his hands flat on the marble floor, which rippled away and knocked me off my feet. Once I fell, he darted for me, but I struck at him with Harlyn's sword, getting in a slice deep enough across his lower legs that he cried out and fell forward.

He was closer now and grabbed my arm at the same time as I put a hand on his shoulder. This time I was ready, and began pulling strength from him as quickly as I could. He was doing the same, so I began searching for his powers.

"How dare you?" he snarled. "How dare you try to take my magic, after all I've done to get you this far?"

"It isn't your magic, or mine," I replied. "This is fire, and either you or I will burn with it."

I used my free hand to reach up toward the chandelier directly overhead. I pulled it down, steering it so that it landed directly on Joth, barely missing me and crashing across his entire body. His hand that had been holding me released and went lax.

I rolled away, breathless from the energy I'd exerted, and studied Joth's arm for any sign of movement.

When I saw none, I stood and backed away, trying to figure out what I should do next, whether this could possibly be over so easily.

Turning around the room in hopes of sensing anyone else who was here with me, I asked the half-lives, "Is he dead? I need to know—"

My answer came when I happened to see Joth's hand form into a fist, and then the fingers flew apart. I was slammed backward, skidding along the floor. Behind me, every window along the room's glass wall shattered with a violence that shook the building.

I started to get up, then felt a sharp pain in my leg and my head swam with dizziness. Looking down, I realized a shard of the glass had lodged in my thigh. I tried to pull it out, but I was weaker than before, and it was in deep. The edges of the glass cut my hands and even the slightest tug made me cry out in pain.

Joth emerged from beneath the chandelier as if it too were made of dust. "That must hurt," he said, rubbing his hands together as if to gather his strength.

"It's easier to tolerate than a kiss from you," I retorted.

He flinched, but quickly regained his composure to say, "This ends today. At noon, I'll meet my subjects in the palace courtyard. Most of them will bow simply to avoid any trouble."

I tugged again at the glass, biting down on my lip to remain strong enough to continue. Meanwhile, Joth used his hands to raise all the other pieces of glass over my head.

"A few may stubbornly resist. For their benefit, Simon has challenged me to a duel. When I defeat him—and I *will* defeat him—he will kneel or die in his place. Then the rest of the citizenry will be given the same choice. The end of this story has already been determined, Kestra. Please stop fighting me. Reconnect powers with me and let us return to a true partnership once more."

"We never were partners, and this fight is only just beginning." I yanked out the shard of glass at the very same moment as he let the pieces of glass fall. I searched for a way to stop them and failed, but the glass fell in a perfect circle around me . . . as if I were protected by some sort of barricade.

"You half-lives are *my* subjects!" he screamed. "Betray me here and I will never heal you. I will destroy what is left of you, just as Endrick destroyed so many others!"

"Attack him," I said to those same half-lives. "You have nothing to lose now."

Joth attempted to shield himself, but the half-lives pushed straight through his protections, rolling over him and leaving him gasping for breath. He would be vulnerable now, as vulnerable as I had been last night down in the tunnels. This might be my only chance.

I stood again, though I was limping as I moved toward him, my sword out and ready.

He leaned up on his arms, raising one hand in a defensive position. "If you intend to strike, do so with mercy. Kestra, this isn't me. Surely you will not be cruel when the same corruption is in you. We are both victims to its power."

"Kneel to me," I said.

He glanced at my injured leg. "You need help, or that will bleed out."

"My leg is fine."

"It's not. Perhaps you should kill me now," he said. "Otherwise, when I get my strength back, you know that I will attack you again. With that injured leg, I will easily win."

I did know that. This is how I must have been last night, in the tunnels with Harlyn. But I struggled with the memory. My mind had been playing tricks with me down there. Right now, full of strength and magic and once again within reach of great power, wasn't this what I wanted?

I looked up at the Scarlet Throne, unscathed despite the battle Joth and I had just waged. The throne was mine.

Yet something last night had changed me. I was prepared to kill Joth here, if necessary, but I had no wish for that, nor would I find any satisfaction in his death. I preferred to show him mercy and hope he accepted my terms.

"I've got to weaken you further," I said to him. "If you cooperate, you will live, but I need you to be unable to use your powers until your mother discovers a way to withdraw the corruption. Go to your knees." That way I could reach his neck without him being in easy reach of me.

"If my mother succeeds, will you connect with me once more?"

"No, Joth." My voice was gentle, but his body contracted at my words. I had not wanted to hurt him, but there was clearly danger in any connection between his magic and mine. "Now please, go to your knees and live."

He obeyed and lowered his head, his hands in his lap. I approached him cautiously and put my hand on his neck, but the second I began to pull strength from him, he muttered, "Or you will go to your knees, and die."

Joth twisted around with one leg, and I was swept off my feet, landing hard on my shoulder and injured leg. I rolled to one side to gather my breath, then felt myself being sent backward toward the shattered windows. I tried to find anything to hold on to, anything to slow the speed at which I was headed toward the edge.

Then I went over it.

I'd escaped the throne room this way before, but Basil had been ready with a net below to catch me. Now there was nothing, only a long fall to the hard ground. I passed treetops and leaves and lost consciousness somewhere on the way down from a limb of a tree.

My last thought was that I was nowhere near the ground. But I soon would be.

FORTY-ONE

SIMON

Shortly before noon, the palace courtyard was so packed with people that a gnat wouldn't have fit inside. Few of them would have chosen to be here, but nobody wanted to be reported as absent, should Joth win. And if I was being honest with myself, he likely would.

In the center of the courtyard, a raised platform had been built so that everyone would have an easy view of the events. Or I hoped they could see us. My only chance today was to get the public on my side.

Once I stepped onto the platform, I made a full rotation, surveying each group in attendance. Most of the Alliance members were here, but I also saw Dallisor nobility, former Dominion soldiers, and a surprisingly high attendance of civilians, the majority of whom I assumed had been Loyalists. I wondered how many of them would quickly claim allegiance to the victor of this duel, simply as a means of survival.

"Listen to me now!" I hoped my voice would carry to the farthest corners of the courtyard. "I will be the first to stand against Joth Tarquin today, but I hope that I will not stand alone. Joth can attack one or two or maybe three of us at a time, but hundreds of us are here. Fight with me, and his reign will end today."

The enthusiastic reaction I had hoped for was more of a light applause. Less confident now, I continued. "You deserve a ruler who will fight for your lives, not threaten them with every breath he utters. Who will protect your freedoms, and serve you more than you serve him. That is not Joth Tarquin."

The crowd's cheer was instantly diminished by cries behind me when light burst from out of nowhere and, from its center, Joth marched toward the platform, his arms raised as if he were already the victor. He made the same rotation as I had done only seconds ago, then widened his arms overhead for silence.

"Lord Endrick is dead. You have been freed from his oppression!" A muted applause went up from the audience, with the exception of those who had been true Dominion Loyalists. They only stared at Joth with solemn expressions that masked their true emotions. They had no desire to see me win, but I suspected their feelings for Joth were far more acidic.

Joth lowered his arms, his hands now in fists. "I must admit, I expected more enthusiasm to greet your new king. Perhaps that is because you do not know me, and maybe you fear me. You will know me in time, and it is right that you should feel this fear because I have powers that extend beyond even what Lord Endrick could do. However, as of this moment, I have no quarrel with any of you, so there will be no revenge on Dallisors, on Halderians, or on Antorans. For that reason, I alone can bring us together."

A more enthusiastic applause followed. If it was sincere, then I was already in trouble. Hadn't they all heard the part about fearing him?

Joth raised his sword and pointed at me. "This so-called Halderian king has no royal blood, nor even a drop of the blood of the people he claims to lead. The most he can offer is yet another battle in which many of you will die today. Or if you step forward now and remove him from this platform, the war is over. Accept me as your king, and there will be no need for any more fighting among us."

Off to the right, where the Dallisors had been standing, a fervor of conversation arose, and movement shifted toward the platform. So the Dallisors had chosen sides after all, and it wasn't for me. I prepared myself to face them, but they had taken no more than ten steps toward me when Commander Reese signaled my cavalry to form a line in front of the Dallisors. Gabe and Basil also led their groups in that same direction, then stood facing the Dallisors, weapons ready.

I had turned to watch it happen, long enough to see the Dallisors back down, but as soon as they did, Joth struck me from behind. As a strange bit of luck, I felt the hard blow against the back of my legs, but he cursed in disappointment. At a slightly different angle, that would have given me a crippling cut.

Still, I was knocked to the ground and rolled away just in time for Joth to stab his sword downward. Based on the force with which it hit the ground, I knew he had intended it to be a death blow.

When I rolled, I angled my sword upward to take a swipe at him, but when I did, his eyes darted leftward and, with them, my blade was forced in that direction and fell to the ground. I glared at him, and he only winked at me. His game had begun.

I grabbed the sword again and stood, facing off with him, but as before, he was quietly using magic against me. This time, my feet felt as if they were embedded in inches of mud. I could move them but only with great effort, making it nearly impossible to swing at him with any effect.

"Surrender now," Joth said. "You're embarrassing yourself, Simon."

"How pathetic it must be to know magic is your only hope of winning. Those who recognize what you are doing will see how weak you truly are."

Instantly, my feet were released, and Joth attacked again, though I was ready for him, parrying his blow and then countering with one of my own, leaving a slice across his arm. The audience gasped, for it was the first strike to draw blood. However, our duel was far from finished, and I had no doubt that Joth would cheat as often as necessary.

We continued to levy blows against each other, though Joth was still using magic in the subtlest of ways. At the moment, the platform floor was constantly changing angles, so slight it wouldn't be visible, but I felt it every time I tried to get a stable footing. And I believed the wind changed direction to come at my face, no matter which direction I turned, while Joth's hair was barely ruffled.

Finally, I got behind him long enough for a strike across his legs, exactly where he had attacked me first, but my sword was turned to cause far greater damage. He fell forward, his own sword tumbling out of his reach. I started toward it, but he turned and raised a hand toward me. I was hit with a force that knocked me backward hard enough to break the ropes that had surrounded our platform. I fell off the edge and into the crowd.

Gasps echoed through the courtyard, and when I climbed onto the platform again, a cheer followed. Angrily, Joth grabbed a knife from his waistband and shouted, "I am your king! Bow to me, or you will die!"

Then he threw the knife directly at me. No doubt it was sent on the wings of magic, which meant it could not miss.

He had no intention of losing.

Neither did I.

· FORTY-TWO ·

KESTRA

There was no explanation for me to have awoken, other than that I now had Endrick's powers and, with them, his near immortality. The wounds in my leg and in my hands had healed, though both were sore to the touch. Although I was capable of standing, I continued to lie in the snow without moving. Joth's attack on me was the nearest I'd ever come to death, and I was still shaken from it. Even Lord Endrick, knowing I was the Infidante, had been controlled in anything he had ever done to me. Joth was untethered from any compass between good and evil. He was sheer venom.

What Joth was, what Lord Endrick had been, would be me in time. That was as inevitable as the rising sun each day. I could see it now in full view, with all its ugliness and stain.

I could see myself now, as if reflected by the clearest mirror, and all I wished was to shatter it, to shatter that part of myself. If only it were possible.

Loelle had said that, for all her searching, she had found no way to pull the corruption from me. Every attempt that Joth had made to take my magic did weaken me, but it always returned. Over and over, I had been assured that with magic would come corruption and that any chance of a cure was hopeless.

Yet deep within my mind, I had always held to one small possibility, something that had not been tried, had not even been considered: If magic could not be pulled from me, could I give it away?

I lay with that thought for some time, rolling it around in my head like a loose marble that shifted with every movement I made, never settling in one place long enough to know if there was anything tangible to my ideas.

And finally I sat up, having made my decision. What I was about to attempt would likely fail, and failure here meant certain death. But in my current weakened state, I knew that I could not continue to live as I had been. I had to take this chance.

Lord Endrick had come to power by killing all those whose magic he wanted, thus obtaining their powers for himself. At some point, he must have begun to sense his own mortality, should someone ever make him the target. So he poured a portion of his magic into the Olden Blade. Whatever thus happened to him would be irrelevant, because the magic in the Olden Blade could restore him.

It was a plan that should have worked, until the Olden Blade was stolen. Then the object that could save his life now became the sole object that could take it.

And I had done just that.

Despite that, Endrick's plan had been a good one. So good, in fact, that I wondered if there was any hope of my doing the same. I wouldn't use the Olden Blade. It already held magic, and I didn't know how the powers already existing there might merge with mine.

I glanced down at Harlyn's disk bow and then remembered the satchel at my side with the two disks. One black and one white.

Perfect.

I set the black disk on the ground in front of me and studied it awhile. Nothing about it was more remarkable than any other disk I'd ever seen. It was a simple metallic circle with a color to designate its purpose.

Black, for death.

The other, white, to separate the soul of the victim from her body, creating a half-life. The eternal punishment.

For my purposes, they both would now have a very different use.

Holding the white disk in my hands, I willed only a single power into the metal, the ability to control the heartbeat of another, as Endrick had used for the Ironhearts. I felt the power empty from me, down to nearly nothing, yet I wasn't worried. As always happened, I knew it would eventually return, as strong as before. But now I had preserved the magic for another use.

The black disk had a higher price, for it was the greatest of all of Endrick's powers, to take a person's magic by killing them. It was the one power I had to protect above all others, and might be the only way to restore myself before this battle was finished.

Sending magic into the black disk felt similar to when Joth had pulled strength from me. I was drained in a most literal sense and was physically weakening. Yet this was different too because I wasn't fighting its release. Instead, I was forcing this element of magic out of me like a fountain would spew its water.

Expelling these two precious powers cost me more than I had expected, but I began to understand why. The first disk was the power over life; the second was the power over death. Nothing greater was in me.

I finally released the black disk when the metal became so hot to the touch that I could not keep hold of it any longer. Etched into the metal was the same symbol that was now a faint scar on my right palm, a square cross, narrowed and slightly curved at the tips. I dropped it into my satchel, then collapsed to the ground, exhausted.

"Kestra!"

Recognizing Darrow's voice, I lifted my head and vaguely saw him running toward me with Rosaleen at his side. While she helped me into a sitting position, he looked up. "Did you fall from the palace windows? How can you still be alive?"

"I had magic."

"Had?"

I gestured to the white disk in front of me. "That one is for you. Should you ever need to use it on me."

Darrow fiercely shook his head, horrified at what I was suggesting. "Do you know what the white disk does to its victim? I never would do that to you, never."

"Take it. And this disk bow too. It's not mine anyway." For some reason, that made me smile. A day ago, I wanted Harlyn dead. Now my conscience was prodded by the thought of having stolen her weapons.

Darrow put his arm around me and helped me to my feet, though I still leaned heavily upon him. Rosaleen stood on my other side, helping to brace me.

"We can get you to Loelle," she said.

I shook my head. "Take me to the palace courtyard."

Darrow stopped walking. "That's not a good idea. Joth is there fighting Simon. It isn't going to end well. Joth will not let Simon win."

"That's why I have to go."

"You can't even stand! What can you do to help him?"

"Joth has the same magic now as Lord Endrick. If the Olden Blade could kill one, it should be able to kill the other."

"You don't know that. And if you're wrong, Joth will not let you walk away from there." I had looked away from Darrow so he counterstepped to catch my attention again. "Listen to me, Kestra. If you enter that courtyard, you will not leave it alive."

This time I stared directly at him. "But I am going to enter because this is my responsibility. I will crawl there if I must, but nothing you do or say will stop me. This may be my last chance."

Darrow sighed and tightened his arm around me, and he and Rosaleen began again to help me walk toward the palace courtyard.

· FORTY-THREE ·

SIMON

Joth believed he was on the verge of victory, but I had no plans to make his claim on the throne this simple.

With his knife headed straight toward my chest, I braced myself, standing perfectly still until the blade was just in front of me. Then I swung my sword at it, connecting with a clash of metals that rang in my ears. The knife careened off sideways, and before Joth had time to react, I raced toward him.

He thrust me backward, but the courtyard had begun to rumble with voices of discontent.

"Make it a fair fight!" someone from the audience yelled.

Joth's face twisted as he glared in that direction; then he responded by pulling his fingers into a fist, corresponding with a desperate cry for help from that same man in the audience. I saw his body collapse and a woman next to him scream out, "What have you done?"

"Kneel to me now." Joth turned to address the crowd. "And no one else has to die."

I used that moment to rush at him, tackling him from behind so that he fell to the ground face-first. He struggled, but I got my hands on his wrists, locking down his body with my legs. Suddenly, I was sapped of strength when Joth rotated one wrist just enough to touch my hand. I fell to the ground, struggling for breath and feeling every cut and bruise in my body swell with pain.

Joth knelt beside me, grabbing my shirt and pulling me into a seated position. "Tell them to kneel," he said. "Tell them or you will die right here."

In the loudest voice I could muster, I said, "Do you see how Joth kneels before me now? He asks that you follow his example and kneel to me as well!"

Furious, Joth reached for me again and surely would have pulled out what life still remained in me, when at my right, I recognized Huge's voice, shouting, "Simon is our king!"

Joth stood, forgetting me. "Who said that?"

"Simon is our king!" another group shouted behind Joth.

"Simon is our king!" So many people began chanting it, Joth didn't know where to place his attention.

Instead, both of his hands clenched into fists and his face tightened into fierce concentration. He was gathering magic such as I suspected Antora had never before seen.

"To your knees!" he screamed, raising his arms, and when he lowered them, the entire audience was forced to kneel. "Now watch as I destroy your so-called king!"

I had lifted myself into a crouching position, still unable to stand on my own, but just as he sent magic toward me, Rawk flew over the platform directly between us, his wings outstretched wide, and Joth fell again. The magic Joth had sent diffused around me, though Rawk had let out a horrifying screech as he was hit by the magic, and his balance wavered as he flew away, injured. I tried to send a thought of comfort to him but could not find him, and that terrified me.

"Protect the king!"

Gabe's words quickly became a rallying cry around the courtyard. Weapons seemed to come out of nowhere and people stood and began pressing toward the platform.

"Protect the king, my brother!"

Above all other noises now thundering within the courtyard, Rosaleen's strong voice easily carried to me, demanding the attention of those who had gathered here. I turned to see her and Darrow pushing forward through the crowd.

For the past several days, I'd been desperate to see her. I'd looked for her around every corner, amidst every group of Ironhearts we'd encountered, and never once had caught a single glimpse of her. Now here she was, but at the worst possible time. I wanted her to be anywhere but in this courtyard.

Unfair as it was to ask, I sent thoughts to Rawk to help Rosaleen, if he could.

This time, Rawk answered. Despite his injuries, he immediately rounded toward us and, with his breath, sent fire down to the edges of the platform, creating a barrier the audience would not cross and which probably created some sort of protection from Joth's magic.

Joth screamed in anger, then waved his fingers, summoning my sword straight into his hands. "When the fire burns down, they will see their king dead by his own weapon."

"They will see a dead king, but it won't be Simon." Kestra leapt onto the platform, untouched by the fire, with the Olden Blade in her hands. Joth turned, but she was charging at him so quickly, he barely had time to react. He grabbed her shoulders as the Olden Blade entered his chest. Something in his touch must have harmed her too, for she let out a cry that pierced the air, pierced my heart. Instinctively, I understood that he was not just taking strength from her. His touch was killing her.

Kestra looked over at me, and I watched the light fade in her eyes, then extinguish. In that same moment, her cry was cut off in a choking silence and then her body went limp. I screamed out her name and ran forward, but even before I caught her, I knew she was dead. I landed on my knees, and when I tried pulling her into my arms, an explosion of light erupted around us and she was ripped away from me.

The light vanished, and a second later, I heard a thud on the ground.

Fearing it might be Kestra, I hardly dared to open my eyes, but when I did, I saw the Olden Blade implanted point down in the platform floor, smoke rising from what appeared to be searing hot metal. Not a drop of blood was on it.

Nor was Kestra anywhere in sight.

Or Joth.

I was alone.

Only then did the fire around me begin to diminish. I realized that no one would have seen what happened, and perhaps with the roar of the flames, they might not even have heard it. They only would have seen a bright flash of light that had instantly vanished from within the flames.

I rose and retrieved my sword. The Olden Blade was still too hot to touch, but I stood near it, desperately calling for Kestra. Fully aware she would not, or could not, answer me. And calling out her name anyway.

With the flames nearly burned out now, the people in the courtyard gasped when they saw I was alone. They probably had no idea what Kestra had just done, what she had sacrificed. They only knew that Joth was no longer here.

Gabe and Harlyn were the first to climb onto the platform. He put an arm around me to offer support, and Harlyn asked, "What just happened?"

As if in answer to her question, moments later, Joth walked out onto a balcony at the front of the palace. He was making an obvious effort to appear as strong as ever, but I'd seen where Kestra stabbed him and he clearly was injured.

But he was alive.

He shouted down, "Victory is mine. The Scarlet Throne is mine. There is no one left to challenge me, so please, my people, accept that and let us be happy."

I stepped forward, shouting back, "Where is Kestra?"

He laughed. "You saw it for yourself, Simon. Your love, Kestra Dallisor, is dead. And so will all of you die if you continue to defy me."

Gabe tugged at my arm. "Come with me. We have to get out of here."

I shook my head, unable to process his words. She had been here only seconds ago, and surely she would return again. Wasn't she immortal now? When her magic regenerated within her, this was where she would come.

Unless she couldn't. Unless she wasn't truly immortal.

Rosaleen reached my side, though she obviously understood

something devastating had happened. She took my arm in hers. "Lean on me."

Joth shouted, "Yes, crawl from here, King of the Banished, King of Nothing and No One. And take your sad Alliance with you. Anyone still here in ten minutes had better be on their knees offering themselves as my servants."

Rosaleen said, "He must be more injured than he is letting on, or he would attack. But that won't last long."

Harlyn pressed a hand against my back. "We must leave, Simon. Please."

By then, Trina had joined us, and I followed her gaze toward the Olden Blade. "Kestra was here, Trina."

"I know, I was in front and heard everything." Trina crouched before the Olden Blade and picked it up with her cloak. "Simon, I know you don't want to hear this, but I think Joth is telling the truth. I think Kestra really is gone."

Gone. Removed. Stopped. All the words we used to avoid saying what really was happening.

I wouldn't say it either, but as my friends and sister led me from the courtyard, the words I was trying not to think about were shattering my world apart.

Kestra was dead.

· FORTY-FOUR ·

SIMON

I truly didn't care.

Whatever the threat, whatever the latest disaster or complaint, I could not make myself care enough to solve it.

Loelle had healed my wounds, and Rosaleen had put a bowl of stew in front of me that I didn't touch. Somehow I had ended up in the Woodcourt library, though I couldn't say exactly how long we'd been meeting, or even what we'd been discussing.

With me was Gabe, who had taken over leadership of the Coracks. Harlyn and Trina sat near him, also Basil and Imri Stout. Closest was Rosaleen, who had her hand over mine, though I couldn't feel it. Each was seated in a circle, all eyes on me, waiting for me to say something.

And I had nothing to offer.

"Did you see the Dallisors kneeling to Joth as we left the courtyard?" Harlyn asked. "I'll bet he invited them into the palace and now they're lying on the floor mostly dead while Joth has made himself whole again."

"I saw them, the cowards." With another squeeze of my hand, Rosaleen added, "Darrow and I were the last people with Kestra before she climbed onto that platform. I think she knew she was going to die, whether the Olden Blade worked or not."

Basil's mind was in a similar place. "If Kestra stabbed Joth directly in the heart with the Olden Blade, then why didn't it work?"

"Kestra was the Infidante tasked with killing Lord Endrick," Trina said. "*Only* Lord Endrick. The Olden Blade contained his magic, not Joth's. Every power that Joth acquired from Endrick probably was damaged when she attacked him, but according to Loelle, he has other powers too."

"Endrick made the Olden Blade to keep himself immortal," Gabe said. "As far as we know, Joth has not created any similar object. He's learned from Endrick's mistake."

"Then we need a new plan." Imri leaned forward. "Surely you have other ideas."

"I don't." My voice sounded as hollow as I felt. "Nobody does."

I stopped before saying what I really believed, which was that Joth's defeat was impossible, especially with our few numbers and thin alliances. And I was no longer content to simply nip at his ankles in a petty rebellion. If we would continue to fight, it had to be for the purpose of winning. Which, as far as I could tell, had no chance of success.

"You have Rawk," Harlyn offered. "He defended you against Joth during the duel."

Loelle had examined Rawk following the duel, or attempted it. He had swatted his tail at her, which for a dragon was no small thing, then flown away. Loelle had assured me he would be all right, but he had no interest in the medicines of man or of magic.

I nodded, barely able to process what that meant for us, if anything. So I stood and said, "You all are welcome to talk for as long as you wish, and I hope you will come up with something useful. Thank you all, for everything you did today."

I started out the door but, behind me, heard Gabe stand and push back his chair. "Hail Simon, my king."

"Simon, my king," Harlyn echoed, also on her feet, followed immediately by Trina.

Rosaleen stood as well. "Simon, my brother, my king. I suppose I have to be nicer to you now."

I glanced back and smiled faintly. Beside them, Basil stood and offered his drink to me in toast. "Well, you're not *my* king, but you are *a* king, and I know you will be a great one."

Still seated, Imri folded her arms. "He is not a true king until he defeats that insolent brat now occupying the Scarlet Throne." Then she looked up at me. "But *when* you do, and you will, you will be a great king."

I gave each of them a grateful nod, then left the library. I didn't go directly to my room but instead wandered out to Woodcourt's yard and called for Rawk.

He was longer to arrive than usual, though when I inspected him for wounds, he appeared all right other than a small chip in a scale on his right side.

"Where do you go when you're not with me?" I asked, then more to myself, added, "Where does anyone go when they are the last of their kind?"

Kestra had been the last of her kind too. I had never truly appreciated how that must have felt for her. I never had fully appreciated *her*. Time after time, she found herself in a position where she could not win, and she had always found a way through it. Always.

Until today.

Rawk's patience seemed to be wearing thin. I had been trying to recall what I had intended by calling him to me in the first place. My only thought was that I wanted to go someplace where every direction I looked didn't remind me of Kestra.

I climbed onto Rawk's back and said nothing, neither aloud nor through silent communication. After a moment, Rawk flew us into the air anyway.

There was nothing specific I wanted to see, and indeed, nothing of any note caught my attention. I did notice a great number of loaded carts headed out of Highwyn, which was little surprise.

On the outskirts of Highwyn sat the two sentries, the enormous rock statues, one to welcome those who came, the other to bid farewell to those who left. Surprisingly, they gave me hope. They had been here before Endrick, survived the War of Devastation, and many battles between the Halderians and Dallisors before that. They would outlast Joth as well.

As we continued, gradually All Spirits Forest came into view. Despite the winter elsewhere, here the forest was alive like springtime. Green leaves budded on strong tall trees, grass was growing, and the air was full of a perfume that I caught even as high as we were.

At my request, Rawk flew us down into the forest, landing near a small flowing river. I slid to the ground and began to wander among the trees, my senses taking in a place that for the first time in a generation was fully alive.

Eventually I came to a small rock home, bearing evidence of someone who had recently lived here. I entered and saw ashes in the fireplace, mice scattering from a table where food must have been, and, on a chair in the corner, Kestra's cloak. The one she had been wearing before Loelle took her away from Nessel in the night.

Kestra had been here.

I picked up the cloak and held it in my arms, no longer fighting my grief. I nursed it until the sadness turned to anger at all those who had wanted her dead for no reason other than who she was, who we had all forced her to become. But when I looked inward, my anger grew. Hadn't I been as responsible as anyone else?

I closed my eyes, imagining her in my arms again, and then hurting all the more because of how impossible it was. My anger was grief, and my grief roared like a tornado within me.

I never should have come here and couldn't stay here any longer, dwelling in despair and hopelessness. So I stood, folding the cloak to carry with me to Woodcourt, another place where every corner would echo with some memory of her. But at least I had distractions there.

In my hurry to leave, I stumbled over a small table beside the chair, knocking a book to the floor. I picked it up and thumbed through the pages, quickly realizing this was Joth's diary.

Curious, I briefly browsed through the entries. He must have had several journals, for the first page on this book was only a little over a month old, and every day contained a new entry.

"Mother has spoken of a plan involving the girl she brought from the Hiplands," he had written. "She believes the girl can help us. I'm wary of her plan . . ."

A few pages later, "The girl, Kestra Dallisor, seems to be able to draw in the curse from these woods. Mother worries what it will do to her. I worry what it will do to Mother, to be so near a corrupted person."

On the following page, "Mother has just explained her ultimate plan for bringing Kestra here. I don't like it. I think it's too risky . . ."

And a few pages later, "Mother insists that I try to connect powers with Kestra. She believes that our people cannot be corrupted by magic, and I hope she is right, but I cannot deny that I am worried . . ."

The final entry was only half-written, but it read, "I have decided to try connecting powers with her. It's our only hope. If I corrupt, may my people forgive me. But if this works, my people will live once again."

I closed the book, incredulous at what I had read. The person who wrote these pages was nothing like the Joth who now occupied the Scarlet Throne, or even the arrogant Joth I had first met at Woodcourt. What I had seen from him yesterday and in recent days was only an evidence of his corruption, but it was not who he really was.

Yet I would have to destroy him all the same.

Just as he had destroyed Kestra, who had been every bit as innocent once.

With that single thought, every ounce of pity I might have felt for Joth evaporated. He would get what he deserved, and sooner than he might have expected.

· FORTY-FIVE ·

KESTRA

I awoke to a searing pain in my shoulder, shooting heat through my arm that brought tears to my eyes and a scream to my throat. A hand instantly covered my mouth, and I heard a whisper, "I know, I know, but it's all right. Please try to relax."

Tears fell to my cheeks, and my breathing became ragged. This was the same shoulder where Harlyn had shot me not many days ago, and that earlier wound had not fully healed.

"You must be as quiet as possible," the voice said. "We're inside the palace."

I nodded, then the hand left my mouth. I fumbled for the disk blade that was lodged in my shoulder, though each miss at grabbing it only made the pain worse. Someone kept trying to push my hand away from the wound. How had this even happened? I must have been unconscious when I'd been shot.

No, not unconscious. I'd been dead. That had been the purpose of this disk, to restore my life.

I tried again to reach the disk. I felt its edge but had no strength to grip it. I needed to do it. The object that had saved my life would kill me if I could not remove it.

Failing yet again, I brushed away the tears in my eyes, frustrated with being weak at a time I had to be strong. When I tried for the disk a third time, Darrow came into my field of vision. He must have been the one who had whispered to me before, and now he said, "I'll pull it out; then you need to take as much strength from me as you can to heal yourself." I shook my head and he added, "Kestra, you must. This wound is serious."

I shook my head again. "I can't. There's no magic."

"Because you're weakened—"

"Joth took it all in the same moment that I stabbed him. He took everything . . . that's what killed me. I have no magic, Darrow."

He crouched near me and took my hands, looking into my eyes despite the low light of wherever we were. "Take strength from me, Kestra, try it."

I obeyed, but it was just as I had told him. I felt nothing of magic in myself, had no sensation of abilities beyond those of any other person, and, most of all, felt none of the heat inside me that had become my constant companion, nor the ice. I was simply me.

Simply me, with a white disk lodged into my shoulder. This was the same one I had given to Darrow earlier, containing one ability only—to control a person's heartbeat. A disk designed to separate a person's body from their soul had reunited mine.

I'd had the idea from the story the Ironheart told me, of how Tenger had once killed Sir Henry, only to find Sir Henry alive the following day. Endrick had the ability to restore life. That was the one power I had put into this disk. Darrow must have understood that I gave him the disk for a reason, and the disk did exactly as I had hoped.

"The disk must come out," Darrow said. "I'm so very sorry."

I nodded and gritted my teeth. After a gentle squeeze to my hands, he stood and put his hands on the blade. "Count to three," he said.

I closed my eyes. "One, two—"

And he yanked the blade from my shoulder. Once again, I felt as though fire was piercing me from all directions. I clamped one hand over my own mouth to keep from screaming out loud; then, when it was over, he immediately pressed a cloth to my shoulder and began tying it. "We've got to get you to Loelle," he said.

I shook my head, but he said, "She's with the Coracks and on their side, not her son's."

"Are we really in the palace?"

Darrow nodded. "I carried you out of the throne room while Joth was on the balcony, announcing your death. We're in a storage room, but he did gain some servants after the duel. No doubt they are searching for you."

"How did you know to use the disk blade?"

"When you gave it to me, you said I should keep it if I ever needed to use it on you. I didn't understand what you had meant until I found you here."

Tears fell to my cheeks again, this time for a very different reason. "I'm so sorry, for everything before. What I was, what I did."

He put a hand to my cheek. "Hush now, that wasn't you."

"Thank you . . . Father," I whispered.

In the room next to us, we heard something topple over. That could only be Joth's minions. "We have to leave," he said, pulling a cloak over my shoulders. "There's another exit from this room."

He scooped me into his arms, and I leaned my head against his shoulder, trying to stay conscious but only doing a fair job of it. He was hurrying so fast, I was jostled in his arms, which hurt furiously, but there was nothing he could do.

"Hold on," he said as he opened the storage room door. "You must hold on."

I didn't see how it mattered. Whatever he did here, I couldn't possibly have long to live, though I couldn't tell him that because he was my father and I wouldn't hurt him with the truth. If Loelle was with the Coracks, then after healing me, I would be given to Captain Tenger, who had already passed a judgment of death against me. Maybe I deserved it; I no longer knew.

Darrow carried me through a servant's passage, and from there we darted from one shadow to another, hoping to be less visible. The next time I opened my eyes, dark skies were overhead. The palace walls still surrounded us, but we had cleared the worst of the obstacles.

Or so I believed, until Darrow said in a low voice, "Someone is behind us."

"Let me down," I said. "See, the palace gates are straight ahead. You will go faster without me."

"You see the gates, then?" Darrow stopped running, gently lowered me to my feet, and pulled the hood of the cloak over my head. "Get yourself there, Kestra."

I shook my head. "They want me, not you. I won't make it anyway."

"They don't know that you're alive, and in this darkness, they've only seen me. I'll give you time to escape, but you must go now."

With a loud cry to draw attention to himself, he began running back the way we had come. When I could see him no longer, I began hobbling toward the exit, one terrible step at a time. Now that Joth had use of Endrick's magic, he could find me beyond the gates. My only chance was that he truly thought I was dead. And for now, my only goal was to get past that gate.

Behind me, I heard Darrow engage in a fight with someone, and I walked faster, wishing my injured arm would allow me to cover my ears. I could not bear to hear the fight and wonder if my father's chance of survival was any better than mine.

After what seemed like hours, I exited the palace walls, then aimed toward the nearest clump of trees, where I hoped I'd be better hidden than if I were on the roads. I made it there, but the effort of walking so fast on the uneven snow had cost me dearly.

My shoulder screamed with pain, and I knew the bandage Darrow had given me had come loose. He wanted to take me to Loelle, certain that she could save me, and maybe she could. But at what price?

I could not return to the Coracks, not with their plans for me.

I wasn't sure where the Coracks had set up camp, but I had last seen them at Woodcourt, so I needed to avoid that place. If I kept to the woods, I might have a chance of getting past Woodcourt without being noticed. And then . . . I didn't know what, or where. Or how I would survive.

I needed Darrow.

I waited in the woods for a long time, hoping he would join me, hoping to see or hear any sign of what had happened to him. When he didn't come, my hopes dimmed. Maybe he hadn't come because he couldn't come.

I rested until my eyes became so heavy that I knew if I shut them, I might not wake. The night was cold, and I felt all of it. I had begun to shiver, and the tips of my fingers were becoming numb.

With no other choice, I put one foot forward and began to walk again. One step after another, I promised myself that I didn't need to fight, didn't need to be or do anything greater than myself. I only needed to take the next step.

And I wasn't sure I could even do that much.

· FORTY-SIX ·

SIMON

My heart felt like lead as Rawk carried me away from All Spirits Forest. Kestra had been in those forbidden woods for weeks, close enough that I easily should have been able to find her.

If I had known, I would have found a way inside, at whatever price, or risk, or effort. And if I had done so, I might have staved off the corruption. More important, I could have warned her against connecting powers with Joth, spreading corruption to him.

I had never in my life felt worse than at that moment, and in the end, what was her sacrifice for? Yes, maybe she fulfilled her task as Infidante, and Endrick was dead, but what good did that do for us?

I sat up taller on Rawk's back, absorbing that thought. Yes, Kestra had fulfilled her task as Infidante. Upon completion of the quest, she had no longer been the Infidante. Stabbing Joth with the Olden Blade might have injured him physically, but only an Infidante with authority to use the Olden Blade could kill him.

We needed a new Infidante.

I sent that thought to Rawk, to hurry us to Woodcourt, and indeed we did fly in that direction, but then we passed directly overhead.

Rawk, go back. I sent the thought first, and when he failed to respond, I said aloud, "Rawk, this isn't right!"

Rawk began a dive, but we were still farther up the hill from Woodcourt, closer to the palace than I wanted to be on my own. With little concern for the danger we were in, Rawk steered us through a narrow breach in the thick canopy of trees. Though most had lost their leaves for the winter, I had no desire to crash through their branches.

He landed us in a small clearing, but I wasn't going anywhere. He knew what I wanted, and I'd wait as long as it took for him to obey me.

Rawk's only response was to widen his wings and arch his back, forcing me to the ground. I stood up straight, furious. "This is important!"

He remained still, leaving me with no choice but to walk from the forest alone, cursing his stubbornness. Finally, I heard the crackle of dried leaves and turned, expecting to see Rawk following me. Instead, from the same position where he'd stood before, he pulled his wings in.

At the very moment Kestra entered the clearing.

Impossible.

My heart crashed against my chest, and time itself froze. This was more than impossible, more than I could make myself understand. But there she was.

Once Kestra saw me, she wrapped her cloak tighter around her body and briefly looked back as if she was considering leaving. I couldn't allow that.

"Kestra, don't go. Please don't go."

She looked at me again and seemed to want to say something, but her eyes were full of tears and she swallowed hard, as if choking on her own words.

There was so much I had to say to her too, but for all I had thought I would say if a moment like this ever came, suddenly I couldn't think of a single word.

Still facing me, she took a step backward, like a frightened deer that knew it was trapped.

That was how she felt then, trapped.

As if I were the enemy.

Finally, she spoke. "Simon, I have to—"

"I thought you were dead." I began walking toward her.

"Listen, I must tell you—"

"I thought you were dead, Kestra."

And like that, I was directly in front of her, staring at her as if she were a forgotten memory from a past life. Maybe she was.

Tears filled my eyes. "You saved my life today. But then I saw you fall when the Olden Blade failed. Then when Joth announced you were dead . . . well, I believed it. I'm so sorry."

"I . . ." Her voice trailed off with that single word. She tried again. "Simon, I—"

"I know. But everything is all right now."

"It isn't." She widened her cloak, and for the first time, I saw the hastily wrapped bandage around her shoulder, bleeding through the fabric.

Immediately, I scooped her into my arms and raced her toward Rawk. I kept a tight hold on her as we flew into the air.

"Woodcourt isn't far," I said. "Loelle is there. She can heal this."

"No one else can know." Kestra's eyes were becoming heavy. "They'll kill me."

"I'll protect you from them, I promise."

But she only shook her head and leaned against my chest, too weak to stay awake any longer. Her final words broke what remained of my heart. "How can you say that? You planned to kill me too."

· FORTY-SEVEN ·

KESTRA

I awoke in a real bed with a thick mattress and soft, warm blankets, and, more important, a familiar bed. I'd been here before. This was the bed from my childhood. Where I'd grown up at Woodcourt.

Suddenly alarmed, I tried to sit up but felt a pinch in my shoulder and had to lie back down. How had I come to be here? Was I a captive? Then I remembered, at least a little.

Darrow had shot me with the disk blade I had created, one with magic to control a person's heartbeat. It restored my life but in time, without care, would have taken my life again. The wound created by the disk had been deep.

I vaguely remembered leaving the palace, though Darrow had stayed behind to protect me. If he had survived that, he was Joth's captive now, possibly an Ironheart himself. And if he was, I had no hope of rescuing him.

No hope, without magic.

But no corruption either.

Someone stirred behind me and I angled my head to see Simon in a chair near the fireplace, asleep.

I remembered him finding me, though I couldn't explain how

he'd known to come to that clearing. He would wonder how I was alive, a far more complicated question.

And it wouldn't be the only explanation Simon would want. I couldn't imagine the number of questions he might have, and certainly couldn't begin to form answers to even the simplest questions in my mind. How could I explain what I didn't fully understand?

I did remember the feeling of corruption—the arrogance, the paranoia, and the way it twisted my mind and my heart. Most of all, it robbed me of the most basic of feelings: love.

If that had cost me Simon's love, I had no one to blame but myself.

Perhaps it didn't matter. If I was here with the Coracks, it would probably also cost my life. Even before I'd had magic, most of the Coracks had already wanted me dead. I couldn't pretend that was going to change now.

I needed to leave while it was still early and I could hope to get out of Woodcourt without being spotted. Hanging from one bedpost was the satchel I'd been wearing when I first came here. Hopefully my boots and cloak would be just as easy to find.

As silently as possible, I pushed aside the covers of my bed but rolled my eyes when I realized I now wore a sleeping gown. I could hardly traipse through Woodcourt in this.

If this was my old room, surely some of my old clothes still remained here.

"You're awake."

I looked back as Simon stood from his chair. His eyes were heavy, as if he had suddenly awoken from a deep sleep, and the tone of his voice revealed nothing of his feelings about me being here.

He must have noticed me looking at my sleeping gown because he gestured to it and said, "Loelle did that. She couldn't leave you in the dress you had been wearing, not as torn up as it was."

My eyes darted. "I need clothes. I cannot stay here."

"Kestra, it's all right." He spoke slowly, as if fearing at the faintest hiccup, I might run. Maybe he knew I was already considering it.

"Nothing here is all right." Every sound from the corridors made my heart stop. I couldn't help but wonder if an army was gathering on the other side, if they already knew I was here and were stringing the noose. Whether they did or not, it was only a matter of time. "Other than Loelle, does anyone else know I'm here?"

"Rosaleen knows. I had to send her to fetch Loelle. But we can trust them. You're safe here."

"Am I? What will they do if they discover me?"

Simon nodded as if he understood. He walked to my door, cracked it open enough to look out both ways, then closed the door and leaned against it. "As soon as possible, I'll ask Rosaleen to begin searching for a place we can hide you until your magic returns."

"It won't return, Simon. It's gone."

His brows pressed low, and he shook his head. "Gone? That's not possible. Our belief was that we could not separate the magic from you if you were to live."

Simon was staring at me as he often had before, his eyes full of hurt and affection, and an obvious worry that if he trusted me too much, I would break his heart again. He was keeping a safe distance, which communicated everything about how his feelings for me had disintegrated. But there was no way around this conversation. I only had to hope that at the end of it, he would still be here.

I said, "Loelle's theories were correct. So long as I lived, magic could not be pulled from me. I had to die."

"You died," Simon quickly echoed. "I saw you die, Kes."

"Yes. When I attacked Joth with the Olden Blade, he returned the attack, taking everything from me, my life, my magic. My corruption."

He shook his head, still skeptical. "Then how are you alive?"

Explaining myself was proving more difficult than I had anticipated. It required me to relive the worst of my memories, and to feel the horrible weight of my crimes. I told him about the black disk I had created, how it contained the piece of Endrick's magic that could restore life, as it had once restored Sir Henry's life when Tenger—

"Tenger killed Sir Henry," Simon said. "He told me about that, or tried to."

"Simon, I'm just me. And I know it's too late to change anything for us. I know about your betrothal with Harlyn. But I'm asking you to believe what I've told you."

His eyes welled with tears, but he swallowed them down before walking over to my old wardrobe and pulling out a deep blue gown with cream lacing at the torso. It was one that had been prepared for my arrival from the Lava Fields months ago, so at least it should fit me, even if it was more formal than I'd usually worn since becoming the Infidante. And it was a vast improvement from my sleeping gown.

"This should be a simple one to get into because it laces up the front," he said. "The Alliance cannot offer you any ladies-in-waiting—"

"I require none."

He hesitated, then cautiously nodded before continuing. "I doubt you'd want Trina or Harlyn's help here either. Or Imri Stout's."

Despite the need for quiet, I laughed softly; then he said he'd find me something to eat while I changed clothes. I was finishing up the lacing when he returned with some bread and cold slices of meat.

"It's simple food," he said, setting the tray on a small table in front of my fireplace. "Nobody here is a cook."

"It's perfect."

He sat across from me, eyeing me like we were strangers. I tried to talk to him, but each time I did, his doubts about me were evident in his eyes. How could I say more when he was struggling to believe what I'd already said? Maybe none of it mattered. If Rosaleen could help me find a place to hide, I'd leave at my first opportunity and no one would ever see me again.

I'd never see Simon again, which created a desperate ache in my heart. But that was better than sitting across from him as he pretended his hand wasn't resting on the hilt of his sword, or that he had clearly left my door unlocked in case he should need to call for help. Anything was better than having to sit across from him now, wanting to be closer to him, to rest in his arms again, but to know that was no longer a possibility.

Finally he said, "I think the best approach is to speak first to the people who are most likely to be on our side. Then we can use their help to convince the others who are most against you."

"No matter who speaks to him, Tenger will never change his mind about me."

Simon lowered his brows. "Tenger is dead, Kes. Joth killed him."

My breath lodged in my throat and I struggled for a way to respond. My relationship with Tenger had always been uneasy, and I had understood nearly from the beginning that he thought of me as little more than a tool to accomplish his goals. Yet it still hurt to hear this news, especially because I knew I bore some of the blame.

Finally, I set down my cup. "I'm so sorry. When I shared powers with Joth, I didn't know any of this would happen. I couldn't see it."

"I know that." His voice was more tender than I'd expected. "And we'll make the people here understand it too."

I shook my head. "We will never get everyone to understand. As long as I'm here, I will be a source of division within the Alliance. I will splinter one person from another; I will divide you from the people you are supposed to lead. We both know that is true."

"We'll just have to find a way!" Simon ran his fingers through his hair, and for the first time, he began to look as anxious as I felt. "We'll talk to them, tell them everything you've told me—"

"Do you believe what I've said?"

Simon stopped, and when he locked eyes with me, my heart stopped, waiting for his answer. Finally, he whispered, "A lot has happened. I just need some time."

"So it's not about convincing the others here to accept me. It's about convincing you."

He leaned forward, and his gaze intensified. "I believe you, Kes, every word you've spoken here. I just need time to understand it all. Most people in the Alliance will feel the same way, and some may never understand. The person we need to worry about most is Gabe."

He was right. Gabe and I had not been on good terms for some time, though, admittedly, Gabe had his reasons. Among them, I had nearly poisoned Simon to death.

"Gabe will not believe there is any chance you could be completely recovered," Simon added, then fell silent as the door opened. I caught my breath in my throat. Gabe was on the other side.

"Indeed, I don't believe it," he said, stepping into the room with three other well-armed Coracks, his eye on me as if I were about to attack.

Simon stood, crossing in front of me with his hand at his sword. "How did you know?"

"Drops of blood leading from where Rawk landed last night into Woodcourt. Someone noticed you loading a particularly large plate of food this morning and taking it to a room other than your own." Gabe shrugged. "It wasn't the hardest thing to figure out, Hatch."

Simon drew his sword, and I stood behind him. "Kestra is staying here, under my protection."

"No, she isn't." Gabe nudged the other Coracks forward. One raised a disk bow at me. Two others aimed at Simon. "Don't make this a fight," Gabe added. "All of us will lose if you do."

Simon huffed, then slowly lowered his sword. The disk archers remained in position.

"We're a fair people." Gabe pulled out the same binding cord as he had once used to hold me prisoner in the Slots, and wrapped it again around my wrists. When I'd had magic, I could have escaped this with a single thought and casual tug of my arms, but now I would remain bound until Gabe released me.

"Is that really necessary?" Simon asked. "She's not our enemy."

"That's what the trial will determine. Whatever is decided, Simon, you must accept her fate. If you refuse, we'll pass sentence right now."

Simon looked over at me, and I felt his concern as a pit in my gut. "When is the trial?"

Gabe frowned back at him. "We're ready for her now."

· FORTY-EIGHT ·

SIMON

Despite Kestra's assurances that she had no ability to attack Gabe, he still insisted that her hands be bound before we left the room.

She eyed him steadily as the binding cord went around her wrists. I wasn't sure what she was thinking, but I knew her enough to know that she was masking a deep fear of what was about to happen.

I could not hide my emotions nearly as well. My legs felt weak as I followed Kestra into the corridor. All I could do was to hope that this trial would be fair, as Gabe had promised, but given all that had happened over the past few days, I doubted that Gabe and I had the same understanding of justice.

We were led to the ballroom of Woodcourt, the same place where, not so long ago, Basil and Kestra had come to be married. I had stood near the far wall, watching for an opportunity to get her out of Woodcourt. Should things go poorly, I might need to try the same escape again.

But it would be impossible this time. The room was full of Alliance members, most of them armed. They parted for us to enter but quickly closed the gap behind us.

I leaned in to Kestra. "You are not here alone. I am on your side."

"You may be the only one," she replied.

A dais was already in place, stretching across the entire front of the room. Five chairs were set in a row on the left side with a single seat on the right that was offered to Kestra. She gave me one final smile of feigned confidence before stepping up. She attempted to sit tall, to seem unafraid, yet she looked so small up there, alone. Her hair was still undone, so it fell loosely around her shoulders, and her eyes intently scanned the audience. Her bound hands rested in her lap with the other end of the binding cord on Gabe's wrist, and she interlocked her fingers to lessen their shaking.

Gabe stood in the center of the platform. "It has been decided that each group here should have a vote. Guilt can be decided by majority vote, but innocence must be unanimous."

"How is that fair?" I asked. "That has never been our standard!"

"But it must be now. The lives of every person in this room, indeed, of every citizen of Antora and beyond, will be affected by this vote. We must have a standard that ensures us all of her innocence. So if you have been chosen to represent your people, come forward."

Trina was the first to step forward for the Coracks, and Basil came next for Reddengrad. I was already tallying votes and believed they would vote in Kestra's favor. Commander Reese of my cavalry came forward for the Halderians and would likely vote against her, as I expected would Imri Stout, from the Brill. An Antoran man came forward, introducing himself as Renn. I knew nothing of him, which made me nervous. Surely he knew that Kestra was raised as a Dallisor, and that would hardly work in her favor.

Five judges, and three likely votes against her. Even by our usual standards, Kestra had already lost this trial.

"I am here for my people too," a woman said, stepping onto the dais.

"We have all groups here," Gabe said. "Who are you with?"

"My name is Halina, and I am Navanese. Until yesterday, I was a half-life. Kestra restored me; I am here on behalf of those she has restored, and those she did not."

Gabe nodded. "Someone get us a sixth chair."

As they did, I glanced over at Kestra, whose eyes betrayed a greater fear at seeing Halina than anyone else. And she likely had a good reason to be nervous, based on Halina's cold expression.

"Let's begin," Gabe said. "Kestra Dallisor, what can you offer us in your defense?"

Gabe had to ask the question a second time before Kestra tore her attention away from Halina. But when she did, she spoke calmly. "I can offer nothing at all until I know who you are putting on trial, and for what charges."

Gabe's brows furrowed. "The answer to who is on trial should be obvious."

"But it's not. Am I on trial for being a Dallisor, for having been raised in the Dominion? Or am I being tried as a half-Endrean, for having a similar bloodline as Lord Endrick? I am also half-Halderian as well as the heir to Woodcourt, which, in the absence of both Lord Endrick and my adoptive father, makes me the heir to the Scarlet Throne. So do you try me as your queen?"

Gabe said, "Defend yourself with whichever of those identities best justifies your actions. For the charges against you are many, and they are serious. You are charged with treason, with the murder of hundreds of Ironhearts, not to mention all those who were assaulted by your magic. You are charged with the attempted murder of Simon Hatch, now a king. And with the attempted possession of a throne that does not belong to you, but to the people of Antora to choose for themselves who will rule there. How do you plead for these crimes?"

"I cannot deny anything that I have done," she said. "But I will deny that they were crimes."

Gabe had been studying the reaction of the audience to her confession of guilt, but now he turned back to her, genuinely confused. "Treason? Murder? Corruption—you deny these are crimes?"

"Is treason a crime when the Coracks seek to replace the ruler?" She looked at Gabe directly. "Are you a traitor, Gabe? Or a patriot?"

Caught off guard, he stumbled through his words. "I am . . . I have only sought for . . . for what I believe is best for my country."

"If that is the standard, then you must either pronounce me innocent or else offer your own neck beside mine when we hang."

I glanced over at the judges. All of them were nodding except for Halina and Imri, who exchanged a brief whispered conversation. That worried me.

Recovering, Gabe said, "There is also murder. Do you deny poisoning Simon Hatch last fall, the effects of which nearly killed him?"

Kestra looked down at me, attempting to remain calm, but I saw the sorrow in her eyes and I shook my head back at her, hoping she knew that I understood why she had done it. She said, "I concede that I was attempting to escape after Simon kidnapped me."

"And what of the Ironheart soldiers you tricked into lowering their weapons only five nights ago? After they did, you and Joth ordered their slaughter."

That prompted Kestra's first big reaction. She sat up straighter and vehemently shook her head. "I swear that I did not know Joth was going to kill them. When I made the offer to set them free, that was sincere."

Gabe's eyes narrowed, and he stared directly at her. "If that is true, then why did you leave with him? If you were truly shocked by those actions, I'd expect you to get as far away from Joth as you could."

"That wasn't possible," she said. "We were about to attack Lord Endrick. If I changed plans then, the attack would have failed!"

From the line of judges, Halina said, "And during that attack, you ordered half-lives into your service. You must have known what Endrick would do to them."

"I didn't know!"

"The judges may not speak," Gabe said, though it was too late. The damage had been done.

Gabe continued. "How many of our own people did you assault with your magic, stealing as much strength as you needed for yourself, no matter the cost to them? Either you killed them, or you nearly did, on more than one occasion."

"I took nothing more than I needed, and only when I needed it." Kestra's tone was becoming increasingly anxious.

"But when was it your right to take anything from them at all?" Gabe asked.

"When I became the Infidante!" Kestra nearly shouted the words, though in frustration more than anger. "When suddenly I became this person who alone could kill Lord Endrick! Did anyone really believe there would be no price for that, that no sacrifices would have to be made other than by me? Gabe, you have seen me in battle, and you have been with me when I have had to make those decisions. You know for yourself that I never touched any life without a reason."

Gabe let the effect of her words settle in the room before he said, "I saw it when the reason was selfishness. What about those who have been killed in your place when you refused to come forward?"

She tilted her head. "Who do you mean?"

"Simon's mother, Tillie."

That seemed to rob her of her breath. Kestra only lowered her eyes, and in a voice almost too soft to hear, she whispered, "Guilty."

· FORTY-NINE ·

KESTRA

I had entered this trial thinking that I was prepared for anything for which I might be accused and had believed that I had defended myself well.

Until this moment.

Gabe had brought Simon's mother into this trial, and suddenly I no longer cared to fight. Maybe while under the influence of so much corruption, I had dismissed her death, but now, my senses had returned to me every whisper of heartache that I had carried since the moment I'd first understood the danger she was in. What was the point of defending myself now, when he had opened this festering wound, one almost beyond my ability to bear? If this was Gabe's route to my conviction, then maybe he was right.

"You admit your guilt, then," Gabe said.

"She tried to save my mother." Simon stepped forward, almost directly in front of me but addressing the judges. "I was there. I stopped her from entering my mother's home. She fought me and begged me to let her go, but we couldn't lose the Infidante." Then his eyes settled on Gabe. "Kestra fought to save you too, once you entered that same home. That's when she finally got her way. Did you know that, Gabe, that she sacrificed herself to save you?"

From the corner of my eye, I saw Gabe look at me, but I kept my head down.

Simon continued. "The consequences of what she did led to Lord Endrick crushing her heart. She needed magic to survive it, something that would never have been necessary had she *selfishly* kept her place while you were killed that night."

Gabe went silent for some time after that. I needed the silence too, to gather my own emotions. Was it possible that Simon no longer blamed me for his mother's death? Could I hope for that?

Finally, in a quieter voice, Gabe said, "Whether she wanted the magic or not, and whether it is fair or not, she has become corrupted. Like any infection, if it is not healed, it is fatal. In Kestra's case, it could be fatal to all of us here as well."

I looked over at him. Nothing in this trial was more important than making him understand this single issue. "The corruption is gone. All magic I once had, that I've ever had, is gone."

"Impossible!" Gabe crossed in front of me, his expression leaving no doubt that he believed I was lying. "Loelle assured us that she investigated every hope for pulling magic from you and none of them would work without killing you."

"It is not impossible." I held up my bound arms. "Do you think I would accept this if with a breath of magic I could pull my hands apart and set myself free?"

"Can you prove the magic is gone?" Gabe asked.

From the far end of the room, I saw a person push forward, his head cloaked, but he lowered the hood once he reached the front of the crowd.

I had already recognized him. "Father!" His face was bruised and his expression was strained, but he was here and alive. That alone gave me hope and a joy beyond anything I could have imagined, even given my circumstances.

Darrow smiled at me, as if to say everything would be all right. Somehow, despite the rumbling pit in my stomach and the persistent throbbing in my head, I believed him. I believed my father.

Standing beside Simon, Darrow addressed the judges directly. "Loelle was always correct. Magic cannot be taken from a person without killing them. That's what happened to Kestra on that dueling platform. She was dead when I found her, but she had left behind a means with which I could start her heart beating again."

"Through magic," Gabe said.

"The magic was used on her," Darrow said. "It didn't come from within her."

"How do we know that?" Gabe turned back to me. "Kestra, none of us here, myself included, wants to pronounce you guilty of anything, I swear that. But if there is still magic within you, then corruption will follow. Can you prove that it is gone?"

A hush fell over the crowd. If I lost the trial, this would be the reason why. But I would not bow down to this fight.

"Prove that you wanted a fair trial," I replied, feeling my temper begin to burn. To the judges, I added, "Prove that your decision wasn't already made long before this trial began, that you came here with every intention of giving me a chance at freedom. If you cannot prove these simple things, then how dare you vote against me?"

"They are not on trial," Gabe said. "Please, Kestra, there must be some way to assure us the corruption is gone. Give us that proof, and I will call for a vote right now."

"How can I prove what is not?" I asked. "Can I prove that I have never seen a falling star? Never danced in the moonlight? Can I prove what is not in my mind, not in my heart?"

"Then how can we set you free?" Gabe shook his head. "I'm sorry, Kestra, I really am."

"I can prove it." Darrow pulled a confused-looking Harlyn forward from the audience and spoke to her. "Shoot me with your disk bow. Somewhere that might be fatal if I am not given the strength to heal."

I stood, shouting, "Father, no!"

"That is my daughter," Darrow said to the judges. "If there is even the tiniest bit of magic still within her, she will use it to save me. If she does not, it will only be because she cannot. And then you must find her innocent."

"No!" I started to run down the dais, but two Coracks behind me each grabbed an arm. I searched for any magic within me to drop the two of them to the ground, I genuinely did. If I had found any at all, I would have done it, no matter what it would have meant for me.

"That is my offer, then," Darrow said to Gabe. "I will provide the proof you require for her innocence."

"Don't do this!" I cried. "Gabe, I confess. I confess to the accusations, every one of them. We all know you were going to punish me anyway. So do what you will to me, but do not allow this."

Simon stepped between Harlyn and Darrow. "Gabe, this has gone too far. If you order Harlyn to shoot this innocent man, I will take the disk myself."

"But I am not targeting you, nor Darrow." Harlyn aimed her disk bow directly at me. "Kestra has confessed, and now she must pay."

"Harlyn, no!" Simon cried.

"If it saves Darrow, then let her do it!" I shouted. "I've lost him too many times already. It will destroy me to lose another person that I love."

The room had gone still, and I had all but stopped breathing. I closed my eyes and waited for the inevitable. I'd been struck with a disk before, I knew what to expect. It would bite, the sting would spread from the wound, then it would be over.

I waited, but nothing happened. And when I finally opened my eyes, Harlyn was lowering her bow. She said, "There is your proof, Gabe. The corrupted cannot love."

If there had been silence before, a single falling snowflake could have been detected in here now.

"Call for the vote," Simon said.

Behind Gabe, Trina stood. "My vote is innocent, on all charges."

Basil immediately followed. "Innocent."

Next, the Antoran stood. "We have no love for the Dallisors, but she is clearly not a Dallisor. We have no love for the Endreans, but there seems to be no magic in her. The fact that this girl has had to bear the weight of both those cursed houses is punishment enough. Innocent."

Halina, the girl who had been a half-life, stood. She had stared at me for the entire trial, without a glimmer of sympathy. I was terrified of what she might say, which only worsened when she began. "It was my plan from the beginning to vote against you. I can admit that because my reasons were just. You restored my life only because our king forced you to do it. And when you did it, you robbed me of my magic, a magic you now claim is completely gone, which means what you took from me can never be restored."

Tears had welled in my eyes, and all the words that came to my mind were inadequate to explain myself. I was so deeply sorry, and yet, if I were in the situation again, I would have to do the same thing. How could I possibly tell her that?

Then Halina said, "If those were the charges of this trial, I would be the vote that determined your execution. But you are charged with treason and murder and corruption. If you are guilty of treason, then so are we all. I was one of those who obeyed Joth's orders to kill the Ironhearts. I cannot find you guilty of murder and justify myself. You are also charged with corruption, and you were corrupt, Kestra. I know the hold it had on you. However, nothing I saw then remains in you now. Reluctantly, I must vote innocent."

I hadn't realized how long it had been since I'd breathed, but finally I exhaled and looked over at Simon, who didn't seem nearly as relieved as I had hoped. His attention was on his commander, who stood and gave only a slight nod at Simon before addressing me.

"Half-Halderian is half a reason to believe your words. I am a father too, and I know what I would risk for the life of my daughter. It is the purest love. Seeing her willingness to sacrifice her own life is a sign of that same love." He hesitated a moment, then said, "Innocent."

I smiled, and then my eyes fell upon Imri Stout. If she was not convinced, none of the votes already cast would make any difference. And I already knew by the sour expression on her face that she had no sympathy for me.

Imri stood. "The question is not your guilt or innocence. It's what we are willing to risk for our vote. There is a great risk if I say you are innocent. If you have fooled us all, then we will lose everything. But there is little risk if I vote for your guilt. Even if I am wrong, all that we have lost is one life that is no longer of any use to us."

I said nothing more for my defense. It was obvious how she intended to vote.

Imri continued. "The Scarlet Throne is now occupied by a person who has declared himself king. He has Lord Endrick's magic, your magic, and any magic that was born into him. What is your plan to stop him, should we release you? If it is true, that you have no magic, then I say you are not worth the risk."

"I wasn't fully honest before," I said, and heads in the audience shot up. "It is true, that I have no magic within me. But I do have magic." With my hands still bound by Gabe's rope, I reached into the satchel at my side and withdrew the second of the disks that I had made last night. "Joth and I shared the same powers. Whatever I had, he still has. Just as Lord Endrick created the Olden Blade, I created this disk. And as the Blade could kill Endrick—"

"This disk can kill Joth," Imri finished. She stared at me for some time, her expression warming with respect. After a deep sigh, she added, "Regardless of my personal beliefs of your guilt, I also believe that we need you alive if we are going to finish this war. Therefore, my vote is innocent."

A cheer rose up in pockets around the room, though there were also plenty of people who eyed me with suspicion. I supposed it would take time to convince them, if I ever did. Gabe frowned at me, but the binding cord released from around my wrists.

Simon ran onto the dais, took me by the hand, and led me from the room.

· FIFTY ·

KESTRA

We had just entered the corridor when Gabe's voice called from behind for us to stop. Simon squeezed my hand tighter, and his other hand went to the hilt of his sword.

"It's over. The trial has been decided," he snarled.

Gabe spoke firmly, without emotion. "Yes, but I have not decided."

Simon turned, putting me behind him and making it clear with the position of his body that he would fight if necessary. "You were the accuser, Gabe. You cannot be that and the judge. Unless you intend to rewrite the rules again."

Gabe held up his hands, keeping distance between us. "She has her freedom, but Joth is still on that throne, and we must decide what to do next." He kicked at the ground. "No, I must decide what to do next. Kestra seems to have a plan. I have to decide whether to follow her. Whether to believe she is the person you think she is."

"Follow us, or don't," Simon said. "You were supposed to be my friend, and until the last few days, you were one of the few people I trusted, no matter what else was happening."

"I'm still that friend, Simon. Haven't you said yourself that your feelings for Kestra would get in the way of making the right decisions? I was protecting you, and everyone on our side, everyone *you* are supposed to be leading! I've proven my friendship!"

"Have you?" Simon's hands curled into fists. "If this is your idea of friendship, then it is one I don't need."

He tried to lead me away, but I crossed in front of him and said, "We need every person we can get. I'd like to talk to Gabe."

"Talk?" Gabe arched a brow. "Are you going to grab my arm and turn me into a puddle on the ground?"

"If I could, I'd be thinking about it. Some of your accusations went too far."

Gabe stared at me without expression, then gestured for the two of us to walk. I whispered to Simon that we would be all right, and he stayed back, though his hand had returned to his sword. I didn't think Gabe would try anything, not after the judges had just decided my innocence. But I had a knife in my boot, and I could get to it if necessary.

After we had rounded our first corner and Simon was out of sight, Gabe said, "If you knew my history, you would understand why I made those accusations. I grew up with the Coracks, fought the Dominion my entire life, considered every Dallisor I encountered an enemy, because they always were. When Simon joined up, he and I fought together, and no matter what, he was always there when I needed him. Then he met you and everything flipped upside down. It didn't matter anymore that you were a Dallisor, or worse, that you were Endrean. He somehow ignored the fact that you nearly killed him. It took the death of his mother for him to finally question his relationship with you. And once you obtained magic, he should have ended any connection with you, but he didn't."

I wasn't sure what Gabe expected me to say to that. He didn't know my history either, yet he had presumed to cast every sort of judgment upon me.

He continued. "I made those accusations because I had to protect the people in that room. Kestra, if you were lying—if you are still lying about your abilities—I had a duty to do everything I could for them."

"I did not lie, not once."

"You are still Endrean, and could reclaim your magic. Then the cycle would repeat itself. We can never fully trust you."

I stopped and stared at him. "Do you think you are immune from any sort of corruption? That the lack of magic somehow shields a person from ever causing harm to another, or abusing their position of power? You have sided against me at nearly every opportunity since the day we met, so how can I ever trust *you*?"

That seemed to affect him. After a pause, he asked, "Will you walk away now? Most people would. They'd count themselves lucky to still be alive and would get as far from this coming fight as possible."

"I bear some blame for Joth being on that throne. So I must be part of the plan to remove him." I shrugged. "Most people would walk away. I cannot."

"Perhaps you should," he added. "Six judges found you innocent, but that does not mean all their people agree with their decision. Can you be sure that a stray disk won't accidentally catch you from behind?"

Slowly, I nodded. "Will it be your stray disk?" It was a sincere question.

"Answer me this: Why did you make that disk you showed us

in the trial? If the corruption was still inside you, why would you do such a selfless thing?"

I shrugged. "It was never selfless. I thought the Olden Blade would kill Joth, just as it did Lord Endrick. But I also knew there was a chance of failure and that he would take my magic. So I gave myself a way to get the magic back. That black disk contains Endrick's ability to take a person's magic by killing them. That was my plan if everything else failed."

Gabe seemed to be sincere in trying to understand me. "It still is your plan, I assume. You'll shoot Joth with that disk, and if it kills him, all his powers will come to you."

"That was my plan at first, but it cannot be me to wield that disk. I am no longer the Infidante. That was proven when I tried to attack Joth with the Olden Blade."

"And why did you do that? You must have known that if you failed, you would lose all your magic."

"That was the most selfish part of all. I knew that Joth was fighting Simon, and that Joth would do whatever was necessary to win." I drew in a slow breath. "I attacked Joth because it was my only chance of saving Simon's life. Whatever happened to me, I could not let him die."

"Why not?"

I wished the conversation had gone in any other direction. I pressed my lips together, then said, "You believe that the corruption took me over, that it was the whole of my identity. And you are almost entirely correct about that. *Almost.*"

Gabe shook his head. "Kestra, I saw you with the corruption. It controlled you."

"You have no idea how strong it was, Gabe. How it filled me, how its weight tried to push out every good part of me. But there was always a piece of me that it could not touch. This fraction of my heart showed mercy to Harlyn in the throne room, tried to warn you in Highwyn of the condors overhead. That piece of my heart could not be touched because it loved so much. I loved Simon with a power greater than magic . . . I still do."

Gabe glanced down, doubting me. But finally, he said, "Well, we have one thing in common. Simon is—or was—my best friend. And you were the girl he once loved. For his sake, we may have to learn to work together."

My smile quickly faded into something far more serious. "We *must* work together, Gabe. Whatever our disagreements, I am not your enemy, nor are you mine. We have one common enemy now sitting on the Scarlet Throne. If we spend all our energy fighting each other, that only benefits him."

"Agreed."

Gabe shrugged and looked as if he were about to walk on, then said, "When I said you were the girl he *once* loved, that wasn't the full truth. He still loves you, Kestra."

My face flushed, though not for the reasons Gabe might have thought. I shook my head, trying to push down the emotions that were rising in me. Hope was a dangerous thing, and I couldn't allow Gabe to threaten me with it. "Simon cares for me, and perhaps he always will, but I know the love is gone. He and Harlyn will marry; that's the plan."

Gabe stepped closer to me. "When Harlyn entered Simon's life, she should have been the most obvious decision. Even though you weren't there, you still stood between them. I went on patrols with her, saw her after she'd leave meals with Simon. I talked with her hour after hour some evenings, trying to explain Simon to her, trying to explain *you*. Simon loves you, Kestra, and if you don't know it, then you are the only one."

I smiled, not only because I believed him, which sent a rush of joy into my heart. But also because I finally understood Gabe as well. I said, "That must be the way you love Harlyn. I hear it in your voice when you say her name."

Gabe opened his mouth to object, then let out a heavy sigh and nodded. "I have learned to love her in silence. She never sees me——"

"I see you now."

Gabe turned and saw Harlyn approaching us in the corridor. She shrugged with some shyness and stepped forward. "I came out to be sure everything was all right. I didn't expect . . ." She glanced up at Gabe. "I didn't know."

Gabe merely stared at her, possibly struck dumb.

I smiled at Gabe. "From now on, you and I will fight together, and on the same side. We will defeat Joth Tarquin."

He stuck out a hand, barely aware of me anymore. "Agreed."

I shook it, then with a backward grin at Harlyn, said, "I suspect you two want to be left alone now."

Simon was waiting around the first corner after I left Gabe and Harlyn behind. I startled at first to see him, but his smile was wide and the warm expression of his eyes pulled me toward him. I glanced back briefly, then said, "Did you hear——"

"Everything." He cradled my face in his hands and kissed me, sending warmth throughout my body, the kind of beautiful heat no magic could ever imitate.

· FIFTY-ONE ·

KESTRA

A ceremony was held that night for the destruction of the Olden Blade. The full Alliance was in attendance, with two notable exceptions: Loelle, who said that while she did not support the actions of her son, she could not strike against him either. Nor was Imri Stout there, although most of the Brill were. She sent an excuse that she preferred to work toward improving the growing technologies of her people rather than to see the dying magic of another people.

A fire was built in the center of the courtyard, stoked with oils to intensify the heat, and indeed, by the time the ceremony began, the fire could be felt from the farthest corners of the courtyard.

As others talked of the battles they'd seen already and tried to anticipate the challenges yet to come, I only stood in front of the fire, staring at the flames. The Olden Blade was in my hands. How comfortable it had become there, like it was part of me. For a while, it had been part of me—its magic was my magic, its purpose was mine as well.

Indeed, the Olden Blade had become the one part of my identity that I could be proud of. It was the one thing I could do for Antora, and I had done it. I was the Infidante no longer.

Which meant I no longer had an identity.

Rosaleen walked up to me. "I never did thank you."

It was difficult to look at her, to think that after every offense I had caused her and her family, she had come to thank me. I only said, "Nothing I've done deserves any thanks."

"You set me free as an Ironheart. I never expected that."

"I didn't expect you would be one of the people who came when I called for help."

Rosaleen smiled. "I'd heard of my brother's interest in you, so I figured I ought to see for myself the kind of person you were."

"I'm sorry that was our first introduction."

"It wasn't." I glanced at her again, and Rosaleen said, "Actually our first introduction was outside All Spirits Forest. I saw what it did to you when Celia died. That's when I began to understand you."

I had no idea how to answer her and felt relieved when Simon joined us. He gave Rosaleen a quick hug before she made an excuse to leave us alone. When she did, he took my hand in his. "Are you ready?"

"I doubt I'll ever be ready," I replied.

"Can you do this?"

"I must."

He gave my hand a squeeze. "Yes, but *can* you do this?"

I wished he would stop asking and try to understand. "Simon, I must. Let that be enough."

"Is it so difficult? I suppose the blade has great meaning for you, because of what you accomplished with it."

"If it were only that, tonight would be a simple end to an object of great evil. But I've been thinking about who I was when I used this. I was becoming an object of great evil myself. And the more I embraced the decay inside me, the easier it became to hold this dagger. I felt nothing for Endrick when I stabbed him, nor for Joth when I attacked him. But it's different now, because I'm different now. When this blade is destroyed, Joth will lose every power that was once Endrick's. This is another step in Joth's destruction." I looked up at Simon. "I feel it this time. How awful it is what we have to do."

"There is courage in facing one's enemy," he said. "But it takes greater courage to *feel* for that enemy."

Simon put an arm around me, and I leaned on his shoulder until we were informed that the fire was as hot as it would get. It was time to act.

A platform had been built near the fire. Simon would speak first, explaining to everyone why this destruction was necessary. Then I would throw the blade into the fire, destroying the weapon, but also destroying all of Endrick's magic, so that no one could ever take hold of it again.

Simon kissed the top of my head and walked onto the platform, holding up his arms for silence. Then he began, "This ceremony marks the end of one battle, and the gateway to the second. Do not deceive yourselves—this is not over, we have not yet won. But we will, and it begins here. I wish to add . . ."

Simon's voice trailed off as he looked sharply upward at the dark skies, then gestured in front of him and said, "Everyone move away, hurry!"

I ran to my left, and others who had been near me scattered as well, in time for Simon's dragon to swoop down to the ground. His roar sounded like an alarm and Simon instantly took a running leap off the platform, and as the dragon prepared to launch back into the air, Simon called out, "Prepare yourselves for battle!"

Simon had no sooner taken flight before something whistled as it fell from the dark skies above, landing somewhere on the opposite side of the fire. After three seconds of absolute silence, an explosion rattled the ground beneath us. The building where Woodcourt's gardener had once worked came down in pieces around us, followed by pleas for help and cries for the various armies to assemble. These were the Dominion fire pellets, and in this darkness it'd be nearly impossible to defend ourselves. With the Olden Blade in hand, I ran to help the injured, but Trina reached me first.

"Kestra, we have to get you inside."

"I won't hide while everyone fights!"

Basil appeared on the other side of me. "Joth wants the Olden Blade. If he gets it, then he retains Endrick's powers."

Immediately, I nodded and began to follow them, but we changed course when another whistling sound fell not far ahead, only to explode on the count of three.

"Run to the gates!" Trina called, but we had only taken a few steps before the gates of Woodcourt burst open and oropods flooded into the courtyard.

Commander Reese shouted an order for his soldiers to mount their horses and try to lead the oropods away, but the beasts had already begun to attack and were blocking the gates. We were trapped inside the walls.

Basil and Trina attempted to steer me safely toward Woodcourt, but another explosion whistled toward us, forcing us to separate. Through the smoke and dust, I couldn't see Trina and Basil anymore, but if the fire pellets were targeting me, it was better for them if we remained separated. I redoubled my grip on the Olden Blade and ran back toward the oropods.

I didn't get far before I heard Harlyn call for help. She had been cornered by five oropods and was firing off disks as quickly as she could, but I saw her reach into her now-empty satchel, then look up with panicked eyes.

Gabe began racing toward her, but in his hurry, he tripped over one fallen oropod, who reared up and snapped its teeth at him. He rolled to the ground to fight it and shouted at me to help Harlyn.

I ran to her and wounded the two nearest oropods before the third let out a soulful cry I'd never heard before from these creatures. It wasn't a cry of pain, but instead seemed to be a warning. The three oropods that remained turned my way, and I raised the Olden Blade. Harlyn suddenly yelled, "Kestra, above you!"

I squatted down low, but it wasn't fast enough and I felt a condor's talon wrap around me, lifting me into the air. From here, I saw the mayhem below as those in the courtyard continued battling the oropods.

I squirmed the best I could within the condor's clutches to get into a position to breathe, but the bird only held me tighter and carried me higher, past Woodcourt's walls and toward the palace. That was unacceptable.

Gripping the Olden Blade tight enough to ensure I would not drop it, I struck its leg. It cried out, widened the talon, and with a scream, I fell into the night.

The last time I had fallen from this distance, it had almost killed me. But that was when I was nearly immortal.

· FIFTY-TWO ·

SIMON

I had been pushing Rawk toward Woodcourt to defend our walls, but without warning, Rawk turned us away and aimed sharply down. I didn't know why he'd changed course, but I trusted him by now, and almost instantly, I understood. Kestra was just ahead, struggling within the talons of a giant condor.

Rawk angled more directly toward her, but another two condors had already targeted us. Rawk attacked the nearest bird with a flame that blew back toward me. Instinctively, I raised my right forearm, which dispelled the worst of the heat around me.

The second condor rounded on us and this time it crashed into Rawk's side, sending us veering sharply to the right. My body slid sideways, but I held to the curve of one wing until Rawk straightened out.

I withdrew my sword, then crouched low on Rawk's back, outstretching my right arm to keep my balance. This time when the condor came close, I swung hard, clipping the condor's wing. It screeched but continued forward, careening into us. The force of the impact threw me off balance, but Rawk compensated for me in the tilt of his body. When I looked up, I saw the tail of the condor as it flew away to nurse its wound. But this was not over.

From farther away now, Kestra screamed and began falling through the air. Rawk raced toward her so fast that even with the balance from my arm, I had to hold on or I would have fallen too.

He veered downward, timing his approach perfectly so that Kestra fell directly above us. I reached up and grabbed her around the waist, pulling her safely toward me. Her eyes widened as she realized where she was; then her attention shifted to the fire we had set before the attack.

From my thoughts to Rawk's actions, we angled toward the fire. The worst of its heat had begun to fade.

"It won't be enough," Kestra said. "Not for the Olden Blade."

In response, Rawk flew lower, searing the ground with flames that destroyed every oropod in his path. Once we reached the fire, his breath grew hotter, and the dwindling fire roared to life.

"Now!" I knew Kestra had heard me, but when she did not act, I said again, "Kestra, drop the blade!"

"I can't do it," she called.

Alarmed, I ordered Rawk to circle around once more. As he made the arc, I asked her, "What's wrong?"

Her breaths were coming heavier, and she stared down at the blade in her hand. "All the magic in that blade, there's great power in my hand."

I tilted my head. "It's corrupted magic. If you take it up—"

"Every bit of magic within this blade came from someone Endrick killed. This magic is their legacy. If I destroy the blade, nothing of them remains."

By then, we had finished the arc and the fire was beneath us again. "If you don't destroy the blade, Joth will get it, and he will have Endrick's powers forever."

"I know. I just . . ." Tears welled in her eyes. "When I do this, I really will be the last of my people."

She dropped the sword, which fell blade-first toward the earth. I breathed again only when it disappeared into the smoke, but my relief had come too soon. A condor swooped up through the thick gray smoke with the blade in its talon. With a caw at the others, it flew away, headed directly to the palace.

In concert with my thoughts, Rawk began to follow the condor, but Kestra grabbed my arm, drawing my attention to Gabe, who was caught up in the claw of a condor, as she had been.

"We have to get the Olden Blade!" I said to her. "If Joth gets it, we're all dead!"

"That's your friend over there!"

I looked over at Gabe, struggling the best he could, but losing the fight. Then I said to Kestra, "Rawk is barely managing the two of us. He can't take three."

"I know." She nodded, almost to herself. Whatever she was planning, it made me nervous. Especially when she added, "Get us closer and we'll figure out some way to help."

I ordered Rawk in that direction. My plan was to force the condor closer to the ground, but I still didn't know how to make it release Gabe without seriously injuring or burning him.

While I attempted to get Rawk at a better angle, Kestra suddenly crouched on Rawk's back.

"No!" I reached for her, but before I could, she lunged toward the condor. She seemed to have been aiming for its body but instead grabbed on to its leg, with Gabe in the talons below.

With the sudden added weight, the condor's flight became erratic. It must have been gripping Gabe tighter than before, for Gabe was shouting out and trying to force the talons apart. Kestra was working her way down the condor's leg, obviously to pry Gabe loose, but with the condor tilting so wildly, she was having trouble.

Finally, the condor crashed into a copse of trees. I heard the crack of heavy branches and their thuds as they fell to the earth, then one louder thump that must have been the condor itself.

"Let us down!" I ordered Rawk. Exhausted, Rawk's landing was nearly a crash as well. I jumped off his back, then raced into the trees. It wasn't only me. Basil had also seen what was happening and had entered the copse with a few of his soldiers.

I saw the felled bird from a distance, and a large branch that had fallen on top of it, likely what had killed the condor. But my horror grew for what might have happened to Kestra and Gabe.

The condor's wing was stretched out, and beneath it I saw the hem of Kestra's cloak and Gabe's boot. Basil knelt and lifted the wing, then frowned at me, far too solemn.

Cautiously, I stepped around the bird, holding my breath for what I might find. There in the snow was Kestra with her arms wrapped protectively around Gabe.

I barely dared to ask Basil, "Are they—"

Gabe moved first, and his movement brought signs of life from Kestra, though her eyes were slower to open. Once they did, she released Gabe, and her eyes darted about as if embarrassed.

Gabe only smiled. "I knew we needed to become closer friends, but this goes too far, Kestra. Simon is watching."

Her smile at him was forced, and when I helped her to her feet, without looking directly at me, she said, "Rawk is injured. Tend to him. I'm all right."

Something was bothering Kestra, but she didn't appear to be in any danger, so I ran back to Rawk and found him licking one wing. I inspected it and saw what appeared to be a break in the bone.

"We can fix this," I said. "But you'll have to be nicer to our healer."

Harlyn ran to me, having seen what had happened. "I'll get Rawk to Woodcourt. He knows me. Maybe Loelle can help him."

I nodded and patted Rawk's neck affectionately before Harlyn began leading him away.

When I found Kestra again in the trees, she was on her knees in the snow, one hand over her mouth and head slumped downward.

"We failed," she said. "No, *I* failed. I should have dropped the blade when I had the chance."

"Then the condor would have grabbed it a second or two earlier, that's all."

She shook her head. "I could sense the echoes of all those people Endrick killed for their powers. Destroying the sword would be their final destruction." Now she looked up at me. "But how many more people will die to retrieve the Olden Blade?"

That worried me too. So far, Joth hadn't seemed to explore most of Lord Endrick's powers. But he must have begun to access them, for he understood the importance of preserving the Olden Blade. And now that he had it, he would explore his powers further. We were all in terrible trouble.

She took my hands in hers. "We must end this fighting, Simon. No more death, no more destruction."

"Then let's end it. You've had a plan all the way along. Please tell me you have a plan now."

Kestra sighed, then said, "I do. But no one is going to like it."

· FIFTY-THREE ·

SIMON

Another meeting was held that night, this time in the Woodcourt ballroom. Nearly everyone within the Alliance who was still on their feet attended. Even Loelle came this time, though she stood in the back, clearly uncomfortable and no doubt keenly aware that the conversation was entirely focused on our single goal: removing her son from the Scarlet Throne at all costs.

Every leader stood to account for their group's condition and needs. Thus far, the Brill had fared the worst, and my cavalry had the fewest losses, though we still had too many names listed among the dead. While most of them had been caused by the half-lives, there were also reports of Dallisors attacking Alliance soldiers from behind. I couldn't understand that. If anything, Joth would be even crueler to former Dominion members, to those who had helped trap the Navan in the forest before they were cursed. But they had chosen sides again and would have to pay the price for it.

Once all our leaders had spoken, it was my turn. I stood before the group, feeling all eyes on me. Kestra came to my side, and I took her hand in mine.

"We have had far too many losses," I said. "But we cannot think of them as Reddengrad losses or Corack losses. Every fallen soldier is a loss to the Alliance, to all of us who remain. You and I, we are the Brill, we are Reddengrad and the Coracks, we are the Halderians, and"—I lifted Kestra's arm in the air—"every one of us is the Infidante! We fight as one people, with one mind and one goal. Though it may seem like victory is far from our reach, if we stop now, we may never get this chance again. Every moment we wait is the chance for Joth to entrench in Endrick's powers. We must attack tonight, while Joth sits on the throne. His defense is thin, only a small band of half-lives and a few Dominion cowards on his side. We will attack, and we will win!"

A cheer thundered through the room, though when it fell silent, a Brillian near the front frowned at me. "It's a good speech, but how is this to be done?" He waited for an answer, and when I did not provide it, he pointed to Kestra. "At least when she had magic, she could restore those half-lives so that we could fight them, one mortal to another."

"We all know she still has magic," a man next to him said. "There is no way to rid a person of magic!"

Kestra sighed, then reached into her satchel and withdrew the black disk blade. "This disk will do to Joth Tarquin what the Olden Blade did to Endrick. But it requires an Infidante to use it. The purpose of this meeting is to identify the new Infidante."

"That must be you," Trina said. "If it's like the Olden Blade, then only the Infidante can touch it, just as you are touching the disk right now."

I hadn't considered that. I walked over to Kestra and held out my hand for the disk. Kestra offered it to me, but I hadn't yet wrapped my fingers around it before I felt the heat coming from it, hot enough that I knew it would burn me if I attempted to touch it.

I pulled my hand away and frowned at Kestra. "Trina is right. You are still the Infidante."

Kestra shook her head. "No, it can't be me." Her eyes widened. "It's not me, Simon. I completed my task."

Trina stepped forward to test her hand against the blade and withdrew it as fast as I had done. She said to Kestra, "Not so long ago, the only thing I wanted was to be the Infidante. How foolish that was. I understand better now what it means to carry such a burden. I'm sorry, Kestra. I know you don't want this."

Kestra looked over at me with tears welling in her eyes. "I can't do it. I can't go through that again."

"We made mistakes before," I said. "We fought magic with magic, corruption with corruption. But we know how to fight Joth now, as we are." Then louder, to be certain everyone heard me, I added, "We were a divided people, and no one was truly on the side of the Infidante. But that will not happen this time. So listen carefully. When we attack, it will be with one purpose only, and that is to remove Joth Tarquin from the Scarlet Throne. There will be one strategy alone, and that is to follow the lead of the Infidante. You will accept these conditions without contest or you will withdraw now. There is no other way for us to succeed. As king of the Halderians and leader of the Alliance, these are my orders."

Silence followed my words as each person passed a look from one to another, making their guesses as to who might be the first to leave, if anyone. After several seconds without a single person withdrawing from the room, I thought we might have a truly united group.

I hoped so. Kestra had been betrayed enough for a thousand lifetimes.

Then Loelle walked forward, the crowd parting for her until she stood before me and Kestra. She looked as empty as I had felt after the death of my mother, but with a pleading in her eyes that bored straight into my heart. With clear respect and humility, she nodded first at Kestra, then at me. "Give me one more chance with Joth. If anyone can reach him, I can."

I shook my head. "You've tried, Loelle. And he will be more volatile once he begins to absorb the magic within the Olden Blade. I won't risk your safety."

"Your mother gave her life for you. Would I do less for the hope of saving my son?" I didn't answer right away, and she said, "That is the plan, correct? To kill him?"

I glanced over at Kestra and was about to respond, when Darrow stepped forward. "I'll go with her. I've been a half-life before, and he knows me."

"That won't matter to him," Kestra said. "I've been exactly where he is now, and I know what is happening in his mind. His every instinct will be to protect his power. He won't care that you were a half-life; he won't even care for his own mother if she threatens his power. He won't see any difference between you coming to him with open arms and me coming at him with a disk bow in my arms."

Loelle huffed and was about to reply, when a cry came from the far corner of the room. I couldn't see who it was or what had happened, but heard a body fall to the floor, then two words emerge from the screams around him: "He's dead!"

Kestra and I locked eyes. Horror filled me as I understood what she had not spoken. That had to have been Joth's work, and he would have done it for only one reason: to warn us to back down.

I leaned toward her and whispered, "How was Joth able to do that?"

She began scanning the room. "He must have half-lives here. They're here, Simon."

"I am going to him!" Loelle said. "Give me one hour, and if I do not return, then you may do whatever you must do."

Darrow frowned at Kestra. "I cannot let her go alone." He finished with a glare at me. "See that nothing happens to my daughter."

He asked for a promise I would give my own life to keep, but before I reached for Kestra's hand, she was already following her father, still protesting his going.

Loelle opened the ballroom door, then drew back, seeing Amala Fingray standing there, the young cavalry woman who had briefly been my commander a few nights ago. I hadn't noticed she was missing from our meeting earlier.

But something was different about her now. She stood stiffly at attention, except for one hand pressed against her chest and pain evident in her eyes.

Joth had made her an Ironheart and taken her for a servant.

Amala focused on Kestra, clearly resisting every word she was being forced to speak, and gritting her teeth against the pain it caused her to fight. "My master has the Olden Blade, ensuring him immortality and all powers once belonging to Lord Endrick. Surrender now, or every person in this room will die."

Kestra looked over to me, and my mind raced for an answer. Joth had proven he was capable of killing remotely, and that he was willing to do it. He might target anyone without notice, and we had no way to save ourselves.

Blinking hard, Amala's attention shifted to me. "Will you surrender?"

"Allow me to send a delegation to your master for formal negotiations," I said.

"Send Kestra Dallisor," Amala said. "The king of Antora has unfinished business with her."

"No, Amala." I stepped forward. "He has unfinished business with me."

Amala shook her head, like a warning that I had gone too far, and indeed, immediately a slight wind brushed over me, bringing a pinch to my chest, fierce enough that I collapsed to my knees. Several others in the room did the same, including Trina and Huge and Gabe.

"I'll go with you!" Kestra cried. "But your king must stop this!"

The pressure on my chest lightened, though it was still there. At least I could breathe again.

Kestra glanced over at me and sadly shook her head, then said, "I will bring with me Darrow and your master's mother."

"Agreed."

They started out the door, but at the last moment, Harlyn ran forward. "I'll come as far as the throne room door, to ensure you all get there safely."

Amala stared at her a moment, then said, "That pleases the king."

Harlyn followed them out of the room, gripping her hands together with worry, and for good reason. Why would Joth be pleased that Harlyn was coming?

· FIFTY-FOUR ·

KESTRA

In less than a minute, Joth had dismantled all our plans for an attack against him. I was now forced to go forward with an army of four. My companions included a father who would sacrifice our mission before putting me at risk, a mother who would not under any circumstances harm her own son. And our fourth member, who for all I knew might still consider my death her prime mission.

I gave Simon a final glance before rushing out the door. He remained on his knees clutching his chest, a stark reminder of how a single misstep might cost me everything. I'd made so many mistakes already. I hoped this wasn't another.

Amala led me out of Woodcourt, with Harlyn and Loelle following and Darrow behind them. Outside, a wagon was already hitched to horses to carry us to Woodcourt. We climbed into the back, and Amala went up front to drive us the short distance to the palace.

As we rode, the four of us exchanged looks, but none of us dared speak. We all knew it was possible that half-lives were listening or watching. But with an air of nonchalance, Harlyn shifted positions to sit by me. She opened her disk pouch, showing me several disks inside, then gestured for me to give her my satchel.

I understood her intentions. I had only one disk and she wanted to be sure I was well armed to attack Joth. She must not have fully realized that the black disk I carried was the only one of any consequence. Nothing else would win this war, and to be sure, this was war.

Still, I could not communicate that to Harlyn, so when she persisted, I gave her my satchel. No matter how many disks she added to my bag, my black one would be easily identifiable by the markings created upon it when it absorbed the magic.

Harlyn looked more closely at my disk and then suddenly closed up the satchel, holding the ends tight with her fists. I locked eyes with her in understanding and then nodded in agreement with her unspoken plan.

While Harlyn worked, Darrow caught my attention, motioning toward his disk bow. Did I want it?

I shook my head. My intentions would be far too obvious if I walked into the throne room thus armed. But I would need it eventually. Darrow would have to find a way to get it to me once we were in the throne room.

Loelle had quietly observed everything that was happening between us, and I was relieved that she had not said anything to Amala or called attention to our actions. But there were tears in her eyes, and I ached for how she must have felt, knowing what would happen once we entered the throne room.

Except that just as before, my plans were thwarted. Once we arrived and Amala led us inside the palace, she said, "The king wishes to see Lady Kestra alone."

"I am her protector," Darrow said. "Where she goes, I go."

"The lady needs no protection from the king," Amala said. "As long as she does as she should."

That was hardly my plan. I looked at Darrow with my heart suddenly racing and with sweat on my palms. I had always known that ultimately I would have to face Joth, but the idea of being in there alone with him again was terrifying.

The doors to the throne room opened, and as we began to walk through, I whispered, "Who am I speaking to right now? Are you a Halderian cavalry woman, or am I speaking to Joth?"

Her response was equally soft. "Surely you know, my lady."

Yes, I knew.

With an entire wall of exploded windows, the throne room was as wintry cold as the outdoor air, and a light falling snow was collecting at the far end of the room. I gathered my cloak around me, recalling how, only days ago, I would have welcomed this cold. Only days ago, I had been this cold myself.

Amala left me at the bottom of the steps leading up to the Scarlet Throne, bowed low to Joth, who was seated on the throne, and then exited the room, closing the doors behind us.

Joth studied me in silence, his mouth slowly widening into a smile. "My lady Kestra. Kneel."

"I've come to bargain for the lives back in Woodcourt."

"Of course you have, and we can discuss that . . . after you kneel." I hesitated, and he said, "We both know that with the powers I now have, I can force you to your knees, and I will do that if necessary. But it would mean more if you choose to obey."

His threat was similar to one I had made to Harlyn when I had sat on that throne. I understood better now how difficult it was to make oneself kneel to a ruler they had no intention of following.

Stalling, I asked, "And what does it mean to you, if I kneel?"

"It means that you recognize I am the king of Antora, and that I am *your* king." He stood and walked down the steps until he was directly in front of me. "But I am a king without a queen. We were connected once, Kestra, and I feel your absence. I must have you for my queen."

I shook my head. "That will never happen, Joth."

Disappointed, he clicked his tongue. "It will. But first you must kneel." He swiped one hand downward, and immediately I fell to my knees. The same power held me there now.

With his other hand, he made a cupping shape, then smiled down at me. "My hand appears to be empty, but it is not. In fact, it contains something I believe you will think is quite valuable. This is Simon Hatch's heart. I know you care for him. Despite your assurances otherwise, I suspect he is the reason you were never able to fully connect with me. But if he is no longer alive, then I will have your full loyalty."

With sudden desperation, I looked up, ready to beg at any price, if necessary. "Please don't."

He compressed his fingers slightly, and I could almost hear Simon's cries from here.

Taking his hand in mine, and thus stopping his use of magic, I quickly said, "I will be your queen. But you must let the people at Woodcourt live, all of them. Do this, and I will accept you."

Joth smiled and pulled me to my feet, then kissed my hand. Keeping hold of my hand, he said, "Soon we will reconnect, and I will restore magic to you, though I hope you understand I will be selective in the powers you can have, and how you can use them."

"Restore them now," I said, absolutely serious. Despite what it might mean for me, magic might be the only way I could still win.

"Soon, my dear. We have another job first." As if on cue, the doors to the throne room opened, and Amala led in Loelle and Darrow, but this time, she remained in the room, closing the doors behind her.

Joth waited a moment, then asked, "Were there not four of you who came?"

"Yes, Harlyn Mindall was here," Amala said. "But when I returned from delivering Kestra, she had disappeared."

"Find her," Joth said. "Go and find her and bring her to me, or you will take her punishment."

"Don't do anything to her," Loelle cried. "Please, my son—"

"You should consider me your king, not your son," Joth said. "Because you are now only a servant with no particular importance to me."

Loelle tilted her head. "Oh?"

"Among his other powers, Endrick could heal himself," Joth said. "Your powers do not benefit me any longer."

"My powers?" Loelle stepped forward. "Is that all that matters to you?"

"Of course not." He leaned back in his seat. "What matters is that you chose a side. You are working with the Coracks again, using that power of healing on my enemies."

"If the sick or injured are set before me, I will heal them first and ask which side they are on later. If any of the restored half-lives are injured here, I will heal them too."

Joth's smile became ice. "I restored those with the magic I wanted. They are of no benefit to me anymore."

My heart stopped as I realized what he meant. Loelle was slower to put the pieces together, but gradually, her understanding showed on her face. Joth must have followed Endrick's pattern of obtaining powers through the deaths of those whose magic he wanted.

Hence, those he had chosen for me to restore. That was always his purpose.

Loelle shook her head, still in disbelief. "Please tell me you didn't."

Joth stuck out his hand unapologetically. "I have acquired the powers of all our people of Navan, except those in my service inside Woodcourt. And you."

Loelle stepped backward with widening eyes. "I am your mother."

"Yes, but I do not need you anymore either." Joth put his arm around my waist, pulling me close. I tried to put any possible gap between us, though every time he noticed, he pulled me in again. "Soon, Kestra will be my wife. She will become the mother to a new race of Navan. Each of them born with magic of their own."

I looked over at him in horror as Darrow said, "Kestra is my daughter, King Joth. I request a moment in private with her to assure myself that she is marrying you of her own choice."

"That is not necessary, because you see, the marriage is not her choice. That will change eventually, once I restore her magic. All I need now is her loyalty." Joth turned to me. "Prove yourself, Kestra. There is someone who needs to die, and I need you to do it."

"Who?"

Joth smiled. "You'll see."

· FIFTY-FIVE ·

KESTRA

I felt frozen. Not with cold and certainly not corruption, but I could not move. I absolutely would not harm Darrow or Loelle, or anyone upon his orders. But the consequences of my refusal were equally horrifying.

Joth withdrew a dagger from the belt at his waist and set it in my hands. "You wish that this was the Olden Blade, no doubt," he said, winking at me. "But as that particular weapon is obviously a threat to me now, I have that in my protection."

I stared down at his dagger. "I can't do it this way. Not so close."

"Then how will you do it?" Joth asked.

"Darrow has a disk bow."

"I have no disks," Darrow said, for Joth to hear.

"Yes, you do." Joth nodded at his satchel. "Give them to me."

Darrow slowly reached into his satchel and pulled out two disks, one black and the other the white one that had restored my life. He placed them on Joth's flattened hand.

"These won't do," I said to Joth. "You could always restore someone from a white disk's effects. And the black disk will work too fast. If you wish for me to prove my loyalty, then give me a red one."

"Creating a wound that cannot be stopped up?" Joth said. "Is that because you still have magic and hope to save your victim?"

I must've hesitated a second too long, because he grabbed my hand and suddenly his even tone became a snarl. "How are you alive, Kestra?" When I hesitated again, he said, "There's a rumor from one of my half-lives, about a disk that contained a power to restore life." He showed me the two disks that Darrow had given him. "Which of these is capable of that?"

"These disks will kill, nothing more." I tried to squirm away from him but failed. "You're hurting my arm, Joth."

He released my arm, then threw both disks against the wall of the throne room, shattering them. Then he looked up at Amala as she was reentering the room. "We will take no chances. Bring me another black disk."

Amala bowed and left the room, and while we waited, Loelle said, "My son, do you remember our time in All Spirits Forest?"

His mood seemed to soften. "Of course."

Loelle stepped forward, subtly motioning to me to move away from him, which I did. "Do you remember the way you cared for the half-lives, watched out for them?"

"I remember."

Her eyes filled with tears. "I care for you too, more than you can imagine. It is a mother's love, and the power of it is greater than the corruption within you."

"Love is weakness!" he shouted, then with an eye on me added, "A soft heart is a pierced heart. Didn't you teach me that once?"

I stared back at him, surprised to be feeling sympathy for what he had become. "A pierced heart can be shared. One that is hardened remains alone."

Loelle finally reached his side, placing a hand on his arm. "Release the Ironhearts at Woodcourt. Give them a chance to kneel to you, even as we do."

She knelt at his feet and motioned for Darrow and me to do the same.

Darrow said, "If we kneel, will you release those still at Woodcourt?"

"I have loosened my grip on their hearts enough that they can come here to bargain for their lives." Joth reached out his hand to summon me to him, but I pretended not to see it. "Together we will build a kingdom with the Alliance as the first of our servants. At least, those who are allowed to live."

At that moment, Amala returned to the throne room holding a black disk. She dipped her head at Joth, who held out his hand for the disk. Once he received it, he passed it to me.

"Now get the disk bow for her," Joth ordered.

Amala obeyed, placing it in my hands.

I took the bow but asked, "Is there no other way to prove my loyalty?"

Joth turned to me. "Reconnect with me. We are stronger when we are together."

"I have no magic," I said. "There is nothing to connect."

But he held out his hands, inviting me again to repeat with him the process of connecting. The thought of what this might mean made my stomach roll, but I had to do it. Taking his hand in mine might provide the very opportunity I needed to switch the black disk in my hand with the magic disk in my satchel. But I feared it would come at a terrible price.

I placed the disk bow over my shoulder and the black disk from Amala into the satchel, then forced a smile to my face and walked to him. He was only a few steps away, but I worked for every single one.

Joth took my hands in his and pulled me close. He studied my face, seeking any possible sign of my disloyalty. Here I was, on an errand to kill him. Disloyalty was the least of the crimes he might find in me.

He pushed his fingers through my hair, then let one hand slide from the back of my head down to my neck. "This was a place of power for Lord Endrick, was it not?"

I tried to keep my breaths even, tried to hide the shaking of my legs, the tremor in my voice. "For his enemies, it was."

"And are you my enemy?" He brought me even closer to him, and in his eyes, I saw anger and a thirst for revenge. "Let down your defenses. Let me into your heart, into your mind."

At first, the magic coming from him had merely pressed in on me, but within seconds, it began to crush me and I had no defense against it. His magic took hold of my heart, not to control it but to dissect the emotions I was guarding most carefully there. Then he found what he was looking for, what I had been terrified he would find.

"Ah, I see that your feelings for Simon are more than simply caring. You love him."

"Please don't harm him." A tear fell from one eye. "Please, Joth."

"I think that I must." Joth cupped the side of my face. I wanted to push away, but feared if I did, his hand would go to my neck again. He added, "Otherwise, I think it quite likely that your love for one king will interfere with loyalty to another. The black disk must be saved for him."

"I will connect with you right now," I said. "Then you know you will have my loyalty. Let that be enough."

I hoped that would be enough. If I was the only sacrifice today, I could live with that.

Indeed, Joth smiled at me, and I felt the tendrils of his magic reaching for me again, but then his smile faded into a thin, cold line. "That is not nearly enough, my dear."

I shuddered. *My dear* was the term Endrick had used on me. Hearing it echoed once more, in this room, sent waves of fear through me.

Joth released me and added, "Do you still have the black disk I gave you?" I nodded, and he said, "Good, because your banished king has arrived."

At that very moment, Rawk flew into the throne room, his full wingspan easily fitting within the wall that had once been all windows. Joth and I each backed up to avoid his fiery breath, though in this dampened room, it quickly extinguished. As Joth's attention shifted to Simon, Darrow ran forward to pull me away from Joth.

Still on the dragon, Simon held up his sword and said, "We never finished our duel. Little surprise from a coward, a false king. You are an embarrassment to your people. Or all people, for that matter."

Simon stopped there, clutching his chest as Joth squeezed on his heart, but put his eyes on me. I quietly pulled the disk bow off my shoulder. This was my chance.

"How dare you?" Joth shouted. "Kneel to me!"

"Finish our duel," Simon said through clenched teeth. "The loser will kneel . . . to *me*."

I reached into the satchel to find the disk I would need to complete my task. I had placed the black disk from Joth in front. The one I had brought was behind it. I withdrew the one I wanted and placed it in the pocket of the bow. My heart pounded. If this went badly, all was lost.

"I will gladly finish our duel," Joth said, still watching Simon. "But I will use all of my magic, for it is as much a part of me now as your skills with a sword are to you."

Simon dismounted, keeping his sword ready. "I suppose that's all you can do. Obviously, before you had Endrick's magic, you were rather insignificant."

Joth straightened up taller, and I quietly took aim as he said, "I have always had magic. What I have now is simply more."

"You have borrowed magic. You are an actor who seeks respect simply for dressing in the costume of a king." Simon raised his sword, but his eyes flicked over to me. "I do not fear you, Joth."

I released the disk. It flew straight and direct, but Joth rotated at the exact moment the disk should have hit him, and caught it in his hand. He turned to me, and his eyes blazed with anger. "That is hardly the loyalty I had hoped for, my dear." Then he crushed it to pieces, black dust falling from his hand.

Simon looked equally crushed. He had only talked with such bold language in hopes of distracting Joth. But now he would have to pay for those words.

As I would have to pay for my actions.

I just wasn't sure which of us Joth would punish first.

· FIFTY-SIX ·

SIMON

Kestra's attempt had failed. That black disk had been my last hope for Joth's death. If he intended to use the whole of his magic against me, nothing I could do would offer more than a few seconds of defense. But I raised my sword anyway.

"This is your last chance!" Harlyn yelled as she burst through the doors of the throne room. Joth's attention shifted to her, and I sent an order to Rawk, who immediately laid a line of fire directly at Joth, though he raised a shield to protect himself.

Harlyn shouted, "You may have the power to harm us separately, but you will never get us all, not before one of us gets you!"

"The five of you and a young silver bird with smoke?" Joth widened his arms with mock concern. "Where do I begin?"

Harlyn grinned. "Begin with any of our hundreds!"

Instantly, both doors into the throne room opened, and Alliance soldiers poured inside, all of them running directly toward Joth. Caught off guard, he backed onto the steps leading to the Scarlet Throne. His hands were busy defending himself or attacking wherever he could, but he couldn't see everywhere at once, and with little experience in actual battle, he remained vulnerable, something we were all too happy to exploit.

He created shields in front of him, forgetting the soldiers who advanced behind him. Desperate to protect himself, he threw one soldier against a wall on the right without noticing how close Commander Reese was at his left. He raised one hand to squeeze on a heart but needed the same hand to mount a defense. He couldn't stop us all, and he was clearly weakening.

Finally, he had backed all the way to the top of the stairs, at nearly the same time as Harlyn approached from behind. He grabbed her arm and forced her down directly in front of the throne, then shouted, "Everyone go to your knees, or I will make her suffer."

To emphasize his point, he pressed the back of her neck, and Harlyn screamed with pain.

Kestra and I were on opposite sides of the throne, but we immediately locked eyes. Endrick had given Kestra a similar punishment once, though with only a small portion of his power. Based on Harlyn's cry, what she was receiving must have been worse.

Immediately, most of the Alliance soldiers went to their knees, Gabe among them. The Brill knelt, and once I went to my knees, so did the members of my cavalry.

In fact, only one person still refused to kneel: Kestra.

Crossing directly in front of the Scarlet Throne, she lifted the disk bow with another black disk in the pocket. My heart both lifted and fell in the same moment.

Obviously, she had used the wrong disk before, perhaps testing the extent of his powers, or knowing that he would detect her attack. But if she had the real disk this time, the one containing Endrick's ability to destroy a person's magic with their death, then how could she hope to succeed where the other attack had failed?

Distracted by Kestra, Joth's attack on Harlyn paused, and she slumped forward at his feet. Joth walked down three steps before folding his arms and laughing. "So a magic disk was indeed made," he said. "And you expect to kill me with it now?"

"Surrender to us," Kestra said. "Joth, I beg you to surrender before it's too late."

"Oh, it's already too late." He raised his hand, palm up, and closed his fingers in. Kestra cried out, and I knew he was attacking her. When her hand flew to her chest, the disk bow automatically fired, though her erratic movement threw off the aim. Joth broke off the attack on Kestra so that, as before, he could catch the disk in his hands.

She fell to the ground, and I rushed toward her, which put me directly in his line of sight. "King of the Banished," he said. "Now is the time when you tell your Alliance to surrender. Do it now and all those who prove themselves to be my servants may live."

I straightened up. "It is not in us to surrender. No, Joth, for as long as you reign, we will strike again and again and again, never stopping until you are nothing more than a bad memory."

"Every attempt will end the way this pathetic disk did. I will always see the attack coming."

"Not this time!" From behind, Harlyn leapt to her feet with a black disk in her hand and slammed it down on Joth's shoulder. He straightened up and cried out, clutching wildly at the disk, but the damage was done. He thrashed about, knocking Harlyn over the back side of the steps. The black disk grew white-hot as it pulled magic from Joth's body, even as the injury drained him of life.

He slumped to his knees, and for the first time, I saw the boy who had recorded a simple journal in All Spirits Forest. The prince of Navan who had spent his entire life caring for his people in their cursed state.

"I'm so sorry," he mumbled; then his body collapsed and rolled down the stairs. By the time he was on the floor at my feet, he was dead.

· FIFTY-SEVEN ·

SIMON

The eerie silence that had fallen in the throne room lasted only a few seconds. It broke into utter despair when Loelle cried, "My son!" and ran toward Joth's body, kneeling before him. I'd stepped aside to give her space, and from this new angle, I realized the black disk wasn't lodged in his shoulder nearly as deep as I'd imagined. Which meant the disk had done exactly what Kestra had hoped. It had used Endrick's power to pull all the magic from Joth, killing him.

While Loelle cried for Joth, I hurried toward Kestra, who finally straightened up, though one hand remained at her chest. She began anxiously looking around the room, but I said, "It's safe; he's gone."

"Yes, but where's Harlyn?"

I followed her around to the back of the throne platform, where we found Harlyn crumpled at the bottom of the stairs. Maybe unconscious. Maybe worse, a thought I couldn't bear to consider. She had slammed the disk into Joth's shoulder with her bare hands. Had the disk's instinct to take life affected her too?

Gabe ran around the platform from the opposite direction and froze when he saw Harlyn. Kestra knelt at Harlyn's side and gently rolled her onto her back. After a brief inspection, Kestra shook her head, and I immediately feared for the worst. Wordlessly, Gabe knelt across from Kestra and took Harlyn into his arms and ran one hand through her hair. He appeared on the verge of collapse too.

"I wasn't the Infidante," Kestra said, still kneeling on the floor. "I could hold the disk because I had created it, but Harlyn always was meant to do this job. We figured it out when Amala drove us here in the wagon. Harlyn opened my satchel to be sure I had enough disks, then picked up the disk containing the magic. It flashed with light, but she closed the satchel before Amala noticed. Then she took the disk for herself, waiting for the right moment."

"And sacrificed her life for it." Gabe pulled Harlyn closer to him.

"Not if we can still help." Kestra looked over at her father. As if he understood what she wanted, he walked away only to return a moment later with a large piece of the shattered white disk. The piece was no longer than his thumb, but Kestra seemed satisfied with it.

I knew right away what that disk was—it must have been the same one that restored life to Kestra. She was offering its use to Harlyn.

But just as Kestra took it, Harlyn coughed and moved one hand. Gabe pressed her fingers to his lips, tears streaming down his cheeks. He nodded at Kestra with something that looked like true respect, then picked up Harlyn and began to carry her from the throne room.

He paused when he passed me and said, "I was wrong about Kestra. She has a warrior's heart, but a soul within her that you may take a lifetime to deserve."

"I know that." I nodded at him. "Harlyn may need a day or two to recover, but I think she'll be fine. Rawk will take you both back to Woodcourt if you want."

Gabe chuckled. "We'll take the normal way to Woodcourt. You and Kestra can use that fire-breathing bird for a victory flight over all of Antora."

"Maybe we will." Though this certainly didn't feel like a victory. I smiled over at Kestra. She couldn't possibly know everything I was thinking, but she smiled back. Even so, a sadness remained in her eyes. I wondered if that would ever leave.

Gabe left, gradually accompanied by most of those who had fought in here. Basil walked up beside me, staring down at Joth's body. "I can't believe it's over," he mumbled.

"We couldn't have done it without you and your soldiers," I replied.

Basil smiled. "Remember that when we meet again as rulers of neighboring countries."

"When we meet again as friends," I said.

My attention shifted to Joth; Loelle knelt beside him, holding his hand. For the last few minutes, she had been trying to heal him, but every effort had failed, as I suspected it would. Most of the time, Loelle could keep a person from death, but she could not restore life.

Loelle appealed to Kestra, who had joined me by then. "Surely there is something of magic left in you, even a whisper."

Kestra gently shook her head. "There isn't, Loelle. I'm so very sorry."

Loelle wiped away a tear as she stared down at her son. "He was a good person, the kind of young man a prince should be. He cared deeply for the Navan like a father would, and even the Halderian half-lives as if they were his own. When you connected your powers, it introduced corruption to him in a way he couldn't possibly have been prepared for. I don't think he knew how to fight it."

"I did that to him," Kestra replied.

"But it was me who gave you the magic," Loelle said. "And it's because of me that the corruption grew within you so quickly. I didn't anticipate any of this happening. It's not your fault, child; it's mine."

Kestra locked eyes with me, but this time there was a purpose to them that I didn't entirely understand. Then she glanced down at the shattered piece of white disk in her hands, and I knew exactly what she was thinking.

Kestra limped over to Loelle and held out the shard of broken disk. "You must leave Antora. You and all the Navan, if any remain."

From deeper inside the room, Trina said, "Reddengrad might be willing to discuss terms for bringing you into their borders."

Basil gave me a wry smile. "Trina and I are still discussing the terms of *her* coming to Reddengrad and she's already inviting guests?"

I chuckled, but ahead of us, Loelle nodded. "We will leave Antora. That is more than fair."

Loelle took the disk, and Kestra said, "Place this in the wound at his shoulder, with every intent of bringing him back."

Loelle's mouth opened in disbelief. "After all we've done, you'd do this for us?"

Kestra only smiled. "You'd better hurry."

She wiped tears off her cheeks, closed her eyes, and inserted the piece into Joth's wound. A full minute passed in which nothing happened; then he suddenly cried out, attempting to reach for the disk.

I knelt across from Loelle, grabbing Joth's hands until Loelle whispered assurances that he would be all right. He looked at me, and his eyes widened. "You're here to kill me."

"That was already taken care of," I said. "But you must be still now."

Kestra knelt beside me and asked, "Is the corruption gone? Is the magic gone?"

Joth's eyes rolled back in his head, and a single tear drew a line down his cheek. "Everything is gone. What have you done?"

"She saved your life. She saved us both," Loelle said.

After a moment, his harsh breathing began to settle as he understood more fully what had happened. When he opened his eyes, they shifted to Kestra. With a most solemn expression, he asked, "Can you possibly forgive me?"

"I need forgiveness too," she said. "I cannot ask for it in one breath and refuse it in the next."

He reached for her hand and gently pulled her toward him. She leaned in, and he whispered in her ear; then she softly replied. Basil eyed me questioningly, but a moment later, she stood and walked up the dais to the throne.

She stared at it for what seemed like a very long time, running her finger over the garnets and rubies embedded into its posts. Then she lifted the cushion seat and withdrew the Olden Blade.

"Not the cleverest hiding place, I admit," Joth mumbled.

Kestra held the blade in one hand and, at the bottom of the steps, took my other hand to leave the palace.

"Did he say anything else?" I asked.

"He told me that if it were up to him, we would still be connected." She smiled over at me. "But he and I never were, not really. Not when I already loved someone else."

Now it finally felt like a victory.

· FIFTY-EIGHT ·

KESTRA

A ceremony was held the following night in the courtyard of the palace. My palace, I supposed, for many of those who passed me addressed me as their queen. But I did not feel like a queen. I was no queen.

The grounds had been cleared of any signs of the fighting that had taken place here over the past several days, though I found it difficult to look in any direction and not think of the terrible price so many had paid for us to be standing here now.

As full as it had been on the day that Joth and Simon had dueled, tonight the gathered crowd stood shoulder to shoulder. Alliance members blended with Antorans, and even the Dallisors made attempts to blend in. All of them, no doubt, wondered what the future held for them.

Didn't we all wonder that? I wasn't even sure how this ceremony would end.

Our main purpose in gathering was to destroy the Olden Blade and also the remnants of the two disks that I had created, gathered in a fabric satchel. Rawk provided a grand fire that burned bright enough to be seen even as far away as All Spirits Forest, and warm enough that cloaks were not needed within the courtyard.

I stood beside Simon with the satchel in one hand and Olden Blade in the other. He had made the appropriate speeches, the audience had cheered or applauded in response, and I had stared into the fire, barely aware of any of it.

Finally, Simon nudged me and whispered, "It's time." I pressed my lips together, ignoring the question intruding in my mind: What if this was a mistake? Whether it was or not, after a deep breath, I threw the items into the fire. A mighty cheer rang throughout the courtyard, but I only heard an echoed cry as the last remnants of Endrick's magic were scorched by the flames. The last of any magic within Antora.

Simon's arm curled around me as we watched the metal gradually melt, then drip in long threads deeper into the fire. Then it was gone. The magic was gone.

"Will magic ever return to Antora?" I whispered, mostly to myself.

After a moment, Simon replied, "You are still half-Endrean. If it ever returns, it will likely come through you."

I turned in his arms to face an expression of obvious worry. I understood why he felt that way, but there was no reason for it. The idea of getting close to magic again had become repulsive to me. I was strong enough as I was now.

Instead, I placed my hands around his neck and kissed him, then with a broad smile said, "At this very moment, I have everything that I could possibly want. There will never be a need for anything more, including magic."

Simon leaned forward to repeat the kiss, but we were stopped when someone behind us called out, "Hail to the queen of Antora!"

In return, many in the group echoed his words and went to their knees. All of those gathered bowed to me, this time out of choice, without force or fear. I hardly knew what to do with it. They were offering me a respect I hadn't earned, and a title I certainly could not accept.

Not everyone knelt, of course. Understandably, those from Reddengrad and Brill would have loyalties to their own countries, but the Halderians did not kneel either. Instead their focus was on Simon, making their loyalties clear.

I expected Simon would have appreciated their gesture, but instead, I saw a tight grimace on his face. He squeezed my hand, and when our eyes locked, I believed we were thinking the same thing.

I hoped so, for there was something I had wanted to say to him since I had returned to Woodcourt, but the time had never been right. I knew how hard he had fought for the Scarlet Throne. I knew he had promised the Halderians that he would take the throne for them. And if it was what he wanted, he would be a wonderful king.

That single thought almost persuaded me to delay our conversation again, but Simon was staring at me in the way he used to do when we were first at Woodcourt together. His eyes were so intent that I knew he was attempting to decipher my thoughts, if such a thing was possible. Then he smiled, and I wondered if he understood what I had not spoken.

"What sort of trouble can the Coracks get into now?" Gabe approached us with Harlyn at his side. "I'm the leader of a rebellion with nothing to rebel against. Should we fight the new farming methods in the south, or rebel against the very long length of our winters?" He smiled at Simon and then at me. "We need suggestions, for Harlyn and I have agreed that we will never rebel against our new queen, and her king, if Kestra will have you."

"If Kestra will have me, that is enough. There is nothing more that I want." Simon turned to Harlyn. "But we have another problem, one I hope you will solve for me."

Harlyn shrugged. "If I can, then I will."

"Only you can solve it." Simon glanced at me and smiled. "Five minutes from now, I will make an announcement, ceding my short and mostly miserable reign as king of the Halderians to you, Harlyn. You will lead them better than I ever could. They will follow you, as they should."

Harlyn's mouth fell open. "You want me to rule over the Halderians? But that doesn't make sense. Kestra is still queen over the land."

I caught the smile on Simon's face and grinned at him. Then it was my turn to address Harlyn. "That is true, and a problem I will address in ten minutes. At that point, I will cede my even shorter and far more miserable reign as queen of Antora. The person who occupies the Scarlet Throne must be able to unite the kingdom. That is you. And if you will have Gabe, he will make a fine king as well."

Harlyn looked over at Gabe, the smile widening on her face. When he nodded at her, with a more solemn expression, she nodded respectfully to each of us and said, "If I have half the nobility that either of you has shown, I will consider my reign a great success." Then she gave us each a quick and enthusiastic embrace, ending with a kiss to Gabe that was hardly quick and much more than enthusiastic.

When they separated, Gabe offered deep bows to each of us, and said, "So, what happens now?"

I took Simon's hand in mine. "In fifteen minutes, Simon and I will leave Highwyn on his dragon. We will fly until we come to a land where nobody knows his name, or mine. Where there is no war, nor magic. Perhaps where there is no one at all but us."

"Once we are settled, we will send word to her father," Simon said.

"And to us as well." Gabe offered his hand to Simon. "So that your friends may visit once in a while. We are friends, Simon."

I took Harlyn's hand at the same time. "We are friends indeed."

As promised, fifteen minutes later, Simon and I left the palace courtyard, likely for the last time ever. We walked to a clearing while we waited for Rawk to arrive. But there was no rush.

We were finally alone.

Simon pulled me into his arms. "After we land, who will we be? No longer a king and a queen."

"No longer a rebel and an Infidante."

He kissed my cheek. "No longer traitors."

He kissed my jaw next, and I whispered, "From this moment on, I leave behind my Dallisor name. I will honor my Endrean mother and Halderian father, but I will not claim that blood. I will only be Kestra."

"And I will only be the boy who loves her."

He leaned toward me, a breath away from a true kiss, when Rawk landed behind us, with an impatient snort that suggested he was not about to wait any longer than he had to.

Simon helped me onto Rawk's back, then sat behind me as we launched into the air. I had no idea where we were going or when we would get there, and I didn't mind that at all. We had a lifetime to finish that interrupted kiss.

· ACKNOWLEDGMENTS ·

The Traitor's Game series was my first foray into true young adult writing, and I never could have done this without the expert guidance, advice, and patience of my editor, Lisa Sandell, and my agent, Ammi-Joan Paquette. If one day I win the lottery with a double-your-winnings coupon, from a tax-exempt territory that delivers my prize encased in dark chocolate with a literal cherry on top, that will still not equate to the great luck I've had in being able to build a career with these two amazing women.

Additionally, though I'm always astonished by the high level of skill and professionalism of everyone at Scholastic, I wish to particularly thank the marketing department, who have worked miracles through their talents and efforts.

My eternal love and affection goes to my husband, Jeff, who is the strength behind all that I do, and to our family—all five of you now—who are the purpose behind all that I do.

Finally, I wish to thank all of you who read; blog; attend book signings, conferences, and classes; teach; manage libraries; and share and recommend books to your friends. You are the reason I'm able to continue on this amazing journey.

And the journey will continue. I cannot wait for what comes next!

• ABOUT THE AUTHOR •

JENNIFER A. NIELSEN is the critically acclaimed author of the *New York Times* bestseller *The Traitor's Game* and its sequel, *The Deceiver's Heart*, as well as the *New York Times* and *USA Today* bestselling Ascendance Series: *The False Prince, The Runaway King,* and *The Shadow Throne*. She also wrote the *New York Times* bestselling Mark of the Thief trilogy: *Mark of the Thief, Rise of the Wolf,* and *Wrath of the Storm;* the stand-alone fantasy *The Scourge;* the critically acclaimed historical novels *Words on Fire, Resistance,* and *A Night Divided;* book two in the Horizon series, *Deadzone;* and book six of the Infinity Ring series, *Behind Enemy Lines.*

Jennifer collects old books, loves good theater, and thinks that a quiet afternoon in the mountains makes for a nearly perfect moment. She lives in northern Utah with her husband, their children, and a perpetually muddy dog. You can visit her at jennielsen.com.